A derang   a judge and puts her on trial—
in a grotesque mockery of justice . . .

"Fascinating medical details, a unique murder method, and effective use of multiple points of view . . . For fans of Patricia Cornwell and Kathy Reichs."   —*Booklist*

BITTER INSTINCT
*A serial killer known as The Poet is writing
a deranged new verse—in human blood.*

"A very frightening police thriller . . . captivating."
          —*Midwest Book Review*

"[An] intriguing villain."   —*Publishers Weekly*

BLIND INSTINCT
*A bizarre series of crucifixion murders haunt
the darkest corners of London . . .*

"If you're a fan of Patricia Cornwell, you'll enjoy *Blind Instinct*. Ingenious."   —*San Francisco Examiner*

"Chilling . . . gruesome . . . *Blind Instinct* is really different."   —*The Sunday Oklahoman*

"A satisfying and disturbing thriller."   —*Booklist*

continued . . .

EXTREME INSTINCT
A psychopath on a satanic mission is terrorizing the American West . . .

"Robert W. Walker combines the best of Cornwell with Koontz."
—*Midwest Book Review*

DARKEST INSTINCT
From Florida to London, a copycat killer strikes, as Jessica Coran faces double jeopardy . . .

"Walker takes you into a world of suspense, thrills, and psychological gamesmanship."
—*Daytona Beach News-Journal*

PURE INSTINCT
New Orleans plays host to the notorious "Queen of Hearts" killer . . .

"Perfect for Patricia Cornwell fans."   —*Mystery Scene*

PRIMAL INSTINCT
The Hawaiian beaches are awash in blood. The relentless "Trade Winds Killer" is loose . . .

"A bone-chilling page-turner."   —*Publishers Weekly*

FATAL INSTINCT
Jessica Coran faces a cunning, modern-day Jack-the-Ripper nicknamed "The Claw" . . .

"A taut, dense thriller. An immensely entertaining novel filled with surprises, clever twists, and wonderfully drawn characters."
—*Daytona Beach News-Journal*

Titles by Robert W. Walker

UNNATURAL INSTINCT
BITTER INSTINCT
BLIND INSTINCT
EXTREME INSTINCT
DARKEST INSTINCT
PURE INSTINCT
PRIMAL INSTINCT
FATAL INSTINCT
KILLER INSTINCT

COLD EDGE
DOUBLE EDGE
CUTTING EDGE

Visit the author's website at RobertWWalker.com.

UNNATURAL INSTINCT

ROBERT W. WALKER

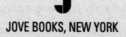

JOVE BOOKS, NEW YORK

This is a work of fiction. Names, characters, places, and incidents either are the product of the author's imagination or are used fictitiously, and any resemblance to actual persons, living or dead, business establishments, events, or locales is entirely coincidental.

UNNATURAL INSTINCT

A Jove Book / published by arrangement with
the author

PRINTING HISTORY
Berkley hardcover edition / August 2002
Jove edition / October 2003

Copyright © 2002 by Robert W. Walker
Excerpt from *Retribution* copyright © 2003 by Jilliane Hoffman
Cover design by Jill Boltin

ISBN: 0-515-13529-1

A JOVE BOOK®
Jove Books are published by The Berkley Publishing Group,
a division of Penguin Group (USA) Inc.,
375 Hudson Street, New York, New York 10014.
JOVE and the "J" design
are trademarks belonging to Penguin Group (USA) Inc.

PRINTED IN THE UNITED STATES OF AMERICA

10 9 8 7 6 5 4 3 2 1

For the gentle and loving spirit who fills me with inspiration, who lifts my soul, who gives me will, strength, and love to carry on in the face of any adversity. For these reasons, I dedicate this novel to the one I love and cherish, Angelina.

PROLOGUE

*Love is impatient; love is unkind and envies everyone.
Love is ever boastful, or conceited, or rude; ever self-
ish, and quick to take offense. Love keeps scores of
wrongs. . . . There are some things love cannot face;
there are limits to its faith, its hope and endurance.
Love will always come to a bad end.*

—FROM A PRISON LETTER BY JIMMY LEE PURDY
TO HIS PARENTS, A BASTARDIZATION OF THE
BIBLICAL LINES OF I CORINTHIANS 13:4

FROM an extremely limited vantage point, her head duct-taped to the face of a dead man's cheek, the slightly overweight woman could only see her left hand—tied as it was—to the right hand of a decaying corpse.

Pounding of someone's heart so loud in her ears. Her own heart . . . pounding itself against the chest wall. Her gasp flowing into the open mouth of death to which she is lashed.

She studied the width and texture of the brown orange leather tie that bound her—wrist to wrist—to the deceased.

Her heart sent out a surge of power all its own.

The ties wound several times around in figure-eight fashion between the two wrists—live wrist to the dead wrist.

Strange mix of commingled pleasant odors of earth, hay, and sweet pine with the unpleasant: urine and feces, and decay. Sensation of large space wrapped about her, but all senses overpowered now by the pounding heart that threatened to wake death beneath her, where it lay cold and unresponsive.

A lengthy, flesh-cutting rawhide strip allowed only her fingers to rise off the dead man's skin. She could feel but not see that her right hand was likewise lashed to the dead man's left hand. Her torso had been wrapped about the corpse in what felt like larger, wider bands of rawhide, and she felt cold and nude against the ties. She and her dead executioner both nude, strapped together at the midsection.

Her heart wanted to explode to find silence.

Nerve endings in her feet told the same story for her other extremities. *Someone had lashed her feet to the dead man's feet, her right to his left, her left to his right, all in an obscene gesture of lovemaking, her atop him, him facing up.* She guessed the dead body to be that of a man by the size of the single hand she could view, that and the size of his blunt nails. An aroma of burned flesh filled her nostrils as well.

Heart now like a crazed, frenetic bird fighting to break free from its cage, all flutters and palpitations.

"Jimmy Boy said it best, said he wanted to fuck you till you were dead . . . said it in open court, didn't he?" When had she heard this grotesque question that now coiled about her brain for a voice, a face, and features to go with it? She remained drowsy, as if she had been drugged, but her heart insisted she pay attention. It also continued its own threat. She sought relief from the insistence of her heart, her lungs, her very breath. She recalled once having made a trip across country with Miss Wiggles—her cat—named for her inability to sit still. She had doped up the animal on advice from a vet friend. Bad idea, for the animal had gurgled and moaned and bitched all the way, every night, not allowing Maureen any sleep.

Maureen . . . that's my name. Now where the hell am I, and what the fuck am I doing lashed to a dead guy? This is too much to bear, too much for anyone to bear. God in heaven, help me or kill me, but put me out of this misery. And what's become of Miss Wiggles? Who is going to feed Wiggles?

"Ogod-how'd-Iget-f-f-f-uck-king here'n dis wretch-edestate-aaah," she moaned under the duct-tape gag, unable to enunciate.

There was a stir of a response like soft feathers being punched from a pillow. Someone heard her mangled plea. Then silence, save for the telltale heart. Then a deep, guttural laugh from a male diaphragm and voice box, coming from the darkness somewhere out of her vision. A laughter filled with derision at her plight yet mysteriously in sync with her drumbeat heart and tortured circumstances. The bastard monster who had done this to her had also been listening to her churning and vexed heart.

A deep, abiding hatred began to build and replace bewilderment and agitation inside her heart and soul, when suddenly the unseen figure standing overhead plunged a three-pronged, rusty pitchfork into the earth inches before her eyes. Simultaneously her body rippled in response, animating the body lashed to her.

"Kinya dig it?" he asked and paused to spit a wad of brown syrup from his mouth to her face—chewing tobacco. "My gran-pap always said a chaw of tobacco could cure any hurt. Course he never reckoned on anythin' like this."

"Youuu-summa-bitch'll payfar'isbygad," she cursed under the gag.

"Dancing with death takes on a whole new meaning for you now, don't it little dear?" He again erupted in an ugly derision of sound, a twisted laugh.

Still feeling the effects of whatever drug he'd used on her to keep her submissive, Maureen thought she recognized her abductor's voice. Could it be the old man? Jimmy Purdy's prune-faced, skin-puckered father? From halfway across the country?

He spat another mouthful of dark liquid, and it slapped her bare behind, trickling down between her legs. "Jimmy always liked a good chew. Prefers Cherokee Red. He'll like my spicing you up for him, so's he can take whiffs of you— all up through eternity."

"Fut you-you-you motherfutt-king-sonofa-hog's-pussy!" she cursed beneath the gag, knowing that all the withered, old creep heard came out as a single, angry animal keening.

She also knew that it was exactly the response he'd wanted.

She tried desperately to hold on to her sanity; she did so by thinking of her adopted son, two daughters, her grand-daughters, and mentally chorusing 1 Corinthians 13, perhaps the loveliest attempt ever to define love. She must hold on to her love. *Love is patient; love is kind and envies no one . . .*

Already he had stripped her of any similarity to the woman she had been. She must hold on to her mind and soul.

The blood and heartbeat thrumming madly through her calmed in her ears, and she gasped and fainted into an oblivion she'd earlier prayed for.

ONE

Canst thou not minister to mind diseas'd,
Pluck from the memory a rooted sorrow,
Raze out the written troubles of the brain,
And with some sweet oblivious antidote
Cleanse the stuff'd bosom of that perilous stuff
Which weight upon the heart?

—WILLIAM SHAKESPEARE (*MACBETH*)

DR. Jessica Coran, FBI medical examiner, had almost forgotten that the letters M.E. followed her name. The two months off since Richard Sharpe's arrival at Dulles International Airport had been a godsend—and amazingly enough, no calls from the office or the lab. Nothing but a blissful opportunity for her and Richard to orient themselves in a new life that would change and align their futures, most certainly for the better, Jessica believed.

Richard had relocated from England to be with her. As a former police detective at New Scotland Yard, with expertise in working with Interpol, the largest crime fighting organization in the world, Sharpe had looked into and gotten consulting work with the FBI. He had told her in no uncertain terms, "I have been self-sufficient and independent since my divorce, seven years now, and I have no intention of becoming Mr. Jessica Coran, M.E., thank you."

"I can accept that," she'd told him, laughing in response.

They had had a wonderful reunion after he had landed. They had wined and dined at Anatole's Riverfront, and he stayed the first week with her at her Quantico apartment, but since then they had been house hunting, both of them knowing they needed far more space than the apartment provided. Jessica's and Richard's books alone would need an additonal room.

"I have known relationships and marriages that have overcome great obstacles and painful hurdles," Richard had told her, "but none can overcome shoulder-to-shoulder crowding."

Richard's height rivaled her own, and they seemed so well matched in so many other ways; they both loved the theater and their taste in music proved to each admirable, and they both held a keen sense of right and wrong, justice and injustice. Both had devoted their lives to law enforcement, and while he was twelve years her senior, she had long ago accepted the fact that she found older men far more to her liking and far sexier than men her own age.

So they had spent these past few weeks house hunting, and they had come upon the perfect place: a lovely little farmstead with tie-ups for cows and horses in a well-lit barn, and the house itself something out of a Norman Rockwell painting. It was within a half hour's drive to Quantico, Virginia, where both of them now worked. It appeared and felt too good to be true, down to the white fence that ran the length of the forty-acre ranch-style farmstead. Already, Jessica was trying to determine a good name for their home.

"It reminds me of Donegal, Ireland, a place I always planned to retire to, until I fell into pursuit."

"Pursuit?"

"Pursuit of you . . . pursuit of real happiness. Real happiness is never about a place; it's something we can only derive from the one we love, and only then if one is loved in return."

Jessica dared to believe that here, finally, stood a man who could give and give, and the well would never be empty; in fact, it seemed the more he gave, the more he had to give. She could hardly believe that the one thing she could never fully achieve with anyone, the idea of complete and true passion in its most literal sense, could be hers.

She had kissed him then and told him, "We'll name our

home Pursuit then, so that neither one of us ever forgets that we're in this for the pursuit of happiness."

"Lovely," he replied. "Then it's done. Now we can take our time and populate the place with some livestock. I love horses and riding."

"So do I, but I was thinking of populating the place with children."

"Children . . . at my age?"

"And why not?"

"Good show. We'll all ride together, you, me, the children." He smiled. "Yes, all of us in pursuit at Pursuit."

Their laughter drifted over the valley and down to the realtor, who had patiently allowed them an opportunity to walk the entire property. The house itself was expansive, with six fireplaces. It was built to last in the 1880s.

To celebrate their sharing the first down payment, they went out for an elegant meal in nearby Washington, D.C. There they dined at Cressida's, a fine restaurant with Greek cuisine.

In the middle of the finest Greek lobster she had ever eaten, a waiter placed a phone at the table and plugged it in, saying, "Dr. Coran, there is a phone call for you." He placed the phone before Jessica.

"I don't want to take this call," she said.

"We both knew it was coming; only surprise is that it didn't come sooner."

"How the devil does Eriq Santiva know I'm here?"

"He's been good to us, Jess, and we've had a wonderful run."

She sighed and took the phone from its hook. "Hello," she barked.

"Jess, it's John Thorpe."

Jessica pictured Thorpe, her right hand at the lab, with whom she had shared years of confidences. He knew more about her than anyone at Quantico, so his tracking her down, even here, didn't surprise her. "I've been calling everywhere for you. It's urgent, otherwise—you know I'd never interrupt love, not for the world."

Jessica imagined her best friend's tortured countenance.

John Thorpe and she had worked for a decade side by side. They had seen some of the most bizarre criminal cases in recent history. "All right, John, what's got you all fired up?"

"It's Judge Maureen DeCampe."

"Not that bitch."

"Listen, Jess, she's been abducted."

"Abducted?"

"From the underground garage, when she was going to her car."

"At the g'damn courthouse?"

"Right outta the garage!"

"Wait a minute. Are you telling me that somebody abducted the judge from the courthouse parking lot?"

"The judges' parking section doesn't have a firewall between it and the public section, Jess. And at night, it's a cave. Damn place was always a crime waiting to happen, so it's no surprise when you think about it."

"J. T., what are you saying?"

"All the fried brain cases and psychos those judges in D.C. deal with on a daily basis? Are you kidding?"

"Jeeze, an appellate court judge abducted." She said it loud enough so that Richard and everyone in the place might hear. This kind of news would be headlines in an hour. "Any ransom demands, any notes?"

"Nada, so far. Not a word."

"Where's Eriq Santiva?"

"On another phone, searching for you."

"Why me, John? Why not half a dozen other capable forensic experts in the organization?"

"Eriq's got marching papers to get his number one person, Jess, and you know who that is. He's covering his ass, though."

"Meaning?"

"He's called Kim Desinor in as well. She's already walking the grid at the parking lot. If you want, just say so, and I'll tell them I couldn't find you. I know there isn't any love lost between you and DeCampe."

"She pissed a lot of people off—and not just the criminals. Remember the Van Lefler case? Remember the McGregor case? Manslaughter my ass."

"The media will have the story spread across the continent in an hour, Jess."

"Imagine if the media put as much effort into every Missing Persons case."

"She's an important cog in the judiciary system of a major American city, that's for sure. A year ago, she was profiled on a *20/20* episode called 'America's Most Ambitious Women.' Like it or not, Jess, it's going to be a high-profile case if ever there was."

"Don't I know it." Jessica now looked across the table at Richard. She stared for a moment, saying nothing.

"I quite understand, Jessica. It's your work; it's what you do. Go." Richard lifted his glass of Merlot and toasted. "To the only woman that the FBI cannot do without."

Jessica laughed in response. Then she said into the phone, "Send a car for me, J. T."

"On its way."

She hung up, reached across the table, and took Richard's hands in hers. "Are you going to be able to put up with my being gone for long periods of time, Richard?"

"It'll only make me want you more."

"They say that absence makes the heart grow fonder, but I wonder."

"I'll not be that far from you, dear. And don't forget, in a week, I start teaching that class on international cooperation among law enforcement agencies at Quantico myself. Of course, I will miss you . . . terribly, despite my being awfully busy. But as far as tonight, I want to stay with you. I'll look over the crime scene with you."

She moved around the booth to be near him. She kissed him, and he returned the kiss. "No kissing at the crime scene," she said in a tone clearly playful and warning.

"I promise."

"It's been such a wonderful interlude—this time we've had, free of everyone and everything. I despise its ending."

He pulled her to him and nestled into her. He followed with a kiss to her throat that then traveled to her mouth.

"Yes, it has been rather amazing," he whispered.

"Rather," came her breathless reply.

JESSICA'S success rate over the past several years with high-profile cases had proven nothing short of phenomenal. Still, she had twice had ill-fated run-ins with Judge Maureen DeCampe over Jessica's so-called bending of the rules—seen as a misstep in the chain of evidence protocol or simply some blunder with regard to the rights of the accused. While the problem remained behind closed doors, not for public record, everyone in the FBI family seemed to know. As J. T. had put it, there was no love lost between the now-missing judge and the M.E. Jessica had repeatedly butted heads with the liberal judge, whom she thought a closet libertarian.

Any hard feelings had to be put aside, however, and their roots, while well established, needed plucking for the time being.

Riding in the back of the Washington PD squad car sent to pick her up, she asked Richard, with a cocked-eared Patrolman Stanley Hanrahan listening in, "J. T. says they don't know exactly how long the woman has gone missing. But why all the suspicion that she has been abducted if it's only been a few hours or not even that?"

"She logged out at just after midnight," said Hanrahan from the driver's seat. "I hear she had a routine on Thursday nights to work late."

"So she never made it to her car; so it was sometime just after midnight. And why still no ransom note, no phone call to the family, nothing?"

"The vic's simply disappeared."

"How awful," Jessica whispered into Richard's ear, "to have your *sum total self* reduced to the abbreviated form of *victim*."

He squeezed her, and Hanrahan watched via the rearview mirror. Richard said, "What do we know so far? A D.C. appellate court judge has vanished from a downtown parking lot, and whoever has the judge apparently cares nothing for money and—"

"And even less for the suffering of loved ones."

"And there's a major push on to find her."

Jessica nodded at this. "Authorities have wasted no time in pursuing this as a suspicious disappearance. Any number of other disappearances, police—and most certainly FBI involvement—would take twenty-four hours before beginning a manhunt."

"This DeCampe must be well connected," he volunteered.

She laughed hollowly. "Firmly entrenched in the top levels of society here in D.C., even though she's not been in the city for long."

"Oh, really? And just how does one pull that off? By spending money?"

"Yes and no. She was born and raised under wealthy family circumstances. She climbed to the top of the legal profession as a lawyer and was a judge in Houston, Texas. After nearly twenty years on the bench there, she moved to D.C. and took a position as an appellate court judge here."

"So, Officer, you saw the crime scene, right?"

"Yeah . . . sure did."

"Any theories as to who has her?" she asked Hanrahan, who'd been chewing on a Snickers candy bar.

He took a moment to swallow. "Not a clue, Dr. Coran, but you know how many loonytunes go through the system and are carrying a hard-on for . . . I mean a grudge against the judges? And DeCampe in a short time has managed to piss off everybody, the good guys as well as the bad guys, so . . ." He let his words hang in the air.

She imagined how worrisome the entire matter would be to the other judges once word got around. "So perhaps my first instinct is right."

"And what would that be, Doctor?" asked Richard as the car came within sight of the courthouse. A roaming wispy but spirited ground fog played about the windshield like a ghost from a wishing well, while the black emptiness of the abandoned street gave Jessica a fleeting chill.

"My intuition tells me that some sort of sociopath has her. Someone who isn't in it for any sort of ransom, some-

one out for some sort of vengeance, some kind of hate motive."

Richard replied, "Sounds like a normal thing, the way
you put it, Doctor."

"Sociopathic reasoning may resemble our so-called normal reasonings and motivations, but it never rises to the
level of daring to think about itself ... or to think of its
consequences." She realized instantly that she had lost Hanrahan in the serpentine, labyrinthian thought when he replied, "Say what?"

Richard said, "Then don't look for a rational motive."

"So, you're going to consult on this case, are you?"

"If I can get assigned to it, I will."

"Assuming you are assigned to it, what kind of motive
would you suggest, Richard?"

"Some sort of revenge motive, likely a quite twisted
one."

Somehow Officer Hanrahan had gotten his feelings hurt,
and now he took a turn too fast, tossing his occupants to
one side, but they only luxuriated in one another and were
back to kissing as the car came to a careening stop inside
the garage below the Washington, D.C., appellate courthouse. "Strange place for this," she told him.

"Never too strange surroundings for love," he replied.

"God but I love you."

"I love you," he countered.

"We're here," Hanrahan announced, switched off the motor, and climbed from the car. Then Chief Eriq Santiva,
Jessica's immediate supervisor with Unit Four, Behavioral
Science Division of the FBI, snatched the back door open
and pried them loose with the obligatory greetings, followed
by J. T. with more of the same.

"Jess, she's vanished without a trace," Santiva assured
her, taking her by the hand to help her from the car. "Not
so much as a hair so far."

"We're thinking it may've been someone with a grudge
against her," said J.T.

"Someone pissed over one of her rulings." The two men
were talking over one another.

"Wow . . . that narrows the field," she joked. "And who would possibly be upset by one of the woman's rutting rules?"

"Still, they're right," said Richard. "It's quite likely that if no demands are made, the culprit has other punishment in mind."

"Richard and I discussed it and have as much as agreed on the same point. Richard ought to be brought in as consultant, Eriq. What's the alternative? That he go back to the restaurant and demand a container to box up my lobster?"

Chief Eriq Santiva grimaced. "Sorry to cut into your honeymoon."

"Honeymoon? Eriq, we haven't even set a date."

"Preamble then to your honeymoon . . . whatever you two are calling it. Sorry to cut it short."

"Honeymoon sounds good to me," Richard replied.

She looked at Richard, and he smiled back. "I only meant that it . . . well, it's just that the word doesn't quite apply, like *Missing Persons* being applied to this case will likely prove inaccurate."

"Trust me, the heat put on to solve this thing immediately and now . . . it necessitated we call it a Missing Persons case."

"I see." Her eyes widened with realization. She explained to Richard, "Makes it far easier to rationalize FBI involvement in an otherwise police matter. So we've already taken full charge of the case, right? WPD is cooperating with us, rather than the other way around?"

"You've grasped the political nature of the case with your normal brilliance, Agent Coran," replied Santiva, a little edge to his voice. "Absolutely, we've taken those steps. No one in the WPD is going to give a rat's ass about what happens to a judge, especially this judge, don't you see?"

"As saviors, we had no choice."

"Something like that, yes."

"Done deal as you Yanks say," interjected Richard, trying to defuse the moment.

Eriq, his Cuban features twitching now, his black eyes like cold marble, said, "We moved ahead on this for all the right reasons. Trust me, this is no casual snatcher. She may've run into a psycho serial killer."

"What're you saying? That this guy targeted her and her only? That tells us a great deal right from the get-go."

"Yeah, he's out for revenge, not ransom."

J. T. joined them, adding a word. "Which will likely involve torture; out of torture, he will gain some sense of control over her, break her down, make himself feel more powerful as a result."

Jessica had heard the familiar tale too often. "The abductor wants to feel superior to his victim—to a woman—and he will, despite all her titles."

The four seasoned veterans had all dealt with the worst crimes in recent history. They were well aware of each other's capabilities, but they were equally aware of the depravity they might well be facing. "How long?" asked Jessica.

"We figure her absence was not felt until three hours after what occurred here. Her daughter was holding a late-late surprise hot meal for her at home—the judge's place. Couple of friends, relatives who were planning an intervention."

"An intervention? Was she on the bottle or—"

Eriq waved his hands. "No, no! Nothing like that. They thought they could break her of her workaholism. You know, the caring children wanting the aging mother put out to pasture, all that."

"Gee, wish I had friends like that," muttered Jessica.

"We could arrange for an intervention for your obsession with work," teased Richard. But the remark left Jessica frowning, Santiva staring, and J. T. simultaneously scratching his ear and scrunching his face up as if deciphering where and when.

Santiva said, "Jess, you do have friends like that, but they're so busy that they can't find time to intervene you, you see?"

"Richard's only kidding, you two! Get off it. Funny, Richard. Now let me have a look at the crime grid, will you?" She pulled away from Richard's hand on her arm, and she pushed past the other two men, going for the location of the crime, saying, "If only these walls could talk." She meant to read the crime scene and come away with some useful, guiding clues or patterns, or a direction in which to take the case.

"Look, we'll need to get Lew Clemmens to look into the judge's caseload records for anyone who even smells bad."

"Can do, but there're men here at D.C. headquarters who can handle that."

"I trust Clemmens to be always right on, Eriq. And we don't have time to work with skeptics and people who're going to second-guess our moves, not if we want to find this creep before he kills her. Not if we want to bring her back alive."

"Shhh . . . family over there."

Jessica saw the grieving handful of people all huddled in one corner, two pretty young women who looked like younger versions of the judge among them. She'd heard the judge had two daughters and three grandchildren with one on the way. Jessica wondered who had the little ones, and her heart sank at the thought of pain brought on the innocent grandchildren.

JESSICA now approached the cordoned-off area, the grid of the crime scene. She saw that Kim Desinor, FBI agent and psychic, was well within the grid, attempting to pick up any psychic vibrations or hits that might defy both the skeptical onlooker and reality itself . . . at least reality as most people knew it.

"How long has she been in trance?" asked Jessica.

J. T. replied, "Going on twenty minutes."

"She say anything?"

Eriq piped in with, "Before she went under, she touched the gun and the shoe." He pointed to a shoe and a gun lying about the rear of a car tagged for impound—the judge's car. "Said the shoe and the gun belonged to Judge DeCampe. But then even I could've told you that."

So far, Kim Desinor's efforts had remained unimpressive. Still, Jessica had worked previous cases with the psychic detective, and she sometimes proved to be uncannily accurate. "She say anything while under?"

"Naaah . . . lot of nothing so far. Couple of grunts maybe."

The moment Eriq said this, Kim Desinor screamed and stumbled forward, as if in a drunken stupor. She was caught by Santiva, only moments before she might have cracked her head on the dirty, oily pavement. Back of her, near the car tagged as the judge's, Jessica momentarily focused on a large .45 Remington revolver—a Texas weed eater some called it—a set of keys, and a single high-heeled, stiletto-style shoe.

"Get her some water, enough for drinking and splashing," Jessica told Richard as Santiva collapsed to the floor with Desinor in his arms. "Eriq, J. T., get her topside where there's some cold air. It reeks of stagnant exhaust fumes in here."

Santiva saw to helping Kim Desinor away. The psychic agent looked in a state of shock, her knees bleeding from having scraped the concrete floor. The results of the fall might have been far worse. Jessica wondered if there would be any significant results of another kind, the psychic kind. Dr. Desinor had in the past conjured miracles. However, Jessica knew she must rely on science and not magic, even if that magic might well have a basis in fact.

A team of two evidence technicians with the Washington PD stood about watching, ordered to hold until Dr. Desinor had completed her reading of the crime scene area, and further ordered to stand down until Jessica could complete her examination of the crime grid. The snickering from the WPD techs over what they had witnessed with Dr. Desinor could not be masked in this underground tomb where every word echoed and bounced.

Normally, no one was to touch a thing until the lead forensic investigator assigned to the case arrived. Dr. Jessica— "Her Highness," as many had taken to calling her behind her back—Coran had now arrived to give the place a thorough look-see and walkover. She'd done that much; she was on deck, at the scene as soon as ordered, and she had taken it all in at a glance, while a piece of her mind wandered back to Richard.

The last time she'd been called to a crime scene it had also cost her an expensive meal. That time, her friend and colleague, Dr. John Thorpe, J. T., had come along with her, as they'd been dining together at the local Caribbean Sin on succulent mahimahi steak dinners, which had been left cold and standing.

On staring across the taped-off area, Jessica felt a sense of dread and déjà vu, and she said to herself, "Sometimes I feel like Eriq's hired bloodhound."

"You can bet WPD'll want this one. It is their jurisdiction, and they're going to fight for it," said one of the D.C. police crime techs. "Dr. Sleezac's contesting jurisdiction as we speak."

Jessica knew Herbert Sleezac, M.E. for the city. She felt no surprise at his contesting jurisdiction. If she were in his position, she'd fight for her jurisdictional rights as well.

"Kidnapping is a federal offense. We don't need an invitation, with a federal appellate judge having been kidnapped."

"All the same, you know how the Washington PD works. Going to be like pulling teeth for you to get any cooperation."

Jessica knew what the guy meant. The city police still thought it was 1940, but they couldn't argue with the FBI taking over, not on this one. They wouldn't stand a chance in a court of law, and they knew it. "Suspected kidnapping of an appellate court judge is a far cry from your ordinary Missing Persons case."

Jessica had developed a reputation among her colleagues for an uncanny ability to "read" the signs of a violent crime scene, and whatever bread crumbs an assailant or a killer left behind. She'd proven it many times over. She not only had the good "blue" sense of a fine detective, but she also "divined" from another place in her psyche that few other women or men could touch. Some called it mysticism. Jessica called it a knack, a Yankee intelligence that came with the DNA. Reading people was a gift passed on to her by her father, a forensics man for the U.S. military. Still she had no illusions about being the kind of psychometric reader Desinor was.

While Jessica had lost her father many years before, she had never lost his spirit, or what he had passed on to her: patience and hard work, how to find out what one needed in any circumstance, how to use time wisely, how to discipline oneself to a task, and how to question and then question the question. All lessons hard won and never to be forgotten, and in never forgetting, she kept her father alive as well. As a result, her father had never completely left her side.

J. T. had remained with Kim Desinor on the outside, while Richard Sharpe and Eriq Santiva had returned. Eriq whispered in her ear, "The absolute absence of a trail or a clue of any sort has dictated, at least in my mind, the need for your special talents, Jess."

"As a forensics guru or as backup to Kim Desinor?"

"And tracker, and cunning person," Santiva added. "We both know the absence of a trail would leave any other forensic investigator or techie Washington cop scratching his head for months or until a body washed up in a storm drain. With this one, the clock is ticking furiously, Jess. We all sense it. Dr. Desinor sensed it strongly the moment she stepped into the garage."

Jessica Coran now crouched over a mini–debris field that spoke of a confrontation in the capital courthouse's underground parking lot—a modern day haunted interior if ever there was one.

Jessica immediately keyed in on the fallen Remington .45, a sterling shiny new barrel looking like an errant piece of a wind chime. The modern version of the old .45 proved far lighter. Jessica had a pair of originals in her gun collection at home, under glass—a collection that had been her father's, which she had added to over the years. Friends who had seen her collection joked that she had more firepower and hardware than did the Pentagon.

Using a pen through the trigger guard, Jessica thoughtfully examined the .45 as she lifted the weapon. Titanium steel and lighter weight notwithstanding, the thing dwarfed her own .38 Police Special; the monster was not nearly so accurate nor easily concealed as her .38 Smith & Wesson. Likely, the former Texas lady judge didn't want to conceal the fact that she packed a deadly weapon. "Why does every man, woman, and child in Texas think bigger is better?" she asked no one in particular as she stared down the enormous length of the .45's barrel, a cannon in Jessica's estimation. "Bitchin' gun."

Immediately on saying this, a naked lightbulb illuminating much of the crime scene began to blink, first creating a pattern of dark ripples across the area and then light-generated shadows.

"She probably used the gun to scare people off," suggested Richard, who stood, hands clenched, nearby, also taking in the bloodless crime scene. "Apparently, whoever has her didn't cringe and slink away on seeing the weapon. Tells us something about her assailant."

"Yeah, right. Maybe he knew her well enough to know it was for show, and that she'd never pull the trigger." Jessica bit her lower lip and shook her head. "Eriq . . . get me a couple of our guys from the lab down here. I want our techs to help me cover the territory, not the city payroll guys over there." She indicated Sleezac's men.

"Of course, will do." Eriq got on his cell phone, but like everything in this underground world, it wasn't working. He had to return to the outside to make his call, bitching about his cell company the entire way.

Jessica reached for Sharpe's hand and stared into his eyes. "There are a lot more places I'd rather be, and all of them with you, Richard."

"I know . . . me, too."

The D.C. techs watched, curious about the lovers as they embraced.

SOME fifteen minutes had passed when Jessica recognized one of the FBI technicians as Phil McMillen, and ignoring the WPD techs on hand, she said, "Phil, I want the firearm in our lab. Give it a once-over for prints now, but bag it and label it as ours."

Phil fought down a gloating look. "Gotcha, Dr. Coran."

Since the city police techs put up no argument, and the city detectives remained mute, Jessica assumed everyone had gotten word from above that she was in charge of the crime scene, regardless of the usual protocol or any jurisdictional *crap,* as Jessica called it when lines between agencies were blurred. Such bullswallop she despised—the jurisdictional quibbling that often escalated into arguments, and later became the sort of loopholes defense attorneys drove John Deere tractors through. All the wrangling also took up far too much precious time, and that would be especially true on this case. *The hell if I'm going to put DeCampe's life at risk over a question of boundaries between law enforcement agencies.* Judge DeCampe was important enough that the governor, the mayor, and most of the city's elite wanted immediate results, and they didn't trust the Washington Police Department for anything requiring speed or overnight results. The same scenario put Jessica and her FBI team on a hot tin roof that would be scrutinized minute by minute.

Referring to the gun she held up, Jessica asked that it get a liberal spraying of Printpoint to highlight any telltale fingerprints. "Who knows," Jessica said, "perhaps her assailant grabbed hold of it at some point in the confrontation. If someone were pointing this thing at me, I think I'd grab hold of the barrel and push it skyward." Jessica looked up on the off chance some evidence of a shot having been fired had chipped the concrete overhead. Nothing. Her nose had already told her that the gun had not been fired, but her brain—starved from having been pulled away from a much-needed meal—was slow to catch up.

"What're you thinking, Jess?" J. T. asked, leaning in over her shoulder and staring at the firearm, studying it and the fact that only the handle showed any print evidence. Phil said even these prints were useless as they'd been smeared horribly with a greasy substance.

"If Judge DeCampe dropped this without firing a shot,

then she may have known the guy or the woman."

"How can you know that?"

"She let down her guard . . . relaxed her grip, possibly at gunpoint, and simply dropped it, which suggests that her assailant got the best of her. Meanwhile, the guy doesn't bother to pick up the weapon or clean up the mess left behind, so . . ."

"He wants *us* to know that he has her," obliged J. T.

"He certainly hasn't gone out of his way to confuse the issue; doesn't want anyone thinking she's on an escape weekend."

"He's telling us he wants us to know she's in his power," agreed J. T., gritting his teeth. "This could get ugly, Jess."

"If it's a power trip he's on, if this is some deep-seated need of his to make us clear on his having her at his will, yeah . . . you're right. Still, it may be something we might take advantage of."

"How so?"

"To turn his need for us to know to our advantage later . . . maybe twist things to our advantage using this need of his."

J. T. breathed deeply. Everyone in law enforcement in the city knew of Judge Maureen DeCampe, and all law enforcement held an unspoken but powerful bond. When someone in the community of law enforcement fell injured or killed, or in this case abducted and possibly dead, a ripple effect of emotion and a call to duty went out like a call to a fire. While neither J. T. nor Jessica called Judge DeCampe a friend, they both respected and admired her, even if they didn't always agree with her verdicts. She had thrown out more than one case on legal technicalities, swatting police authorities like flies, while some criminal smugly walked back out onto the street. Nothing made Jessica see red more than this kind of injustice, to watch the family members of the victims go numb and stunned at such a verdict.

DeCampe had recently made the ruling to release a certain inmate of the Washington, D.C., penal system back into society—due in large part to his advanced age and failing health—and this resulted in a local retired detective on the

WPD taking the law of blood into his own hands, first murdering the released man and then killing himself. It had been front-page fodder for the *Post* for days. DeCampe came under fire of public opinion and members of the press, not to mention police and law enforcement professionals. It had been break-room conversation back at Quantico headquarters as well. The Washington Police Department personnel were particularly pissed with Judge DeCampe afterward. However, DeCampe stood her ground like the Texan she was, never acknowledging any part in the series of events that led up to the murder and suicide. Her supporters pointed out that she tried every case on the merits of that case alone; every case handled as a unique, animal. As a result, few could predict the outcome of a DeCampe ruling. Jessica had to agree that most other judges were so predictable that area lawyers—both defense and prosecuting attorneys—banked on certain outcomes.

Overall, Judge Maureen DeCampe proved a tough, fair, and firm judge, the sort sorely missing in many current judicial arenas in D.C., and Jessica liked her no-nonsense manner, despite not always agreeing with her.

Jessica now coldly stared down on the spot where the woman's keys lay alongside the stiletto-heeled pump, the items just shy of the judge's Mercedes. Judge Maureen DeCampe was known to have used those heels on people who got too close. Jessica momentarily wondered if she'd held onto the other one for any chance to strike back at her assailant at the secondary location.

The rule of thumb among knowledgeable people in law enforcement is that under no circumstances do you allow an assailant to transport you to a second location, one of *his* choosing. Rule of thumb called this *assisting* the assailant in putting him into a comfort zone, one in which he might exercise any fantasy he has ever held, including but not limited to the power over life—the abductee's life. At the second location, the assailant held absolute sway over his victim without threat of discovery or interruption, and 90 percent of the time, this ended in the death of the victim. If Judge DeCampe were conscious, she'd have fought extremely hard before she would allow anyone to abduct her. In addition, Judge DeCampe had a reputation for taking care of herself—Tae Kwon Do, stiletto heels, and .45s—and everyone in and around the courthouse knew her well enough to agree with Jessica on this score. She would never assist in her own abduction.

Everyone from the governor of the state, the mayor, the DA's office, the PD's office, the entire police force, the press, the public—everyone would have a personal and/or powerful interest in the case; she was, in a sense, one of D.C.'s finest. There was no keeping this high-profile case out of the headlines. By the time Jessica got home in nearby Quantico, Virginia, and crawled into bed tonight, Jay Leno would be cracking wise about the case.

Judge DeCampe as celebrity. Weird-assed world we live in with this perversion of what stood for celebrity—victims and celebrity killers, Jessica thought. Maureen DeCampe's disappearance already deeply disturbed Jessica, and it would insinuate itself on any sleep she might hope to get until they arrived at an outcome. Her case would be blazoned across every U.S. newspaper, and blazoned across Jessica's forehead. She imagined the effect of it all while trying to make love to Richard, or while simply trying to find any peace of mind until the judge was located and hopefully returned to her family unharmed. The chances of that appeared slim to none at the moment.

Despite their run-ins and problems—and perhaps due to them—Judge DeCampe had helped Jessica out on more than one occasion. Regardless of where the judge's political and personal leanings were, she remained a stalwart ally to those she befriended. In fact, among the law enforcement community in D.C., few people commanded as much respect as she. Well liked, she had hundreds of admirers and friends. Some said she "owned" Washington—meaning it in a political sense and not always in a nice way. Others called her the city's finest and fairest appellate judge, some saying she earned every accolade, and that nothing was ever handed to her. Jessica respected her because she could easily have simply become another Washington debutante and social butterfly.

"Funny how she had the money and position to do nothing with her life, but she chose to do something with it instead," said J. T. in Jessica's ear.

"Yeah, so I've heard."

"Nothing would've been enough for her parents and immediate circle, but she took the far more difficult road, carving out a real life for herself in a profession for which she harbored great passion."

"Are you writing her eulogy already, John? You're speaking of her in the past tense."

"Jeeze, I didn't mean to . . . I mean, imply that . . ."

"Cool it. We're all thinking it, and besides, you're right about her. You gotta admire her gumption. I think that's what they call it in Texas."

DeCampe had been born and raised on a Texas ranch near Houston. She had risen in the legal system in Texas through several administrations, and she had taken a position in Washington only a few months before, ostensibly to be close to her adopted son, Michael, and her grandchildren as both her daughters worked in politics and had married politicians. "She is a woman of substance and conviction. Can't fault her for being without courage."

"I admire you for the same qualities, Jess," he confided.

Her eyes had closed in thoughtful response; she knew that despite all their ups and downs, despite the squabbles and the tension that came whenever people worked or lived in close proximity, and despite the caustic humor that had taken on the nature of a hallmark between them, J. T. greatly respected her and her abilities—as she respected him. "Thank you, J. T., but never forget that people do not condemn us for our frailties and faults but ultimately for our qualities."

"What's that supposed to mean?" J. T.'s gaze gave away his complete confusion.

"An old truth I once read tells me now that she was abducted because of her fine qualities, not despite them, and not because of her flaws. Whoever took her likely is punishing her for her finest traits, not her weakest."

"That's . . . that's deep," J. T. muttered.

"Well . . . we see it every time someone is murdered. The stalking male who can't function and who has to continue to harass his former lover or wife until someone is dead. He goes after her because he can't have her ideal—the best that she once was in his mind—which no longer exists. He kills her for her finest qualities, not for her worst. Someone who can't leave a celebrity alone does it for the same reason. And Judge DeCampe was, in her way, a celebrity."

Her eyes closed, nearing a comforting moment of pure instinct as her mind played over the chess board of the crime scene. *Twenty-four hours an investigator,* her subconscious scolded, *but now is the time it really counts.* She recalled how often her shrink had told her she must find ways to relax and get away from her work. But even when she did so, her work wouldn't get away from her, as evidenced this night.

When the soft-spoken but firm judge had gone missing, reported by her daughters, it was taken seriously from the get-go. No one working in law enforcement at any level remained far removed from the threat of violence, especially not in a major American city; D.C.'s spiraling skyscrapers and gorgeous skyline might be seen by some as monuments to a civilized camp, but Jessica Coran knew better. She knew from hard-won experience that human beings, whatever the size of their monuments and accomplishments, remained as savage and bestial as the day they were deposited on Earth by whatever powers governed the void. Whether you subscribed to Cherokee creation myths or to Hindu or Christian creation tales, you had to know that the human creature was the most complex and dangerous animal on the planet, given as much to creating art and philosophy and religion as to creating fear and hatred and monsters of their offspring.

Both as a woman and as a detective, Jessica had long understood, even appreciated, how the animal brain of the first men to walk upright operated—fight or flee was not far from that of the bear, the first man in Native American the-

ology, or any other predator. Regardless of add-ons, the late
improvements and refinements to the predatory man-brain,
there was no denying that the original bear-brain remained
intact and working. The refinements had come in layers,
creating an onion of the cerebral cortex, layer upon layer
masking the primitive brain: a core center for growing fur
and fangs and claws, but also a center for spawning ignorance and fear, giving rise to bigoted hatred and irrational
violence.

And so, Jessica's fevered brain played tennis with the
ideas that went back and forth across the net of her consciousness. Something disturbing in the clean crime scene;
something speaking to her of how easy it had been for
DeCampe's abductor. Too damned easy. No blood spilled.
No scuff marks. No car door swinging open. No lock with
a key left hanging in it. Jessica knew of cases in which
killers had taken their prey with the help of a fake cast on
what appeared a broken arm, with trained dogs who faked
being hit by a hasty exit from a parking space, a pair of
fake "blind man's" eyes and a tin cup, or even a helpful
wife with a baby on her arm. This was the con game that
asked the victim to become a willing participant, a perfect
victim. But Judge Maureen DeCampe knew all this as well.
She ought to have been in a unique position to see it coming,
yet she had put up no struggle whatsoever. It could mean
only one thing: She knew her assailant and she felt no fear
of him whatsoever.

TWO

I didn't invent the world I write about—it's all true.

—GRAHAM GREENE (1904–1991)

THE crime scene felt like a cave with an opening at front and back, and the cold Washington, D.C., wind whistled through it with a banshee wail, and still the scene had "abduction" written all over it—but abduction done by a novice, not a trained professional. Although Judge DeCampe had vanished, her car and some personal effects remained behind. Professionals would have seen to the car and any effects; professionals would have created false trails of such personal property. A messy, disorganized crime scene usually meant a first-time offender, a spur-of-the-moment thing, or simply an amateur at work. So what had happened to Judge DeCampe?

The brittle air that bit into the people standing around the crime scene would not say. Still, the question hung in the air like a Pied Piper spirit, tugging at anyone caring to listen to the whisper inside the echoing wind. Authorities had immediately looked for and pulled all camera tapes within a reasonable radius of the scene, but the one most likely to have helped was not in service. They couldn't be so lucky. They wouldn't be handed a gift to uncover the person responsible. In other words, the person who had come for her remained a mystery. Had he admired her beauty, her wit, her abilities from afar? Had he sent her flowers? Offered her compliments? Wooed her and then surprised her with plane tickets to Borneo or the Australian

Outback? Was she this moment off on a cruise with a six-foot-four hunk half her age? No . . . no way, not with the gun and the keys lying here.

God, how Jessica wished it were otherwise, but whoever had the judge had taken her under duress.

"We've located her purse!" shouted a uniformed officer, coming in from a breezeway that led out into the Washington night where light sent shafts of silver through a delicate icy rain that wasn't enough in this dry season. "Was in a Dumpster just outside. Creep didn't bother taking it, but it's been rifled. Took the cards and cash, left the photos and ID."

"We can put out an all points on the card numbers," suggested Santiva.

"Get Lew Clemmens on that," Jesssica insisted. "He's the best we have at tracking credit cards. Trust me."

"OK, if you're sure of him."

"I insist."

Santiva got on his cell phone to make arrangements, but again found the phone uncooperative until he walked toward one of the exits. He called for one of the uniformed cops to walk the elder daughter over to him. He would need access to Judge DeCampe's social security number or personal pin numbers.

Kim Desinor lay now in the rear of a van, still reeling from her trancelike state. Santiva passed the rifled purse to Kim, asking if she would psychometrically read it. Now with the purse, her keys, the recently fashioned .45, and the single shoe, the picture of forced abduction came more and more into focus. Everything fit. Yet, some nagging something didn't feel right, didn't fit precisely. Jessica thought it felt like a missing but crucial element in a chemistry experiment or a missing ingredient in a recipe. Then Jessica filled in the blank with an instinctive suspicion that Judge DeCampe had had some dealings with her abductor before tonight.

Judge DeCampe certainly hadn't left the parking garage with anything resembling free will, unless she had reason to stage her own disappearance. But her closest friends and relatives believed this was an absurd possibility. The two daughters almost went ballistic at the suggestion when a pair of D.C. cops had put it to them. The women had screamed that their mother would never do anything to distress them, and certainly nothing of this nature.

One of the two strikingly tall, darkly tanned women rushed to Jessica and said, "Mother loved her life and the fact she'd become a grandmother. She loved every iota of her life here. She didn't for a moment miss Texas. We were all so . . . so happy with her here with us, finally in the area, you know?"

"We're going to do everything in our power to locate her," replied Jessica, while the woman pulled and tugged at her. "I promise you that."

As to her disappearance, all the family members adamantly parroted the same phrases. "It's totally out of character for Maureen," and "No one was more excited about her life than Maureen."

Finally, Santiva swept the family members out of the garage area and talked them into giving Jessica enough space to work. But there was so damned little to work with. She looked up and saw that the garage attendant's island and ticket booth were well within view of the spot where DeCampe's car remained silent and taunting. "Has anyone talked to the attendant?"

"First on scene took a statement from him. Says he didn't see or hear a thing."

"Where the fuck was he?"

"Claims he had a bad case of the runs—a stomach virus kept him running between here and the men's room just inside the building."

She stared at J. T. "And Santiva and the rest of you bought into his toilet excuse?"

"The guy's a slug, Jess. We're not going to get anything from him. I think he's doing roaches."

"Roaches? Marijuana?"

"Maybe crack. Can't be sure. But he definitely has lost some gray matter over the years."

"Where is he now?"

"Shift was over. Santiva set him on his useless way."

"Christ," she moaned.

"Trust me, Jess, he's useless," J. T. assured her. "He really seemed honestly wanting to help, but he had nothing whatever to contribute."

"No one else on board at the time?"

"Lateness of the hour . . . one attendant . . . taxpayer's money, all that."

"One of us better check on Kim. See how she's holding up," Jessica said, lifting from her knees and going to the van to speak with a more lucid Kim Desinor. Jessica had known Kim now for a number of years, and they had worked a number of cases together, their first in New Orleans, where Kim had grown up Catholic in an orphanage, no one knowing of her gift of psychometry—reading objects for psychic impressions.

As Jessica approached Kim in the van where she lay on a cot with a waiting attendant, Kim asked, "How're you doing, Jess?"

Jess thought her friend looked pale and drained, weary and sleepy-eyed. Somehow Kim looked smaller. The word *frail* filled Jessica's mind.

"More to the point, sweetie, how're you doing? I hear you had quite a long session."

Richard stood nearby, lending support and saying hello to Kim, whom he had met through Jessica.

"What happened during the session? Anything useful?"

"Mostly a jumble of confused images: darkness, a void, choking feeling, claustrophobic spaces . . . hands, feet tied."

As usual, the skeptic in Jessica said, *Anyone could say the same, knowing the victim was abducted.*

"Got a distinct odor of decay. Stronger than I have ever read it before."

Jessica did not know what to say to this. "And did you get anything from the purse?"

"Purse was handled by someone other than either De-Campe or her abductor. That's all I could get."

"The attendant, no doubt," muttered Jessica. "I want to grill his ass."

"As to the fall I took, it was brought on by some sort of flashing pain, like a searing shock."

"A shock? What kind of shock?"

"A sudden zap like I was hit by a lightning bolt, although I have no idea what that must feel like. Scared the hell out of me. Felt it in every cell in my being."

"Electricity?"

"Yeah, I think so . . . but as you know, it could be symbolic."

"Or it could be literal? If he used some sort of electric tensor gun on her, that would explain her being so taken by surprise. He calls out to her, and she stops before unlocking her car, turns, sees she knows him, relaxes her grip on the gun she has already revealed when zap—she's surprised a second time by a shock of some sort."

"That's a pretty good line of suppositions," replied Kim.

"They'll have to serve us for now. So, what about when you were under? Before the shock? Were you getting anything else unusual?" Jessica persisted. "Did you see anything that might help guide us? Anything at all?"

"Nothing else, save that strange odor . . . like the odor of death and decay mixed with earthy odors left by vermin, mildewy stuff, like the smell of a bad mushroom, which when I get . . . well, it usually ends in finding the victim dead, Jess," Kim reiterated.

"My God," Jessica moaned, her eyes closed as she pictured the grieving family.

"I'm sorry . . . but I don't hold much hope for De-Campe."

"Are you saying that you have absolutely no hope? That you believe she is dead already?"

"No, no! Never any absolutes in this . . . I don't get that sensation, but I do get the sensation that this will end in her death, and that she will die a most unpleasant death."

Jessica frowned and held Kim's hands in hers. "Thanks, Kim. And if you have any of those flashback moments coming to you, I'm sure you'll keep me apprised."

"Absolutely."

"In the meantime, rest up. We may need you again and

again on this one. Obviously, the clock is ticking fast here."
Jessica started to leave the rear of the van where Kim now
sat upright, gathering back her scattered energies. But something stopped Jessica in her tracks.

Kim realized that Jessica stood staring at her with an
intensity she hadn't felt before. "What is it?"

Jessica stepped back toward Kim. She stared at a strange
speck of discoloration on her friend and colleague's cheek.
It looked like a beauty spot on her right cheek, but Kim had
never had a beauty spot there before. "Just noticed for the
first time this pinpoint of a freckle you have," she explained.

"I haven't a single freckle on my entire face," replied
Kim. "What're you talking about?"

Jessica then reached out to touch it and wipe away the
mark. "It's likely something you picked up when you fell."
Jessica smiled even as she realized the mark didn't wipe
away.

Kim smiled in return, thinking the gesture a kindness
toward her, a show of sincere concern. The words about a
blemish just an excuse for Jessica Coran to show a bit of
genuine affection. They said their good-byes, and Jessica
marched back toward the garage, stopping short of the structure.

Jessica then snatched out her cellular phone and called
Lew Clemmens back at Quantico. For some time now, Lew
had been Jessica's favorite contact in the computer support
division of the FBI. No magician on the planet could do
what Lew did. He was literally the best computer geek a
girl could have—a consummate information gobbler. She'd
barked out what she needed to Lew without so much as a
how're you doing or how's the wife, but Clemmens, like
everyone in law enforcement, knew what was going on. In
fact, Santiva had already reached him with the credit card
numbers he was to track.

"I've already got it going, Jess. I put out an all points on
anyone using the judge's credit cards. The family readily
gave up both Visas and the MasterCard."

Jessica gave a fleeting thought to the family—how their
privacy became public the moment a crime was committed

against them. The family had to give up all pretense to privacy for a safe and hopefully speedy return of a loved one gone missing.

Lew continued his nonstop tirade about the judge. "Didn't waste a moment. Someone's got her cards, and we need to catch this guy before . . . well . . . ASAP, before it's too damned—"

"Shut up for a minute, will you, Lew?" She pictured Lew at his computer, his stomach spilling over his keyboard, a broad smile generally streaking across his face.

"What? Oh, sure."

"We need to look closely at the cases she was working on at the time of her disappearance. I seem to recall some racketeering case, involving the D.C. Mafia. Then there's that nasty business with the Wainwright case, where the guy may or may not have murdered his sister's husband, after the husband was found innocent of murdering the sister. We need to work back from her most recent cases—things she's involved in now, yesterday's verdicts, last week's, last month's, since she's been in D.C. You got that?"

"Just since she's been in D.C. Got it. Nothing before that?"

"No . . . she was abducted here. Not likely some pissed-off Texan is going to cross the continent to settle a score."

"Unless he happens to be in town, or unless it's a guy with a Texas-sized vendetta," countered Lew.

"Points taken, but—"

"But we can't waste time down a blind alley, so let's begin with her D.C. cases," Lew finished for her.

"Agreed, and thanks again, Lew."

"Gotcha . . . will do."

Jessica hung up, and the click resounded in her ear like the closing of a tomb. Something about what Lew had said, about the judge's cases before she had moved to Washington, D.C. . . . about someone stalking her clear from Texas . . . something about the finality of not finding the right information in time. It all made Jessica ill, to think what might be happening to Judge DeCampe at this moment.

*   *   *

JESSICA had returned to the cryptlike area of the parking garage where court authorities this morning had begun to show up in search of their usual parking spaces. Disgruntled judges and clerks of court and attorneys gave varying degrees of cold stares, some demanding to know the reason why. All of them had been rerouted to another area set aside for them until the FBI—and Jessica in particular—chose to release the crime scene.

Every time a crime scene like this, out in the open, subject to the elements and the traipsing of man and dog was released, it seemed to Jessica an inevitable loss to forensic investigators. No matter how long a crime scene like this was held cordoned off, there was always a need to have kept it whole and intact longer than authorities generally allowed. End result, something was missed. But pressure to resume things as normal always won out, and so losing the crime scene to time demands normally meant tying investigative hands.

However, as it stood and in all outward appearance, she expected that very little else of any use might come of this place.

Still, she combed the area for fibers, hairs, anything that might, under a microscope, lead to a clue or even a DNA match with the abductor once they located him.

Even as her hands worked to gather the minuscule evidence that might or might not have been left by the attacker, Jessica's mind flashed over a deep-seated fear that she had been pushing off since Richard's arrival in the states. *Dare not drag it into the light* was a phrase that kept repeating in her head over this. She only dared to now look at it in a waking dream, a kind of half-life existence that took her back to London, England, where she had met Richard Sharpe. So much time had gone by while she had awaited Richard's arrival at Dulles International for their reunion, and finally the day had come, and finally they were together— truly together. Only apart since then for the time it took to shower and dress and do all the routine things of life. She sensed a horrid dread come over her whenever she thought of separating from him for any length of time, as if to do so meant to lose him. Even now, here, with him nearby, as she did her work, she felt an irrational fear of losing him somehow to her other world, her work. And so she found herself pacing about the corridors of her subconscious, second-guessing every word, every action she'd taken with Richard. How long would he stand for this, for her work being more important than him? What man did she know on the planet who willingly stood second place to a woman's work? A woman's other passion? Pacing the corridor of memory . . . pacing the corridor of old regret, past the foyer and into recent remorse. Pacing even in her soul, her heart turning slowly into a garrison, like a sad and empty room made of mortar and stone. Lonely echoes against walls filled with chinks born there out of past pains. God, the fear of losing Richard now that she had found him might paralyze her.

Then Jessica imagined again the nightmare that was no dream. She imagined the disappearance of Maureen De-Campe. She journeyed down each path of the labyrinth to examine the myriad possibilities. She had already tossed out the one path, a wild, romantic fling with a secret suitor who had whisked her off to some beach shore or cabin retreat. Now she must explore the darker possibilities. Perhaps some sociopathic fiend held her hostage for lust-torture-murder in that sequence. She imagined horrible decapitation and mutilation of various body parts; she imagined wood chippers and blood sent to the heavens, of postmortem defilement, and of shallow graves and animal finds.

She'd seen it all too many times in too many situations. She suspected the worst had happened to the judge; she expected to find her dead in some ditch somewhere along some abandoned highway. Friends and relatives would hold out hope till the end, like a twisting hand cloth that comes to tatters in the end, the stress and horror of it all taking its toll on all those who loved the victim. Jessica's own friends had told her how jaded she'd become after over two decades of chasing monsters.

Still, something different about this case mercilessly nagged at her gut, tearing at it the way a vicious animal might rip apart a beautiful bird caught in a snare. Past villains she had known—their features and their crimes played inside Jessica's head. Violins also played inside her head—a song of sadness so deep and abiding that it created a black, empty hole where life ought to be. The violins played for the victims, always the same refrain, one that spoke of an endless well of pathos for the human condition, a condition that often created angels but just as often created monsters. The violins played for a world in which mankind did so much good and yet so much evil in the same breath, a world in which fast-moving clouds in a moon-and-star-filled sky, or a full moon rising over a silver ocean, stood shoulder to shoulder with child molestation and cruelty of all sorts. The sound of it was something she felt more than heard—vibrations on a tuning fork—and they disturbed her core being more than she dared admit until a near mental breakdown had sent her to Dr. Donna LeMonte for psychotherapy some years back. Even so, even today, after several years of professional help, the tuning fork continued to disturb her more than she understood.

She hadn't felt so much unleashed fear since the night she'd been trapped and strung up by her hands and feet to die in the manner of Christ on the cross in an underground cavern below London. And while that fear had been for herself, this new, awful fear was for Maureen DeCampe.

Jessica's knees now began to hurt where she had been kneeling over the few clues left them. She stood to straighten her legs, and she looked about the cold institutional gray walls of the underground parking garage. There seemed a solitude here that felt eternal. "This fucking place feels like a goddamn mausoleum."

Richard appeared next to her and squeezed her hand, whispering, "It must feel like a horror chamber for a woman alone at midnight."

While she squeezed Richard's hand in return, Jessica's eyes registered the quiet, thoughtful faces surrounding her. She simply said, "We're done here." It came out as a statement of fact, as if to say there was nothing whatever left to examine at the scene. "Anything else we do here this morning will add up to a complete waste of time and energy."

"We're done?" asked J. T.

"There's nothing more here that's going to talk to us, John."

"But we still haven't dusted the car or—"

"Do it if you like, but he never touched her car. Neither did she, for that matter."

"Yes, from the look of it, she never got that far," Richard added.

"So there's absolutely not a damned thing left for us. The answers to this one aren't going to be found in the fibers or the prints or the dust."

J. T. only stared at her, wondering what was going through Jessica's mind. She knew he could not imagine the terror of a woman alone with her captor.

THE next day, Jessica stared out the window of the spartan office turned over to her at FBI headquarters in D.C., where she could remain in close proximity to the case. Her office overlooked a section of the D.C. Beltway, now that some old tenements had been demolished and reduced to ashes to make way for construction of more new high-rise upscale apartments. If you lived inside the Beltway, you likely worked for one of the many companies supplying services and goods to the government. Jessica could see a strip of Beltway bandits, companies that lined the Beltway and did almost exclusive business with the U.S. government. Scam in D.C. was a way of life.

As a result of having to take up temporary residence in D.C., she'd had to say good-bye to Richard and her new Quantico farmstead, at least for now. She'd driven back to the apartment with him, and they'd talked about the situation as well as the Missing Persons case that had so suddenly changed their plans.

"Circumstances like these can't be ignored," Richard said at one point on the drive back.

"Santiva and his special cases always seem to screw with my life."

Richard puzzled over the remark for a moment before saying, "Oh, yes . . . as in screw up."

"Yeah, you've got that right, darling."

They both laughed. Richard's response was one of interest in the case. He encouraged her instinctual response to the lack of any evidence of a struggle pointing to either a surprise grab or that the woman did not fear her attacker. He also agreed that the lack of concern on the abductor's part in leaving her keys and the .45 lying there was an act of defiance against authority, likening it to the criminal who defecated at the scene just to piss cops off.

"And what sort of bugger uses a cattle prod to control his victims?" Richard had asked. "I mean if your psychic is right, then he's using a stun gun or a bloody cattle prod of some sort, don't you think? That might make 'im either a farmer or a cop himself . . . maybe."

"Nowadays anyone could get hold of a stun gun, Richard. Doesn't have to be a cop."

"So true," he'd agreed.

"Anyone with a computer can order any damn thing that might come to mind these days." They'd arrived at her Quantico apartment, and they promptly went up and inside. Richard hadn't any of the reserve of fear she had felt well up inside when she thought of how much time away from him this case meant.

"It's your work, dear, and who does it better? Just promise me one thing."

"What's that?" she mirthfully replied.

"That you'll come back to me . . . home safe."

"Promise."

They had made passionate love then, and afterward, she packed a bag and returned to D.C. All of the evidence-gathering and lab work would be handled out of the D.C. field offices and crime lab. Until the case was solved, she'd be living in a D.C. apartment at taxpayers' expense. To complicate her life, it appeared D.C.'s dry season had ended. The rain had come down the night before in a steady, calm downpour, leaving the streets awash, sewers drinking it in.

And now Jessica watched the light rain that J. T. had exaggeratedly characterized as "The Flood." It barely washed clean the windows. She had gotten six hours' sleep, and she continued to work at clearing her mind of the overwhelming fear growing by the hour that Judge Maureen DeCampe would not be found alive. To fend off this negative and depressive thought, she abandoned it long enough to count the now evaporating raindrops on the windowpane of her temporary D.C. office in a building filled with files on missing persons. Jessica couldn't clear from her mind that creeping, familiar sense of clawing claustrophobia overtaking her. The room filled with a thousand dead voices and dead stories—all the innocent women and children who had ever disappeared without a trace, all seemed to cry out with the rhythm of the raindrops against the windowpane. And yet the cry was all of one voice.

And all the voices had one other thing in common: Here in the city resided countless unexculpated murders. The files of victims that lay silent and unanswered in D.C., as with each major American city in the nation, finding voice, would drown out the living, she imagined. Hardly a new story— *not enough manpower to begin to do the job.*

However, Jessica had been working with Lew Clemmens on an electronic answer to give true voice to the dead of D.C., and if successful, to carry the plan to other major cities throughout the country and possibly abroad. She had modeled her idea on a Houston Police Department program called COMIT, run by a Cherokee Indian detective named Lucas Stonecoat with whom her friend Kim Desinor had successfully worked a case. As a result, Jessica felt confident that very soon ancient necrofiles nationwide would be placed on computer files, and any one of them could be accessed from anywhere in the country. This would save countless hours and manpower.

However—and there always was a however—it had proven a tedious process, and still some 60 percent of D.C.'s cold files had as yet to be revived in this fashion; the 40 percent that had been scanned to disk and transcribed onto the Washington Police mainframe database under USA-COMIT had not been read by anyone human, except for Lew Clemmens. For the time being, it had been for electronic eyes only. Today they could plug in key words to flag any cases that might now be solved via DNA evidence, new fingerprinting techniques, photographic imaging, or any other new technology. In many ways, the tide was turning in favor of the crime fighters and away from the criminals, thanks to modern scientific police and forensic detection. Once the old file transfers were completed, anyone anywhere in the world who might be working a cold case could conceivably do searches for unsolved murder investigations, which might now be reassessed on grounds of new technologies designed to combat crime.

The trouble was the sheer number of cold cases. *Any* death investigation with moss on it could benefit from current scientific knowledge and techniques *not* available to earlier law enforcement—an unpleasant fact shared by every police agency in the world. Jessica imagined a time-traveling modern medical examiner who might go back to significant moments to unravel mysteries surrounding deaths that, at the time, could not be solved, from Jack-the-Ripper to Lizzie Borden. The thought recalled a fascinating book that her mentor, Dr. Asa Holcraft, had insisted she must read when only a fledgling student in his classes. The book was *Century of the Detective* by Jurgen Thorwald, a fascinating attempt to survey the history of crime detection and the science that had built up around it. The book put a great deal into perspective, not the least being the question of guilt or innocence of a man convicted at a time when animal blood and human blood could not be separately identified, a time when there was no microscopic evidence since there was no microscope, a time before fingerprinting was discovered as a viable crime-fighting tool.

Jessica had stepped away from the window, the sadly anemic rain, and her thoughts. She held her hand against her chest, an acidic pain rising there to threaten her. Her team so far had uncovered nothing new, and the case was stalemating quickly. She walked out of her temporary office and into an adjacent one where Lew Clemmens sat at a state-of-the-art computer, working away.

Jessica joked with Clemmens about the notion of a time-traveling crime fighter, since Lew had earlier talked up a blue streak about some TV program named *Time-COP* with the same premise.

"Hell, even Jack-the-Ripper could be discovered with the new technologies," Lew Clemmens said over his shoulder as he worked at the screen. She thought them finished with the subject then, but Lew kept up chatter about the idea.

Lew, like her, had set up shop in D.C. at Santiva's insistence. She now went to stand over his hefty shoulder, where the young man worked at bringing Jessica caseload information lifted from the courthouse where DeCampe had worked.

"Old Jack wouldn't stand a chance against the crime-fighting tools we have today," Lew said.

"Can't argue with you there," she agreed, her mind now set on the present, on the DeCampe case, which had seen zero progress so far.

Clemmens continued, adding, "Imagine if we could go back in time and hand over our crime-fighting tools to London authorities when the Ripper was at large and taunting police."

Jessica knew how Lew's mind raced with two and sometimes three subjects at once, and while he worked on the DeCampe case, he could sit about and talk on another topic as if his brain simply partitioned off the separate jobs needing to be done. He was amazing for this.

Clemmens continued, "Yeah . . . if even they'd had only a laser blue light to follow the blood trail, they would have caught the guy. History's most infamous serial killer."

"Are you kidding?" she finally asked, a bit miffed. "Today, Jack's career would have been cut extremely short. The man left a slime trail as wide and as obvious as a walrus dragging his ass over a mud puddle."

Lew looked young enough to be delivering Jessica's newspaper. *He hardly looks the part of a fellow whose job touches so many lives,* she thought.

"Still, if Jack were alive today," countered Lew, "he'd know to be a hell of a lot more tidy, wouldn't you say? I mean like the creep that got hold of Judge DeCampe?"

Jessica liked Lew's enthusiasm for a subject he warmed up to—war-pathing over it, as Lew professed an Ojibwa heritage along with his flinty Irish looks. As the young man's eyes—reflected in the computer screen—lit up green and luminous, he said, "Today's serial killer has more readily available information at his disposal about what we know and how we work." Lew's fingers seemed to operate independently over the keys. "Thanks to the TLC channel. Still, crime makes you stupid; I've heard you say it time and again. Jack isn't necessarily more intelligent today than he was in 1872 when he killed that string of prostitutes in Whitechapel."

Jessica smiled at this. "I'm telling you, today the Ripper would be apprehended."

"Only because of the poor condition of criminal detection in his day, he was never caught. If he were alive today, Jack would have to bone up big time," countered Lew.

Jessica snickered and added, "Yeah, you're right. Today's criminal can and sometimes does study criminology right alongside the criminologist. I take your point."

"And they gain much of their information off the Internet, from FBI public relations officers, from police bulletins, law enforcement gazettes, Ann Rule and other true crime books, as well as novels and films depicting criminal behavior, police procedure, profiling, and crime-scene detection. Ever read *The Handyman* or the *Decoy* series?"

"Price of a free and open society; price of democracy: freedom and access to information." Jessica snatched an office chair and wheeled it to a stop beside Lew, and she slipped into it, groaning at a spasm of pain that cut knifelike through her back. "Like a double-edged sword," she agreed.

Lew glanced at her, wondering if she meant the pain in her lower back, evidenced by Jessica's grimace, or if she meant the double edge of freedom. He snatched at the back of his neck as if to rip some pain of his own from it, and then he continued downloading cases which had been tried by Maureen DeCampe.

The printer was abuzz with information spewing forth. Jessica picked up a stack of papers and said, "Damn, we're going to need an army of readers. I'll have to put together a small task force to review DeCampe's cases." Still, she began reading, scanning, hoping to light on something useful, a verdict, a name, a clue of any sort.

The phone rang, and Jessica grabbed for it; anything to end her staring at the reams of paper that made up the bulk of DeCampe's cases in just the last month.

The call was for Lew, his wife, sounding pissed off. Jessica handed him the phone and tried not to watch him squirm. Jessica liked Lew, but she thought the man ought to show a little firmness with the woman on the other end of the line.

Clemmens hung up, shaking his head. "Sorry . . . she has no idea why we have to be in D.C. I had to leave a message at home for her. She wasn't pleased."

Again the phone rang. This time J. T. came on the line, going on about how the newsies had gotten the entire story of Judge DeCampe's disappearance and still no ransom note, nothing whatever, in fact, from the abductor. J. T. sounded as if he might hyperventilate.

"And everyone's gunning for you, Jess. They think you're not moving fast enough on the case. Can you believe the crap that—"

"Slow down, J. T. Take it easy, and take a deep breath. I'm working on the case. I've got Lew Clemmens here, and we're searching electronically through old case files that have anything to do with Judge DeCampe. Going to take it back incrementally to her first year out of law school if necessary to find any clue as to what sort of phantom we are chasing. You tell all the whomevers that. Give it to Santiva. He'll kick it upstairs."

"Yeah . . . good thinking. He'll run to the end zone with that. Gotcha. I told them you were on top of it."

"Thanks, John. And John—"

"Yes?"

"Don't let the bastards wear you down."

"Situation normal, all fouled up," he replied and laughed.

"And let Santiva know that Lew and I have been at work at HQ for two hours this morning on this."

"Right . . . check . . . count on it. Lew's with you already?"

"Picked him up on my way back from Quantico. Tell anyone busting our asses that we are busting our own asses and don't need any help. See you back here when you can get here."

"Will do. You did the right thing calling in Lew."

"Tell them that. I wouldn't trust anyone but Lew with this. He knows the COMIT project like no one else aboard, so if this guy's MO is in any of the files, open or unsolved, that we've poured into the system to date, then we'll get him."

"Just a matter of time."

"Nice of you to say so, J. T."

She hung up. Lew stared up at her where she now stood. "Thanks again, Doctor, for the confidence. I'm correlating any unsolved murder cases in the system with the judge."

"Who knows? We might get lucky. Meanwhile, I also want you and Steve Conyers to work on/off shifts so there's no slowdown on this info gathering. And Lew . . ."

"Yeah?"

"Do the same for solved cases as you're doing for unsolved cases, and cases that resulted in threats on the judge's life."

"Let our fingers do the legwork," he replied. "Why not?"

"It's the time element that's crucial here. Guy abducts a woman and does not make a ransom demand . . . well, you figure it out. Not much hope that time is on our side here. Maybe the computer can even the odds a bit."

Lew fell silent for a moment. The personal aspect of this case called on them both to work especially hard to locate a female judge whom they both knew from stints at the courthouse. They were at war with the clock. And time had no beginning and no end here; instead it took on the nature of a runaway train.

"What're we really looking for, Jess?" asked Lew.

"In the Native American scheme of things, Lew, a wrong done at the beginning of time still festers because it may as well have been done today. Now, all things in nature being cyclical, even human nature and actions are understood as circular, and time is no exception."

"I see . . . I think."

Jessica continued, not missing a beat, talking over Lew. "Nor is revenge. It's the same kind of thinking that has kept the ancient, tribal belief in avenging one's brother by one's own hands an absolute trust. But the belief is not limited to Native Americans. It's one that has come down through the ages through all cultures."

"Is that why Native Americans view the atrocities of the Indian Wars as having just happened like yesterday?"

"Same holds true of black men who'd never lived under the institution of slavery, yet they still often act as if wronged personally, because it was a kind of slow death meted out to their ancestors. Easily understandable, really. Who can blame a black man or a red man for not putting a time limit on such atrocities?"

"Little wonder the Indians take such glee in victories like the Little Big Horn."

"While Wounded Knee continues as an open sore for Indians and an embarrassment for whites."

Jessica, who had always had a fascination for Native American culture and art, had joined some friends who had gone to the small reservation town of Wounded Knee with its long history of bloodshed. Wounded Knee's largest cemetery cradled the murdered Sioux who had died there, victims of a bloody massacre at the hands of the U.S. Cavalry in 1890 that proved to be the last major encounter between the red man and the white man on a battlefield. Then, on February 27, 1973, absolutely frustrated with conditions at the reservation town of Wounded Knee, American Indian Movement leaders staged a takeover and an encampment to bring national attention to the plight of Native Americans and the deteriorating reservation conditions everywhere. They occupied several buildings to dramatize their com-

plaints. FBI and Bureau of Indian Affairs police surrounded
the AIM camp. During the next seventy-one days, gunfire
was exchanged, until AIM members could no longer go on.
Trapped without food, water, or electricity amid the bitter
winter, the noose was drawn, not unlike the Sioux before
them. Two members of the occupying force—Anna Mae
Aquash and Joe Stuntz—became martyrs to a cause for
which most Americans took no heed. Nine other people
were wounded, including a federal marshal, who came away
paralyzed.

Jessica had felt an overwhelming sense that the judge was
the victim of a kind of justice, or injustice, not entirely different from the kind of injustice that came with "blood"
vengeance—Native American style.

Jessica had had DeCampe's Western-style pistol brought
into the task force room to keep focused on who they were
working to locate.

The cold sight of the .45 brought Jessica back to the
present, full circle. "How long has she gone missing?" She
recalled having asked the WPD detectives the night before.

"Long enough to alarm her family; they waited dinner
for her after she'd called to say she was out the door, on
her way home after working overtime. It was her 'overtime'
night as she called it, Thursday nights. But it went unusually
long, and then she didn't show up at all. Finally, she was
not answering her cell phone, so her son-in-law comes down
to investigate when midnight rolled around," Jack Dane, a
longtime veteran of the department who had no love lost for
Judge DeCampe, had replied.

"Found her cell phone in her purse," added Dane's
heavyset partner, Joe Myers. Jessica had taken one look at
the pair and instantly understood why the higher ups wanted
an "independent" brought in to lead the investigation. These
men were emotionally involved, yes, but in a negative sense;
in fact, they were so negative that they might have done the
deed themselves, if Jessica didn't know better. It appeared
that DeCampe had managed to offend every working cop in
D.C. at one time or another, even to the degree that some
in the city would as soon leave her to her fate. In fact,

officialdom didn't believe they could scrape two Washington cops together who could devote themselves to De-Campe's case without some prejudice. As a result, Jessica felt certain that the bureau could and would do a better job of finding the judge than the D.C. police for more reasons than manpower and technological support.

"And so her son-in-law comes down to investigate, and what'd he find?" Jessica asked after staring down the men, a small gargoylish creature lurking at the back of her mind to tell her that she would, despite any feelings toward the victim, do her utmost to find DeCampe—dead or alive.

"Peter Owens," said Dane, "House representative." He handed over his pocket notebook where his address and phone number and remarks were jotted down. "Said he found her car in her spot at the courthouse. Some suspicious items scattered about."

"Cell phone and her purse were missing," added Myers. "Looks like a simple abduction, straight up, no-nonsense snatch and grab."

She wondered how much they had already disturbed. She stared them down before saying, "We'll keep you apprised of every step of the investigation from our end, detectives, and would appreciate it if you reciprocated."

"Recipro-cated . . . sure," said Dane.

As they walked off together, talking of a place to grab some breakfast, the two laughed over Jessica's use of the word reciprocated.

Something told Jessica that Maureen DeCampe faced an even worse fate than a simple abduction. Was there ever such a thing as a *simple* abduction? She didn't think so. Still, she didn't know exactly what her intuition meant to tell her, or if this instinctual feeling that the judge's abduction had to do with her being a judge had a name, or even if it were right. Still, something kept hitting that nail, that this abduction had to do with who the victim was, that it was tied to an official case, one of her courtroom decisions. So, did it have a name and a number, this case?

As luck would have it, at the same time that the judge had become a victim for the first time in her life, Jessica was heavily invested in the Claude Lightfoot case, the murder of an Indian activist that appeared complicated beyond the norm. The case involved the death of a Blackfoot Crow Indian activist and civil rights worker, who had overcome serious physical handicaps his entire life only to be killed in a vicious attack in the early '80s that nowadays would go for the most heinous and brutal of racially motivated hate crimes. The murder had gone unsolved all these years, what police called a cold case. Claude Lightfoot had been twenty-seven when he faced multiple attackers. No one was ever apprehended in the case, and few were questioned in the murder that had happened at a closed-down drive-in theater. Pieces of his mangled body had been hung from the marquee and discovered at daybreak by passing motorists. This all in Sioux Falls, South Dakota, where such ugly things weren't supposed to ever happen.

In effect, after much beating and torture, Lightfoot had been lashed to two cars, his feet to one bumper, his wrists to another. A bumper of one vehicle remained behind in a spray of blood, a souvenir to the night's violence. The young man had been literally torn in two when two cars drove off in opposite directions. According to the local coroner's report at the time, Claude Lightfoot likely felt nothing, as he was unconscious from a severe beating and trauma to the head with lacerations to the brain, but he was alive when his body was literally ripped in two.

It had occurred out at a lonely moor surrounding an abandoned old outdoor drive-in called The Apache Theater. It had been far from any town lights or houses off the main arteries leading to Sioux Falls. No one save those responsible had seen a thing, and no one else heard Lightfoot's screams—none but the coyotes and the scrub cactus, and recently a man named McArthur, who was now dealing in information.

Anyone hoping to solve such a case would have a hard time jogging memories lurking so long in the darkness of a decrepit guilt and a crippled remorse, but perhaps somewhere out there in South Dakota's heartland, there lived a gnawing, unrelenting regret, a flicker of positive humanity burning like the last wisp of a candle. If there were any hope whatsoever, Jessica wanted more than life itself to avenge the voiceless young Crow man who had died so horribly at the hands of an obvious pack of rabid racist jackals.

Jessica's old curse was a simple one: her obsessive and near maniacal seeking out of the truth to help the underdog, the beaten, the dead, who had no one to speak for them; this all warred with her desire to have a life. Her enormous tolerance for things, her Job-like patience to learn and uncover truths, and her relentlessness—all her best qualities—proved to be her worst qualities as well, especially for those who got close to her. Preordained by some unseen force or hand, she felt a constant gargoyle perched on her shoulder, gnawing and ranting and sullen until she provided it with answers. This had been the case now for almost two decades, when her mentor and lover, Otto Boutine, had died on the altar of her relentlessness. It had been her first major case as an FBI agent, and Otto had so believed in her. Since his passing, she had been driven to prove that his faith in her abilities as a medical examiner extraordinaire had not been misplaced.

Time and again she had had to prove her worth to the FBI, and both her physical self and her mental state went through repeated reassessment by her superiors. Try as some might, they could find no fault with her performance, and she still remained the best shot with a handgun the boy's club had ever produced. Still, she knew they were less interested in her ability with a weapon and even a microscope than in being assured 100 percent that she had overcome all of the emotional pain brought on when one's life amounted to chasing monsters. She had convinced her superiors anew that she was psychologically fit to continue doing what she did best—only a partial lie, for truth be told, she knew that the mental anguish would pursue her to her grave, despite the bravest effort on her part. It was for this reason that she so empathized with Kim Faith Desinor, whenever Kim faced down a killer inside her visionary readings of crime scenes and objects and photos associated with a murder investigation.

She had learned to appreciate Kim's gift and the inherent dangers associated with it. She was not far removed from the same dangers herself. But she had learned also to appreciate the best efforts put forth by her friends and coworkers to help her. She also felt good about working with the new FBI shrink with whom she'd had an instant rapport. All of these people she allowed close knew her for the liar that she was when it came to her own well-being, and there was comfort in that; comfort in the fact that others knew how deep she had traveled into the abyss and had managed to keep her sanity intact and her priorities in focus.

Still, the superiors worried about Jessica becoming a crack-up case, so from time to time, they saddled her with duties that kept her pinned down to either the lab or more recently to a computer. The restoration of dead files, to keep her both busy and off field duty for a period, was when she came across the Lightfoot file.

Dealing with the COMIT plan on a national level primarily meant a desk job, a prison to a woman of her nature. But then the DeCampe thing happened, and her superiors couldn't help themselves. They knew her as the best. They demanded she take charge of the case, despite any earlier misgivings about Jessica's sanity or loss of humanity or any such thing. DeCampe had people in high places, friends and family alike. Her case demanded the best and the brightest.

THREE

A man whose blood
Is very snow broth; one who never feels
The wanton stings and motions of the sense.

—WILLIAM SHAKESPEARE

NORMALLY speaking, everyone but Jessica was happy about her taking time off the job, of her slowing down, her periods of personal leave, but now with Richard and their plans going forth, she was the happy one, and she didn't particularly want to be bothered by any other reality, especially the job of hunting down monsters. But the FBI was like a force of nature—a mindless chaos unto itself—and the force had come to her again. They had strongly encouraged her to take on the DeCampe case, but she comforted herself in believing she could, if she wished, decline the case, that she did in the final analysis have the strength of reputation and power within the "family," as many called the FBI, to have the last word. But she wasn't so vain as to truly believe that if push came to shove, she could win against the top echelon in such a disagreement. And besides, with Richard's encouragement, she did find the case important and tugging at her. So once again, she was heading up perhaps the most important case of the year, as it were.

At least she had had the last say as to how they would proceed and with whom she would be working, and she was pleased with the speed with which Santiva had arranged everything. "Good to be needed," she'd confided to J. T. at a moment when she had first come on board.

She kept no secrets save those of the heart from J. T.

Only one other person understood her anger and resentment
at her superiors, and that was her new shrink, Patricia Phelan. Patricia knew her to be a ticking bomb if she felt unduly
cooped up or hog-tied. Pat daily proved to be a no-nonsense,
fiery-tongued petite redhead who had skillfully worked
around FBI officials to arrange for real investigative work
for Jessica, assuring Santiva and other higher ups that it was
just precisely what the "patient" needed: work. No one else
knew it, but Jessica certainly did know how influential Pat
Phelan had been in Jessica's decision of whether to take on
the case or not. Jessica knew herself well enough to know
that she did indeed need to work. Work was like breathing
for her. So she was, after all, glad to have been called up
to bat on the DeCampe case.

While Jessica's first curse was the painful realization that
she was as obsessed about finding the facts and ending the
careers of murderers as Ahab was with the whale, her second curse was also a simple one: She simply could not abide
injustice of any kind, but especially injustice toward the
helpless and the weak.

She thought of the Claude Lightfoot case. She'd been
obsessed with it before Richard had arrived in America. She
and Lew Clemmens had been digging up the bones around
that old case.

"Where do you begin to search for such Gila monsters?"
Lew Clemmens had asked her when he had brought the
twenty-year-old case to her attention.

"Under the nearest rock," she'd replied.

Jessica had been poring over the file since Lew had pro-
grammed the computer to red-flag hate crimes—anything
smacking of a racially motivated crime. This was his job,
but he was also looking for anything that might rival the
ferocity of this murder, anything similar in the least that
might point them toward a suspect or suspects, first within
the same geographical location and then expanding from
there.

It took time, but they'd found two men who had served
time at Folsom State Prison for hate crimes similar to what
had occurred in the Lightfoot case. The two had discovered

the Aryan Brotherhood in prison, where they'd also found one another, and when one was released, they stayed in touch until the second stepped out of prison. Together, they went to Sioux Falls, South Dakota, ostensibly following a job, working day labor on a construction site. Joseph Ireland and Montgomery Nestor had become Jessica's primary targets as a result of computer snooping.

Jessica had not left her Quantico, Virginia, office for Sioux Falls, but with Lew's ingenious help, she had put out an ever-widening electronic eye on the two former convicts with ties to the Aryan Nation. But they needed eyewitness information, and so they began building information from acquaintances, a Malcolm McArthur in particular.

Jessica knew just the right man to call, a field agent in the Sioux Falls area. She had made some calls and had sent the perfect man for the job: a very scary, huge black man named Hosea Crooms, who would frighten a bounty hunter. Crooms was told to look under all the rocks and to ask some tough questions of McArthur, and early reports back said that McArthur was definitely in the know and was willing to talk for immunity and a place in witness protection and for a hefty sum. Negotiations had gotten under way.

It was a hate crime Jessica still wanted very much to do something about. She was well aware of the foolish debate going on nationally over the semantics of the phrase *hate crimes*; some people believed all crimes of a violent nature were inherently crimes of hatred. But law enforcement people knew better. Hardly a country on the face of the planet was unaffected by racism, bigotry, and all its courtiers of ignorance and stupidity. Hate crime in the legal sense implied a premeditation to harm another based on his race, religion, sexual preference, or cultural heritage, and this "evil intent" ultimately meant a judge or a jury could add more time onto a convicted man's sentence for his display of hatred on the basis of dislike for a whole population of people. A hate crime on the books, whether before or after hate crime legislation, looked and smelled like violence directed at an individual *because* of the color of her skin, or his sexual orientation or religious preference. The spirit of

hate crime legislation meant to more severely punish those
ape men still involved in clubbing to death anyone who did
not appear to squat about the campfire in the exact fashion
of everyone else seated around the campfire.

Hate crime legislation intended, like laws made since
men began making laws, to end fear, ignorance, intolerance,
and hatred based on fears. Regardless, fear continued as the
great leveler of mankind, despite all his technological
accomplishments, and part of his growing fear was incul-
cated now through his own technological wonders, such as
neo-Nazi cyber domains, where hatred and bigotry were
preached to whole new generations and whole new populations of people via the Internet. *Any crackpot with a laptop* . . .
Jessica mused. Anyone could set himself up as a guru of
truth or religion with the push of a few key strokes in cy-
berspace, where none of the rules of decency or even laws
of ethics and tolerance applied. So hate crime legislation
came into being as perhaps a futile act, an attempt to muzzle
the human race. The law of mankind, especially in a dem-
ocratic society, was indeed an ambitious creature. So, using
key search words, the computer had obliged with the Lightfoot case and hundreds more, but Lew had also included
mutilation by ripping apart of limbs as a key phrase, and
Lightfoot's case itself came up among these.

So it had caught Lew's attention first, and Lew had
hoisted it on to Jessica with a kind of challenge. "Bet if
anyone could solve this horrible crime, it'd be you, Jess.
What a horrendous way to die."

After studying the file, Jessica shivered at how young
Lightfoot had met his end. She'd muttered to Lew, "Some
plains tribesmen ripped apart their especially hated enemies,
only they used horses instead of horsepowered Fords and
Chevys."

"So . . . where would you begin?" asked Clemmens,
pushing it, his eyes dancing, curious, intelligent.

"In a hate crime, you begin with the bottom feeders and
you work your way up."

However, the Lightfoot case, like so many others, had to
be placed on hold, at least for now. So Jessica had pushed

it aside, shunted it off. For now, Jessica's entire attention must be devoted to the DeCampe case. She must concern herself with the here and now, with the living case and not the dead one, with the live Judge DeCampe, *who had to be alive!*

ISAIAH James Purdy's brain felt too heavy inside his cranium, as if the jar of his skull had become filled with fluid, and worse yet, his mind, as well, had been turned over to the clawing, nonstop agitation that he must do what his God and his dead son clearly told him to do before the execution. He'd gone down to Huntsville, Texas, alone, clear from Iowa City, Iowa, to sit in a straight-backed folding chair to watch them electrocute Jimmy Lee until his poor boy was gone, as fried as a chicken wing by what they called executive order, as the governor had granted no reprieve.

Isaiah had grown up on black-and-white, tough-guy gangster movies from George Raft to Jimmy Cagney to Bogey duking it out with police in frantic shoot-outs, the hero bad guy always getting it in the end, sometimes via the electric chair. But nothing Hollywood could create could possibly have prepared the old man for what he had had to witness; nothing in Hollywood could ever match the sheer horror of a man sitting before a glass case and watching his son literally brain-fried and tortured to death, as burned at the stake as Saint Joan of Arc had been, and by whom? The authorities.

Isaiah had watched with the tears of Jimmy Lee's mother in his eyes. Jimmy Lee's mother could not have been there for the execution, even if she were alive, because she could not have borne up under the crushing horror of such emotions that flooded in on Isaiah, watching his own flesh and blood destroyed before his eyes in such a fashion. Destroyed like a rabid animal by the state, and on less evidence than it took to free that black man who was some big-shot basketball player and movie star.

When Jimmy Lee's mother had died, it was then that the voice of her son came full-blown into Isaiah's head, all the

way from the prison cell in Huntsville, Texas. Isaiah had at
one time decided not to go to the execution, had decided no
man should sit and stare at what the sovereign State of Texas
planned for his son. He could not leave his ill and dying
wife, Eunice Mae, who had never wavered in her devotion
and duty to him. He couldn't leave Eunice in her state, not
for the likes of Jimmy Lee, not for a moment.

Still, Jimmy Lee's words came creeping, seeping into
Isaiah's head through his mother's mind first: clawing,
snatching start-stops, stutters, and pleas. Toward the end,
he'd thought that perhaps, just perhaps Jimmy Lee had
found peace, but maybe in the end, Jimmy Lee simply didn't
want to be alone . . . in the end. Something about how he
had done as his daddy had told him. That he'd confessed
his sins before Christ and had discovered the healing power
of the Word.

Isaiah had pleaded with young Jimmy to read the Bible
his mother had sent him, simply to read the Bible and to
read it closely, and to find its message, and to deliver himself over to Christ his Savior, for many a battle was won
with the Bible in hand, and those reading the Bible over the
ages had been so taken over as to go out and win wars
against Philistines and Muslims and all manner of infidels
and soldiers of the Antichrist, to wage war on the Antichrist
in whatever form he next chose to appear. And if whole
races and populations could act out what they read in the
Bible, if it had that power over the minds of multitudes,
then why not over the individual, and why not Jimmy Lee,
the most lost soul on the planet?

Isaiah thought it a strange debate going on in America
as to violence on TV and film, when in fact for countless
generations the Bible had depicted more true violence than
any film imaginable. Still, there it was, and if the Holy Book
could affect the passions of nations, why not the dedicated
individual who sought to understand its deeper purpose?

So with Eunice Mae now at peace, deep in the ground,
a Bible passage she herself selected and impressed upon
Isaiah as the sure way to vengeance to see her over to the
other side, beyond the River, he had pulled up stakes for

the greater Houston area. He'd been on the road for hours without sleep. He feared he would miss the execution, his final good-bye to a son who had been born a bad seed, born with the mark of Cain. Cain slew his brother Abel, and while Jimmy Lee never had a brother nor ever killed a man, he had killed some women: six in all, and all of them loose and no account. Even the police reports said that much.

It was the last thing Isaiah Purdy meant to do before he died: give something back to his son, his only son born with a fevered brain, an agitated soul, and a broken heart. Be there in the end for him, a show of support they called it.

The drive was lonely—utterly so. No amount of music or talk radio could end the metallic, hard, awful-tasting emptiness that exuded an odor like death surrounding Isaiah there in the cab of the van he'd purchased for the trip. And why shouldn't everything smell of rot and decay and death? Death now stalked his little family like some rabid hound of hell. Here he was leaving his wife in a lonely grave that he'd dug with his own hands, followed by a journey toward his son's execution, followed by a claiming of the body, followed by what Jimmy Lee kept telling him *he*—and by extension *they*—wanted.

His cross-country journey was one of a modern day black hearse pulled by an engine fueled by vengeance. The Lord called for vengeance in a place inside Isaiah's head that he had no previous knowledge existed, a place where contact with voices of a purely evangelical hatred dwelled. Eye for eye, tooth for tooth, blood for blood, flesh for flesh. He need only gather the parts for the ageless, timeless ritual, and like Jimmy Lee and God kept repeatedly telling him, he could do this. He could be the hand of God, the instrument of His wrath.

A fitting ending to a life that had had no specialness about it, a life of a simple man without dreams or aspirations above working the land. Sometime during the journey to Huntsville and to Jimmy's execution, Isaiah began to wonder how the boy got the way he did. "How'd my boy come out so bad?" he'd asked the air.

Isaiah, with Eunice's considerable help, had raised

Jimmy Lee in as strict a biblical sense as possible, always mustering up the courage to punish the boy with the rod as the Bible said. Isaiah had beaten the boy whenever he did wrong, so why had he come out the way he had come out? Had to be a bad seed.

As the white lines and road signs whizzed by, Isaiah continued to ponder the question of his troubled son. The more he rolled it over in his mind on the long, empty blankness of highway leading out of Iowa City, the more he believed in his deepest recesses that Jimmy Lee had one of those gene defects the scientists talked about on that TLC television show that Eunice Mae would stare at for hours late in the night. Late in life, Eunice Mae had discovered her liking for such, that and the animal stuff. He chuckled, recalling how it'd been Jimmy Lee who had insisted on putting in a satellite dish and a brand-spanking-new twenty-five-inch TV. Regardless of all his vile and admittedly wicked ways, the boy had always been good to his mama and in his way to Isaiah, his papa; regardless of all those women they said he had harmed, he had never once taken on devilishly or evilly toward his own . . . at least that much could be said of the boy.

Isaiah swerved to avoid the headlights of an oncoming Mack truck that blared its horn at him. He turned hard to avoid the truck, sent up a shower of debris as he hit the shoulder and grass off U.S. 20 outside Sioux City. He'd buried his wife this day and had begun his journey, and now he'd almost joined Eunice in the hereafter. The minivan careened to a full stop, but not before the van rocked to one side, nearly going completely over an embankment, but somehow righting itself with a bounce onto all four Firestone tires.

He sat there for a moment with the engine idling and the headlights piercing the emptiness of a wall of black trees. For a long moment, he wondered at the fickle hand of fate in a man's life and why he had not been killed. The truck had come within inches of smashing into his left front end. The embankment had been just steep enough to have easily reached out its arms to pull him into the waiting creek twenty feet below. He imagined the van upside down in the creek, him upended with it, unable to free himself, and drowning in the muddy bottom. Maybe it'd been best had it happened that way, he thought, anxious as he was to join Eunice, and besides, it would end this strange, unbidden pilgrimage to Huntsville. Death would have brought an instant solution to his immediate problems and an end to Jimmy Lee's voice in his head, a voice like a bull terrier that had clamped down on his brain, holding firm and taking control, without letup, day and night, night and day, over and again, endlessly tumbling in-out-around-through the pathways of Isaiah's skull.

"Maybe I best ought to park it right here and get some damn sleep," he said to the photograph he had pinned to the overhead visor, a picture of himself with an arm draped over Eunice's bony shoulder. The photo had been taken when they had gone to the Jersey shore to see the Atlantic Ocean for the first time. It had been a wonderment of nature the likes of which neither of them could muster words for, and so they had asked a stranger to snap a photo of them with the ocean as backdrop, and Eunice had said that every grain of sand on the beach was special and unique, and that she regretted that they had never found that special uniqueness that seemed buried in their boy, Jimmy. Still, they had smiled for the camera even then, even knowing that their only son had that same day been placed on death row and placed on the schedule for execution. The trip had been Eunice's swan song, he told himself; she had somehow known that her heart would give out, just as the doctors had said: a condition of the heart. Isaiah wondered how much of the condition was brought on by the situation her son now found himself in.

"Sleep . . . best to sleep til dawn rise," he said now to the photograph. Beside the photo of Eunice and himself, a photo of Jimmy Lee stared back. Short-cropped head of sandy blond hair, narrow eyes too close to each other, a beaked nose, and a freckled face. The chin was weak, near nonexistent, while the ears poked out from each side of the head like some strange pair of Brussels sprouts. He'd been a damn homely infant with the look of an opossum, and he'd not improved since.

One other photograph accompanied Isaiah on the long journey to Huntsville and later to D.C., and that was a photograph ripped from a Houston newspaper, a photograph of Judge Maureen DeCampe, posing with some other fancy judges on the steps of the courthouse.

Isaiah shut off the van lights. He'd taken a slight blow to the head against the dash. He tried to refocus and found himself staring into the rearview mirror. Behind him, he saw the shell of the van as if it had been carved out with a giant knife. He'd taken out the seats in the rear and had made a pallet of the blankets from his and Eunice's bed. Even if Eunice were alive, she might not be on the trip to see their son executed. But even in death, she was here in the spirit, inside Isaiah, and he took comfort in knowing this. "For a fact," he muttered as he shut down the engine, locked the doors, and worked his thin, small frame to the back of the van. Once there, he lay down in his clothes and pulled the blankets up around his chin just as he and Eunice had done for forty-four years.

He lay there on his back, missing her spooning up against him. He lay there, looking out through the side tinted window at stars overhead, thinking out loud. "Eunice . . . this here universe is too much for me. All them stars . . . makes me feel so damn small. Wish you was here to see them . . . to see me through all this."

He felt a tug at his old heart. He felt so alone. Still, he knew that he could never truly be alone anywhere, not in this life, not since Jimmy Lee had gotten into his head through some magical projection that had come through Eunice Mae, had somehow leaped full-blown from out of her head and into his, and it was him, Jimmy Lee come a-calling.

Jimmy Lee had sent him a mental picture, full-blown and frightful, of himself in the death chamber where they meant to throw the switch on Isaiah's boy. Isaiah watched from outside a giant glass jar inside a maximum-security prison where they officially and efficiently killed people.

Isaiah didn't begin to think he could ever understand how Jimmy Lee's voice got into his head from such a distance, except to say that perhaps it had been something like divination or sorcery; perhaps a kind of witchcraft associated with Christian curses and the Bible, something tangible though, like a cream or a gel or a jam, that oozed from Jimmy Lee's letters to Eunice's hands and then to Isaiah's head. Whatever or however, this power crept unseen and unknown into Isaiah's brain via the cells. After all, Jimmy Lee had miraculously begun reading his Bible, but Isaiah could not be certain just how much the boy had been getting from the Word until that first contact, when Jimmy Lee might as well have been in the rocker across from him on his falling-down old farmstead porch.

When Jimmy Lee's words came into his brain, only ten minutes after Isaiah had buried Eunice Mae, Isaiah had no hope of denying Jimmy or to *not* hear his last wish, and certainly to *not* act on it.

He'd buried her with a Bible passage suggested to him by Eunice Mae herself, but she might have gotten it from Jimmy Lee, in Jimmy's last letter to home. Eunice could read, and she'd read all his letters to Isaiah, but he knew she'd leave out any unpleasantness. Jimmy's kindness toward his mother and Isaiah in his last letters proved he'd been reborn, proved that his words were sincere, that he had come to that plateau of spirit that would indeed cleanse him in the next life, while the State of Texas made its feeble attempt to do likewise through several hundred thousand odd volts of electricity. *Sonsabitches*, he thought, *one and all, and especially the judge who refused to show a stitch of mercy to my boy.*

"Just go to sleep, old man," he told himself, there where he'd nearly been killed, there in the ditch alongside the road, his voice thin, bony fingers running over a scrub board of a face.

But he'd still remained wakeful. "Get some rest. You'll be needing every ounce a' your energy, so get some damned rest." He now ordered it, willed it, wishing to end the agitation and unrest that had created of his mind a chaotic

whirlwind. His eyes closed on the dark road that lay ahead
of him, and they closed on the barn, where he sat on the
stool, and they closed on the image of the judge in her
bonds. He had done it. He had lashed her to Jimmy Lee's
body.

JESSICA Coran found Washington, D.C., a city of contrasts.
The tourists' finds and traps abounded, of course, the city
being the so-called capital of the free world, but it also
housed crime, poverty, pestilence, and the usual infrastruc-
ture problems. This along with its soft underbelly where
drugs flowed freely, where an overburdened police and judicial system tolerated prostitution and other crime, and
where politics meant everything and public outcry demanded more out of the current White House administration
than the latest scandal.

This time of year, the cherry blossoms all along the main
thoroughfares were sadly gone, and the cold chill of a fall
that promised a frigid winter left homeless people in door-
ways within the shadow of 1600 Pennsylvania Avenue. The
city had earned the reputation of D.C.—District of Crack.

FBI Headquarters in Washington, D.C., was nothing
whatsoever like Jessica's country club atmosphere at Quantico, Virginia, where people showed attitudes more positive
and goal-oriented. And the pace and stress set here proved
mind-boggling, as did the number of ringing telephones. In
order to think, she had to close two doors that led into the
office turned over to her.

Despite the distractions and the *vibes* here, Jessica had
immediately set out to take action. She called in all the D.C.
field agents assigned to her, and she ordered them to work
closely with local authorities, and to put out a street request
for anyone knowing anything about the disappearance of
Judge Maureen DeCampe. "Anything coming of such inquiries," she told them, "gets reported to the task force and
posted on the electronic bulletin board in the operations
room."

"Where's that? The ops room?" one of the agents asked.

"Where you're standing." It was a room that hadn't seen use in at least a decade, but the ancient furniture was enhanced by state-of-the-art phones and computers for the operation. The room stood adjacent to the office they'd given Jessica to work from, and the moment she had stepped into the room, she had felt something, a kind of ghostly history to the place that had seen no use in such a long time. In her mind's eye, she saw a busy, frenetic office with old-fashioned furniture and dated telephones and a teletype machine in the corner. No computers. A lot of noise and movement, all in an empty room. The room begged to be put to use, and since every other room in the building that might serve was already in heavy use, she had selected this one to be outfitted for their needs, and an army of technicians had made it so.

"Secondly," she added to her task force people, "I want a complete rundown on everyone Maureen DeCampe would have or could have come into contact with on the day of her disappearance. Add to that anyone she came into contact with on a daily basis."

"A judge comes into contact with a lot of people in any given day," said George Marks, a tall, clean-shaven agent, hand-picked for his knowledge of D.C. streets and street life.

"We're hauling in the usual suspects," Jane Cardinal, his younger partner, added.

"We need to focus on specific suspects. That means we don't have the luxury of interrogating useless suspects for hours on end," she countered. "We need to zero in on someone we like for the crime or someone we catch in a lie and to quickly focus our search. We need to think clearly about what comparison points to use to narrow the field."

"I'm not sure I follow you," replied the young female agent named Cardinal. She'd been selected to be on the team due to her expertise in Missing Persons cases.

"Which of the usuals has proven violent? Which is or has been capable of abduction in the past? Twenty questions, people, will reduce the numbers. Those who forced themselves on another person reduce the pile by one-third. Which of the usuals has ever used a weapon in the commission of a crime? We know that the judge showed her assailant a .45 but was overpowered or outgunned. This reduces the pile further. So who is left? Which of the usuals has ever threatened the judge?"

"That just might tend to increase the pile," said Cardinal, drawing a laugh from the others. For a moment, Jessica recognized a little of herself in the younger agent. *Give her ten years, and if she continues as an agent, she might have learned something,* Jessica thought.

"Look," began Jessica, "I know that DeCampe is relatively new to D.C. and that she didn't waste any time creating enemies here, and that she's not everyone's favorite D.C. judge, but she deserves our best effort, same as anyone else abducted off our streets. As things stand, we have zero ideas on how to proceed, people. Get me some leads; if you can do this through your snitches, it may save us more time than collaring and interrogating the array of lunatics you call the usual suspects. That's all I'm saying."

Richard Sharpe stood to put in his say. Everyone's eyes turned to the tall, handsome Englishman. Everyone knew that he'd retired from New Scotland Yard and had come on as a consultant to the FBI. Everyone also knew that he and Jessica were seriously involved with one another. "Where I come from, the usual suspects are called the street nasties, but in either case, they're called the usual suspects for good reason, but we don't believe this is the usual case. Besides, this is D.C., and the list of perverts in this city is endless, not unlike London."

"So, your thinking is that we'd be wasting our time with the street nasties, as you call them?" asked Agent Marks.

Sharpe paced the room as he spoke. "Canvassing them all . . . well, we just don't feel the judge has that kind of time, and we fear it would be a waste of time, energy, and manpower, you see. We believe the judge's assailant knows her in some capacity, and that this is about what you Yanks call *payback* of some sort. Otherwise, ransom demands would have long since been made by now."

"To that end, we're electronically canvassing court documents and records," added Jessica.

"In the meantime, what do we do?" asked a second female agent taller than any man present.

"As I said, put out feelers with your usual snitches. There has to be something on the street about the case, something useful."

"We need to know where this rat is holed up," added Sharpe.

"Someone collects his rent." Jessica paced toward Richard, and together they stood as a united front before the agents assigned to her. The usual protocol would be to put the entire team on the track of known offenders—kidnappers and rapists. But Jessica and Richard had discussed this fact and found such an exercise wanting. "So, get your noses to the pavement and get me something I can use."

After the others left, Richard asked, "What about that pending case you were looking into, that Native American thing?"

"All other pending cases will just have to *pend* longer," she replied.

"If it works . . . fix it anyway." Richard stated the oft-repeated, unofficial motto of the division, a phrase she had shared with him one evening when he'd been asking questions about how the bureau worked or failed to work in some cases.

Jessica found a chair and fell into it, squishing the air from its cushions. "It doesn't appear to be or even feel like the judge's disappearance was a random act of violence."

"Agreed." He joined her, placing a hand on her hair, stroking it. "Everything points to a premeditated plan, although the crime scene was a bit messy."

"A bit messy, yes, but the perpetrator collected up what he wanted."

"Her, yes."

"Her—and vanished without a trace. What does that say about him?"

"That tells me he made exacting plans."

"Right. Whoever did this staked out the judge's home, her office, stalked her, knew her habits, and took her at her most vulnerable."

"You think he knew she was in the habit of eating in chambers and working late every second Thursday of the month?" asked Richard. "Only her family knew that."

"And her working family," Jessica countered, "including the parking attendant. It was no big secret, after all."

"Do you think the parking lot fellow had something to do with it?"

"No, too stupid."

"Stupid might be why we ought to look closer at him," countered Richard. "Sometimes you can learn a great deal from a stupid man."

"What's that? Shakespeare?"

"Scotland Yard."

"OK, explain."

"Just suppose the attendant spilled some details of when and where someone might catch the judge, thinking the guy just wanted to talk to her."

"And suppose he took a few bills for the information? Then the judge turns up missing, possibly raped or killed . . ."

"Now he's shitting his pants."

She agreed. "He's got to be thinking it's his fault and that he's an accomplice to the crime."

Sharpe went to a coffeepot that had been burning too long, poured himself a cup, and asked if she'd like one. She declined with a wave of the hand. He returned to her, sipped at his steaming cup. A well-proportioned man, he had an easy, rolling gait. He continued pacing the room. "We need to send a patrol car around to bring the parking attendant in for questioning."

"Do it."

Sharpe made the call. After he hung up, he said to Jessica, "Maybe it's a jealous old suitor who's nabbed the judge."

"How old?" asked Jessica. "How old you think this suitor is, Richard?"

"I'm not talking old as in age; I mean, an old boyfriend."

"Yeah, but how old? How many boyfriends do we have to go back to? Besides, the family is adamant that she was not involved with anyone who could be construed as violent or obsessive, and you met her current boyfriend. Nothing there. From everything we could turn up along those lines, we suspect that if the motive is an obsessive fixation on the judge, it's come from a source the family and likely the judge herself knew nothing of."

"You mean like someone who saw her in the media, maybe," he replied.

Leaning across her desk, her hands going through her auburn hair as if to assist her thinking, Jessica said, "My suspicion is that either he knew her, so she let her guard down, or he looked harmless."

Richard considered this for a moment, his chin propped up by his right hand and elbow on the chair where he now sat across from her in the operations room, the conference table separating them. "But no one she would have had a personal relationship with."

"Agreed. The abductor may think he has a relationship with the judge, that in his head, he does have a full-blown relationship with her. Get into that."

"You're right on about the media, Jess," he replied, toying with a pen as he spoke. "They have a name for that sort of thing."

"It's called a media fixation," she filled in. "Some Joe gets it in his head he has a special connection to a news anchor or other TV personality, movie star, or other public figure. Listen, Richard, get hold of any old tapes we have of the judge from media sources."

"What'll you be doing in the meantime?"

"Praying."

"Praying?"

"Praying we hear from the abductor or get a ransom demand." Jessica now went for coffee only to find that Richard had emptied the pot, leaving it on to burn the bottom of the glass container. She returned to him and took what was left in his cup, drinking it down. "We've got the phones at every possible contact point bugged. We're just waiting to hear his demands."

"After all this time, Jess, I doubt he's interested in contacting the family."

She sighed deeply. "Gotcha."

"I feel so damned helpless. What can we do to find her, Jess, and how do we know which path down the maze to take? How do we keep from wasting a minute?" He took the cup from her and studied its emptiness, a reflection of his gut feeling about the progression of the case thus far.

"We work round the clock," she replied. "We keep running down leads, as in any case."

"Meanwhile, we dodge the media and the brass?"

"Nobody's asking you to dodge Santiva or anyone else, Richard. But . . . but . . ."

"Yes, of course, I appreciate what you're not saying."

"Trust me. I have an ill feeling about Judge DeCampe's disappearance, and I fear it can only get worse, but if she has an iota of a chance, it can easily be lost if, say, Santiva or someone over his head decides to take the case out of our hands and changes horses in midstream or begins to dictate what direction our investigation ought to go in."

"What exactly do you mean, Jess, by an ill kind of feeling?"

Abandoning her chair, she again paced the operations room. "Gut feeling is all."

Richard knew by now that her pacing actually signaled either a characteristic impatience at the lack of leads or her frustration with the four walls closing in on them, time being so short. "Texas may have some input here, you know," she now said. "Before the judge was an appellate judge here, she was a criminal judge in Houston, Texas. We've got friends in Texas; field office SAC is George O'Leary, right? And there's this Lucas Stonecoat with the Houston Police Department."

"Stonecoat?"

"Texas Cherokee . . . worked a case with Kim Desinor a couple of years back."

"Oh, yeah . . . the case that was shaping up as another Atlanta black boys murder thing. I recall reading about it and hearing about it on the telly."

"The case took a real toll on Kim, but nothing like this has . . . Who knows, maybe our friends in Texas could jump-start us on any cases Judge Maureen DeCampe tried in Houston."

Richard nodded, agreeing. He somehow sensed that this time Jessica's pacing meant more, that she was searching for any errant clues in her mind. Sharpe's eyes followed her movement; as always, she fascinated him, and as always, he resisted her fascination at the moment with cold caution. He thought of how quickly they had come to a full-blown, rich relationship that was more than that of simply lovers but that of friends. He'd be the first to admit that his sexual interest in her remained as high as ever, but his fascination for her keen scientific mind and what the two of them shared in this world was just as important to him. He understood that her work had always been her first love, that she was positively obsessive about the hunt, and so in a sense she was involved with another lover, but he accepted this as part of the person he loved, one of the major reasons he loved her. Aside from this, she was a Scorpio to boot.

She caught his eyes on her. She quickly asked, "What does your gut tell you?"

"Doesn't tell me anything unless I've just swallowed a pepperoni pizza."

She didn't laugh at the joke. "Me . . . I have a tick. An uneasy tick . . . like a ticking bomb in my head."

"So you think she is alive?"

Jessica turned to him and forced direct eye contact. "Yes, but I fear her time is limited, and maybe. . . ." She hesitated to say more.

"Maybe what?"

"Perhaps she'd be better off if she were . . . dead."

Richard's jaw quivered. "What makes you say that?"

"Just a sense I get. Revenge motive, you said it yourself. If this guy knows her from her court dealings, he's going to hurt her, right? He's out to hurt her badly. That's what revenge is all about. In its way, it's as horrid as any hate crime because of the level of hatred involved."

"Well then, we'll just have to hope that her abductor

instead fell in love with his victim, that it's that media-fixation thing at work, right?"

"Yeah, maybe we can do a better job focusing on that scenario."

"But you don't think so."

"It's certainly a possibility."

"But if it's wrong?"

She nodded. "If it's wrong, it could cost her precious time. Fact is, any move we make down a wrong path will cost her precious time."

FOUR

Tis man's perdition to be safe,
When for the truth, he ought to die.

—RALPH WALDO EMERSON

M Y *goddamn hands are tied to the lifeless hands of some*
dead guy, lashed to them by—she could not think—
rawhide strips; my legs and body're lashed similarly to the
corpse. My face has been forced into the decaying face of
death, right cheek to his left. A sick mockery of the dance
posture, this horrid nightmare; a nightmare from which she
had awakened only to find herself once again *here*, lashed
to the dead man. His decaying process was slowly, torturously breaking down the bonding tissues of her own flesh.

Her mind had shut down on itself more than once since
coming to the realization that her predicament was not a
nightmare, but a nightmare reality. She had not—could
not—awaken from the nightmare, because it proved to be
no dream at all.

Someone had drugged her—no, stunned or traumatized
her in some manner as to render her helpless; stunned first,
drugged afterward. That had been the sequence. Maureen
could not recall the particulars, but she had a vague notion
of the small man behind this mad revenge on her.

All because she had excused herself from any further
dealings in the old man's problem, his son, James Lee
Purdy, who she had put on death row after his first trial.
With his appeal filed, all the time that had passed, almost
ten years, she had become an appeals court judge, and
Jimmy Lee Purdy's appeal should never have come before

her. She'd had to recuse herself and step away from the case; it only made sense. The judge who presided over the original trial, the judge who had condemned Jimmy Lee to death in the first place, could not be the same judge to hear his appeal.

Anyone who knew anything about the law understood the enormity of such prejudice and conflict of interest, but for some strange reason, Jimmy Lee and his father both had wanted her on the case. The old man had come to her office and pleaded, saying, "It'll be Jimmy Lee's last wish for you to stand in judgment on him a second time. And since he's what they call at the prison 'a dead man walking,' then you gotta give him his last wish. We'd do it in Iowa. What kind of people are you Texans?"

She had flatly refused, and then the wizened old man placed two clenched fists on her desk and sternly said, "It's not just Jimmy's wish. God told him it had to be you, Judge DeCampe. God, do ya' understand that? God's wish."

"God does not dictate here, Mr. Purdy. The court system does. I can't break the law to enforce the law. Now, please, I have no more to say on the subject."

"I have lived in perdition all these years Jimmy's been on death row. I won't apologize for taking up a half hour of your life, Your Honorable Judgess."

He'd stood, rail thin, bony, emaciated, haggard, and sickly. He'd come like a visit from Death himself to her chambers there in the Sam Houston Central Courthouse. That had been almost a year ago, long before she'd taken the position in Washington.

"He'll get a fair appeal, Mr. Purdy, before Judge Raymond Parker," she had assured the scarecrow before her.

That had been the last she'd seen of the old man, but this Jed Clampett parody continued to wander the courtroom halls like a ghost, sitting in every day of his son's doomed appeal, just as he had for three months during the original trial. She had caught glimpses of him, and she also caught moments when his eyes staked her with their mix of frustration, sadness, and a kind of fire that spoke an angry and sullen language all their own.

Even though she had no choice but to recuse herself from the case in Houston, Texas, she'd secretly blessed the fact she did not have to hear Jimmy Lee Purdy's bullshit ever again. Further, she never wanted to see his ugly face again. She'd begun to feel exactly the same toward the old man.

The state by and large had to bury death row inmates using large sums of taxpayer dollars, and they were interred in a sad potter's field. Judge Parker, with whom she'd remained in contact primarily through E-mail, had confided to her that on sentencing day, Mr. Isaiah James Purdy had asked for only one thing from the court before he'd ended his plea for leniency for his son. He had asked that the boy's body be returned to him, to be shipped back to Iowa, where Mr. Purdy meant to inter his son on the family farm.

That had all been a lie.

The wizened little old man wanted the body for a far more grim and sinister reason; he wanted it to wreak its slow revenge on Judge Maureen DeCampe; he wanted to watch his son's decaying flesh eat away at her, to eventually murder her in a slow and agonizing fashion not heard of in modern times. Something he'd muttered about Romans . . . and something about the biblical injunction of an eye for an eye, a tooth for a tooth, but she hadn't gotten it all. *Flesh for flesh,* she imagined now. She failed to dredge up some words he'd read to her from his Bible. She was unable to recapture every word, far too busy as she was with the horror of the moment, lashed to Jimmy Lee Purdy's decaying, shrinking corpse, the odor of it certain to drive her insane long before her body would turn to rotting mush. *Die, let me now . . . now let me die*, she mentally pleaded.

The duct tape around her mouth worked twofold: to silence any screams and to hold her head into the deadly, flesh-eating decay. It was all too horrid and heart-sinkingly terrifying to contemplate. Mercifully, her mind sent her into a spiral of unconsciousness, her only means of escape.

THEY began the tedious process, requiring a small army of agents, of reinterviewing everyone, starting with the parking

lot attendant. But Jessica soon learned that the man could
not be located, and that it appeared Arthur Collins had
packed his belongings and had vacated his apartment. He
might be on a plane, a train, or a bus bound for anywhere.
His suddenly fleeing the area told Jessica that her instincts
about the creep had been perfectly right all along, and now
she cursed herself for allowing Collins the time to vanish.
She immediately ordered an all points bulletin for his apprehension and return.

In the meantime, they spoke to the judge's youngest offspring, her adopted son, Michael. Michael, a law clerk, tearfully told them that he meant to follow in his mother's
footsteps. At twenty-five, Michael blamed himself, saying
he'd wanted to stay late in the building and go out with her
that night for dinner and drinks, but that she had insisted he
go on his way when it became extremely late. He'd met his
fiancée at a restaurant, and he'd wanted the two women to
get along, so he had the date set for weeks, but his mother
hadn't really wanted to meet with them. She'd begged off,
using her usual excuse: work.

"She is a workaholic, you know," Michael had said during the course of the interview. "She'd been happy for me,"
he said. "I didn't know anything was wrong until the following morning, when my sister called."

The daughters had been the ones to initially cry foul.
Further discussion with them amassed no new information.
The family was at a total loss as to how anyone could pos-
sibly want to harm their mother.

Hours passed like days on this case, a case that had
nerves frayed from the lowest civilian to the governor of
the state. Information of any useful sort simply failed to
materialize; every person questioned seemed unable to supply a single helpful clue. Jessica's anger at herself for not
cornering the parking attendant when she had had the
chance threatened to explode. Richard Sharpe's detailing of
the suspect from his unique perspective, from what few giv-
ens he'd had to work with, while not adding anything star-
tlingly new, did corroborate Jessica's own worst fears for
Judge DeCampe, that her abductor was in it for revenge,

that his motive must be to inflict pain and suffering on the woman. Such evil revenge might come in any number of cruel ways. The revenge motive, in the experience of the people running the investigation, proved the worst possible scenario for the victim. The only crime that rivaled it was lust-torture and lust-murder done by a psychotic killer who had created some fantastical notions of right and wrong in his head in order to come to sexual release. A typical rape— if there were such a thing—was by contrast all about power and domination, while a lust-rape-murder had also to do with the mental state of the killer who must take life to feel alive or to fulfill some demented commands made on him by Satan or some hound of Satan's, or some other "outside" force he could not fully control.

Still, murder for revenge could be as savage as any. It certainly predated most reasons for murder.

Richard had agreed. He had cast aside all other possibilities, just as Jessica had on reading Richard's profile of the abductor.

"A media stalker is usually an amateur, who is a great deal sloppier," Richard had assured her, once again corroborating her own feelings. She knew her abductor.

Jessica and Richard decided to drive back to the scene of the crime, where they hoped to speak to anyone who had come into contact with her on the night of her abduction. Now, as they made their way to their waiting car, they talked.

"I've contacted Eriq Santiva," she informed him, "and he's convinced that bringing you on board, Richard, lends a certain air of respectability to the investigation." She laughed lightly at this.

"And why does this make you laugh?"

"Don't you see? He can tell the governor and the mayor that he's got a bona fide Scotland Yard investigator on the case alongside his best profiling team."

"I'm here merely as a consultant on the case."

"You're Richard Sharpe of Scotland Yard. Your record speaks for itself."

"And the Yard has handled countless abduction cases, and I've certainly had my share."

"You know a great deal about the psychology of abductors, as well as being an expert on stalkers."

"I'm sure the official thinking is that you Yanks can use all the help you can get, Jess."

"Some people are going to say it was the only way I could get you over here, Richard."

"Really?" Now he laughed.

"That it took a fee to entice you to me. That you are a kept man."

He laughed louder, his tone rich and resonating. Then he said, "Fuck anyone who says so."

"Thanks. I needed that."

"You hungry?"

"I could eat."

He turned right. "Do you know of a nearby useful place?"

"Funny . . ." she muttered as they turned down the side street that took them out of the madcap traffic of downtown D.C.

"What's funny?"

"I feel guilty doing things like eating, sleeping, breathing . . . knowing that Judge DeCampe is likely being deprived of basic needs and possibly being tortured."

"Nonsense. We don't know anything of the kind. You're just . . . What is it young people over here say? 'Laying a trip on yourself,' Jess. Besides, you *gotta-hafta* keep your strength up."

"I know you're right, but . . . Hey, turn in here!"

He quickly pulled into a parking lot fronting a sign that announced the place as St. George's Potato Patch. "I have a feeling we're going to be pulling an all-nighter. What is this place, by the way?" He jerked the car to a halt and shut down the motor.

"St. George's Potato, a pub and grill. We're still pretty near the agency building and Police Precinct One. Police and others working in the area of the courthouse frequent the place. Everyone at the bureau and nearby precincts hangs out here."

"Let's give it a go then."

They exited the car for the restaurant.

Everyone in law enforcement in the area had gotten comfortable with the idea that the FBI and not the WPD would be running the show in the DeCampe case, and most in the WPD were glad the FBI had taken the leadership role in the Missing Persons case. So walking into this lion's den would be no threat, Jessica assumed.

"You sure you want to be in this place?" he asked her.

"When in Rome . . . all that."

Inside, once seated, Jessica stared across at Richard. He had been a stalwart and honest friend since their first meeting in London, where they'd worked the case of the Crucifier. It seemed so long ago; they had shared so much since then. She often thought about how she could have used such a friend when she was chief medical examiner for the city of Washington, D.C., before joining the FBI, when her life had unraveled before her eyes in a matter of days. Her father's health had suddenly declined, when a series of strokes first left him paralyzed, then comatose, and finally she had had to decide on life support or death. She had chosen as her father would have wanted: no heroic efforts to save him in his vegetative state. She had had few friends then, having devoted herself entirely to the job. Dr. Asa Holcraft, her mentor all through the final stages of her education as an M.E., was the only one at her father's funeral for whom she felt any affection.

As if losing her father were not enough, Jessica lost a series of politically motivated battles with the city commissioner and assistant to the mayor, and despite her spotless record and determination to keep the Office of the Medical Examiner above and beyond political rancor and the influence of politicos, she failed. The writing was on the wall, and when FBI Division Head Otto Boutine, recognizing the fine work she'd done as M.E. and noting the work she'd done during a horrendous airplane disaster at Dulles International, offered her a job with his FBI Behavioral Science Division, she readily accepted.

Otto had explained that they needed someone with great

talent to create psychological profiles of both killers and
victims. Serial killer profiles proved difficult, but doing profiles of victims tore at the heart of anyone with feelings.
Still, she leaped at the chance to do more forensic psychology.

Now her standing with the department, her badge, her
insurance package, it all meant a great deal to her.

"Where's Kim Desinor? Isn't she still on this case?"
asked J. T., who suddenly appeared at the table beside them.
It appeared J. T. had already eaten, and out of the corner of
her eye, Jessica saw others on the task force exiting the
place.

"Keep this between us, J. T., but I think she's somewhat
burned out, at least on this case. Something she saw or felt.
I think it was too much for her."

"Hence your fear for DeCampe."

"Frankly, I felt that fear long before I knew Kim held
similar feelings. I've been trying to reach Kim, but she
hasn't answered her messages, either at her office or at
home. Getting a little worried about her."

"I see. But earlier, you did discuss your feelings with
her, about DeCampe's fate, I mean?"

"Yes, we discussed it somewhat."

He saw that she didn't want to go any deeper into it, so
he switched to her favorite subject instead. "So, I understand
Richard Sharpe wrote the book on stalkers and what goes
on in the mind of a stalker."

"That is my forte, yes," replied Richard, a smile creasing
his features as he lifted the salt cellar on the table and idly
twirled it about in his hand. The thing was a winking pirate
with a similar grin. Richard had long since determined that
while J. T. and Jessica had enjoyed a long professional and
personal relationship, J. T. was a good man and to be
trusted.

Still, J. T. had remained a bit unsure of Sharpe, and he
now took notice of Sharpe's interest in the salt cellar. This
prompted Richard to comment, "Sorry, I'm one of those
chaps who must keep hands busy at all times."

"Since taking on this case, I don't blame you."

J. T. slid into the booth alongside Jessica, informing her that everyone on the team had determined that her and Richard's talk of that morning had fired them up. They then sat for a moment in silence, the piped-in music wafting over them, the mild tones of the oldies playing softly, reminding Jessica how fleeting time actually was.

J. T. broke into her thoughts with a question. "You two are absolutely convinced that we are working under the correct assumptions about the incident, right, Jess?"

"That she was taken by someone who had carefully planned her abduction?"

J. T. asked, "Perhaps that he stalked DeCampe for some time before acting?"

"I think that's quite possible, J. T."

"And that she knew her abductor?"

"Knowing DeCampe, I'd say that anyone else she drew a weapon on would most definitely be in the morgue with a .45 slug through him, and we'd be busy with autopsying him, rather than searching desperately for her."

J. T.'s laugh was light but genuine.

"Hear! Hear!" commented Richard.

J. T. agreed, adding, "Yeah. You've got that right. We'd be working to keep her out of prison for murder, and you know Santiva would be up our asses to find evidence to save her, no doubt."

"We're following every lead, J. T. Every possible suspect."

"And you've got Lew Clemmens reviewing every thread in every case DeCampe ever worked. What else can Santiva ask of you? Miracles?"

"Every thread and every threat," Sharpe replied.

But Jessica said, "Santiva? Why're we discussing Eriq Santiva every other breath, John?"

John Thorpe looked from Richard to Jessica, his eyes like those of an animal's just caught in the headlights. "Just think he and the top brass expect miracles from us, Jess, is all."

She sighed heavily and put her head in her hands for a moment, trying to fend off a headache. "Unfortunately, there've been hundreds of death threats made against

DeCampe over her long career both as a prosecutor and a judge."

"Right, her career goes way back—"

"All the way to Texas."

"And whoever snatched her here," interjected Richard, "may have been a recent acquaintance, but he may well have been an old acquaintance from Texas who—"

"Houston," added J. T. "Am I right?"

"He may have seen her in the newspapers here, one of her high-profile cases like that child murder case last fall," Jessica said.

"Bad business that one, I remember."

"Lew's still pulling off information." Jessica sipped at her lemon tea and thumped the plaid tablecloth. "Maybe we'll get lucky."

Richard swilled down his iced tea as if it were beer. The Washington humidity had shot to eighty percent. Jessica thought she could water her flowers at home by simply wringing out her blouse.

J. T. stood and excused himself, saying he'd see them later back at headquarters. After this, the waitress came with their hot sandwiches and refreshed their drinks. They had just begun their meal when someone's shadow fell across their table. Jessica at first assumed J. T. had returned, something on his mind that he'd perhaps forgotten.

"What can you tell me about the disappearance of the judge, Dr. Coran?" It was Tim O'Brien of the *Washington Post*, the police beat reporter with whom both J. T. and Jessica had maintained a fairly good working relationship. He had on more than one occasion contacted them at Quantico either by phone or in person in pursuit of a story. The pursuit seemed all the man lived for.

"Not a damn thing." Jessica did not make eye contact with the reporter.

"C'mon, Doc! My readers're going to want to know something by the evening edition. You gotta give me something."

"You're so wrong, Tim. You're interrupting our meal,

and no, we don't owe you a damn living, thank you," replied Jessica.

"Hey, it's just an expression. Still, you gotta give me something, or my dildo of an editor is going to make my life hell." His body language said that he wanted to sit down, but neither Richard, whom he glanced at—wanting an introduction but not getting one—nor Jessica responded to the silent request, neither budging over to allow him room to sit as Jessica had with John Thorpe.

"That's your editor's problem, not ours," Jessica replied.

"Do you two have any clue, any idea? Do you understand the freaking enormity of this story? The feeding frenzy that's going on right now over Judge DeCampe's disappearance?" He paused for a breath. "I mean this goddamn business is big news—front-page stuff. Sidebar, every beat cop in the city who's ever been embarrassed by the woman in court is suspect."

"That's taking things a bit far, even for you, O'Brien," she calmly but firmly replied.

"What about you?" O'Brien turned to Richard Sharpe. "Obviously, you're working the case with Dr. Genius here, so what's the word? Guy's obviously a nutcase, but is he, you know, a sex pervert, or what?"

"Yeah, yeah, that's it, Tim," countered Jessica. "Our guy is definitely a pervert."

"So the judge was snatched by a pervert!"

"That's all we know."

"Any leads?"

Richard finally exploded with, "Yes indeed, we're canvassing all the perverts in the city at the moment, beginning with your relatives. Do you think you can concoct a story around that?"

Jessica laughed, but O'Brien, picking up on Richard's English accent, only frowned, turned, and left, defeat written into his step.

SOME four hours had passed since she and Richard had eaten at St. George's Potato, and since then, they had again walked the scene for anyone or anything that might shed some light. Jessica now paced the ready room where all pertinent information for the task force flowed, and she didn't like the fact that the river of communication had log-jammed.

She dropped into a chair, exhausted, others watching her, reading a certain defeat into her body language, when Chief Eriq Santiva briskly walked in and came directly to her. He stared down at her, shook his head, frowned, and then slapped down an evening edition of the *Washington Post* with a front-page story by Tim O'Brien. "Who wrote this? You or O'Brien?"

Jessica only had time to glance at the headline: "FBI Pursues Sex Pervert in DeCampe Disappearance."

"Where do you get off, Agent Coran, in doling out information like this to the press before I get it? I have to read about the case in the papers?"

"Chief, it didn't happen that way," began Richard, coming nearer Jessica, attempting to defend her.

"Then enlighten me!" he shouted.

Everyone's eyes now riveted on Jessica for an answer. More than one on the task force sided with Santiva. But Eriq continued rampaging, not allowing her a word. "Jess, it says here you are hot on the trail of a sexual pervert who has Judge Maureen DeCampe at his mercy. You know what this will do to the family?"

"I had nothing to do with O'Brien's fictional concoction."

Santiva didn't hear her or chose not to. "Says here you are following leads to every sex pervert in the city. Is that true? No one's shared this with me. I thought this was an abduction for revenge motive case, so tell me, just what the fuck's going on down here?"

"What can I say, Eriq? O'Brien's misrepresented what I said."

Jessica gave Richard a stern look to tell him to keep out of it.

"What precisely did you say to the press?" Eriq pursued.

"Nothing, I tell you."

"All the same, now Sex Crimes at WPD wants in. Cap-

tain Halstrom in Sex Crimes is all over my head about this
and—"

"I told O'Brien nothing. Two words to shut him up."

"Oh, I see, and let me guess what those two words were."

"Man, this sucks," Jessica roared while scanning the
story. "He's managed to blow everything I said out of all
proportion. Tim must've been on 'ludes when he wrote this
shit."

"Any truth in it? This has got to sting the family, Jess.
This is just thoughtless and insensitive."

"You can't blame me for O'Brien's actions."

"Are you and your team chasing a sex-lust-murderer here
or not?"

"Who knows? Maybe, maybe not. Frankly, I think not.
We're of the same opinion as Richard. This creep is out for
revenge-murder not lust-murder."

"Gene Halstrom is sending over a shrink-cop from his
Sex Crimes Division at the WPD. Is that what I tell her?"

"Turn the whole damn case over to them, Chief. They're
a special unit. You can wash your hands of it quite easily,
if that's what you want."

"Don't test me, Jessica, or I just might do that."

"It's not about sex," shouted Sharpe, who came to stand
beside Jessica, defending her. "We all know it."

J. T. joined in, standing behind Jessica. Others in the task
force now did the same. It was a silent show of unity and
conviction.

Santiva replied, "So you are all of one mind now?"

"We are," said Sharpe.

"That's good . . . good."

"And it's not *all* over the press," Jessica replied firmly.

"Thank your lucky stars, Jessica. Someone always runs
interference for you. But this time, all our heads are on the
block if we don't deliver and deliver quickly. So how do
we know for certain that it's not a sexually motivated abduction?"

"You tell him, Richard," suggested Jessica. The others
remained silent.

"Well? Give it to me straight." Santiva stared into Sharpe's eyes.

"We believe there's . . . there was some history between Judge DeCampe and her abductor. It doesn't on the surface warrant the label of a sex crime. We are leaning toward a revenge or hate motive, and that the perpetrator carefully premeditated the abduction. We believe she's been targeted for some time out of revenge, hate."

"Hate . . . revenge . . . but no perversions of a sexual nature?"

"We don't know enough yet, Chief," J. T. confessed.

Jessica offered an apology of sorts, lifting her shoulders. "I'm sorry for whatever I may have said that set O'Brien off, but at least our true investigation isn't being laid out in today's headlines."

"But they may well be in tomorrow's," countered Santiva.

"I have a full profile on the abductor," Sharpe told him. "Sent a copy to you via interoffice a half hour ago. It has taken into account all we have, and the profile attempts to make sense of it."

"Look, Eriq," said Jessica, her hands in the air, "I'm sorry if I screwed up, but my words were taken out of context, as usual."

Richard's stare at Jessica told her in no uncertain terms that he did not like it that she had assumed the brunt of Santiva's accusation when in fact it had been Richard who had chosen to throw the reporter a bone in order to get rid of the pesky fellow. Still, it was a rarity to hear her apologize for anything, and now she'd gotten herself in this deep, he held back.

"I hope it doesn't hurt the family," Jessica added.

"Hers or ours?" he asked, referring to the FBI's reputation.

"Theirs, of course. Please, tell them it's just to get a dig in at the abductor, maybe stir him to some foolish action, like perhaps contacting us or the newspaper."

"It already has hurt the family, Jessica," replied Santiva. "It already has." Santiva stared about the room, did a bit of pacing and rampaging, mostly muttering to himself. "So now you're all dug in here?" He didn't wait for a reply. "I just got heat from the police commissioner who just got the mayor off his back. Everyone upstairs wants results yesterday, people." He lifted the newspaper and slapped it down again with a rifle shot result. "And this kind of crap can only worsen our public appearance, unless we're all in agreement on content that goes out of here. Is that clear? Say not a word to the press that isn't cleared through channels. Repeat it back, both of you." His eyes settled on Sharpe and Jessica, even as murmured *yessirs* wandered the room like so many blind birds.

Jessica remained silent; Richard almost broke the silence, but Jessica jabbed him in the ribs. Santiva stormed off, a section of newspaper taking wing in his wake. Sharpe exchanged a long stare with Jessica before J. T. got between them, saying, "Gee willikers, you handled that well, Jess." J. T. lifted the newspaper and began scanning the story for himself.

Jessica laughed lightly, but it was a hollow laugh at best. Sharpe put an arm around her, bolstering her and saying, "All in a day's work, sweetheart."

She tilted her head upward and they kissed while J. T. gave them a firm frown.

"Are we absolutely sure it isn't some sex pervert with sexual intentions on his mind?" asked one of the other agents. "Maybe we locked down on the notion of revenge motive too soon."

"Yeah? How do we know?" she replied. "Maybe that asshole O'Brien—the Newly Established Irish Anti–Sexual Perversion League—can define sexual perversion for us."

"What kind of game are you playing, here, Jess?"

"Is that the best you can do, J. T.?"

Now it was Sharpe's turn to frown at Jessica.

J. T. asked, "What's-at supposed to mean?"

"Hey, what if our guy reads the *Post*, or the *Enquirer* for that matter? What'll be his reaction to the news that he's being called a sex pervert?" Jessica asked her longtime friend and Richard.

"You tricky devil, Jess," replied J. T., squeezing her hand. "Smart move." A big laugh escaped him. "You *meant* for O'Brien to plant this in the newspaper, didn't you?"

"You were there, Richard; you heard what I gave O'Brien: *nothing*. I gave him zip. The fact he ran with it, well, he ran to my goal post is all."

Going along with things now, Richard added, "A newspaperman is easily guided when he's given to think an idea originated with him."

"Gotta handle him like you would Chief Santiva is all," Jessica put in.

"So if our abductor sees or hears the news that he's some kind of aberrant sex offender, you think it might shake something from the proverbial tree," J. T. surmised aloud as if it would be clearer if he could vocalize it. "Not bad."

"I have a gut feeling that we don't have a lot of time for niceties or anything else where this guy is concerned, my friend," Jessica replied. "We certainly don't have time for petty concerns and petty politics. Understood?"

FIVE

When is death not within ourselves?

—HERACLEITUS (CA 540–CA 480 B.C.)

HOME, her daughters, her son, family, friends, her passions, her work, her passion for her work, the safety of familiar surroundings, more about family, friends, full circle to home, then inside her home with the doors locked, roaming familiar corridors, loving a place of mortar and wood, windows drawn, a hot bath drawn—warm and soothing against her skin—music playing in her ear, the smell of candles and incense she'd bought on a trip to India, a teasing, pleasant incense—all of these wonderful thoughts felt now like lost treasures, promises. But could she believe the promise of ever seeing or feeling any of these special things again? *Is that what heaven is comprised of,* she asked herself, *you get back all you've lost?*

Maureen DeCampe thought of everything that ever meant anything of real value to her, and all that had been stripped from her: all sense of security and faith in the ground beneath one's feet, replaced by fear, uncertainty, and horror in its rawest sense. She imagined having been drugged and kept in a state of unconsciousness, taken across country into a maze of farmland, hills, and paths, into a heartland that was crisscrossed by seemingly endless, anonymous blacktop roads. A place of wheat and cornfields that went on for endless miles, fields on a grand scale, a grand place to lay train track and raise children on little farms amid a paradise called Iowa; a place where nothing bad ever happened until now, and it was happening to her.

He'd abducted her and had transported her from the nation's capital to here, somewhere Iowa . . . Iowa Falls, Iowa. Wasn't that where Jimmy Lee had been raised on a farm? She had never seen it on a map; she had no idea of the geography of Iowa, knowing only the clichéd facts: Indian name, flat terrain, nothing to interest the casual traveler, sleep-inducing wheat fields, and close-knit neighbors who didn't bother locking doors or windows at night. In the midst of this, a dark little farmstead that reeked of animal slaughter and feces, a dark little place where she would die a horrid death not heard of in the modern world.

How did I get here? How was I made so stupid? Turned into a victim—a g'damn victim, me! A thing I swore to never, ever become again after walking out on Stewart after three months of being the teen bride he so liked to victimize! How did I wind up thrashing atop a vile corpse in a black place in the middle of no-fucking-where?

"Go on," came his voice out of the gloom surrounding her. Bastard sat on a three-legged milking stool in the gray gloom, just within her sight if she squinted; sitting there watching her struggle, no animal sounds but her own sad whine.

She could not form words. The tape choked her.

Attempting to form words took too much effort.

Still, she strained against her bonds and cursed him just the same.

"More you thrash around like a sturgeon on a pike, faster the bruisin'll pop up all over Little Jimmy; I say *little* 'cause he's done shriveled up so since they threw the switch on him. Body's just a shell of what he once't was, but it's full of dying cells, you can believe that. Hell, you can smell it. My old pap always told me what you can smell, you can believe in."

Despite her gag, she cursed him in no uncertain terms.

He ignored her feeble attempt to curse him, adding, "Like an overripe apple, Jimmy Lee is. He'll decay faster if'n you help it along that way, and so you'll catch the decay from him more quicker, so's you can end it that much sooner. So, you just carry on, little Miss High and Mighty Judgess."

Again she thrashed and cursed under the gag.

"You thought it was cute, first time I called you Judgess in your courtroom office, way back when you was still just a judge in Houston. I could tell you thought it was cute. You still like it some?" he asked, a hissing snicker escaping him. "Treated me like dirt when I come to speak to you personal about taking on Jimmy Lee's appeal case, remember?"

She lay perfectly still and silent, thinking. *I'll be damned if I'll put on a show for this motherfuckin' throwback son of a motherless fucking pig.*

He laughed hollowly, as if he understood her silent curse. He lit a lantern and studied her and his dead son where they lay like some kind of game with four legs and four arms. He hemmed and hawed for a few long minutes, then, taking his lantern with him, he left her in the empty darkness of what felt like a barn, alone with the diseased thing that meant to kill her in flowing ooze and in slow motion. Only a small light was left burning, a single flame that dipped and rippled with the intermittent wind through the cracks. The old man had left a small candle burning on the stool where he'd been sitting earlier.

Just enough light to create grotesque shadows.

While her eyes focused on the flame, her ears told her that there were no chickens, no sound of sheep, no cow's tail thumping against a stall. She remained perfectly alone, except for erratic slithering noises that came and went—curious vermin, brought by the odor of decaying flesh; that and the sound of her own breath remained all there was. She gagged repeatedly as she took in the awful odors through her flared nostrils.

How long? How long will the process take if this sick fuck allows it to continue to its natural—or is it unnatural—resolution? Two days, six, twelve, a month? At what point will I begin to feel the inevitable pain? The horror of my own rotting flesh? The stench of flesh as it loses its bond, the unrelenting odorous horror of inhaling my own dying flesh? Will it be distinguishable from the flesh that takes my flesh into its maw? At what point will I feel no more? At

*what point do I go sinking and melding into Jimmy Lee's
decaying body? At what point do I go insanely insane?*

The old man had left the candle burning on a holder on
the stool. It only required a moment's thought to prefer
burning to death to what Purdy had in mind for her. She
slowly began to rock Jimmy Lee's body beneath her. It was
easier getting momentum going than she had imagined. The
old man was right. Jimmy Lee was no longer a large man,
no longer much mass left to him. Still, she would have to
roll with great momentum to make Jimmy and herself a
missile for the stool. She didn't care at this point if she
would or would not come out atop the dead man. It would
only take a half roll to send the candle onto the hay-strewn
floor and possibly, just possibly, set the two of them, Jimmy
Lee and herself, ablaze. She believed it a far, far better way
to die than by the slow and painful degrees the old man
wanted to see and relish.

She got the body rolling back and forth with great force
now, and suddenly the bodies lashed together hit the stool,
but at the same moment, the old man lifted the candle into
the air. He'd been standing in shadow, watching, inwardly
laughing at her struggle. The candle had been left to test her
and to offer false hope, so that he could take it away.

Bastard. . . .

She was under the corpse now. The old man kicked out
at his son's dead body and sent it back over to its original
position, she on top.

"Wouldn't do to have Jimmy on top," he said. "He'd
decay you too quick thataway. I want this to last."

She cried as darkness completely enfolded the barn,
while the old man waltzed out this time to the tune of her
complaints. The old man made a noisy show of rattling the
door, locking her inside.

ISAIAH Purdy, determined to make his destination, had continued on toward Huntsville, Texas, at dawn, even after the
near-fatal crash into the ditch that had acted like a hammer
blow to wake him up at the wheel. That night he'd been

nearly killed, having been run completely off the highway by a road hog truck driver, who didn't so much as slow down. *Like a goddamn ocean liner running down a man in a rowboat.* This all happened just outside of Sioux City, Iowa, where one turn would take him to South Dakota, another to Nebraska. He'd needed the exit for Nebraska, and having almost missed it, he'd veered into the path of the truck, which was passing him on the right. When he'd come to his senses, it was too late, and the trucker had no sympathy for his indecision. "Indecision kills," he'd muttered to himself once the van had come to a complete halt.

Purdy then continued on for the border exit out of Iowa altogether and, using the interstate, was soon having breakfast in neighboring Nebraska.

The long journey had given Isaiah time to think clearly about his plans, and to again and again condemn that bitch judge who had sent his child to his death.

At the time of his going to Huntsville, Jimmy Lee's execution was imminent, looming in Isaiah's mind like a predatory bird picking at his brain whenever he gave the least thought to the adult boy he had raised on the farm. He recalled how he had taught the boy all he knew about raising pigs for slaughter, and how Jimmy Lee learned to slit a pig's throat and drain the blood from the carcass in the most efficient manner. How the pig must be boiled in water to scrape off every whisker and hair, and how to dismember the animal limb by limb, and how to use every strip of flesh and organ. At first, the boy proved reluctant and a slow learner. Isaiah had had to shame the boy into his first slaughter of a pig the boy had become fond of.

The boy's mother joked on more than one occasion as to how Isaiah loved his pigs more than he did her, and more than he did his own son, that he spent more time with his pigs than he did his family. But how else to make a go of a pig farm? It took time—lots of time—to make money off of a slew of piglets raised to become pork on the hoof.

The Nebraska state line had come and gone, and still Isaiah had miles to go before he slept that night if he were to make his son's execution by the appointed time. "What a cursed life it's become," he moaned, and his stomach and sore heart lurched in unison, bringing a sour pain to his chest. *Acid indigestion, a lifelong problem, rearing its ugly head,* he thought. "Miles to go before I sleep . . . miles to go before I sleep . . ."

That had been only a week ago. Now he had completed the journey to Huntsville, and he had sat stone cold and rock-hearted as they strapped Jimmy Lee into that chair and they played out their little ritual like they were the military, and the order was given and all those many volts of electricity were sent coursing through Jimmy Lee's horrified body, turning the boy into a stiff board. He'd then claimed his boy's body, and had gotten the needed extra coffin loaded into the van alongside Jimmy's. All the paperwork was filled out, and then he'd gone looking for the judge. Miss High and Mighty. Jimmy Lee's choice to spend eternity with. It was the boy's final wish. And Isaiah believed it was the least he could do for the boy at this terrible time.

He reasoned that his fulfilling the boy's last wish would make up for all the time he'd not spent with Jimmy Lee as a child. Maybe . . .

That was only a week before.

Now Isaiah had set Jimmy Lee's final request in motion. Now Judge DeCampe lay helplessly strapped to Jimmy Lee's decaying corpse.

Now . . . now it was set in motion, he kept telling himself, because sometimes he didn't believe it himself. Sometimes, the idea of time itself meant nothing to him. Sometimes nowadays time had no linear meaning to the old man; one day did not follow another, and there were no increments of time, no minutes, no hours, no days, no weeks, months, or years—not any longer.

Sometimes inside his head, Isaiah still had the journey to Houston to complete, still had to kidnap the woman there in Houston, even knowing now that she hadn't been in Houston but in Washington, D.C., where he had found the woman who had for so many years occupied Jimmy Lee's dreams. In his mind, he had not yet kidnapped the woman, but he would. And he'd do it without a hitch whatsoever,

so sure was he of his plan. And why not? After all, it was foreseen and foretold by Jimmy Lee before his execution in one of the boy's visions—visions that had come to him after his incarceration. The visions came along with Jimmy Lee's sudden realization of how his life—even his life in prison— could be softened and helped by a steady reading of his Bible, the one his mother had sent him.

So while he drove to Huntsville to fetch Jimmy Lee's corpse and then to Houston for the judge's soon-to-be-corpse, he was also simultaneously turning the woman's flesh to a gangrenous Jell-O. All in due time . . . all in time, but all time was relative, after all.

His pocket watch read three A.M. Everybody was a little crazy at three in the morning. He had returned to the barn and now regained his seat on the stool facing DeCampe. She lay helpless in Isaiah's power, but in truth, it was due to Jimmy Lee's power, the power he had found in the scriptures. If truly in the faith—as old white-haired Samuel Putnam said every Sunday at prayer meetings—Jimmy Lee could move mountains even in death. Hell, he had moved his old man clear across the continent and back. Proof positive the boy had come to know that he could not go through this life without help from those who loved him, had loved him his entire life, had forgiven him his horrid deeds, had forgiven him his murdering ways, had forgiven him his unthinkable, unspeakable acts, because in the end he had accepted Christ as his Lord and Savior. This above all had moved his mama and papa to stand by their only begotten son. The Lord *moved* in mysterious ways . . . the Lord moved *people* in mysterious ways.

The humming of the van's engine all along the winding roads, which took him closer and closer to Huntsville and his "walking dead" son, conspired to give more and more credence and time over to Jimmy Lee's secret life inside Isaiah's head. Still, he had resisted long and hard to control the voice and to beg for a sign or a word from Eunice Mae, where she stood in all this now that she had crossed over. However, Eunice Mae had not stirred from the grave and

had not visited inside Isaiah's head, as had the living, prepared-to-die Jimmy Lee.

Life, death, the passage of time, the stars, the universe, God, and the tree of life, how men chose to live their lives, all of these questions Isaiah had had time to ponder and sift through his brain on his long and twisting journey to the Huntsville, Texas, penitentiary. Other more worldly concerns also occupied his time; on more than one bleary-eyed stop, the old man feared he would not make it in time to see his son alive again, but rather that he would arrive only to collect up the body that was of his flesh.

As it turned out, he'd gotten there on time for the execution, which had been a surprise—but hardly a pleasant one.

Saints and snowstorms had always converged at that one corner of his farmhouse, back of the barn, the whiteness of it covering his Iowa land to form a huge lake of purity that blinded a man. He burst out in a rattle of laughter that tasted good but lasted only a moment. He'd suddenly recalled having discussed the beauty of the old place and what his son mockingly called "the palace itself." It was at a time when Jimmy Lee had turned to God for answers as to what to do with the rest of his incarcerated life. Jimmy Lee had gotten a peaceful look on his face and had replied through the glass partition that had separated them, "You think God ever really sends any saints down to Earth along with the snowfall like mama always claimed?"

"He sent your mama, didn't he?" was Isaiah's instant reply, and it had shut the boy up on the topic. "Sure, son, we beat you when it was called for, but your mama was a saint if ever one lived."

"I 'spect God would send a saint to a lonely old backwoods Iowa farm to live out her days."

"Modern life being what it is, you think he'd send a saint into someplace like New York City, boy?"

That's when Jimmy Lee's voice took on the tenor of a god and he bellowed out, *"Sodomy and Gay-mor-aaa!"*

To pass the time and distance between Iowa City and Huntsville, the three of them—Iowa farmer, death row in-

mate, and God—talked of theology, the nature of time and space, of man and spirit, of the anima and fate, karma and vengeance. They spoke of death and life and the cycle in between, and they spoke of rebirth, renewal, and regeneration, and Isaiah wondered about regeneration of tissue and limbs like he'd seen in frogs and tadpoles, and he asked God why men couldn't do that, and he asked why God had created mosquitoes and mites, pestilence and disease, and he asked about pain—pain from physical harm and pain of the emotional and mental sort. He asked why such things existed in the world, and God and Jimmy Lee pondered these questions, and neither of them gave the old man a straight answer. So he continued to drive on.

The entire way to Huntsville across America's highways Isaiah asked questions that no one—not even God—could provide an answer for, until finally Isaiah decided that God had nothing to do with the way things worked out, that while He set things in motion, He could not have known that out of the muck of the original mire from which mankind dragged itself a seriously screwed-up brain would come about alongside polyps and viruses and no-see-ums.

Then Jimmy Lee's laugh would fill Isaiah's brain; sometimes the laughter was followed by a sneer. Sometimes Jimmy Lee would tell him he was an old fool to bother God with such stupid questions. While it had been exhilarating at times to sense Jimmy Lee traveling over space and time to enter his mind, Isaiah often feared the power and clarity of his son's voice in his head. This he felt was what the young folks called intensely "cool"—that his son, sitting on death row, awaiting certain execution, had not waited until death had overtaken him to astrally project his anima or spirit to the back wall of Isaiah's head, to live inside the old man full-blown, and to direct him in these actions. His brain, encased in his skull, had always been a comfort to him, but now it registered a discomfiting feeling, and he was no longer at ease with his own mind. Not since Eunice followed her sister Emma Tilda to the grave. His beloved wife Eunice had been first to hear their son, Jimmy Lee, as clear as ringing a Wisconsin cowbell. But Jimmy Lee had not sounded his words alone. He had come in the company of his God, and they were awful and all-powerful in their combined voice and message of death.

Driving the byways of Nebraska, crossing into Kansas, heading toward Arkansas and parts south for Texas, zigzagging downward across the states, fearful now of the big interstates, Isaiah Purdy simply no longer felt at ease. His agitation came on scratching claws and unsettling words; words that spoke of a cruel revenge, something he had never thought himself capable of. Yet the evolving plan—Jimmy Lee's unfolding wrath—would not leave his brain. It came that first night to mark his mind, like a knife slicing across his forehead to make itself clear, like a firm fist pounding on a bolted door, clamoring to get in.

Strange how it had gotten into Eunice's head first, but then not so strange after all; Jimmy was always more partial to his ma than his pa. And the old man could well understand. After all, it had been his father who had had to punish the boy repeatedly, every time he broke a commandment. Jimmy Lee usually took a horse-hiding to come into line. And the favored instrument used on the boy was a harness.

Maybe it had all been for the best, his beating the boy. The boy was, after all, finally traveling in the company of his and Isaiah's Maker.

Isaiah looked up from the steering wheel and stared over it at the endless stretch of Texas highway, the center white line at the center of his hood, and once again he knew he was veering into an oncoming car. He snatched the wheel and brought it in line as the highway coalesced into a hay-strewn barnyard floor upon which lay a nude woman strapped to a dead man, to the corpse of his dead son.

Isaiah wondered what time it was. He'd been dozing on the stool set up alongside the suffering woman. "Time for a soft bed up at the house," he told himself and Jimmy Lee, who, in the old man's head, agreed.

"Time for bed, old man. . . ."

* * *

JESSICA Coran had been unable to reach her friend Kim Desinor by phone, by fax, or by E-mail either at her office or home. Kim appeared to have disappeared without a word, and such behavior was unlike the woman. Jessica then learned that Kim had told Eriq Santiva that she wanted nothing more to do with the DeCampe case. She put in for time off. The sudden turnabout in Kim's behavior, her interest turning to disinterest, worried Jessica, so she asked Richard to take her to Dr. Kim Desinor's door an hour from D.C.

This necessitated a drive out to Quantico, Virginia, to Kim's apartment home, a beautiful place carved out of a hillside, now mushroomed with single and multiple duplex homes and apartments. They'd had a bit of a holdup at the gate when no one answered the buzzer, but they had convinced the security guard to let them pass. Outside Kim's door lay several untouched newspapers, and blinds and curtains were drawn against the gray, overcast day, which was just beginning to see patches of blue and sunlight.

Kim didn't readily open her door when she heard Jessica's voice on the other side of the stout, white-coated wood. Richard had remained behind in the car, reading some of Judge DeCampe's case files, sifting for information, anything that might click.

Alone at the door, Jessica sensed that Kim had, for whatever reason, chosen to hole up here like a wounded animal. Jessica wanted to know why.

"Come on, Kim. You don't keep your friends standing on a doorstep. What's up with you, sweethearts?" It was an old joke laced with truth. Jessica had once told Kim that her heart seemed so large, open, and giving that she must have two hearts, so she'd begun to call her *sweethearts.*

The door opened a crack, and Jessica saw that the interior was semidark, the drapes pulled against any Virginia sunlight that might dare attempt to enter the room. Kim's normally bright and cheery surroundings appeared to have been turned into a mortuary or mausoleum. Uncharacteristically inhospitable, Kim held Jessica at the door, where she grimly stood; Kim also tilted her head to show only her left side. "Are you going to let me in or do I have to—"

"Go away, Jess. I'm not feeling well, and I'm not receiving visitors, and I certainly don't . . . feel sociable right now."

"Eriq said you want off the case."

"Wanted off, past tense. I choose my cases carefully. I have to. I don't have the luxury of psychological distance, not like you and the others have, and at the close range I am at, I can't as easily maintain a mental balance in the face of such horror, Jess. Now, if you don't mind. . . ."

Jessica sensed there was more to it than what Kim had to say, far more. But Kim didn't wish to confide, and in an impulsive move, she pushed the door closed, but Jessica just as impulsively shoved her foot in and pushed back, knocking the door open. It stood wide open now, sunlight pouring through as the two friends glared at one another. The sunlight created a halo around Jessica where she stood in the doorway. Jessica's action had surprised Kim, revealing that the psychic's right cheek appeared badly bruised. "What the hell's happened to you, Kim?"

"I walked into a door," she bitterly replied. "Now, please, leave."

"Who the hell's struck you? That cop boyfriend of yours, Sincebaugh? I'll kick his—"

"No one's battered me, Jess!" Kim wrapped her head and face in a large scarf, revealing an area on each wrist that looked like age spots or the spots of leprosy. "You've got no right storming in here like some savior. I want you to leave now, Jess."

"My God, Kim, tell me what's going on! Your hands, your face are—"

"Despicable, I know." Kim's eyes swelled, and tears flowed. She turned away. "You're stating the obvious, Jess."

Jessica grabbed hold of her friend's shoulders and stared at the awful discoloration on her right cheek. She gasped when realizing what she stared at was diseased tissue—decay, even. She helplessly shrank back, recoiling for a split second as she might with a leper. But how had Kim contracted leprosy?

Kim recoiled away as well, flailing her way to a chair,

her shoulder hurting from where Jessica had touched it. "I'm decaying, Jess. Literally decaying."

"My God, has it been diagnosed? Who're you seeing?"

"I'm seeing DeCampe! She's decaying, Jess; she's somewhere fucking decaying, and I can't go near her, not . . . not again, not ever."

Jessica stepped closer to Kim, one hand extended, yet fearful of touching her friend. "Are you telling me that your symptoms are due to—"

"My only hope, if it's not too late, is to rid my mind of this goddamn case, to rid my mind of DeCampe and her condition."

"I've never known your psychic wounds to be so . . . this severe, Kim. I absolutely agree. I just need to understand. Are you saying that DeCampe is in the process of decaying and that you somehow tapped into her dead body and—"

"Yes, damnit. DeCampe is decaying, by the hour in some hellish grave."

"She's buried somewhere? But where? Have you got a location, Kim?"

"She feels buried alive but decaying at the same time. I see her in a coffin."

"Decaying alive," Jessica repeated.

"I don't know . . . it makes no sense . . . but she just doesn't feel dead . . . rather she feels like she wants to be dead."

"But she's not dead yet."

"Nor am I, Jess." She turned and faced Jessica. "I keep sensing that she is somehow being tortured with her own flesh."

"My God," Jessica gasped once more at seeing the discoloration on Kim's cheek, and now at her wrists.

"That's all I know about DeCampe. Now you've got the information you came for, so please go."

"I appreciate your insights on the case, Kim, but I came here out of concern for you. No one's seen you."

"I know that you came out of concern, but now that you have seen me, please, go!" Kim fell into a chair.

"You know I can't just walk away from you and leave you here in this condition."

"Leave, please."

"I love you, and I want what's best for you. Have you seen a doctor for . . . what kind of medication you can use?" Jessica had gone to her knees before her friend, reaching out, caressing her forearms, careful to avoid any malignant spots.

"Medications don't work on mind-altered states, Jessica. You know that as well as I. All I can do is keep away from Maureen DeCampe, wherever she is."

Jessica sighed heavily. "I'm so sorry, Kim. I had no idea."

"No one does, and please, I would like to keep it that way."

Jessica reached out and embraced her. Kim tried to hold back the tears, but in a moment, she erupted, her body quaking against Jessica's, until she pulled away and rushed from Jessica, shouting, "Go—get away from me. For all we know, this *psychic leprosy* could be contagious."

Kim now firmly took hold of Jessica's arm and ushered her to the door, and there put her out, closing the door between them.

Jessica called out. "Let me know if there is anything— anything—you need, Kim. If you need someone, let me know."

Silence. No answer.

It felt like the silence of a cavern behind the thick white door, the silence of suffering. Jessica felt angry with herself at having involuntarily recoiled at first sight of Kim's cankerous facial sores. She could not take that back, but the surprise and shock were understandable. It had only been a day since she had last seen a healthy Kim Desinor, and now this.

Agitated, pacing at the doorstep, not wanting to abandon Kim, Jessica saw that Richard was staring at her, that he must wonder what was going on. Her eyes returned to the blank door, which stared back, and she heard the soft crying of the woman inside. The sound made Jessica weak and angry with herself that she'd allowed Kim to manhandle her out the door. She now wondered what she ought to do. She then shouted through the door, "You know me, Kim. I'm going to meddle. I'm going to call Dr. Roy Shoate—best physician in the city. He'll make a house call on my say-so. There's got to be something we can do."

Again silence.

Jessica felt a twinge of fear; she didn't want to leave Kim alone, but she also knew how fiercely proud the woman was, and she must respect her wishes. She stepped away from the door, feeling as if she were letting Kim down, that she and the FBI family had already let her down. She feared Kim might do something to harm herself.

Halfway back to the waiting car and Richard, she dialed Dr. Shoate on her cellular phone.

SIX

Fair is foul, and foul is fair.
Hover through the fog and filthy air.

—WILLIAM SHAKESPEARE

JESSICA had learned never to discount Kim Desinor's visions or suspicions, and never to read one of her visions literally. If she said Judge DeCampe was in some place of decay, this could have many interpretations, that there were many rivers to the ocean. Decay had many connotations and images attached to it, and the place where DeCampe was being held might simply be a "place of decay" such as a cemetery or burial plot or even a cold storage meat packing company. The fact that her abductor had "confined" her could point to a decay of movement as in wither, ebb, crumble, dwindle, fade, fall off. In the most hideous sense, however, it meant spoil, corrupt, perish, degenerate, decompose, deteriorate, disintegrate, putrefaction, and adulteration. Then again, adultery came out of adulteration, so the association could go on endlessly, and therein lay both the strength and the weakness of the psychic and psychic imagery. The psychic vision might not in and of itself be useful, but in the psychic's interpretation, a use might often come of psychic information. Kim had proven herself time after time as an able and capable interpreter of her own visions. If she said that Maureen DeCampe was "in a state of decay," there was some truth to this, but it could well mean that she was in a state within the contiguous United States that was in a state of decay, such as a farm state in a nation that no longer valued the private farm and its family of caregivers. Or it might be taken literally, that DeCampe might well be buried alive in a coffin this moment. Decay meant decline, decadence, failure—all adjectives perhaps better applied to DeCampe's abductor. Decay stood for collapse, for waste, breakdown, and breakup, dissolution, corruption, and mold, blight, and rot—perhaps the condition of a man gone mad. All these horrid images Kim had internalized, and the result was disease overtaking Kim's own body—a strange psychic malady somehow connected to DeCampe's circumstances. Psychosomatic illness taken to the tenth power, Jessica imagined.

Dr. Roy Shoate had contacted Jessica to tell her that he had never seen a healthier person exhibiting signs of Ebola virus. That's what it looked like to him. He had run no tests, but he said she was literally being eaten up, and it was ongoing unless they could find some way to arrest it.

"She submitted to your examination without a fight?" Jessica had asked.

"She has little strength left. She is dying, Jessica."

Tears welled up in Jessica. "Do all you can to arrest it, Dr. Shoate." Jessica did not confide in the doctor that Kim's condition was psychically induced. She knew that no doctor could completely stop it until Jessica brought an end to the DeCampe case, the case Kim had been so diligently working on when the strange malady overtook her.

"This appears a public health issue to me, Dr. Coran. Will you be notifying Atlanta?"

Jessica had no intention of alerting the CDC or anyone else about Kim's condition. "I'll take every step necessary, Doctor, and thank you," she lied.

"Meantime, we have her sedated and isolated. We will proceed under the assumption it is the Ebola but will administer no meds until we have isolated the virus itself, to be certain. That's the best we can do for now—hospital policy—now that we live in such a litigious society."

"How long will further tests take?"

"Twenty-four hours for initial tests, forty-eight to be certain."

"Thanks for all you've done, Dr. Shoate."

"Absolutely. I know you have your hands full. I've been reading the papers."

Jessica hung up, her friend's life very much on her mind. She paced the office and stared out the window, weighing the news from Dr. Shoate. The ante had been significantly raised now, with Kim's life in the bargain.

J. T. stepped in, shouting, "The parking attendant has been found dead in Detroit, Michigan, as far as he got."

"How?"

"Killed in a flophouse."

"Christ help us. We'll never know the extent of his involvement."

"What's up with Kim Desinor, Jess? I couldn't help but overhear. Is she ill?"

"She's somehow contracted some sort of bad case of . . . not sure what it is, but she believes it came directly from her psychic journey into Judge DeCampe's mind. She's . . . she's not good." Jessica began to cry. "But J. T., keep this information between us, please."

J. T. fidgeted. He had rarely seen Jessica break down, certainly not in a public place. He awkwardly went to her and held her. He promised what he could not possibly deliver. "Kim's going to be all right; don't you worry. She's a fighter."

"I've got her under the best care in Quantico. Still, I wish I could do more. If we could locate Maureen DeCampe, put some closure on this case, maybe . . . it might have a beneficial effect on Kim, but as of now . . . Kim is slowly dying of wounds she feels are empathetic in nature. They're like the open sores of a leper, J. T. In all my career, I've never seen anything like this before, except—"

"Except where?"

"Except on an autopsy slab."

"What are you talking about?"

"I drove down to Quantico to see her, and I tell you, she's exhibiting leprosy-like spots, like we see on decaying corpses. She even smelled of decay. Her whole apartment did."

J. T. could find no words of comfort now. Instead, he

offered her a shoulder and continued to hold his friend.

"I got Roy Shoate to see her, and he admitted her to Washington Memorial. He's the best in his field."

"He's a rare disease man, isn't he?"

"Yeah . . .'fraid so."

J. T. said no more.

MAUREEN DeCampe, judge of the First Appellate Court of Washington, D.C., believed her mind had always had a perverse liking for frightening her; it played games all the time. So why should a moment in a darkened underground parking lot be any different?

Her logical left side of the brain told her right side how foolish it was being, and that she was not about to pay heed to the false instinct to flee from the stranger in the parking garage. Such an act would make her appear foolish; in the end, it would amount to twaddle, what her career Navy father called bilge-rot, malarky, drivel, and she would, in the end, senselessly appear nonsensical.

She hated to be embarrassed or made the butt of a joke.

Still, a distinct odor of fright—a thought of horror winging shadowlike out to her car—or was the shadow him? Shadowing in her shadow?

Shadow . . . such a positively lovely word when properly sounded out; it played melodic over the concave surface of the mind . . . shadowlike in a shadowed land that smelled of ancient, earthy, red dirt and rotting ears of corn and of hay and of more odors than she could enumerate, all commingling here in this place of her captivity.

Something brought her around to a startling realization, an epiphany: What at first had felt like a dishonest emotion was in fact a righteous paranoia, after all. Despite her self-assuredness, her directed and fast gait from stairwell to waiting car, and the fact she was armed and capable of bringing down a tundra yak with her Remington .45, a sense of vulnerability cast itself over her like a Maine fog. She felt the touch of this blanketing vulnerability; felt it the way an animal at a watering hole knows it is being stalked. *Death, the ultimate stalker* . . . She felt the fear of an animal about to be devoured whole and with pleasure.

She'd felt it then, and she felt and feared it even more now. Now that she sensed him close by, observing as before, watching her terror, enjoying her slow spiral into insanity and despair and fainting and recovering and what must come soon—her final death. She'd given little thought to life or the possibility of some savior crashing in to free her.

She willed herself to no longer contemplate long on her family, what they must be suffering. She willed herself to think only of mercy and prayer.

There in the underground lot, she had wheeled and brought her weapon into the stalker's face, but the man's sheer fright lessened her resolve. It was a passing homeless fellow looking for a warm corner to sleep it off in. She scolded him. Told him to get himself together as she pushed a five dollar bill into his hands, turned, and continued to her car, while the tall homeless man ambled off.

Then someone tapped on her shoulder, and she reacted, bringing the firearm up to eye level on the white-haired man with the gray-stubbled chin.

"Please, don't *shoooot,*" pleaded the little man in the rumpled old suit. He was shorter by a head than she. This old coot must have witnessed her generosity toward the other fellow and wanted some shown him, she had guessed. His skin appeared as rumpled and loose as his clothing. His country drawl made him a simple fellow, and when he'd thrown up a pair of wrinkled hands in the universal posture of defeat, Judge DeCampe almost felt sorry for his having startled her into putting the muzzle of the .45 in his face. Then she recognized him with a startled shock.

"Mr. Purdy? James Lee Purdy's father?" she then asked, somewhat amazed to find the man so out of place and time.

"You couldn't forget the likes of me, now could you?"

"No . . . haven't forgotten, no."

"Guess that goes a long way to show your guilt, Your Honorable *Judgess.*" He uttered her title as if spitting battery fluid.

Still, her recognition of the quiet little man who had sat

for almost three months in her courtroom nearly nine years ago, month after month during his son's murder trial, listening to testimony condemning his son to die in a Texas electric chair, told her she had nothing to fear from this sad Iowa farmer. "What the hell're you doing here? In Washington? Wasn't your son's execution scheduled and carried out?"

It came as a surprise to find him here, seeking her out. His son's case had come full circle, the final appeal, and through some strange judiciary coincidence, it had fallen on her desk when she was hearing appeals in Houston. Of course, she'd immediately refused the case on grounds of conflict of interest, since no judge could try the same case twice, even if she had become an appeals judge by then and even if Jimmy Lee Purdy had kept up with her career for some perverted reason. Still, at that time and now, she suspected, the old Iowa farmer must be absolutely confused about the judicial system. A simple Iowa farmer lost amid Houston's court system with its winding, twisting corridors until he found her office.

He had entered her chambers and there he stood the entire time, pleading with her to handle the appeal, that Jimmy Lee wanted it that way, so there could not be any real conflict of interest due to Jimmy Lee Purdy's final wishes. "A man's final wishes are a sacred thing," the senior Purdy had told her then. Of course, no amount of magical thinking on Purdy's part could convince anyone in the Texas judiciary system to break generations of protocol for "a man's final wishes."

Now here stood old Purdy again before her in an underground lot in D.C. Part of her mind asked why had he sought her out again, here, now. She knew that his son's execution had occurred over the weekend, and this knowledge only made her clench tighter to her Remington.

"I know your son's execution was set for the weekend," she told him. Colleagues in Houston didn't let her miss much, and besides, it'd made national news and had sparked new debate on the capital punishment issue and the State of Texas's penchant for using the chair often and often again.

She had recalled how the worn-out looking little man had abandoned his crops and life on the farm to be at his son's trial, and it had surely proven an ordeal for the father of the accused and convicted defendant. The fact was that the young defendant had no defense; he'd left enough DNA at the series of rape-murders to convict hundreds of men several times over. He'd been careless and messy, meaning to be, taunting law enforcement to stop him, as if it were all a game, and he killed with the thoughtless abandon and impunity of a natural disaster, and he ought to've been put to death the day after his conviction. Instead, they had run him through all of his civil rights until finally he had no more, and Judge Parker had—just as she'd known on the day she'd handed the case over to him—found Jimmy Lee guilty on top of guilty. He'd just been executed over the previous weekend.

So seeing the father here now did not completely surprise her, yet it did surprise her, all the same.

"Mr. Purdy, you startled me."

"I sure don't want that, ma'am, Your Judgess."

"I'm sorry for your loss, Mr. Purdy," she said without sincerity.

"I 'preciate that . . . coming from you, Your Judgess." Aside from this wizened old man, no one gave a whit for Jimmy Lee Purdy. Even the opponents of the death penalty had remained strangely silent on Purdy and his execution, as if to say they'd give the state this one since Purdy was— or appeared by all rights to be—a natural born killer. Certainly, he did not make a good poster boy; he cursed, spat, and made filthy gestures whenever and wherever given the opportunity.

The old man appeared his exact opposite. The old man had sat straight and stiff throughout the proceedings like a staff, an ancient, worm-eaten wooden staff, erect and unbending, proud and sad all at once. Judge DeCampe could only imagine how a parent might react under such stress as God, Texas, his son, and circumstances had placed on him and his absent wife. DeCampe had come to think of the elder Mr. Purdy as a biblical character like Lot or even Job—the Job of Iowa Falls, Iowa.

She relaxed her arm along with the weapon, pointing it downward just as her father had always taught her. "Mr. Purdy, you damn near got your head blown off. You startled me."

Then he grinned a twisted and grimacing grin and mocked her words, "Mr. Purdy, you startled me. I plan for a heap more'n to startle you, Missy."

Now she felt real fear of the sort that went without the blink of second-guessing, but too late! Maureen DeCampe didn't see the electric cattle prod he shoved into her abdomen from somewhere deep within the rumpled coat, through a hole in a pocket. She saw a flash of the silver tip, like the giant sting of a wasp, even as it remained somehow attached to the inner lining of his cloth overcoat. She only felt its report as it sent her into a confused convulsion, a sense of burning material and flesh filling her last thought before passing out.

"You had your chance, woman. You done sat in judgment twic't on my boy, and you done kil't Jimmy Lee, but he ain't going outta this life without company. Electrocution . . . How's it feel? My boy and me're now gonna teach you a little about old time religion and justice. Call yer-self a judge. *Hawww!*"

Her gun had fallen immediately, her hands reacting violently to the electric bolt sent through her every cell. She had slumped forward into him, unconscious, her weight against the frail figure nearly knocking Purdy over. He then must have used some sort of drug on her, she now surmised. Likely used a premeasured dose from a hypodermic.

"I lifted your body, carried you to my waiting van, and there I deposited you . . . inside a pine wood coffin, same as Jimmy Lee's. You rode here right alongside one another in the back of the van. After I put you into the coffin, I nailed shut the top of the thing."

She had a vague memory or sixth sense of having been shut up into a black inkwell.

Darkness complete.

                    *   *   *

ISAIAH Purdy had grown tired, his eyes so heavy they had
closed, his ears no longer registering the whimpering and
animal cries of his victim. He dozed on the three-legged
stool that sat in the barn. He half remembered, half dreamed
now, rewinding his experience through the mechanism of
his mind. What had happened? How had he found the courage and strength to carry out his dead son's wishes?

He recalled again how he had taken the woman in the
garage in Washington, D.C., after he'd made a cruise by the
White House and the Lincoln Memorial—places he'd always wanted to see. He recalled standing in a crowd of
tourists, feeling he needed a bath or a shower.

He recalled next going to the courthouse, and what had happened after he'd jabbed her with the cattle prod and injected
her with the drug. He had then banged tight the coffin lid over
her unconscious form, nail after nail. When he had turned to
climb from the van, he was shocked to see a vision standing
there, a biblical character if ever there was one, a giant, bearded
prophet, asking, "What're you doing there, mister?"

The unexpected man wore tattered clothes, sported a long
beard, ragged hair, and confused eyes. With mouth wide
open, he gazed at Purdy and past him to the coffin into
which Isaiah had deposited Maureen DeCampe's benumbed
form. Purdy thought of Moses and John the Baptist when
he stared at the homeless man, who now asked, "Do ya'
think you're doing the right thing here?"

"I'm about doing the Lord's work. And you? You have
come from God as a messenger, like John out of the wilderness, and you, sir, are a sign!"

"A sign? Me?"

"Yes, a sign that I am doing exactly as God intends me
to do."

"Really?"

Purdy's arms went up as he spoke, making him look like
a preacher. "I am following the dictates of the One True
Lord God. And you? Are you one of his prophets?" Purdy

opened his palms to the homeless man. "Be at peace, brother."

"Then you're taking care of her, you mean?" The homeless man indicated the two coffins with a single finger. "Or them . . ."

"Precisely, yes."

"Can I have her purse money?" The homeless man indicated where DeCampe's purse lay alongside her gun, several feet from her car.

"Take it; render unto Caesar that which is his."

Purdy closed the van's rear doors on one coffin from which a slight groan erupted, and on one silent coffin. At the same time, the homeless man shuffled off for the purse DeCampe had dropped, but he first stared at the long-barreled gun, lifting it in his greasy, food-stained hands. His heart said *use it,* but his logical side won when he lifted the purse and carefully placed the gun back where he had found it.

"I ain't been nobody's hero for a long time," the man muttered to himself.

Purdy walked around to the front of the van and stared back at the homeless man. Purdy simply waved at the old prophet, climbed into the van, put his keys into the ignition, turned the motor on, and then slowly pulled away. The homeless man had already disappeared into the gray walls.

"Well, Jimmy Lee . . . our undertaking's been blessed . . . blessed by Ol' John the Baptist himself," the old Iowa farmer muttered as he arrived at the ticket booth, where he calmly paid his bill and continued on, the attendant so strung out on drugs that he had seen nothing and had heard less. Purdy, at Jimmy's urging, had brought plenty of drugs— mostly animal tranquilizers—to bargain with.

As for Judge DeCampe, she was past caring, at least not for now. Purdy would taunt her with the story of her would-be knight in shining armor, who turned out to be Purdy's prophet. He'd share it all with her in detail when she next regained consciousness and when he next awoke. He knew the story well, but she had yet to hear it.

*   *   *

MAUREEN DeCampe now lay amid hay and dirt in an open
room filled with dust, mites, and pollen. She could only imagine being in the coffin which was standing in a corner alongside Jimmy Lee's. The old man had told her all about how he
had transported her here in it. He'd also begun to hint that it
had all been a plan concocted in Jimmy Purdy's fevered brain.
DeCampe at this point would prefer the safe confines of the
coffin and a death by asphyxiation to that which the Purdy men
had in mind. Had in mind was the right phrase, for the old man
had his son's dead voice filling his mind, or so it seemed to her.

She would readily have chosen being buried alive to what
torture she now endured. She felt her skin crawling with the
decay from Jimmy Lee's body.

For now she was in some sort of large area where animals
had once been kept, some sort of a barnlike structure, she
realized.

"Am I'n I-o-wa?" she asked under the gag, realizing the
tape around her mouth protected the only area of her body
touching the dead man's flesh—and grateful for this two-
inch-wide swath of freedom from the desiccation. *Unclean
tissue . . . contamination,* these words swam in her mind like
feeding piranhas, but these toothy microbe fish ate away at
her sanity and soul as well as her flesh.

The only response from the nearby darkness was a hearty
laugh at her attempt to speak; she wondered if the old man
could understand anything she said, that she had guessed at
her whereabouts. If it were Iowa, how did he transport her
without anyone knowing or seeing something? As if to answer her thoughts, the dark little man, Purdy, stood and
lifted a kerosene lantern and turned the light up. She wel-
comed the pungent kerosene odor into her; for half a nan-
osecond, it masked the overwhelming odor of decay that
had caused her to pass out more than once. Worse thought
yet, she had gotten somehow used to the odor.

Her father had been a cattleman rancher in Texas, and
his father before him, and she had often wondered how the
DeCampe men could get used to the smells that came with

slaughtering cows, but they did. In fact, it seemed to have lodged in their genes. Her grandfather had once sat her down and told her that men could, given the circumstances, get used to anything—anything at all. Any odor, any deed, any sinful behavior, if exposed to it long enough. He pointed to the slave trade, the Holocaust. She began to feel that she'd reached that point here, the point of no return, in which her senses, so assailed by the decay, simply had shut down. She could tolerate it, at least long enough to hate this man Purdy strongly enough to want to live to wreak vengeance on him.

Why was the old man turning up the wick on that damned kerosene light of his? At first, she thought he simply wanted a better look at the progress of his gruesome art. However, in the next instant, the light shone on the two white pine boxes with cheap chrome handles: coffins. One had held his son's electrocuted body, and now she recalled the horror of having awakened inside her coffin. He'd lifted the lid, smiled down at her in grotesque, toothless fashion, and then he'd shoved a cloth filled with chloroform over her face, and when she next awoke, she was lashed to his son's decaying corpse.

And my brain is beginning to accept this shit? she inwardly screamed.

How long? How long had they journeyed from D.C. to this godforsaken place? Had she been lying unconscious for the duration of a trip that had taken her near lifeless body from Washington to Iowa, where the old man resided? Had she been out that long? Had he managed to bring her back to his private property—to the safety of his homestead amid the nothing void of rural Iowa, where the only other soul to set foot in his barn might be the occasional postman, or Jimmy Lee's mother, the old man's wife? Did he have a wife? Did she condone what was going on out in her barn? Had she masterminded the entire abduction from her front porch rocker? Was it a ma and pa operation? Or was ma out of the loop?

It felt unseasonably warm for an Iowa fall; even the nights had felt somewhat warm. The warmer the weather, the faster the decay, she knew. What was the cause for the warmth? Was it part of that large thing they called global warming, Indian summer come early? Or was it simply the heat of her own decay?

She wondered these things and why the old man was hovering with the light over her, studying her again. She wondered all these things before passing out again.

SEVEN

I will ransom them from the power of the grave:
I will redeem them from death . . .

—HOSEA 13:14

ISAIAH Purdy had gone to his son's execution with no expectations save to see the thing through and to follow through on Jimmy Lee's requests—appeals made in his psychic visits.

After the execution, which had been handled with an eerie and perfunctory precision, Isaiah made his way down an institutional green and yellow corridor that felt like a tunnel out of *The Wizard of Oz,* at the end of which, he could view the body. It was a cold and stony Jimmy, his boy, whose head had been shaved, and whose temples were bubbled—marks of the boiling brain that had been scrambled by the electrocution. He didn't want to know the number of volts they'd fired into the boy's head. *Poor Jimmy. Poor boy. . . . Last of his lineage . . . end of the line . . .*

After this, they told Isaiah to drive his van around the back to a sign indicating the prison wood shop, where he could take possession of the body. Once at the wood shop, he requested the extra coffin, telling them he'd pay for it, and telling them that it was meant for himself. The shop foreman readily obliged, saying he couldn't take any money from any father of Jimmy Lee's. This made Isaiah proud to know that his son had still managed to make friends here, even as a death row inmate.

They had carried Jimmy Lee down on a stretcher to the wood shop, just like as if he were a side of beef, and they

lifted him from the gurney and into the pine wood box that'd
been awaiting him, throwing his arms and legs in last. The
men in the shop loaded Jimmy's coffin into the van, and
then they loaded the one meant for his bride, the judge
who'd sent him to the electric chair so many years before.
Jimmy Lee meant to travel into eternity with his chief ac--
cuser.

Once the two coffins and his boy's body were loaded,
the old man solemnly thanked all involved and waved a
good Iowa wave to the incarcerated men, wishing them all
good luck. Moments later, the wood shop's loading platform
door ratcheted down and came to a metallic, screeching halt,
leaving Isaiah once again alone. But he was hardly alone.
Jimmy Lee's body might be in the coffin inside the black
van, alongside the pine box awaiting the judge, but in point
of fact, Jimmy Lee himself was inside Isaiah now.

"Taking you home, boy," muttered Isaiah as he stepped
from the loading dock and down the stairs. "Home to your
Lord and Maker, son."

Isaiah snatched open the van door and climbed behind
the steering wheel. He turned the engine over and switched
on the radio, which was playing a Gordon Lightfoot song.
The words wafted through the cab of the van: "If you could
read my mind, love . . . what a tale my thoughts would tell."

It was Isaiah's favorite song of all time, but now, with
Jimmy Lee actually crawling around in his head, the song
made more sense for Isaiah Purdy than ever it did before.

HER interrogations for twelve hours had netted little save
heartburn and mental heat stroke. No one knew anything,
and Jessica's team's usual sources on the street, from paid
snitches to prostitutes, had nothing to barter. It was as if
Judge DeCampe had literally vanished from the planet, like
one of those weird alien abductions that Whitley Streiber
had been writing about for two decades.

Poof, and she was gone.

"We're not getting anywhere this direction," Jessica confided to J. T., who had stood around making time with Dr.

Shannon Keyes, an FBI psychiatrist on standby should they need any psyche evaluations done or any psychiatric advice on a given individual as they processed suspects called in for questioning. Only Jessica and Santiva knew the complete truth of the situation, that Keyes was Kim Desinor's replacement, at least for now.

"I fear whoever has her, he's an amateur at this and just lucked out, leaving us nothing," Jessica told J. T. and Keyes.

A cop's worst fear was the crime scene that left not a single trace of victim or assailant—exactly what faced them now. Either the perpetrator had planned his every move, rehearsed his every line, or it was a crime of opportunity, a random violence. Hard to tell at this point which. While they leaned toward the judge's having been a victim of a carefully crafted stalking attack, they had zero suspects who posed an immediate threat to the judge before the abduction. Court records were being pored over, some by Lew Clemmens and his supercomputer, some by other members of the team, including Richard Sharpe.

In the meantime, Jessica had put out a general call to locate anyone who had ever made the remotest threat against Judge Maureen DeCampe, and anyone capable of acting on such a threat, and anyone available to act on his or her threats.

"It's just remotely possible that some guy she put away arranged for all this," suggested Keyes. "Being incarcerated nowadays doesn't stop a person from being violent on the outside, not if he's got contacts."

Jessica looked across at Keyes, a beautiful ash blonde with an hourglass figure and penetrating gray eyes. Keyes had come up through FBI ranks via the Chicago field office, and by all accounts, she had seen a great deal in her capacity as a profiler there. She had been instrumental in capturing the infamous serial killer who called himself Doctor O, when she was just a fledgling police officer with the Chicago Police Department.

"Then we need to scrutinize everyone she ever put away who's still alive," offered J. T., looking mesmerized by Dr.

Keyes, who normally worked with the Washington Field Bureau of the FBI these days.

"And perhaps interview a few people around them," added Jessica. "And that's going to take a great deal of time, and time, I fear, is the scarcest commodity we have right now."

"Certainly likely that time is the scarcest thing DeCampe has," added J. T.

"What other choice have we?" asked Keyes.

J. T. agreed with Keyes next, saying, "Yeah, guess we don't have any other choice, Jess."

Jessica tried to ignore J. T., going to Keyes and saying, "You're the expert on the way the mind works, Dr. Keyes. What do you think the abductor wants? You've had time to review what we have. Any conclusions?"

"She's only just arrived, Jess." J. T. gave Jessica a fleeting grimace. "Cut her some slack."

"You think the killer's going to cut DeCampe slack, J. T.?"

"Why're you assuming the abductor is going to kill her?" asked Keyes.

"Are you kidding? We believe he has her buried alive somewhere."

"I see. . . ."

"Maybe your first impulse is right, Dr. Keyes," Jessica offered while pacing the operations room. "Perhaps if we can target someone at the state pen as possibly out for revenge against Judge DeCampe," suggested Jessica, easing her tone, "then you can do some psyche work on him."

J. T. added, "We're also looking at inmates in the Texas penal system as well."

Keyes nodded. "I'm open to anything you suggest. I only want to help."

Lew Clemmens, who like the other Quantico people on board had moved to D.C. to be on call, burst into the room, waving a printout over his head, saying, "I have the last of the judge's decisions for the past year. Maybe we can sort out the worst cases and the worst threats she'd ever received and work from there. I can pull off the court records from the file numbers and cross-reference with the words *verbal threat* now."

"How long will it take, Lew?"

"Less than an hour, and we'll have some targets," he replied.

"Run your program," said Jessica.

"Already done. It's running solo as we speak."

They ordered in Chinese food and were soon looking over Lew's results. Most of those who threatened the judge in the past year—on the record—were behind bars, serving jail terms, many facing the chair, and some had already passed on via that route. She handled the worst cases; she'd known and worked with Dr. Morrissey back in Houston, Texas, who only a year before had been targeted and murdered by one of his own psychiatric patients, a killer who had been released to a halfway house against Judge De-Campe's ruling, thanks to a weak parole board and an overcrowded prison system.

"I'm out of here for a couple of hours," Keyes told them. "Have a meeting I have to attend, but I'll try to get back before sunset, OK?"

Exhausted, Jessica waved her off, and then she herself stepped back from the case long enough to find the women's room. Once there, Jessica popped some pain pills and threw water in her face.

When she returned to the ops room, it was to a jubilant Lew Clemmens. "I think we're onto something here, Jess." He handed her a prison profile of a man named Lester Goddard. Goddard had repeatedly threatened Judge DeCampe, and his threats had been vehement and filled with rage and gore; details informed her as to exactly how he meant to kill and mutilate her entire family, starting with the pets, running through the children, and working his way up to her: "The blood of your loved ones dripping from the knife I use on you, bitch!"

"We've got to run this creep down, then. Make him sweat," J. T. said.

"Where is he incarcerated?" asked Jessica.

"Huntsville, outside of Houston, Texas."

"So who do we know in Texas?"

I came back for the Moo Goo Gai Pan," said Shannon Keyes as she reentered the operations room that had been set aside for the task force, where the others stood about a conference table littered with paper ware and plastic cups and forks and chopsticks. "I'm Keyes," she told Clemmens, taking his hand and vigorously shaking it. "Dr. Shannon Keyes, FBI field office shrink and profiler, previously of the Chicago Field Office, prior to that, the Chicago Police Department," she introduced herself. "All my apologies for being blunt, Mr. Clemmens, is it? But Goddard is *not* your man."

"Why?" asked a confused J. T.

"More important, how did you learn of our interest in Goddard?" asked Jessica.

"FBI's a small family. Word gets around fast."

"Too fast. There's a goddamn leak in my task force."

"I'm on your task force now, remember?"

The two women stared hard at one another.

"All right, tell me why you think Goddard is a wild hair to chase?"

Richard Sharpe had been sitting quietly in a corner, reviewing what little they knew of Goddard. He introduced himself to Keyes and asked, "Is this your belief because Goddard is in a Huntsville, Texas, prison cell, over half a continent away?" Jessica had already made contact with people in Texas who might help uncover any plot on the part of this man Goddard to wreak havoc in the life of the judge.

"No, because he's a blowhard. Anyone who makes that many threats and makes them that loud and loutishly . . . well, we who are in the business of predicting who will and who will not deliver on threats, suffice to say, first one dismissed is the Goddard type."

"How can you predict he hasn't paid someone to abduct and kill her?" asked Jessica.

Keyes dipped into the Chinese food and, building a plate-
ful, she complained that she loved Chinese too much—
especially the dumplings—before answering Jessica. "Goddard is what we call a stalemate threat. He makes threats
like most of us make plans for the day. He loves to hear
the sound of his own voice. He much prefers the threat itself
to the actual carrying out of the threat."

Sharpe asked, "We're wasting our time with pursuing this
Goddard?"

"Let me see. How can I put this more clearly? Goddard's
full of shit; he's not your man," Keyes firmly said. "He's
what's known as a loudmouth, for lack of a technical term.
Likes the sound of his own threats, he knows they're hot
air, and so should we."

"How can you know he hasn't acted on his threat to harm
DeCampe?" asked Jessica.

"Aside from his being incarcerated on death row, you
mean?"

Jessica clenched her teeth before saying, "Yes, aside from
that little problem."

"He's too over the top; he's venting his spleen. Look, I
make my living by reading threats and dangerous situations.
I worked with the Secret Service for six years. No one who
reads threats as often as I do would take Goddard seriously.
Be much more wary of the single sustained curselike threat.
I make my living predicting when words of menace might
become actions of menace."

"Are you saying Goddard is harmless?" asked Sharpe.
"I've made my reputation on such cases in Great Britain,
and I can tell you, I'd pay attention, a lot of attention to this
fellow, indeed."

"Not at all. I'm sure he would cut DeCampe's throat if
he found himself in a locked room or dark alley with the
judge," countered Keyes.

"Whoa up there," said Clemmens. "You're contradicting
yourself, Dr. Keyes."

"I'm saying that given the opportunity that maybe . . .
maybe he'd act on his threats, but he's not going to carry
on a long-term vendetta or stalk against her, nor plan out a

complicated move that would involve a third party."

Jessica looked Keyes square in the eye and asked, "How can you be sure of that? That he's not involved in her disappearance?"

"He doesn't know a damn thing about her; hasn't bothered to find out, for one thing. A real threat is the enemy who knows your every like, dislike, whim, and collectible."

"I don't get your point."

"He says he's going to kill her pets and her children."

"Yeah?"

"Been my experience that the real threat—the guy who acts on his fantasy to harm another person—isn't into mental anguish so much as physical anguish for his victim. A real threat focuses on her physical pain; besides, she doesn't have any children living at home. Goddard assumes much because he's really just reacting to a verdict he dislikes. You'd be wasting time zeroing in on him as your prime suspect, but being on death row and having threatened the now missing judge, you might persuade him to talk about who else he might know who might have harmed her, but even there it's problematic, since you have so little to bargain with. His life is already forfeit but . . ."

Jessica nodded and said, "But to a man in prison certain privileges that seem small and insignificant to you and me, well . . . he might just bargain his brains out for."

Jessica grudgingly admitted to herself that Keyes's outward appearance hid a keen, analytical mind. The woman was very on, very good. Jessica began to warm toward the FBI shrink.

A phone had been ringing for some time, and Jessica grabbed it up, barking, "Ops room, Coran! What can I do for you?"

Jessica had been sitting on the edge of the conference table, but now she pushed off it, asking, "When? Where? Are they . . . is he in custody? Meet you in interrogation." She hung up and said, "We just got a break. Keep your fingers crossed."

"What's happened?" asked Richard.

"The monitor on Judge DeCampe's credit cards. They

got a hit, and the guy using her cards is in custody. It could be our man."

"Good news," Richard replied. "Who is the chap?"

"Some older man; they think he's homeless, a transient."

"Then maybe her attack was a random crime of opportunity, after all," said Clemmens.

"Maybe . . . maybe not. The guy swears he just stole a wallet out of a purse he found lying in an underground parking lot." Jessica started for the hallway and the elevator. She wanted to be first in line at this new lead. "Washington PD's bringing him in now. Let's have a talk with the guy."

INTERROGATION of the homeless man who might have witnessed something in the parking lot had to be carefully handled. Jessica and Richard both immediately decided this on seeing the shaking, hulking figure in the interrogation room. The man's face seemed catlike—rawboned and pointed. Richard agreed with Jessica's quick assessment of their possible witness/suspect. "Ganging up on the frightened figure with too many in the room will only terrify the poor, bedraggled devil more than he is already."

The man stood as tall as a grizzly bear, and he had a mountain man's scraggly appearance, replete with out-of-control hair and beard. He seemed bent on hiding himself away in a large overcoat as well. The general impression and smell was that of a cave dweller out of time or an Old Testament prophet newly stumbled from the desert.

Jessica asked, "Richard, I would like you to stand aside for Shannon Keyes to join me inside the sweat box with the suspect."

Keyes, standing near enough to hear the request, jumped in at the chance, showing her eagerness to question the lead.

"Whatever you think best, Jess." Richard's tone remained calm, mild. If he were upset, no one could possibly know.

As it turned out, Jessica's choice was a good one. The frightened man fixed on the two women as friendly faces; he smiled back at them as they entered the room. The chain from his handcuffed wrists rang out in a metallic clang whenever he moved slightly. *Like a toneless human wind chime,* Jessica thought.

Jessica had stopped J. T. at the door along with Sharpe, knowing J. T. had limited experience in interrogation, and when Eriq Santiva, hearing of the break in the case, appeared at the interrogation door, Jessica asked him to remain outside; when he tried to bully his way in, pull rank, she challenged him at the door, saying, "You said I would be in charge of the case if I came on, Chief. What's changed?"

Chief Santiva's eyes said that he had every intention of entering and confronting the suspect.

Jessica eased him out of the room and closed the door behind her, leaving Keyes alone for a moment with the suspect. "Shannon's a lot easier on the eye and a great deal less threatening than you, Eriq, and with this guy, we need to be less threatening, not more. He's squirrelly and jittery as a starved cat," Jessica told Santiva.

"Oh, and you're not threatening, Jess?" asked Santiva, his eyes challenging her now.

"I didn't say we shouldn't lean on the guy. Just trust me. I think Keyes might give us some insights we might otherwise miss."

"You told me you didn't need her help, remember?" he whispered just before she turned and reentered the interrogation room, closing the door on him.

Jessica felt great relief that Santiva hadn't managed to bully his way past her. He could easily have pulled rank, but perhaps even he knew that he'd have scared the hell out of the possible witness, and in doing so perhaps shut the frightened man completely down. So J. T., Santiva, and Richard now listened and watched via the one-way mirror, while the stranger, Keyes, took a bold run at the only man who might shed some light on what had happened to DeCampe.

"Tell us what you saw just prior to finding the purse, sir," Keyes asked the man.

Jessica felt a stifling heat inside the interrogation room, and this, combined with the suspect's body odors, made her slightly ill.

Beneath the layers of hair and dirt, Warren Paul Marsden had the facial characteristics of an aristocratic man who'd stepped out of time, and he was huge and daunting, even while sitting, where his head came up to Jessica's breast-bone. With Jessica at almost six feet, this placed Marsden at nearly seven feet high, and yet this grisly Grizzly Adams lookalike had somehow escaped the attention of the parking garage attendant? The question begged an answer, and it further corroborated a growing suspicion that the attendant was either on drugs and busy the entire night on a binge of his own, or knew a hell of a lot more than what he'd given up. Now that the attendant was reported dead, it appeared his secrets would never be revealed, making Mr. Marsden here even more valuable to the case.

"You've got to tell us what you saw in the garage, Mr. Marsden," Jessica began cajoling the man in her most en-couraging tone.

Marsden's straight mouth twisted into a wry grin, and his keen, twinkling, intelligent eyes, which seemed at odds with his condition, traveled from one to the other of these people who were suddenly interested in him. "Been some time since somebody called me *Mr.* Marsden. Hell . . . one time it was *Dr.* Marsden. Was a choirboy before I lost everything. Model citizen, not a day of debt, and a nice home and Millie meeting me every night at the door with . . . with her un-conditional love. She was all the family I had."

"I'm deeply sorry for your loss, sir," Shannon Keyes of-fered.

He gulped back a tear and said, "Funny how things turn on a dime."

"Isn't it so," agreed Keyes.

Jessica had lost all patience with the man. She stood and paced around him, fuming, working to control her anger.

"I was a school superintendent. You believe that? Re-spected, you believe that? Not as if I expect you to, not looking at me now."

"Where was this, sir?" asked Dr. Keyes.

"Everyone in Jasper, Georgia, held me in high esteem, even though they all called me a damn Yankee."

"Then you're not originally from Georgia. I didn't think so," said Jessica from behind him.

"You got that?" he asked. "How'd you know, no accent?"

She frowned and from behind his back threw up her arms for Keyes to see.

Marsden continued spottily speaking. "I was born in Zion, Illinois. Went to college at Northwestern. Went through the ranks of teaching. Got my Ph.D. on the job. Took the position in Georgia. It was my dream . . . a dream come true, but it all came apart, as you can tell from my current situation."

Jessica, having gotten hold of her anger, commiserated, saying, "I know how that goes. Things fall apart. Three years ago, I was on my back in a hospital, out of money, out of a job, shafted by my employer, when my hubby tells me he wants a divorce," she lied.

"Life sucks rocks, like the kids say, huh?" he replied, his eyes now fixed on Jessica, who had come around to face him while telling her make-believe tale of woe, designed to put them on the same side.

"With me, it all went to hell when . . . when Millie . . . when she died."

Keyes bit her lower lip and stared across at Marsden, who saw her struggling to hold back her emotions. "We're all very sorry to hear of your loss, Mr. Marsden," she offered.

"In my private time with Millie . . . well, she was all I had, my whole life outside the job, but I should've given her more of my time, you know?"

"Sure . . . sure," replied Jessica.

"Should've devoted myself to her. She certainly did as much for me. Before the disease struck."

"Disease?" asked Shannon.

"She contracted a rare disease. Blood disorder. Ripped my heart out to watch her slowly succumb. Doctors all said it was only a matter of time; best I could do was make her comfortable in the end." Marsden rose as if under some invisible force. "She came into so much pain in the end, so I . . . I put her down myself, you see, and afterward . . .

I couldn't just go on with life as if . . . as if everything were the same as before. No way of doing that. . . ."

"Easy, Marsden," cautioned Keyes through clenched teeth, hissing, when suddenly the huge man came up out of his seat. Jessica had to reach up to put a hand on his shoulder, but she was right up with him, toe-to-toe, eye meeting eye. Something in Jessica's stern gaze caught firm hold of the lean giant, and he dropped back down into his seat, almost toppling it with the sudden impact of his weight against it.

Once righted, he allowed his legs to fully extend and relax beneath the table. With a shaking hand that he balled into a fist, he muttered, "I-I-I put a bottle of painkiller into her. A whole fucking bottle. Figured the more I used, the quicker and faster and less pain that way, you see?"

Keyes tried to get control back, saying, "You don't have to relive these events here and now, sir. We are only interested in what you saw in that parking garage at the courthouse where you stole that woman's purse."

"Millie . . . she went just as peaceful as nightfall then . . . after I took it on myself to . . . to . . . you know. . . ."

"I'm sorry for your loss, Mr. Marsden . . . really. But we have a situation on our hands here and now that requires our full and undivided attention. Do you understand?" Keyes firmly asked.

Jessica continued to be impressed by Keyes's approach.

Leaning into his space, Keyes added, "How you came to be in that parking garage, and how you took Judge De-Campe's purse off the floor and emptied it. That's what we're interested in here and now, sir."

"If we have your full cooperation, Mr. Marsden, you're outta here in the time it takes to answer a few questions." Jessica's lie would have to suffice for now.

The others all knew that with a confession of having killed his wife, they would have to return Dr. Marsden to the Georgia judicial system, likely to stand trial for mercy killing.

The broken giant, tears in his eyes, asked, "You want to know how that man got her, don't you?" Marsden thanked

Keyes, who offered him a handkerchief from her purse.

Impatient again, Jessica held herself in check, saying, "Go on, Mr. Marsden."

"I saw how he zapped her."

"Zapped her?" Jessica perked up at this.

"I heard the buzz and smelled the flesh burn. I was that close. In my usual corner."

"Go on," encouraged Keyes.

"She fell like a piano with no legs. After he zapped her, she went to her knees and right into him. She almost knocked him over with her weight. He dragged her to a van, put her inside, and drove out. That's all I know . . . all I know."

"Zapped her? Zapped her how?" repeated Jessica.

Marsden looked again directly into Jessica's eyes. "One of them rods, an electronic gizmo you might use on a cow."

"A cattle prod?" asked Keyes.

"That's it."

Jessica, who had remained standing at Marsden's side, now stared across at Keyes. She had watched Dr. Keyes closely and again felt pleased with the woman's technique. She gave Marsden the feeling that he was the only person in the world she wanted to be with at the moment. She shrewdly nodded at everything he said, not flinching once, and her body language didn't give her away either, not even at the worst moments in the interview. At the same time, Keyes listened intently for every nuance, studying their only witness to the crime.

"Are you sure of what you saw, Mr. Marsden?" asked Keyes, her glasses playing hip-hop with her eyebrows.

" 'Cause, he was a little guy . . . scrawny as a scarecrow. Clothes hung on him. No way he coulda overpowered that woman any other way."

Jessica asked, her eyes burning into Marsden, "At what age would you place the man who attacked her?"

"Old . . . way old, you know."

"Old, how old?" asked a surprised Keyes, who, like the others, had been going by the usual profiling measures,

which statistically placed the attacker at between the ages
of eighteen and forty. "Define old."

"Granddaddy old. Looked like somebody's grandpappy.
Wore a suit, but it looked like he'd slept in it more than
once. All skin and bone, you know, sun-baked hound-dog-
leather skin, you know, like they say in Georgia."

"Do you think you could describe him to a sketch artist,
Mr. Marsden?"

"For a hot meal and some coffee? Sure."

"Deal, sir. I'll just arrange to get an artist in here," replied
Jessica.

"*Sir* . . . used to be my name . . . *sir*. Then the thing with
Millie . . . hit me so hard, first her sickness, dealing with her
mortality, and then . . . then having to do what I had to
do. . . ."

Jessica girded herself for this uncalled-for confession.
She gritted her teeth before staring into Keyes's eyes, and
then she stared at the one-way mirror at the back of the
room. "Maybe we ought not say any more about Millie, Dr.
Marsden."

"Yeah," agreed Shannon Keyes, "let's keep that between
. . . among us for now, OK? We can get you a court-
appointed lawyer to discuss that with you."

Jessica added, "And Dr. Keyes here is a psychiatrist. You
can tell her all about Millie later. How's that?"

"Pains me to talk about it."

"I absolutely understand," replied Keyes, smiling warmly
and adding, "I think we all understand, Dr. Marsden."

"It's been a long . . . way down . . . a whataya call it . . .
free fall." The big man had a feminine, even childish air
about him. "Just walked away . . . right off the face of my
life. Stopped making payments. Walked away . . . got on a
bus, then a train . . . don't recall how I got to D.C., not really."

"I'm sure Millie was in a lot of pain," offered Keyes.

"Pain . . . we're talking horror. She had a rare form of
cancer in the blood you don't often find in canines."

Both Jessica and Keyes found their mouths had dropped
open. Now, staring at one another, they knew they had been

had, not intentionally, but had nonetheless. Keyes falsified a coughing jag to cover her mirth.

"Did you say canine, sir?" asked Jessica.

"Millie was my support, my linchpin, my fulcrum, my unconditional love, and all round best friend. It's true what they say. . . ."

"But she was a dog, sir?" pressed Jessica. *They shoot horses and dogs, don't they?* ran through her mind.

"She wasn't just a dog, detectives. You people . . . you all pretend to be so understanding and sensitive, but that's only a means to an end. With Millie and me . . . there was never any inkling of that, *ever.* Not even when I put her outta her misery."

But Millie licked your face for food, thought Jessica; still, she censored herself, saying instead, "Well, sir, we certainly understand how much you must have loved Millie."

"Love . . . still do."

"Yes, of course. . . ."

Keyes, still crushing out a full-blown laugh directed as much to Jessica and herself for being so gullible, added, "That's . . . painfully obvious, Mr. Marsden."

Jessica imagined Richard, Santiva, and J. T. behind the one-way mirror, likely laughing it up on learning that the mysterious, ailing Millie had turned out to be a dog and not the man's wife or lover. For a moment, she wished herself to be behind the mirror, where she could safely vent her feelings at having wasted so much time over this interrogation. Still, Jessica felt both the room and the outer room fill with great relief that Marsden had not killed his wife but had put down his dog instead—animal euthanasia—still not a crime in America, despite all the lobbying to make it one by certain animal rights groups. One chimp in the news had his own lawyer now.

"Ahhh, Shannon . . . Dr. Keyes, will you arrange for a Boston Market meal for Dr. Marsden while I arrange for a sketch artist?"

"Absolutely, right away, Dr. Coran." Keyes's rolling eyes told Jessica she could not wait to get out of there.

"We'll want a complete description of the van the old,

cattle-prodding guy used, too, Dr. Marsden. Did you get a clear look at it?"

"Not real clear, no. A dark van, tinted windows. Didn't get the license plate, but it was curious, since it was out of state."

"Out of state?"

"Yes, ma'am."

"What state was it?"

"Something like Iowa."

"Something like Iowa, or Iowa?"

"Iowa, yeah . . . it was Iowa."

"Anything else distinguishing about the old man or his ride?" pressed Keyes, now held up at the door by the turn of the conversation.

"It was spanking clean and brand new, one of those newest models, foreign-made for sure. . . . Couldn't tell you which, but large enough to hold two caskets side by side. Man looked like the Grim Reaper himself."

"Truly, sir, you do have a way with words," replied Jessica, picturing this image. A van large enough to hold two caskets.

"Did you ever at any time think that maybe you ought to . . . you know . . . intervene, Dr. Marsden?" asked Keyes, an edge that had not been there before now creeping into her voice.

"Hell, I can't straighten out my own life. I wasn't about to get involved, but I did kinda sorta confront the old man."

"You confronted him?" asked Keyes.

"You had words with him?" asked Jessica. Both women approaching the old man anew, their eyes pinning him to where he sat. "How?" asked Jessica, her eyes telling the old man that she wanted every single word of this latest revelation, and she wanted them now.

Marsden's voice quaked a little bit, a small anxious crackling sound, as if he might go either way, explode with words or contract into himself and say little or nothing. "Just after . . ."

"Just after what?" *Damn this man,* Jessica thought.

"Just after he . . . he put her into it."

"Into the van?"

"Into the casket . . . the casket in the van."

"Whoa, wait up there, sir," replied Jessica. "Are you saying that he actually did have two g'damn coffins in back of his van?"

"God's honest truth, yes."

Again the women exchanged a long, amazed look. The conversation had held Keyes planted in the room, and she, like Jessica, had turned her full attention to Marsden. "Tell us, sir, how you actually confronted the abductor."

"Well, maybe not confront . . . that may not be the word."

"What is the damned word?" Jessica felt on the verge of slamming her fists onto the table. The man infuriated her. Keyes must have sensed this. Shannon placed a soft hand over Jessica's and asked Marsden to go on.

"I . . . I mean we had words. We spoke to one 'nother."

Just like that? Jessica wanted to scream. "What precisely did you say to him, sir?" she pleaded.

"I asked him . . . let me see . . . asked if he thought . . . if he was . . . you know . . . if he was doing the right thing here."

"Jesus," Jessica muttered.

"To which he replied?" asked Keyes calmly.

"The old feller said something from the Bible straight out."

"What . . . what from the Bible did he say?" pressed Jessica, her back now like a staff.

"He stood there eyeballing me like I was an old friend the whole time, but never letting his eyes off me, burned a hole through me." Now came the explosion of words out of the former Georgia school principal's mouth.

"What did the old man say to you?" Jessica again pressed.

"Said, 'Fear not, for I am about the Lord's work, and you'—he said to me straight out—'you have come from God as a messenger, John out of the wilderness,' and how I was a sign . . . yeah, a sign."

"A sign?" asked Keyes.

"A good sign that he was doing exactly as God intended him to do."

"Damn," cursed Jessica. "We not only have a lunatic on our hands but one that is inspired by God's divine message."

"The worst kind," agreed Keyes.

Jessica's hand meandered across the table in Marsden's direction, stopping short of his. "You say he put the woman into a coffin in the van?"

"Yes ma'am."

"And you let him leave without another word?" demanded Keyes, finally losing some of her control.

"He had a look about him that told me it wasn't *none* of my business. Fact is, he had a strange look in his eyes."

Jessica kept eye contact with Marsden. "What kind of look is that, sir?"

"Like he was doing what he said he was doing."

"God's work, you mean?" asked Jessica.

"The business of God's work, yes, and his eyes . . . that look he had . . . told me I wasn't to interfere, that no one was to interfere."

"Is there anything else? Did he say anything else to you?" Jessica was glad the interrogation had been taped.

"There was one other thing he said. He said, 'Who can know or judge God's work,' he said."

"I see." Jessica stood again, turned, and spoke to the others behind the glass. "Sounds like our man is hearing voices from God."

"Or reading too much into 'Vengeance is mine, sayeth the Lord,'" added Keyes.

Jessica had to control her anger with Marsden. She sucked it up and returned to him, sat, and calmly asked, "You didn't think to call the police?"

"He had two coffins in the back of his van!" Now Marsden began to show some agitated anger, weakly defending his inaction. "Damn it, I didn't want to be put into the other coffin beside her, and that van . . . it smelled . . . smelled of a horrible odor."

"What kind of odor?"

"Like decay and death all balled up into one."

"And you aren't exaggerating about the size of the van," asked Keyes, "or that it contained not one but two coffins?"

"Two coffins, side by side."

"This means she could be buried alive somewhere," said Keyes, trembling.

Marsden began to prattle, "I thought it was some old guy come to carry his woman or maybe even his child on back to a home she run from. I saw an old Iowa farmer come to fetch what belonged to him. Maybe she was his runaway wife or daughter, I told myself. Maybe he was rescuing her from a cult or something. How should I know?"

"Daddy come to fetch his little girl with a box to restrain her in, all to save her from the big bad city, huh?" asked Keyes, shaking her head.

"That's 'bout what I was thinking, ma'am," replied Marsden to Keyes. "Like that, yeah. I didn't get a fair look at her to determine if it was the wife or daughter, but yeah . . . that's why I didn't get involved. Thought it was family business, you know?"

"Family business," repeated Jessica, feeling weakened by this process of getting information out of this man. Still, she felt great relief that she had excluded Santiva and the other men from the questioning. Perhaps not Richard or J. T., but Santiva most certainly would have shut Marsden down like turning off a faucet. At least she and Keyes had been patient in finding and turning that faucet on. Eriq Santiva would most likely have sent the mole scurrying to the dark underground of a splintered personality that existed deep within him, and they would have gotten little or no information from Marsden. Even J. T. might have exploded on learning that Marsden had wasted their time with a doggie death, while all this vital information about DeCampe's abductor remained off the table and inside the man's head.

"Family business," muttered Keyes.

"That's 'bout what I was thinking, ma'am," repeated Marsden, his eyes glued on Keyes yet vacant. "Like that, yeah," he repeated.

"Were you drunk at the time you witnessed the attack?"

asked Jessica, looking for something mitigating about the sheer cowardice of the man.

"Not nearly drunk enough. Bothered me some that I didn't help out that woman."

Jessica released a long breath of air. She had smelled Marsden's odors long enough. She stood beside him, where she slapped Marsden on the shoulder as if they had been lifelong friends, telling him how much he had already helped them. His worn, tattered coat reacted to the slap on his shoulder by sending up a flurry of dust and mites. Jessica backed off, saying, "Now you just quit blaming yourself for any of this, Dr. Marsden. If you'd gotten involved any more than you had, you might be down in our morgue right now and unable to help us one iota." *Certain amount of truth in that,* she thought. "As it is, you've put us onto the right track."

"I have done that, haven't I?"

"Yes, sir, Mr. Superintendent. Now relax here, and one of us'll send in some coffee and a meal and be right back, Dr. Marsden."

As Jessica hustled Keyes out and let the door close on Marsden, the man said, "You don't have to call me doctor no more, and I don't hold title to superintendent no more; I know it's just your technique to get friendly, but you don't fool me any, detective."

Not smart like Millie at all, am I? Jessica thought and felt a moment's relief to be away from the strange giant she'd left alone in interrogation.

EIGHT

And when the thousand years are expired,
Satan shall be loosed out of his prison.

—REVELATION 20:7

JESSICA felt as if she had been in a marathon run when she stepped from the interrogation room. She wanted to grab hold of Richard and hug him, but instead, she told him, "Keep your eyes on this nutcase. He can't be allowed to waltz out of here."

Richard stood alongside J. T., who stood beside Santiva at the one-way glass, where they had seen and heard the entire story. Santiva wore a smirk on his face.

"What's so funny?" she asked Santiva.

"Been a while since I've heard a good dog-saves-man story."

"I think he's mixed his milk toast with his rye once too often," replied J. T.

"Pitiful wretch, actually," added Richard, his eyes still on Marsden.

Keyes got in Jessica's face and asked, "Are we sure Millie's really a dog, Dr. Coran?"

"No . . . Guess we can't be a hundred percent."

Santiva, biting his lower lip and shaking his head, replied, "Yeah, maybe somebody ought to contact authorities in Jasper, Georgia."

"Just to be sure?" asked J. T., a wide grin making him the Cheshire cat. "Did you get a load of that red scar along his neck? He's obviously been in some back-alley scrapes."

"Yeah, this dog will fight, but he didn't raise a hand to

help the judge that night. Why?" asked Jessica, still angry with Marsden.

Keyes raised an index finger and said, "Something about the old man's demeanor. All the biblical talk may well have frightened anyone, and if he had an insane look about him, carting two coffins about with him . . . not sure I'd get involved, either. Would you?"

"Damn straight I would."

Keyes didn't blink. "I think Marsden may well have been half or fully blitzed at the time, and so that much more easily convinced that DeCampe's abductor was in fact doing the 'Lord's business,' as he put it, and with Marsden's pitiable self-esteem issues . . . hey, who's going to go out of his way to piss off God?"

"Or his servant," added Richard Sharpe.

Jessica bowed to this notion, letting Marsden off the proverbial hook for now. She then turned to John Thorpe. "OK, J. T., you're my main expert on rural America types. Look into Marsden's Jasper, Georgia, story. See how much of it checks out."

"Gotcha."

Jessica stared through the glass at the Rock Hudson–sized man inside. "Cleaned up, he might look like a Baptist preacher or a school superintendent."

"Yeah, Jack, why don't you check his story out," Santiva, who liked calling J. T. Jack, piped in. "Keyes, see to getting the man some hot food and drink. Jessica, we need to talk." Santiva asked Richard to cuff the strange man in the interrogation room to the table. For a moment, they all stared through the one-way window.

"Yes, sir, Chief."

"I need a sketch artist inside with him, Eriq," Jessica said.

"Already called; she's on her way."

Jessica nodded as he took her arm and guided her out of earshot of anyone. "I'm getting a great gob of loaded heat from upstairs. They want some bone thrown their way, Jess, something—anything—I can take back. How much of this guy's story do you believe?"

"I think he's telling us all he knows."

"But he could have hallucinated the whole damn thing, right? I mean with the caskets, the cattle prod, all of it. Could be just filling in blanks you laid out, Jess."

"I don't think so. He's . . . he comes across as telling the truth, Chief."

"Murphy's Law at work, huh?"

"I don't follow you."

"If something can go wrong, it will, right? So if I report what we know from Mr.—ahhh—*Dr.* Marsden in there, it could come back to clip me at the knees."

"We really don't have time for this kind of hand-holding with the politicians, Chief. Not with DeCampe's life in the balance, not with the time clock ticking as it is. DeCampe doesn't have the time. We don't have the luxury of holding meetings with lieutenant governors and deputy mayors and—"

"Now hold on, Jess."

"We need to pursue this Iowa license plate on a huge dark van with two coffins aboard the thing. We need every field office between here and Iowa on it."

"You'd think such a thing would be obvious or at least curious to someone out there."

"I need more people, Eriq, to call every law enforcement agency in the goddamn country for anything smacking of such a report. Can you get me that kind of support here?"

"I'll get you more people."

"When?"

"Today."

"As for someone out there seeing two caskets in a dark van with tinted windows, how weird is that, Eriq, in the grand scheme of things in the state of this nation? Besides, even if someone saw the caskets, say at a Waffle House stop this old man made, do you think the average John Q. Citizen is going to bother getting involved? I don't know why I was so angry with Marsden. He's just typical of all of us."

Eriq tried to calm her. "I know . . . I know, Jess."

She relented. "People might simply take it for a hearse; after all, according to Marsden, it's black and the windows are tinted."

"I still need something to take upstairs. We're going to hold this guy for as long as we can, right?"

"On suspicion he's somehow connected to the abduction? Are you really going to announce to the world that this poor bastard's the perpetrator?"

"We need something, Jess. If it comes to that, yes."

"Damn it, Eriq, we need to know what triggered this old man's vendetta against the judge. We need to know who he is, how he is linked to her. And we don't have the luxury of time, so we really don't have time for any g'damn games."

"We're talking about keeping the fucking governor of the District of Columbia and the mayor of Washington apprised, Jessica, and now the governor of Texas and the mayor of Houston. They have all sampled party favors together with the judge on many occasions. Their interest is not purely politically motivated. They all genuinely liked—or at least respected—the woman."

Lew Clemmens found them, a cell phone in his hand. "I've got someone in Houston, Texas, willing to run out to Huntsville and interview Goddard. Goddard's on borrowed time, waiting to hear if his appeal is going to go forward. If he's shut down, he dies by the switch in seven days."

"Who've you got?" asked Eriq.

"Guy that Dr. Desinor recommended, Detective Lucas Stonecoat with the HPD. He knows something about Goddard, and he has a special place in his heart for Judge DeCampe. Says she busted his chops more than once."

"When did you speak to Kim Desinor?"

"She called in. Wanted to know if we were any closer. I told her about the Houston, Texas, connection."

Jessica took the line, holding her hand over the mouthpiece for the moment. She knew something of the Texas Cherokee Indian detective's recent history with successfully closing out a string of unusual cases in his home state and beyond. Kim Desinor, acting as the FBI psychic consultant on the case, had spent time in Houston working with Stonecoat and the police psychiatrist Meredyth Sanger there. Jessica recalled that Kim had once urged her that if ever she

needed insight into Texas and the Texas penal system, that
Lucas Stonecoat was her man. "Hello, Detective Stonecoat,
this is FBI Medical Examiner Dr. Jessica Coran. We appreciate your help."

"I'll interview Goddard with the help of our resident police shrink, Dr. Meredyth Sanger," he replied. "She's the
best Houston has. If anything can be shaken loose from
Goddard, she can do it."

"Excellent news, and thanks."

"No thanks necessary. Let's just find Judge DeCampe.
Underneath that scaly, rough yet too-liberal exterior beats a
beautiful heart. She's good people."

Beats a beautiful heart still, we hope, Jessica thought but
replied, "Yes, yes, she is."

"I'll call you back the moment we have anything."

"We're working up a sketch of the abductor now. We'll
fax it to you. Clemmens will take your fax number, and
again, thanks."

"Hold on. You've got a witness who can ID the abductor?"

"We do."

"Excellent work."

"Lucked out."

"Not from what Dr. Desinor tells me about you. She tells
me you are the most intuitive detective she has ever known."

"She's being generous."

"The state here just executed a guy named Purdy three
days ago. Purdy's original trial played out with Judge
DeCampe presiding—one of her first trials, long before she
became an appellate judge."

"What's so interesting about this guy, Purdy?"

"He was in the same cell block as Goddard. They had to
have known one another. Now Purdy has been fried. It could
have something to do with your case, maybe . . . maybe
not."

"This fellow Purdy by any chance from Iowa?"

Stonecoat's stentorian voice silenced. "I . . . I'm not sure.
Will look into it. What does it matter? I mean, does it matter?" He quickly answered his own question with, "Of

course it's important; otherwise, we wouldn't be discussing it, right?"

"Suffice to say, it could be vital, yes."

"We're looking under every rock in Houston. Trust me."

"I'm sure you are. We'll forward the artist's sketch as soon as we have it. Hasn't actually been created as yet."

Lucas Stonecoat replied, "We've begun with traffic records, any tickets, maybe DMV and also have my computer whiz kid cross-reference between the DeCampe caseload and anything to do with threats."

"We're doing the same here. That's how we focused on Goddard."

"I'll have him cross for anything doing with Iowa and Purdy then."

"Same here." Jessica hung up, sighed heavily, and leaned into an institutional gray wall. "Man, I hope something substantive comes of Marsden's interrogation. For all we know, he's making it up as he goes. That's what one voice is telling me; another voice is telling me he's our best shot yet."

Santiva, who had listened intently in on her side of the conversation with Detective Stonecoat, now said, "Jess, keep me posted on what you learn from Texas and from Jasper, Georgia."

"Course, will do."

"And Jess . . ."

"Uh-huh?"

"You sure got some second sight or something."

"Meaning?"

"I'm sure glad you kept me out of the interrogation box and away from this guy, Marsden."

"And why's that, Eriq?"

"I might've strangled him when he dropped it about the dog."

Jessica laughed lightly, and Eriq, shaking his head, went in search of his office, a little privacy with his phone, paperwork, and coffee, no doubt. "It's going to be a long night," he muttered back at her from the elevator where he now stood.

Aren't they all? Jessica thought but only waved Santiva off.

She turned to stare at the interrogation room where Richard Sharpe, now one of Santiva's agents, continued to study Marsden through the one-way; but overhearing Santiva's last remark, he heartily agreed in her ear as she came close, saying, "The boss is right. It's going to be a long night, dear heart." Sharpe had made his presence felt on the case, and at the same time he had often put Santiva at ease, acting as a kind of right-hand man for Eriq. Jessica's only fear was that Richard might get assigned to direct duty alongside Eriq. *That would be a nightmare come true,* Jessica thought. Richard would not own his own time if that should become the case. It would be like the relationship she had with Santiva—always on call. Like her, Richard would never know peace. "Yeah, long night," she agreed.

Eriq disappeared via the elevator, and Jessica imagined him, instead of rushing back to his stuffy office, going straight for a set of doors that opened onto the world outside. Air, a clean breeze, something Jessica herself wanted right now so badly. Instead, she turned back to Richard, taking him in her arms, saying, "I could sure use a hug about now."

"I'll take one as well," he replied, obliging. They stood that way in the corridor outside the interrogation room. "I think I've seen enough of Dr. Marsden to last me."

They kissed. "Strange case," he muttered when their lips parted.

"And getting stranger by the moment. Meanwhile, the clock is ticking, not just for the judge but for Kim."

"Did she really appear as bad as you say?"

"Worse."

"But if they're psychosomatic lesions—"

"No, no, these were as real as knife cuts."

Keyes stepped off the elevator and came through a milling crowd of agents and toward Jessica. "I'll write up my notes on the interrogation," she said, her hands full with some food in a bag from a nearby Boston Market. "Your captain requested a copy pronto. Caught him on the way out."

Jessica momentarily wondered what words had transpired between Santiva and Keyes, and if Keyes were working for Jessica or for Eriq. She wondered if Keyes might not be the eyes and ears of the upper brass, peeking over Jessica's shoulder. It wasn't unheard of in the organization.

"Yeah, me, too," added Jessica, looking weary and shopworn. "Poor Eriq needs PR fodder, and he needs it badly." Jessica smiled, then frowned and shook her head. "The eyes of a nation are on our every move, Dr. Keyes. Imagine if we fail. Who's going to be the first to blink?"

Keyes gave her a firm glare and replied, "Certainly not the most famous forensic detective in the history of the bureau, not Dr. Jessica Coran."

TIME relentlessly reminded them with each passing hour that Judge DeCampe's life hung in the balance. Only Jessica, J. T., and Richard knew that Kim's life, too, hung in the balance. The situation gave Jessica pause, and she wondered if Kim's eerie malady might not simply disappear with Judge DeCampe's demise. If the judge were dead, then why wouldn't the psychic leprosy simply end? It made Jessica hopeful on the one hand that DeCampe might yet be found alive, but it also twisted a dark key in Jessica's mind as well. If the logic proved true, that with the Judge's death Kim might be released from her pain and suffering, Jessica could not help but choose Kim's life over that of the judge's.

She confided these thoughts to no one save Richard, who had held her firmly to him when she finished speaking. They had found a moment in her office.

Meanwhile, the hunt for the appeals court judge continued. No one was idle. Every lead was followed. The team narrowed the search after gaining new insight into the case, thanks to information coming from different sources, which all began to converge. Aside from what they'd gathered from the hobo thief, that a man old enough to have been the victim's father accosted DeCampe, a sketch-artist likeness had now been put together from Marsden's befuddled brain. The likeness, which Jessica prayed was likeness enough, now circulated to everyone in law enforcement nationwide. A call to John Walsh's producer at *America's Most Wanted* had gotten instant results. The story was run on an emergency basis, and now the media everywhere had both the story and pictures of Judge DeCampe and her suspected abductor, as well as a description of the suspect vehicle. But even Walsh called up to complain that the man in the composite looked like everybody's grandpa. In fact, the likeness drawn of the man they were so desperately seeking closely resembled George Burns. Add a cigar and a baseball cap as when Burns portrayed the role of God in the film *Oh God*, and it proved a perfect likeness. Some law enforcement people openly laughed at the depiction. It certainly didn't look like a desperate criminal; in fact, it looked cartoonish.

Jessica and Richard returned to the operations room.

"Get me Detective Lucas Stonecoat in Houston, Texas," Jessica ordered the civilian secretary who had been turned over to the task force.

"It's only seven A.M. in Houston, Dr. Coran."

"I don't give a damn what time it is. Get me Stonecoat."

"Yes ma'am. Will see what I can do."

Jessica reached for the bottle of Tylenol someone had brought her earlier, and she downed three tablets with a swill of Coca-Cola.

In a moment, the secretary tossed back her hair, saying, "Stonecoat is on one. They patched us through to his home."

"Did you get the likeness we sent of the suspect?" Jessica said into the phone. "We laser-faxed it an hour ago."

"Got it, yeah. Some old geezer, I'm told. How sure is your information?"

"We're certain of it. We think he's out for some kind of revenge motive. You guys turn up anything since last we talked?"

"We're planning a ride out to Huntsville, see what went on there with respect to Jimmy Lee Purdy's execution and body. With the sketch, we'll have something for show and tell. Been my experience that most cons respond to pictures a lot sooner than words."

"Keep us posted. The clock's ticking."
"Yeah, understood."
Jessica feared the Huntsville, Texas, execution and this guy Goddard, awaiting execution, would be just another blind alley.

NINE

Startling, like the first handful of mould
cast on the coffined dead.

—P. J. BAILEY

Texas State Penitentiary, Huntsville, Texas

Lucas Stonecoat feared that a visit to the state penitentiary would likely uncover little or nothing. Most convicts had little reason to cooperate with law enforcement, and few did so without inducements of one sort or another. Lucas had come to the fortress of stone and barbed wire with no authorization to barter with or OK any promises he might make to an inmate on death row. Along with Lucas, police psychiatrist Meredyth Sanger had come, but so far, only rumor filtered to their ears, something about a dead man reaching out from the grave—a story of how Jimmy Lee Purdy meant to get vengeance at whatever cost after his execution. Purdy certainly appeared the most fixated inmate bent on DeCampe's being punished. Warden Jerold Gwinn characterized Jimmy as he led them toward Purdy's only friend inside prison walls.

"Purdy was a Bible-thumping so-called born again," began Gwinn. "Jimmy Lee condemned any use of the Lord's name being taken in vain, but he called up unholy hellfire to rain over his enemies, and no one cursed more or longer than Purdy. Still, the idea that Purdy—executed on the Sunday before Judge DeCampe's disappearance—could have had any hand in the judge's disappearance . . . ?"

"We don't know for certain that he had anything to do

with it, Warden Gwinn, but we're trying to keep an open mind," explained Meredyth.

"Inmate Goddard!" shouted Gwinn, rousing the shackled prisoner as they stormed into the interrogation room where Goddard had fallen asleep while waiting for them.

Goddard laughed at the warden.

"You show these people respect and answer their questions as best you can, Inmate Goddard, and you'll get two merit points, two demerits if I learn otherwise."

Lucas wondered what kind of a kindergarten Gwinn was running here.

"You reap what you sow," replied Goddard, and this biblical injunction seemed to appease Gwinn, who turned to Stonecoat and Sanger and said, "He's all yours. Good luck."

"Inmate Goddard is ecstatic about DeCampe's suffering, if that's what you want to know," said Goddard before they had time to sit. "But I don't know jack-shit about what happened to the bitch or who's behind it. I had nothing whatever to do with it. So, are we done here?"

"The warden apprise you of what we're here for?"

"Got it through the prison grapevine."

"Ever hear Jimmy Lee Purdy threaten the judge?"

Goddard laughed uncontrollably. "Do rats shit? But hell, I don't have to talk to you, and I ain't about to rat out my only friend in here."

"He's no longer in here," countered Lucas. "You can't seriously believe that you can rat out a dead man, do you?"

"The hell he ain't, and hell yes, I don't rat out nobody, not even the dead. Besides, like I said, Jimmy Lee's still here in the cellblock. Talked to him just last night. He's a haint now, haunts the place. I hear him talking in my ears when the lights go off. He tells me what hell's like. Fact is, it don't sound so bad after all." Goddard, a hairy chest peeking from his prison shirt, grinned throughout his little speech.

Meredyth raised a hand and said, "Cooperate with us, Mr. Goddard, and—"

"And what? What can you do for a walking dead, sweetie?"

"What're your chances you'll ever kiss another woman before you die?"

He laughed. He snorted. He stared into her eyes. Then he slowly formulated a reply. "They say I can't have no contact in here with my visitors. Any contact, and I'm in the hole."

"You willing to chance that for a moment's pleasure?" she asked.

"What about a touch. One touch, here," he bartered, standing and holding his crotch.

"Only if my partner can stay and watch over me."

He glared at Lucas now. "Shit. All right."

"Then you'll tell us what you can about Purdy?"

"All right . . . all right."

Meredyth indicated to Lucas to watch out for the guard. Lucas started to protest, but she put a finger on his lips and said, "It's for a good cause."

She then turned and seductively moved to within inches of Goddard, who stank of Old Spice shaving lotion and cigarette breath. She ignored the sickening odors and the man's ugly little gnome appearance and beehive-shaped head and alligator-gray skin. She passionately kissed him and allowed him to guide her hand to where he wanted to be touched. "Easy . . . easy," she cautioned, feeling his grip tighten and his body shiver in one wave after another.

She broke it off, and Goddard stumbled to his seat, holding his privates and looking as if he'd been given the greatest gift of all time.

Lucas and Meredyth returned to the interrogation table, its oak surface again a barrier between the officials and the condemned man. "All right, you got what you wanted, now it's our turn," instructed Meredyth. "Out with it. Anything and everything you know about Purdy and his hatred for Judge DeCampe."

"Yeah . . . a deal's a deal." He was aglow now, his eyes riveted to hers. "You're some lay, Doc."

"Never mind that. Out with it."

Goddard took a deep breath, still touching himself, as he spoke. "Hell, every other conversation we had, he was going to fuck her over, until he started getting really weird."

"What do you mean, really weird?"

"Ahhhh, mouthing off how he'd like to be fucking her while she's straddling him on The Chair—Old Surefire we call it in here. Jimmy Lee got quite graphic about it. Want to hear more?" he asked, leering at Meredyth. "Said it'd be one hell of a fuck, you know, his penis frying up in her at the same moment they both are electrocuted together. Her pussy electrified along with his organ, and them fusing together like that."

Lucas grabbed him by the arm, shouting, "That's enough bullshit, Goddard! Get to the point."

Goddard snatched his arm away and growled, bearlike.

"Just get on with it," Meredyth firmly said, her green eyes pinning him.

"All right, and after that, Purdy started talking even more weird shit than that."

"Like what?" demanded Lucas.

"Look, I got no reason to say no more against Jimmy. He was a stand-up guy. Cut two bastards bad who run up on me."

"What's the worst weird shit he told you in connection with the judge, Mr. Goddard?" pressed Meredyth.

"Look, I'm no fool. I watch the TV news. I know what you people want, and it's going to cost you."

"We had a deal, Mr. Goddard," said Meredyth.

"I want my appeal heard."

"We don't have any juice there," said Lucas.

"But we'll do everything we can in that regard, Mr. Goddard," Meredyth replied, holding a hand on Lucas's arm when he had come out of his seat toward Goddard.

"All right, if you're sure you're going to go to bat for me, I'll tell you what I know."

"Please, go ahead."

"J. P.—I called him J. P.—he said shit like, 'When I'm dead, I will have her.'"

"Her? The judge, you mean?" she asked.

"Have her in what manner?" asked Lucas.

"Said he would share his coffin with her. Said it was all

arranged. Said God told him how to do it. Said his father
in heaven had arranged it with his father here, on earth. Said
it was ordained, foretold, all that shit. He even believed it
was coded into his Bible that DeCampe would lie down with
his dead body and follow him into the next world. Crap like
that. I only listened and agreed with him and went along
because he never done me no harm."

"So . . . what about you, Mr. Goddard?" asked Lucas.
"Do you want to see Judge DeCampe dead?"

"Jimmy wanted to ride her into eternity. Me, I just
wanted her to die slow and suffer. I guess maybe he had
more imagination."

Lucas produced the faxed artist's sketch of the suspect,
the aged man who had abducted DeCampe, according to FBI
sources. "Take a close look at this. Do you know the man
in the picture?"

"Ahhh . . . looks roughly like Jimmy Lee's old man,
yeah."

"How would you know what he looked like?"

"Old Isaiah? Hell, Jimmy Lee showed me his picture
more'n once. Claimed he loved his mama and papa. Seen
her picture more than the old man's, but yeah, that looks
like his old man, all right."

"That fits with the old man with the van and two coffins,"
said Lucas.

The interview came to an abrupt halt when Meredyth
stood, rushed the door, and banged for the guard to open it.

Goddard shot to his feet, shouting, "What about my appeal? What're you going to do for me?"

Lucas, who stood a head taller than Goddard, intercepted
him with a threatening glare that halted the man. "We'll do
whatever we can," he lied and then rushed out after Meredyth.

Outside the interrogation room, Meredyth held up the
artist's sketch and said to Lucas, "If this is James Lee
Purdy's father, and he's been here to collect his son's body,
then Warden Gwinn can ID him. We don't need that low-
life belly crawler Goddard."

*   *   *

"HELL of a show you put on back there, but are you OK?" Lucas asked Meredyth as they approached the warden's office in the company of a guard who had been assigned to them. Already the prison was abuzz about their visit and why they were here.

She breathed deeply. "I'll survive. Been through worse, and I think Goddard did definitely put us onto the right path. I'm not exactly a stranger to the James Lee Purdy case. The guy was a classic megalomaniac. Some kind of weird complexes that it might take a lifetime to unravel, but he had a definite fixation on DeCampe, if Goddard's to be believed."

"Yeah, big *if*. If Goddard can be believed."

"Trusted no, but believed, I think so. He seemed a little afraid of Purdy himself, if my reading between the lines is as accurate as I think."

"So we need a far more serious talk with Warden Gwinn, the keeper of this asylum, and this time, we'll put the tough questions to him." Lucas grasped his aching neck in his large right hand and massaged it as the winding way to Gwinn's office came to an end.

Gwinn, a thin, sickly looking man, stood to greet them. "I told you . . . wasting your time with Goddard."

"Not entirely," replied Meredyth.

"Oh?"

"He had a lot to say about another of your inmates, a Jimmy Lee Purdy," Lucas added.

"Purdy died last Sunday in Old Surefire. Again, you're barking up the wrong tree, Detective Stonecoat." Gwinn displayed a self-satisfied grin on feeling a step ahead of them.

"We don't think so."

"I see, then you think that Purdy arranged for something to happen to Judge DeCampe after his death?"

"How about on the evening of his death?" replied Lucas. "Who came to claim the body?"

"Purdy's father."

"Did he look anything like this?" Meredyth pulled the police sketch of the old man from his breast pocket.

Gwinn studied the face. "Doesn't look like the same man, no. Eyes are all wrong. That turn at the mouth upward. No . . . I'd say Purdy's mouth was pulled down, like gravity had a-hold."

"But it could be Purdy's father. He had the same general features?"

"You could say that."

"All right, but it *was* the old man who took possession of the body after the execution?"

"Yes, correct."

"And he had these general features."

"Generally speaking, maybe yes."

Meredyth thought how this man qualified everything he said, a typical politician. She asked, "What about the old man's vehicle?"

"Wouldn't know. I had left before then. Did not meet Mr. Purdy Senior except to see him through the glass, sitting like a zombie up front during the execution. Didn't make eye contact. He didn't seem or appear capable of it. May've been on drugs for all I know."

"Who takes care of turning over the remains?"

"It was taken care of by a guard and honorary inmates who've earned the respect of the guards."

"I see." Lucas realized now that Gwinn had not seen the old man face-to-face, nor had he talked to the elder Purdy. That all the dirty business of cleaning up after an execution—once the show was over—fell to inmates and guards.

Meredyth broke the uncomfortable silence. "According to the only eyewitness we have, Judge DeCampe's abductor shapes up to be old man Purdy."

"And that old man left here with two pine box coffins in his van," finished Lucas. "One housed his fried son's body, and the other was intended for the judge."

Meredyth added, "Goddard corroborates our worst fears, that the old man means to bury his son and the judge, and she most likely alive."

Visibly shaken, Gwinn's mouth moved, but only an unintelligible utterance sounded.

Lucas stormed at him. "Last time I looked, the State of

Texas still supplies pine boxes for death row inmates, but somebody had to have given or sold the old man that second coffin. Any guesses who?"

"Pine boxes can be had at any funeral home. You just have to ask."

"Do you really believe that is how Purdy came to have two coffins in back of his van, Warden?" asked Meredyth.

He bridled and puffed up as if every fiber had filled with air. "All right, we build pine boxes with gold-chrome–plated handles in our inmate wood shop. Keeps idle hands busy. Takes some stress off to work a plane and a sander."

"We'll want to talk to your man in charge of the wood shop where they make the coffins for death-row inmates."

"There're three of 'em. Each on different shifts. As for the coffins, we supply them to public funerary homes all over the state, and some out-of-state locations. It's the only alternative to those high-priced Cadillac models, and there're a lot of sharecroppers in the state who don't want to go broke over a funeral."

"So a coffin or two going out the door wouldn't necessarily be missed?"

"You'd best talk to my men."

"Before we talk to them, let me see their records," suggested Meredyth Sanger.

"If you wish, Dr. Sanger."

"We're trying to win a race here, sir, against time. Perhaps we can save some time by my going over the records. Sometimes it's in the ink—the handwriting. I'm something of a handwriting expert," she explained. She had taken up the science of reading handwriting after learning how it served Kim Desinor, when she and Lucas had worked with her on the Snatcher case two years before.

The warden only frowned at this, punched a button on the intercom, and shouted, "Shirley, I want three personnel files in here stat. Bill Lowry, Karl Tubbs, and Jake Pascal. Got that?" He then turned to his visitors and said, "I trust every one of my guards here at Huntsville. They're the best."

Before even meeting the three guards who rotated overseeing the wood shop, Meredyth Sanger had a fix on Jake Pascal as being the rascal who had sold a second coffin under the table to the old man, based on his handwriting. They didn't bother speaking to the other two men. Summoned to the warden's office, Pascal was immediately apprehensive and defensive, and spilled his guts the moment Meredyth displayed the artist's sketch of the elder Purdy.

"I thought it'd be OK, you know. The old man said it was for himself, for when his time would come. Said he didn't have nothing in this life but the van he'd just bought. When we loaded his son into the van around by the shop, I just had the boys toss in another for him at no charge."

"No charge?" asked the warden.

"Sir, I swear, I didn't take a cent for it. You can ask Fletcher and Columbo; they were the ones who helped load the coffins. No mystery about it."

"What kind of van did the old man drive?"

"Ahhh, fancy, large, expensive, well carpeted. Roomy. Both the boxes fit in side by side. He'd taken out all the backseats."

"What make and model?"

"Chevrolet, I think. Big American job. Maybe a Ford. I didn't pay any mind to that. But I wondered where he'd put the seats he'd removed so the boxes would fit."

"So he anticipated getting two coffins before he ever got here?" asked Lucas.

"Look, we all knew Jimmy Lee pretty well after ten years. Jimmy asked me as a favor to him to cut out a coffin for the old man. I . . . I was expecting the old man and his request."

"But you took no money for it?" repeated the warden.

"Not a cent, sir. Honest."

The warden waved him down.

Lucas wanted the warden to leave the room, but he knew making such a request would only anger the man. "Did you notice anything unusual about the license plate?"

"Wasn't one of ours. Out of state. Indiana, I think."

"All right, Officer Pascal. You can go now," said the

warden, seeing that Lucas and Sanger were finished with the guard.

"I'm sorry, Warden Gwinn, sir."

"I'll deal with you later, Pascal. Some tough guy you turned out to be. You allowed yourself to be hoodwinked by an old Iowa farmer."

The phone rang; a call for Lucas from Randy Oglesby, his computer support. Randy had unearthed some fascinating facts, if belated. "Get this, Lucas—old man Purdy had made two previous trips to Houston, the first time was almost ten years before, when Judge Maureen DeCampe, a newly appointed judge, saw his son to the death chamber in a ruling she alone made—no jury trial. Jimmy Purdy was found guilty of sex crimes that had turned to sex-lust-murder. He had opted for a no-jury trial, and his case had fallen into DeCampe's lap."

"Good work."

"That's not all. The old man returned recently when Jimmy's appeal was being heard before Judge Raymond Parker, but not before it first fell into DeCampe's hands. DeCampe hand delivered it to Parker. She recused herself from hearing the appeal since she was, to say the least, extremely prejudiced where Jimmy Lee Purdy was concerned. It was a direct conflict of interest, a no-brainer," said Randy. "However, the senior Purdy made an appointment and saw her before the appeal trial began. What was said during that meeting remained between them. Judge DeCampe shared it with no one."

"And the old man's third trip here," said Lucas, "was to retrieve his son's body." He thanked Randy and hung up. Lucas then conveyed this information to the warden and Sanger. They next stood and said their good-byes.

On leaving the prison and locating the car, Sanger said, "Lucas, as I see it, we have one more stop, and then we call out the armed forces in Iowa to locate one Isaiah Purdy."

"Warrant across state lines can take time," replied Lucas.

Darkness was already descending over Texas when they made their way out to the parking lot.

"Not if the judge is sympathetic to our cause," countered

Sanger, "and being highborn as I am, I have a few friends in high places around here, and so did DeCampe. If Judge DeCampe is suffocating somewhere in a pine box between here and Iowa or back at this guy's property and six feet under, we . . . well, we have to act fast, and even then it may be too late."

"I've got to call this medical examiner with the FBI, tell her what we've got. Maybe she can get a federal warrant to search the guy's property faster than the State of Texas can talk to the State of Iowa."

"I know Judge Parker, and he'll be extremely sympathetic, and—"

"I see. Play on the old saw: There but for the grace of God coulda went Judge Parker, right?"

"With these men, father and son, fixated on DeCampe, I suspect Parker was never in the running. But of course, I'll work every angle on him, Lucas. Meanwhile, you get the feds to jump-start the state patrol in Iowa. Have them at the ready to move in at a moment's notice. One or the other of us, Texas or the Feds, whoever gets a warrant first, we use."

Lucas placed his strobe light over the top of the car and turned on the siren. They raced for the courthouse.

TEN

I advance to attack, I climb to assault,
like a choir of young worms at a corpse in a vault.

—CHARLES BAUDELAIRE

A subdued light filtered into Maureen DeCampe's consciousness, as if she were awakening from this nightmare, a little glimmer of hope that she could willingly, easily step into the light of consciousness, and that within that consciousness none of what had occurred had occurred except in her head, inside the nightmare, and all this horrid time would have been spent in her dream state and all such terror as Purdy represented would be mercifully over. She tried to rouse herself from the nightmare, urging herself into consciousness, and it was working. The light grew nearer and brighter and more real. She just needed to allow herself to move into it. Then the nightmare would end.

The barn odors were gone, too, and even the odor of the decaying had ceased. Thank God for the light. And what was that sound? Footsteps coming out of the darkness, soft footfalls, careful, inching their way toward her along with the light. A door hinge creaked; some small vermin skittered away. The sound of someone gasping for breath directly behind her.

The subdued light became a burning torch in her eyes. *It's a flashlight,* she thought. It was directed on her and the corpse to which she remained tied. She then heard the distinct high pitch of a woman's voice say, "Oh my freakin' dear God-inmerciful heaven-havemercy-on-us-all! I knew that old SOB was up to no good out here, but I didn't know . . .

couldn't know this. My God, my dear God-a-mighty!"

Maureen next saw the blade and handle of a red Swiss Army knife begin sawing at the rawhide strips around her wrist, and she wondered if it could be Mrs. Purdy. With one wrist now freed, she felt the tug at the larger bands about her back. Her savior didn't know where to begin, but with a frantic gasping that threatened to send the woman into hyperventilation, reacting to the sight and the stench before her, and in nervous fits and starts, the brave woman tore at each binding strip. One by one, the little knife struggled through each band until Maureen DeCampe cried tears of hope and joy. The feeling of recapturing her own self in the pulling apart from the ugly unit she had become with the dead, that alone created in her a sense of unadulterated joy.

Was it Mrs. Purdy, another relative? Whoever her savior might be, the woman seemed young, strong, vibrant. *She's no old matron of the farm,* thought Maureen. *But who could she be?*

"I'm Nancy Willis. I count myself an ass for not checking out that old man in more detail. He told me he was a widower. Told me he was lonely and sad. He struck me as an odd duck, but I didn't think he was a psycho-lunatic!"

Nancy now pulled and cut away at the ties that held Maureen by forehead and neck to the corpse's head and neck, and once this was done, Maureen's savior tugged at and cut away the tape about Maureen's mouth. Whoever this woman was, she was not squeamish about Purdy's desiccated body, which gave her fingers a liberal decay bath. "I got my cell phone in the bag. I'll call 911. We'll have this old wicked sonofa-monster's ass in prison before dawn, you can bet. Poor child, poor thing. How utterly awful what that sonofa-bastard's put you through."

Her mouth finally free, Maureen gasped and thought, *Call 911 first,* but her body and her brain screamed to be free of Jimmy Lee's body now. She pleaded, "Just first . . . first get me free . . . of this rotting sonofabitch corpse."

"Yes, of course, first things first."

Nancy Willis continued cutting rawhide with the four-inch blade. It took time, as each strip was thick, and the old

man had wound the rawhide several times around his son
and his victim. At one point, Nancy's knife nicked Maureen's side, but Maureen dared not cry out. Nancy talked as
she worked like a cartoon dwarf out of *Snow White,* Maureen thought. Then a grim idea began to form in Maureen's
head, making her wonder if this woman hadn't been sent in
by the old man just to give Maureen false hope. Anything
might happen in this horrid storybook she found herself in,
an abyss darker than anything in *Alice in Wonderland.*

Nancy had worked her way down with the knife, going
from wrists to back and then waist. When she finished the
waist ties, even though still attached by her feet, Maureen
twisted and rolled off and inched her upper torso as far from
Purdy's body as possible. Nancy next began work on the
ankles.

Maureen only half heard Nancy's nonstop words now.
"When in doubt, check him out, all that, but he paid cash
up front, and he seemed harmless enough, all that spouting
off with Bible quotes, you know. Still, some last instinct
told me he couldn't be all there, wanting this place, the last
hole on the planet, and I was right all along, that nagging
little voice inside my head. Still, I never . . . not all the way
out here did I ever . . . never suspect such an awful result."

Nancy continued cutting strips of rawhide as she spoke,
now freeing Maureen's second ankle from the dead man's,
allowing Maureen complete detachment. "Who else has he
killed? How many? Some kind of serial mass murderer, isn't
he?"

When Maureen pulled completely away, she realized
how weak and stiff she felt. But this was masked by a sense
of freedom that filled her with hope.

Finally, Nancy stared in the half light at Maureen, gaping
at the other woman's wounds. Maureen, shivering in the
cold barn, looked the part of a leper, and now Maureen
reached up to touch the cheek that had been pressed to the
dead man's, and she, too, became more aware of the sores
on her body. Nancy removed her thigh-length jacket and
placed it around the nude woman, asking her what her name
was.

"Maureen . . . Maureen DeCampe," she managed.

"Ohmygod! You're the . . . you're the . . . you're the . . . that woman in the news that's gone missing? That lady judge stolen from the parking lot? I saw it on *America's Most Wanted.*"

"Dial 911 now, please!"

Nancy shakily dialed 911.

Nothing. Dead air.

She redialed 911 several times.

Still nothing.

Maureen flashed on her body tied to Jimmy Lee's again. She desperately feared the old man might come through the barn doors any second and reclaim her.

Nancy said, "I don't fucking believe this. Damn, I knew I should've recharged this thing, and now way out here in the middle of nowhere. Shit. We'll have to get to my car; I can recharge it there on the way to a safe place. My daughter's house is only ten miles east. We can call authorities from there if we can't get the signal."

She tucked the phone back into her bag, and with both hands, she tugged at Maureen, trying to get her to stand. "We've got to get to the road, my car, now!" Maureen allowed herself to believe they might have a chance at escape.

But Maureen hesitated at standing, fearful she would simply topple over. Her legs felt like wood.

Nancy Willis didn't skip a beat. "Why didn't I pay heed to my little voice? No, I went straight ahead with the rental, took his money without so much as a . . . and now this. I shoulda known. He gave me the creeps from the get-go. Something told me I had to come out here and see what he was up to."

"Thank God you did," muttered Maureen, fearing to look at the itchy patches of skin at her wrists and ankles, her stomach and breasts, where she had lain so long against the decaying man. A part of her wanted to stop Nancy for a mirror from that purse of hers; a part of her wanted to assess the damage done to her face. But another part of her screamed for her to get up and get out of here.

Nancy hadn't stopped talking. ". . . now this. Honey, we

gotta get ourselves outta here before he wakes up. Come on. On your feet. I know it's difficult."

Maureen stumbled and broke a rickety old stall when she fell against it, sending her back to a sitting position. "O'dear-o'dear-o'dear!" Nancy's flashlight beam now bathed Maureen's features, and Nancy gasped on seeing the lesions on Maureen's face clearly now. Nancy was momentarily silenced, and she stood over Maureen frozen, her hands hesitating now to touch the other woman. The flash had caught the extent of the blue green tint to much of Maureen's skin. "What has that madman done to you?"

"Slow poisoning . . . with decay of his . . . dead son. I . . . I sent his son to the electric chair."

"And that old bastard is wreaking as cruel a vengeance on you as he can imagine."

"Something out of his Bible. He's completely insane, and he will kill you, too, if he finds you here."

"Don't worry about me. I'm Chicago bred. I can take care of myself."

"Chicago? Are we near Chicago?"

"Heavens no!"

"Shhh. . . . Turn off that light."

Nancy did as ordered.

"I think I heard something. He may be moving around." Maureen froze, petrified of his getting his hands on her again and trussing her up to Jimmy Lee. In the darkness, she thought she saw a glint in the dead man's eye and a rictus smile shone like an Elvis sneer. "Give me the knife," she whispered to Nancy.

"What for?"

"I'll kill myself before I'll let him tie me back to his son."

Nancy took a deep breath and handed the closed knife to Maureen, who latched onto it as if it were a religious icon, clutching it to her breasts.

FROM his bed at the farmstead—the bed he had decided to die in—Isaiah Purdy wandered again in a meander of mem-

ory, searching for his lost identity: the lost self, the lost man
who had been taken over by his dead son and God. One
small corner of his mind held a doubt about God in particular. Jimmy Lee was Jimmy Lee, but this here God he traveled with . . . Isaiah began to wonder about. Maybe this
so-called God was something Jimmy Lee had conjured up,
and maybe it had to do with the black arts, and maybe it
was one of Satan's minions posing as God. But how to tell,
how to ferret it all out, what was he to do? Either way,
justice was justice, and Jimmy Lee had some modicum of
justice coming.

Isaiah snapped out of the ugly thought. *Where is my head
at?* he silently queried. Lately, he'd been asking himself this
question a lot. He had no idea of the answer, not when he
could question whether or not he'd been in the presence of
God or not, in the presence of Satan or not. Perhaps it'd
been neither. Perhaps it'd been an angel. An angel, yes. That
would put things into a clearer perspective, be a lot easier
to deal with. Without this sure knowledge, how could he
have wreaked the vengeance he had helped Jimmy Lee to
find?

He searched for the man who he had been before Jimmy
Lee had gotten hold of his head. Instead, he found only an
empty space staring back, a shapeless thing in coveralls,
faceless and without distinct form.

He rolled over in bed. The old box springs screamed in
reaction, further disturbing his sleep. A birdlike thought flew
through his brain, in and out, that perhaps he ought to end
it all tonight, put the bedeviled woman in the barn out of
her misery. His former self would have done as much for
any ailing animal on the farm. A part of him wanted to leap
from the bed and just go do it, the way he might destroy a
dog with incurable mange. How much more suffering could
he handle? It wasn't easy being Jimmy Lee's eyes and ears.

He questioned who he was . . . why he was even here on
this planet if not to end his life this way, to fulfill a dying
son's wish: Jimmy Lee's mother had said neither yes nor
no to the idea before she passed, but his son's voice in his
head told him that Mother wanted what he wanted. It'd been

left on Isaiah's shoulders to make the decision, as with all major decisions involving the family—at least in this life.

"We're dealing with no less than a miracle," Eunice had managed to mutter when he'd asked her point-blank what she thought they ought to do about Jimmy Lee's request.

After she succumbed to death, Jimmy Lee would not be denied, and he'd given Isaiah strict orders, and very specific details, down to where he could find the judge, but Jimmy Lee had been wrong about that much. When he'd left Huntsville prison in search of Judge DeCampe, he had first looked into a rental property where he could kill the judge right handy there, instead of worrying himself with carting her across the country and back home. As much as he wanted to bury Jimmy Lee at the Iowa farmstead, that was no longer feasible. Meantime, Isaiah had learned the hard way that the judge no longer resided in Houston, Texas. He'd had to investigate where she had gone, and when he found out, he almost quit the entire lunatic plan, but again Jimmy Lee— even more so in death than before—insisted the old man would not live one moment in peace if he did not carry through. Although she had not put it in words, Isaiah had to believe that Eunice had been entirely and wholly for her son's plan.

Jimmy's voice inside Isaiah's head said over and over, *"You've got to do just as Mother wanted."* Jimmy Lee never let it rest. Repeatedly, the words flowed like a river through his father's brain.

On the trip back from Houston, Jimmy Lee startled the hell out of his father when he spoke from within the casket, from within the mortal remains, the electrocuted corpse. "Ice, ice, damn you, old man!" Jimmy Lee ordered up, and his voice almost made Isaiah run through a fence, so startled was he to hear his dead son's voice from outside his head and from behind him. "Keep my body fresh until you can locate Maureen." He always called the judge by her first name.

Jimmy Lee had always wanted to be in charge, and now he was. Mother had simply wanted her boy's remains returned to the farmstead to be buried alongside her, but of

course, Jimmy had to complicate matters. He couldn't just
go off into whatever eternity awaited him. No, he had to
drag this judge lady there with him. It didn't look promising
that Mother would ever lie alongside her boy in the grave,
at least not without a third party involved. Jimmy Lee
wanted far, far more than did Mother. And he had asked
far, far more of his papa than anyone had a right to, but
somehow, the boy knew that Isaiah would do his utmost to
grant him a dying wish.

An alien noise penetrated through the fog of the old
man's disturbed sleep. He sensed more than he heard it:
some disturbance, a faint noise like the crack of a whip but
muffled. At the same instant, he realized that anything large
enough to make such a noise as to wake him from this
distance—the noise coming from the direction of the barn—
that it must be the result of a two-legged beast.

He pushed himself from bed, and in his flannel nightshirt,
he crept across the floor. He next grabbed his shotgun but
thought better of making such a noise here in the middle of
the night. He instead grabbed his pitchfork and the unlit
lantern. Not bothering to dress, Isaiah made his way to the
barn down a worn path. He saw a moving light through the
cracks inside.

Definitely, someone had paid Jimmy Lee and the judge
a visit, but who?

Isaiah inched toward the door, kicking an errant bucket
and frightening a cat as he did so; he then quietly cursed
his clumsiness. Now he had alerted whoever it was to his
presence. Inside, all remained silent and dark, the light
having been doused. Befuddled and only half awake, the old
man wondered if the light might not be Jimmy Lee's doing.
The boy had a nasty playfulness for making mischief, something he seemed born with.

What he felt deep inside he had long held in check, and
the voice of his son in his head made him put one step ahead
of the other to move forward. Jimmy Lee continued to drive
him, and now Jimmy, as dead as the boy was, had awakened
him, telling him he was needed here, inside, to witness every
moment of the judge's suffering.

Isaiah thought of how damnably little sleep he'd had since tying the judge to Jimmy Lee. But the next sound he heard was by no means Jimmy Lee's voice in his head. He heard a woman's whisper. The judge? Impossible. Some third party had indeed entered, and Isaiah wondered how long the intruder had been inside the barn with Jimmy Lee and the judge.

He carefully set aside the lantern, lifted the pitchfork's three deadly prongs to eye level, and he inched toward the door, prepared for battle.

JESSICA Coran didn't know where she was; her only certainty proved a blue veil through which everything was filtered. She saw a pastoral setting, absolutely peaceful, and serenity poured forth with the waterfall in the distance. Flowers in the foreground, flowers that smelled of life and promise. But the waterfall, grass, and flowers were all tinted blue. The same was true for two figures walking through this land of birdsong and bright sunshine, but again all was gauzy, hazy, enveloped in the blue filter, even the burning sun, softened radiation in blue.

The two figures, a man and a woman, looking very much like her and Richard, walked with their hands entwined, their bodies wrapped in one another's. Nearing the curtain of blue, she saw a series of looping, binding ties between them, holding them together like so many horse reins. And now she saw that the hands were not naturally wrapped in one another but bound with rough rope.

Am I dreaming? If so, what does it mean? she searchingly wondered.

Jessica heard a roar and saw the waterfall turn into a gaping mouth. Then the blue veil and the land of dream shattered into black-and-white dots as on a dead TV screen. Someone's hand had reached into her dream, shaking her; someone's voice had infiltrated her brain and had set her eyelids fluttering.

At FBI headquarters, Richard Sharpe shook Jessica Coran, waking her from a nap on the sofa in her temporary office. "It's Houston, that Cherokee detective, on the line for you. Says he has something for us. Thought you'd want to hear it firsthand."

"What? Oh . . . yes, of course."

Jessica listened on one line, Sharpe on a second one, as Detective Stonecoat said, "There's no time to explain, but we have sufficient grounds to issue a warrant for search and seizure at Jimmy Lee Purdy's father's farm home outside Iowa City, Iowa. But getting an Iowa judge and a Texas one agreeing with one another, well that could take some time. We suspect that a federal warrant may be easier and faster to obtain, although Dr. Sanger is at work on Judge Richard Parker as we speak."

"Then your visit to Huntsville turned up something about the case, about the old man?"

"About the son, for certain. It may be that the old man is acting on Jimmy Lee's orders."

"Say that again?"

"From the grave, so to speak. He . . . we believe Jimmy Lee left strict instructions for the old man to follow through on, and they involved sending Judge DeCampe over with Jimmy Lee to the other side."

"Just as we feared."

"What about a federal warrant?"

"We'll get right on it. Send me a full report of your findings out at Huntsville. We'll need every shred of corroboration on this."

"Consider it done. I'll fax you a full report. Meanwhile, someone's got to get the Iowa authorities alerted and descend on that farmhouse, and since I'm in Houston and you're in D.C., I don't think we have the luxury of wasting a moment's more time. Fact is, we fear she may be buried already, fighting for her last breath, if she isn't already dead."

"Then I take it Goddard was forthcoming with what he knew?"

"We convinced him it was in his best interest, yes."

"I'm saying good-bye now, detective, and thanks for the help. I'm off for that warrant."

Stonecoat asked to be kept informed. "Judge DeCampe was well liked in these parts."

"Yeah . . . yeah, same here, detective."

JESSICA called in every favor she had outstanding, and she felt certain that a federal warrant for search and seizure of property at the Purdy farmstead outside Iowa City was just a matter of time. She immediately contacted the head of the Highway Patrol in the vicinity of Iowa City, and after a number of frustrating stops and starts, she finally found herself talking to the man in charge, someone who sounded normal.

"This is Chief of Patrol Virgil Gorman. How can I help you, Dr. Coran, is it?"

"I'm head of a task force in an abduction case, Chief Gorman, and it involves a Washington, D.C., judge who's become the victim of a vengeful relative. Our investigation has recently shifted toward—"

"Wait a minute, you talking about the case I saw in the *Police Gazette* just the other night?"

She covered the phone with her hand and said to Sharpe, "God, he sounds like Andy of Mayberry."

Sharpe raised his shoulders to indicate he didn't know what in the world she referred to. She then spoke into the phone. "Yes, that would be the case I am referring to, sir, and all evidence is pointing at a one Isaiah Purdy, who maintains some sort of farm outside Iowa City."

"Damn, you don't say. These parts are full of Purdys. Isaiah Purdy, huh?"

"His son was recently executed in Huntsville, Texas, and DeCampe put him on death row."

"I see . . . so you suspect his father of abducting the judge?" The chief stated the obvious.

"We have many leads pointing to him, yes."

"I see. So, how can we help you, Dr. Coran?"

"I want you to get out to his place and execute a search and seizure warrant, ostensibly to locate Judge Maureen

DeCampe. We fear he intends burying her alive—if he hasn't already done so."

"Christ . . . sure, we'll do everything within our power to cooperate, of course. Have you faxed a copy of the warrant to my people here?"

"Not just yet, but it's on its way."

"On its way?"

"She doesn't have a moment to lose, sir."

"Lost my last case in court for jumping the gun on a warrant, Doctor. It's not going to happen again. Best I can do is stay in radio contact while I get some units up there, waiting and poised to go in. But I won't order my men in without paper on the suspect."

"It's on its way," she lied.

"Like I said, soon as we have it in hand."

"What about soon as *I* have it in hand, Chief Gorman?"

"Don't know . . ."

"You can trust me."

He hesitated.

"Minutes are like days on this case, Chief."

"I'll send 'em in on your say-so. I'll get them out there soon as I get off the phone. I can promise you that much."

"Keep in constant contact with us, sir."

"As much as earthly possible, I will."

Chief Virgil Gorman immediately telephoned Iowa City Sheriff Chester Dunkirk, who on learning the news, replied, "I'm going to step back, Virgil. You're entirely in charge here."

Virgil Gorman understood. There were a lot of Purdys living in and around the area, and it was an election year. "Do you know Isaiah Purdy? Is he capable of this sort of thing?"

"I've never made the man's acquaintance. Heard stories when his son was arrested in Texas. All I ever heard was he was devoted to his wife, his son, and his pig farm. But he never spent a night in my jail. You?"

"Never heard of him before I got that call from the FBI."

"Well, since you called, I dug out the likeness the Feds put out on the old man, Virgil."

"And what about it?

"According to a cousin, it doesn't look anything like him. The cousin works for us."

"A cousin of Purdy's? Could be useful at the scene. Can you get him out there?"

"He's not too cooperative, Virgil."

Gorman hated to hear this. "Anything? Did he give up anything?"

"Said the old man's a hermit up there, and nobody has anything to do with him or his wife, and no one's seen either of them in months."

"I'll see you at the perimeter, Dunkirk."

ELEVEN

Ruthless as the old devil gods
of the world's first darkness.

—SIR PHILLIP GIBBS

Houston, Texas

INSIDE Judge Raymond Parker's chambers in downtown Houston, Texas, Dr. Meredyth Sanger did not have to plead long for Parker's help. Parker told her a chilling story about how the old man, just after his son's execution, had shown up at the courthouse, ostensibly to talk to Judge DeCampe. He grew somewhat irascible when he learned that DeCampe no longer worked at the courthouse. The old man had then asked for Judge Parker, and so he was brought upstairs by one of the guards to see Parker.

"And what did he want?"

"He wanted to know how he might get in touch with Judge DeCampe, said something about closure, how he was glad it had all finally come to a conclusion."

"Did you tell him how he might get in touch with her?"

"Absolutely not, no! I told him I would be most happy to convey that message on to her."

"Well, it would appear someone told him she was in D.C. He's suspected of abducting her there."

"He didn't learn of her whereabouts from me, but her move was reported in the newspapers, the *Chronicle* in particular. He could have easily accessed the information."

"Then he goes clear across the continent with his dead son in tow alongside an empty coffin meant for her. Amazing."

The Honorable Judge Raymond Parker grabbed up a pen and a preprinted form to fill out. "I'll give you a warrant to search the old man's home in Iowa, but for an Iowa cop to serve it, I don't know. It's not always as simple as signing on the dotted line."

"I'll take any kind of paper I can get," she finished.

While filling out the search and seizure warrant at Purdy's address in Iowa, Judge Parker gave Meredyth more insight into the motive behind DeCampe's abduction. Parker said, "Purdy sat stone-faced throughout his son's appeal months before. The man never said a word. Just came every day and statued himself behind Jimmy Lee."

Parker finished the document with a swirl of the wrist and he said, "So what are you doing here, Dr. Sanger? Why aren't you on the horn to Iowa City, Iowa? Get the State Patrol out to Purdy's farm now!" Judge Parker's order came with his warrant as he pushed it into her hands.

She thanked him.

"I'm not waiting for Sharon to have the papers triplicated. Once you call Iowa, I'll do all the busywork. Make the call. Use my phone." He handed her the phone.

NOT every cop, but very near every state trooper in Iowa, sat poised and ready for Jessica Coran's go directive, and she knew that every minute ticking by could be DeCampe's last—*If the judge is indeed still alive somewhere in the world of Isaiah Purdy,* she told herself. An hour and twenty minutes had passed since she'd talked to Chief Patrol Officer Virgil Gorman in Iowa. "Where the hell's that warrant?" she shouted to the ceiling. No one on the task force had an answer for her.

"Get the guy in Iowa back on the line for me," she told the civilian secretary.

Only a few seconds later, she was in contact again with Gorman. "Look," she said firmly, "if he's already buried her out there someplace on his property, you guys could take hours, even days locating where the grave site is."

"Yeah, that's why we brought dogs, Dr. Coran. Once we

hit the place, we'll find her and find her quick. Promise you that much."

"Can you? This old man is like some devilish fox. I need you to move in on him now."

"Then you have the warrant in hand?"

She hesitated.

"We can't just go on a man's property and search without some kind of warrant," replied Gorman. "Despite all your suppositions about Purdy, Doctor, this is still the U.S. of A., not Moscow."

"The warrant's a formality. It's in the works."

"I have to have it in my blessed hands or at least have a call from the governor. You think you can arrange that?"

"If DeCampe's not already dead, she's still being mentally and physically tortured by him. She could lose her mind. Damn it, we've got to act."

"We've got to have the warrant in hand if we want to nail this bastard. No warrant, and he will in the end get off scot-free," countered the Iowa lawman. "What's more, you people know that better'n we do out here in the sticks."

"I'll get your warrant. Just hold on to this line for a few minutes." She looked across at the task force members in the operations room. Very near the entire team, including Lew Clemmens, had assembled. Clemmens, who'd brought over his laptop, awaited electronic confirmation from either Judge Parker's office in Texas, the U.S. Marshal's Office, or Judge Pauline Fitshue in D.C. Whoever got the paperwork completed first had custody of Purdy: the federal government, D.C., or Texas. Jessica wasn't particular.

"I'm not waiting a second longer," said Jessica to her team, her hand over the receiver. "Fuck it. Lew, send a fax to Iowa now."

"Telling them what?"

"That the federal writ for Purdy's apprehension has been ordered by the U.S. Marshal's Office. Do it! Do it now."

Clemmens hesitated only a moment before sending the message. Iowa dispatch, poised and ready, instantly contacted men at the scene just outside a dark little farmstead in the middle of nowhere, outside Iowa City, Iowa. "Go!"

shouted Jessica into the phone. "It's a go, Chief!"

Sirens responded as the Iowa State Patrol stormed the stark, bleak countryside farm home of Isaiah and Eunice Purdy.

MAUREEN, her ankles wobbly, her limbs weak, unsteadily climbed to her feet and stumbled into Nancy. They clumsily clung to one another, the stench and the horror of this place overwhelming. "You going to be able to walk, honey?"

"I . . . I think so."

"Might even have to run. Think you maybe can run with my help?" asked Nancy.

"I will if it comes to that, yes."

"Good girl . . . good girl."

Unsteadily at first, like a baby, Maureen began to regain use of her legs and feet. She dared not wonder at the gangrenous portions of her body. But she felt faint, weak, and she realized only now that she'd been slowly starving and dehydrating as well as enduring the torture.

Nancy held on, guiding her. "Come on, dear. Let's get out of this awful place." They made their way to the large barn doors, when suddenly one of them slammed into Maureen and Nancy, knocking Maureen off her feet and stunning Nancy. In the next instant, Maureen heard Nancy's startled scream and the thud like a fallen tree, a dirt cloud kicking into Maureen's eyes. Clearing her sight, Maureen saw the awful cause of the dirt cloud. The force of Purdy's pitchfork had sent the other woman's body to the dirt to be pinned there, twitching and alive.

Maureen now stared at the RE/MAX button on Nancy's bloodied blouse, just over her heart. One of the three prongs of the pitchfork had bitten into and through her badge and breast, while the center prong went through her center, and the third through her left breast. Nancy's head slumped melonlike to one side, her now dead eyes staring into Maureen's. Neither words nor sound issued from her now, only a froth of blood and body fluids.

"Kill me! Kill me, you son of a bitch!" Maureen shouted

at Purdy even as she struggled to stand, pulling herself up by the handle of the pitchfork, rocking Nancy's lifeless body in the effort. She tore at the pitchfork, attempting to free it and use it on Purdy. But she couldn't find the strength to pull the thing free before Purdy's hands also grabbed hold of the deadly tool.

In the darkness, she fought for possession of the pitchfork, but his grasp and tug easily overcame his weakened victim. He toppled her with a slap to the face, and now she backed farther into the barn, backed over Jimmy Lee's decayed corpse, where she fell. Screaming and scrambling from the filthy floor and into a stall, she found a large square of blackness in which to hide.

"Can't tell you how much I'm enjoying this little turn of events."

The judge's whimpers in the dark were her only response. Just enough for him to home in on her. In the distance, he heard—and she heard—the sound of a siren, and they both wondered if the dead realtor had called anyone before she had arrived. Maureen thought not, but in her confused mental state, perhaps she was wrong; perhaps help *was* indeed on the way. And fearing this, perhaps the old man would kill her here and now to end this thing before the authorities could.

It was a thing she could never have ever wished for in her past, but now she wished for death to take her, and yet there remained a residual of hatred and anger for Purdy that made her want to kill him first. But how?

AN army of black-and-white cars with sirens blaring descended like locusts on the Purdy farmstead, one running down a RE/MAX For Sale sign as they converged on the house and barn. Two teams moved with precision training, each knowing its objective: one to control the house, the other to control the barn. They easily poured into the house, the doors unlocked and one swinging on its hinges. There, Sheriff Chester Dunkirk immediately felt the utter loneliness of the place, the emptiness of the old farmstead, as if the walls shouted its desertion. Still, he called out for Purdy and Mrs. Purdy to show themselves. "No one's going to harm you. It's Chester Dunkirk and Deputy Bailey Dobbins. The State Patrol's got some questions for you, Isaiah, Eunice."

Deputy Dobbins added, "Come on, now. You know me. I come only to help you out whenever you got problems over this way. Just come on out of hiding now and answer the sheriff's questions. Just step out now."

There was no response, save the pounding of men charging up the stairwell to Purdy's second story. Everyone knew the fierce regard many of the area farmers held about anyone, lawman or not, coming uninvited onto their property and especially into their houses. Every man here understood he could be shot at any moment should old Isaiah come through a door blasting two shotgun barrels full of buckshot at the officers, and given the allegations against the old man. . . .

One patrolman now stuck his head over the rail and shouted down, "All clear up here, Sheriff! Nobody at all."

Others poured into the basement. Again the report came back: no one, not a sign of life and no sign of the abducted judge. "Nobody walking."

Sheriff Dunkirk repeated the words in a mutter of frustration. "Nobody walking. Hope Gorman's team's done better out at the barn."

Meanwhile, team two had a problem getting into the barn. It appeared locked from inside.

"Careful, you men! Purdy may be armed and dangerous!" shouted Chief Virgil Gorman, in charge of the second strike force.

"Place could be booby-trapped as well," came another shout.

Men poured through the back door now and some had scaled through windows they'd broken out, and one had scaled a rope and was into the loft overhead. They brought flashlights to bear on the expansive barn, searching every corner and inch for any sign of anyone or anything untoward or out of place, or any sign of disturbed earth. Nothing save the pantheon of instruments found in any barn: rusty rat traps, harnesses, ropes, cans filled with nails, stalls standing empty, and a floor of mildewed hay.

No coffins.

No one tied to a post.

No blood or bodies dangling from rafters.

A few scurrying mice.

A lieutenant, who had deferred to the town sheriff's rule at the house, had rushed out to Gorman, shouting, "Nothing up at the house. Beds are made; place is neat as a pin, like it hasn't been lived in for some time."

"Sonofabitch!" shouted Virgil Gorman, a sixth-generation Iowan policeman, who purely hated it when an Iowa man broke the laws of man or God. He had never met Purdy, but he knew the area around Iowa City and the Falls; the area harbored Purdys up and down the roads. He'd have to have his men fan out and talk to every goddamn one of them about this man Isaiah Purdy, see who knew what, and if anyone might be harboring him. He tried to imagine anyone cruel enough to conceal and shelter Purdy while the man buried this poor woman alive.

"Fan out with the dogs! By daybreak, I want every inch of this property scoured for anything smacking of freshly dug earth! You got that!"

A chorus of *yessirs* responded. Like a well-trained machine, the men broke into teams.

Gorman shouted at the Iowa City sheriff, Chester Dunkirk, saying, "Chester, you sure we got the right farm here?"

"This is Isaiah's place, all right. Don't rightly know where his wife's got off to. I expected to at least find her up at the house, but she's nowhere to be found. The house is strange, like someone's lived there just yesterday but no longer. Cups, saucers, food scraps, but no people, and no feeling of people."

"Now what?" asked one of the patrolmen, his hat in his hand.

"Now I gotta tell these people in Houston and in Washington, D.C., that their information was wrong and their warrants useless."

The young lieutenant standing by said, "Suppose maybe Purdy's still on his way back here, Chief? Sir?"

"Maybe . . . but we can't take that chance. Search high and low. And Marty, put a cruiser out on I-80 and one on that old dirt road that runs betwixt here and Three Corners. Only roads he can take down through here. Watch for anything smacking of the vehicle the Feds put the APB out on. If he is still transporting this judge, we'll get the damned old fool."

"Right, Virgil. On it."

Virgil Gorman stared Dunkirk down and said, "I gotta call this lady doctor in D.C. and this fellow Stonecoat in Houston with the bad news. Keep everyone looking for anything outta the ordinary, Chester. Don't take anything for granted."

At the same instant, someone shouted out, "Grave site! Gawl-darn grave site here!"

Everyone converged on the shouter and the circle of light his flash beam made over a mound of freshly dug earth. "Break out your shovels, boys!" shouted Gorman. Many of the officers had by order brought their shovels along for the grisly work, and they set the spades to working now, the dirt flying like a black water spray.

Still, they could not work fast enough for Gorman, who wanted this nightmare not to be happening in his rural jurisdiction. "Get that damned generator and field light out here. Get some of them damn car lights on this spot!" he ordered. "Get it dug up, you men! Now! Now! Now!" shouted Gorman, pushing past Dunkirk and the others. "Dig her out!"

The younger, stronger men bent to the work, tearing at the recently disturbed earth. The excited young officer who had first discovered it dug ferociously while saying, "The dogs first picked up animal tracks around it. Told me animals been sniffing around here. Then my light picked up the fact the dirt here 'bout didn't look pat, you know. All stirred up, you know, darkest patch in the moonlight."

A field light came suddenly on, flooding the grave site,

and the men working at the gruesome task of disinterring
the body were suddenly surround by their own giant shadows.

Someone handed Virgil Gorman a cellular phone, saying,
"It's that Texas cop, Virgil. He wants to know what's happening. Told him only you could say."

Gorman snorted like a walrus at this, took the phone, and
spoke into it. "Stonecoat? We got bad news and—whoa . . .
hold on . . . and on top of the bad news, we got more bad
news. First off, Purdy is not here and nowhere to be found.
Second, we've discovered a single grave site and are in the
process right this moment of shoveling it empty for a look-
see. You understand?"

"Gotcha, Chief." At his end, Lucas Stonecoat conveyed
the bad news, a chorus of despair replying and filtering
through the line all the way to Iowa.

"I want to stay on the line until you ID Judge DeCampe,
sir," Lucas said to Gorman.

"I fully understand, Lieutenant Stonecoat. Will keep this
line open. We have the Feds on the other line. I gotta tell
them what's up."

Gorman switched lines and was on the phone with Jessica
Coran now. He brought Jessica up to date, adding, "We have
a faxed photo of DeCampe. As soon as we have verification
she is . . . you know . . . in the grave out here, we will let
you know." He held up the phone to the grunting and the
sound of dirt flying. "We're doing it without benefit of a
backhoe, so it'll take a little bit."

"Thanks, Chief Gorman. Anyone from our field office in
Davenport arrive yet?"

"Negative on that. Sorry we don't seem to have any good
news whatsoever for you folks."

Gorman felt painfully aware of the chorus of grunts,
snorts, cursing, and gravel-tossing relayed through his open
line to Dr. Coran. He felt an acute sense of disappointment
at the situation, at his inability to do anything ultimately
useful, as he assumed the woman was long dead, and at the
depths to which human depravity sank, and in particular one
lone Iowan. He wondered if this Isaiah Purdy might not

actually have been born elsewhere and migrated to the state, but he rather doubted this, too.

IN the pitch-dark stall, Maureen DeCampe, at the same moment that Purdy's farm was being dug up, felt like a cornered and wounded animal, her strength sapped but her mind raging with anger and hatred for her pursuer. In the darkness, she blindly pulled down an ancient horse harness with metal fasteners as large as studs. As Purdy now approached, she readied herself. Taking a mighty swing at the old man's face, she sent the harness and its metal parts into his eyes, lacerating his forehead and sending him to his knees, temporarily blinded.

Disorientated for a moment, he raged and lashed out with the pitchfork he'd snatched from Nancy Willis's body. He next stumbled backward, and she ran past him and out into the night to find herself below the firmament of a star-filled sky.

"My God, I'm not in Iowa," she muttered, realizing instantly that the landscape of rolling foothills and cleft valleys didn't compute. She saw the lonely, old, dilapidated farmhouse on the rise, so she *was* on an isolated farmstead, but this was not Iowa. If she knew one thing for certain, this was not the Iowa she had always her entire life heard about. It was not colorless enough, not characterless enough, and certainly not flat enough to be Iowa. Texas? Were they near Huntsville, where he'd picked up Jimmy Lee for this horror ride? No, the land was not ochre or sand brown. In fact, this area was a mix of boulders and verdant greenery with a forest of black trees standing silent and ancient.

No time to cipher it out.

As she ran blindly away from the barn and scene of her torture, she saw a large collection of faded, whitewashed factory buildings surrounded with ten-foot-high fences. Between these two extremes—silent, dark forest and silent, run-down factory—she opted for the man-made structures in the hope of finding help. However, the old factory looked lonelier than the ancient farmhouse and the barn from which she had run. Still, some lights burned there, sending shards of light and shadow out from its center.

The odor from the factory assailed her nostrils, but it was a welcome relief from the odor of decay from which she ran. Still, the air around the place choked on sulfur-filled gas belching from two enormous smokestacks. She guessed it to be some sort of chemical factory, possibly a paint factory. She might find someone, a guard, a night watchman perhaps, who might help her. A telephone that fucking worked! If she could get inside the fence, get to a phone. . . .

TWELVE

Evil is easy, and has infinite forms.

—BLAISE PASCAL

ISAIAH Purdy had regained his vision and was now fueled with anger, and with Jimmy Lee's horrid laughter piercing his eardrums, he gave chase. With Jimmy Lee's dead voice telling Isaiah that he was made a fool, being bested by a damned woman, the old man, with his cattle prod in hand, raced after Maureen, muttering to himself until she came in view.

He saw that she was heading for that old chemical factory buttressing the property. And even with the distance between them, he could see that she had spotted him.

Then she vanished. One moment in his sight, the next gone, like a deer in a leafy wood. She'd seen him coming, and she had dropped into a shaft of black shadow this moonless night. He carried a rope alongside the cattle prod. He meant to hog-tie her and drag her, like a squealing animal, back to Jimmy Lee.

It's what Jimmy Lee said he wanted now.

"I'll get the bitch, Jimmy Lee, and I'll cozy the two of you up again just as soon's I do. Don't you be worrying none. Not one bit."

Jimmy Lee would make her pay for this in the next life, just as Isaiah had made that snoopy-assed realtor pay in this life. *Felt good to put the prongs of the pitchfork dead through her like I done,* he thought.

*   *   *

MAUREEN DeCampe had seen the old bastard bent on
slowly murdering her as he came over the rise, the man's
frame, rope, and what looked like the cattle prod silhouetted
against the sky when a dry lightning bolt lit up the heavens.
He looked for all the world like a maniacal biblical prophet
out of history. Just then, the moon peeked through an opening in the clouds. She quickly hid among some barrels just
outside the fence gate. A sign proclaimed the place to be
Midlothian Tool & Die, but the sign appeared ancient, and
it remained questionable exactly what sort of place this was,
except that it reeked of petroleum and alcohol and carbide
odors, with a touch of methane. The old sign looked like
something left over from another era. The place could just
as well be a gin mill today.

She inched along the fence, not certain where or how
close Isaiah Purdy might be at this moment. Having taken
her eyes off him once, she'd lost his gray form in the surrounding gloom.

Still, she heard animal noises. Was it Purdy? No, it was
something sounding trapped, the poor creature crying and
whining off deep in the woods. She heard the pitter-patter
of scurrying mice and rats among the discarded boards and
barrels on the other side of the fence. In all the time she
had been here, she had not heard a farm animal, not so much
as a dog bark or a cat meow.

Now she heard someone whistling, and she turned to
stare at a man on the other side of the fence, not a hundred
yards from her, lighting up a cigarette. His bulk stretched
the idea of comfort in a uniform with white shirt and blue
patch, the knit badge of a security guard. Her heart skipped
a beat at seeing the man, as it had at seeing Nancy Willis,
but Nancy lay dead now as a direct result of helping Maureen, and she was keenly aware that approaching the man
certainly put him in as much danger, but she had no choice.
In her condition, without help, she was not going to get free
of Isaiah Purdy. Purdy had made her an expert on helpless-
ness.

She rushed along the fence, banging, calling out, when
suddenly she felt the sting of an electric bolt streak through

her being, toppling her and sending her into unconsciousness, but in one instant before she lost consciousness, she realized that she was again in Purdy's hands.

"Hey, old man! How're you doing tonight?" shouted the security guard. "What's all the ruckus?"

"Damn varmints—rats!" Purdy called back in his most casual tone, while Maureen DeCampe lay in a patch of blackness at his feet.

"Hate the damn things. Why'd God make 'em in the first place? To torment good people like us?" asked the guard, puffing on his cigarette.

"What's it they say? Lord works in mysterious ways?"

"Is that your final answer?" he joked, mimicking a now world famous game show host. "You think the same is true in His creating the mosquitoes and the gnats?" The guard swatted at something that bit his forearm.

"OK, my friend," Purdy added, "God didn't make rats at all."

"Didn't? Then who? Satan?"

"My friend, rats came along for the ride, came out of the evil men do. They're here to remind us of our sinful natures, same as those stone statues—gargoyles. Hell, we're all just like 'em."

"Just like who?"

"Rats! Ain't you listening, son?" Purdy cleared his throat and pulled on his chewing tobacco, one foot on top of the game he'd just hunted down, keenly aware that if the moon should return, or if another lightning strike lit up the place, the guard would see what lay at the old man's feet. He thought on the one hand how he might need to get a few steps closer to the guard, that he might need to zap him with the cattle prod, and on the other hand, he thought, *I gotta get her up and outta here, but I can't so long as this idiot is talking to me.*

"There are some among us who can't help but give in to that nature." Purdy fished for words to extricate himself from the conversation.

"Nature of the rat, you mean?"

"Chinese have it on their calendar—year of the rat." The

old man now wondered if babbling would work, in hopes
that the younger man would grow bored and end it and walk
off.

"Yeah . . . hey yeah, and the Chinese are 'sposed to be
real smart."

"It's what ya might call imprinting from birth for some.
Why, the Lord don't have any more use for rats than we
do, son. Still, the rats among us flourish, and it's a damn
rare moment in this life when a man gets even a whiff of
real home-grown justice."

"I 'spose you're right, old man." The security guard
hadn't seen DeCampe or heard her pleas. A radio played
from a nearby doorway, a loud medley of Johnny Cash
tunes. The old man secretly thanked Johnny Cash.

But now the guard stepped closer to the fence, closer to
Purdy, and he would see DeCampe crumpled at his feet.
The idiot was actually interested in the gibberish Purdy had
concocted to put him off! *Shit.*

Closer and closer he came. Purdy stiffened his hold on
the cattle prod, gauging his reach through the gate; exactly
at what point would he be able to stab the beefy man with
it, to render him unconscious? He would not get a second
chance. The man was not wearing a side arm, but he had a
nightstick and a huge flashlight, which thus far, he had seen
no use for. But this meant he had good eyes, and with each
step, those good eyes came closer to discovering the woman
lying prone at the old man's feet.

One more step, and there'd be hell to pay, but then someone at the door called out the name Frank several times.
Frank stopped and turned, waved and shouted across forty
yards to his boss at the door. "Be right there, Mr. Wainwright." He then muttered under his breath for Purdy's sake,
"Now you wanna talk about rats? That SOB has incisors
longer'n any rat's gonna have."

Frank the watchman then looked over his shoulder and
said to Purdy, "Talk to you again, old-timer. Gotta go. Duty
calls, and ain't that a bitch. Some fifteen-minute break,
huh?" Cigarette smoke trailed after the man as he sauntered
off.

Purdy waited for the man to disappear through the factory
door, taking his flashlight, nightstick, his eyes, and radio
with him.

Purdy kicked the woman at his feet for making him sweat
and for shaming him, as Jimmy Lee's taunts continued in
the old man's brain. She'd shamed him good, breaking free
like this; even if she were recaptured without incident, it
was incident enough to give him ulcers. Not to mention how
things looked to Jimmy Lee. Jimmy Lee would be laughing
in his ears for weeks over this.

Purdy bent and placed DeCampe's limp form over his
shoulder and started back with his prize toward the safety
of the barn. "Some big rat you are, Your Judgess. Had yourself a nice little runabout, but now it's time to go back and
nest down with Jimmy Lee, like two mice nestled in a bur-
row."

With no one to see her, with no one watching him, with
the watchman gone and sirens in the distance not finding
this place, Isaiah Purdy returned his unruly charge to the
safety of the old farmstead. He returned Maureen DeCampe
to the hell he meant at all costs to inflict on her.

Reaching the interior of the barn, stepping over the realtor lady, he dropped DeCampe's unconscious body hard on
the earth beside Jimmy's still grinning corpse.

"A couple few bruises now. You brought 'em on yourself, dearie," he began. "Ought to speed up the process
some, like a bruised apple—jump-start this death by decaying, huh? Whataya think, Jimmy Lee?" he asked the corpse
and cackled, pleased with his own words, even though only
Jimmy could hear them.

He paused a moment to study Jimmy Lee's badly spaced,
badly cracked, yellowed teeth just back of the bloated, mot-
tled lips that'd been pulled by death into the familiar dead
man's smile. Isaiah said to the empty barn, "Always had to
fight the boy to brush his damned teeth. The one thing I
hated seeing was the boy's bad teeth. If only the fool had
listened, but guess it don't matter nary a bit now. Once't
you're dead, good teeth, bad teeth's all the same by then,
huh, Jimmy Lee?"

Isaiah turned from the corpse and its now-decayed eyes
and stepped back to the heavy barn doors, creaking now in
a growing night wind that had turned the tops of pine trees
into giant brushes that painted the underbelly of the crushing
gray clouds that had rolled in. He latched the doors with a
makeshift latch that he must replace with something
stronger—a cord of hemp wasn't going to do it. Miss High
and Mighty Realtor Nancy proved that much. He'd have to
go to work on the latch, use his Iowa ingenuity, his Yankee
know-how.

For now, he pulled the doors tight with the cord and
closed out the world to him, the judge, and Jimmy Lee. Then
he went to fashion some new leather straps. It would cost
more time, but at least his father had taught him how to cut
a tanned hide into useful strips, a job his father learned from
his father and so on down the branches of the family tree.
Those strips were usually used to beat an unruly child, but
Isaiah had found a better use indeed.

LEW Clemmens, FBI computer whiz, looked in on Jessica
to see how she was holding up and to offer his apologies
that things in Iowa had not worked out as everyone had
hoped. "Something good did come out of our liaison with
Houston, however."

"Oh, and what's that?" she asked, accepting the cup of
steaming coffee he had brought as a gift.

"I hooked up with this guy named Randy Oglesby, Houston PD's civilian computer genius, and together we managed to uncover some interesting cyber facts on the case."

She indicated the chair, and he sat down, getting comfortable. "Go on," she said, after sipping at her coffee.

"Well it was mostly Oglesby. He has inroads to the Houston court system. He's kind of a legitimatized hacker, if you
ask me. Any rate, he tapped into the fact that Judge De-
Campe had recused herself on a case recently, and this
caught his full attention, and it led him to search back for
a nine-year-old case, and guess who it involved?"

"Jimmy Lee Purdy?"

"Exactly, a case in which she put a man on death row: James Lee Purdy."

"But she recused herself from his appeal nine years later . . . makes sense. Conflict of interest."

"Yeah, Purdy's case had come up for appeal and oddly, it had fallen on her desk."

"Snafu?"

"Snafu or greased hands? Hard to tell. But coincidence, I find hard to buy."

"What're you saying, Lew?"

"From the way the papers were drawn up, Jimmy Lee asked for her, specifically requested Judge DeCampe to oversee the appeal. I know that's stupid, but people chalked it up to Jimmy Lee's having an idiot for a lawyer and a fool for a client."

"Don't tell me, he was acting as his own lawyer?"

"Yeah, and as it appears to Randy, he was orchestrating a rendezvous with DeCampe. He definitely had an unhealthy interest in her. DeCampe turned the appeal over to a Judge Parker, same one that got a warrant out for Purdy's farm."

The phone rang, and Jessica heard a man introduce himself as Judge Raymond Parker in Houston. "I have issued a warrant for search and seizure to go ahead in Iowa. Anything else I can do, please let me know."

She covered the mouthpiece a millisecond to gather her thoughts. Clearing her throat, she replied, "Yes, your honor, we received word via fax about . . . a while ago." She had had her secretary forward Parker's warrant and the federal warrant on to Virgil Gorman's office, which ought to satisfy Iowa authorities and cover her earlier lie—her jumping the judiciary gun.

"Did they find anything? Is there any news?" Parker asked.

"Their search has uncovered nothing of significance so far, and I am afraid, sir, that Judge DeCampe is not at the Iowa location."

"Have they located Purdy?"

"No, sorry once again, but should the search of the property yield any useful information, well . . . one never knows, sir."

"We appear to be back at square one, as they say." Parker then apologized for the time it had taken to draw up the warrant. "Due process . . . takes time; we rushed it through as best we could the moment I learned of your suspicions."

She again thanked him. "I understand you were the judge who handled Jimmy Lee Purdy's appeal, and that you saw the senior Mr. Purdy in your courtroom." Her last conversation with Lucas Stonecoat had provided a lot of useful information.

"That's true; I gave authorities here a few items to add to the artist's sketch you're circulating. Hope it helps catch this maniac. Frankly, it could just as well have been me targeted rather than Maureen, I suppose."

"Hard to tell. Seemed his son was fixated on her."

"If I could take her place in this nightmare . . . well, I would in a heartbeat."

"Brave of you to say so, sir." *Easy to say,* she thought.

"Do you have any idea where next you will look?"

"I've kept in touch with Houston PD and the FBI there."

"There? You mean Iowa?"

"In Iowa, yes, but also there—in Texas."

"Texas?"

"Everywhere within a fifty-mile radius of Huntsville is being closely looked at, thanks to HPD, Dr. Sanger, and Stonecoat. We're doing the same in the D.C. area, but frankly, other than that, we've come to a standstill."

"Stalemate, I see. If there is anything this office can do. . . ."

"You can be on twenty-four-hour alert, should we need another warrant in the Huntsville-Houston area. And thank you, Judge Parker."

"There's something else you should be clear on, Agent Coran."

Bored by now, she said a sleepy, "Yes?"

Judge Raymond Parker recounted how DeCampe turned

over the Purdy case to him, telling him that all she wanted was to see Purdy die in the chair. While she had to recuse herself from his appeal as a matter of course, since she'd tried him originally, she made it clear that in her opinion, there was no room for appeal of the death sentence in Purdy's case.

"She was clear on that?"

"Expressly. She said that all his Bible-thumping, born-again crap was just that: crap."

"Anything you can tell me about the old man?"

"I'd've sworn the old geezer to be, you know, harmless, but who knows these days anymore? He carried a Bible into the courtroom every day; read passages from it. Lips moved as he read. Used his fingers to help him read. Never a peep."

Another line rang. "I'm afraid I have to go, Judge Parker. Another line, and I'm hoping it will be Iowa with some good news."

"Yes, I do hope you can salvage something out of this."

"Yeah, me, too," she said to herself, after she had hung up the phone.

"What's that?" asked Clemmens who had remained seated across from her.

"Gotta get this other call, Lew. Could be important."

Lew Clemmens nodded, raised his hands, and indicated he would leave her in peace. He made his way to the door and back down the hall.

Jessica took a deep breath and prayed for good news from Iowa, that her patience would be rewarded. She could hardly stand working like this, feeling as if her hands were tied. She'd rather be in a lab or in the field. Working out of a task-force operations room was killing on the nerves.

"It's Iowa," said her secretary.

"Give me half a second to get into the ops room, and put it through there. I want this on the speakerphone for the task force to hear."

"Not a problem."

Jessica saw that Lew had disappeared, likely with a sense of feeling like the proverbial third wheel. She didn't want him or anyone else to feel that way, not on account of how she worked or failed to work. She raced after Lew, grabbed his arm, and said, "Come on, Iowa's back."

"Virgil, you mean?"

"Yeah, think so. I've got it on speaker in ops."

"Let's hear what Virgil has to say."

She nodded, and when they stepped into the ops room, she shouted for everyone's attention. "Iowa's on line one." She pressed the button, and everyone fell silent, anxious to hear if Virgil and his small army of men had come up with anything at all remotely worthwhile down on the farm.

THIRTEEN

Logic is the art of going wrong with confidence.

—JOSEPH WOOD KRUTCH

THE call was indeed from Iowa State Patrol Chief Virgil Gorman, who asked if he were speaking to Agent Jessica Coran.

"Yes, this is Dr. Coran, Chief Gorman. Everyone in my command is listening in on speakerphone. Go ahead, please."

"You sound tired, Doctor. You may want to take this news sitting down."

Jessica looked across at Richard, whose expression was meant to cheer her and encourage her. She was glad to have his support. "The better part of the team is in the room, Chief Gorman," Jessica replied. "We've all been anxiously awaiting news, so what have you got for us?" She fully expected him to say that he had located DeCampe's lifeless body.

"I've got some good news . . . some bad," he came back.

"Go on."

People in the ops room looked about at one another. "We've hit a box . . . pine wood box, Dr. Coran."

"Inside the freshly dug grave, I presume?"

"Yes, buried out back of the farmstead."

"Bastard . . ." Jessica muttered.

"Prying it open now. He's nailed it but good. Don't imagine we're going to find anyone alive. . . ."

"Oh, Jesus," groaned Jessica. Jessica saw the horror of the others in the conference room, each imagining the terror of being buried alive. Had that been the price exacted of Maureen DeCampe? Jessica tried to imagine the ordeal of such a fate. No one deserved to die in such a fashion. The entire team had been affected by the news that Gorman had brought them. With Gorman's voice gone silent, a wrenching metal sound reverberated all the way from Iowa though the wires and around the ops room: the sound of prying metal, the irritating noise of men struggling painstakingly, panting as they did battle with a coffin lid.

"Thought you'd want to be in on the opening," said Gorman. "That noise you hear is crowbars."

Then everyone in D.C. heard a collective, "Ohhh, Jeeeezuuus" float through the line. Jessica promptly asked, "What is it? She's dead, isn't she? That sonofabitch's succeeded."

"No, Dr. Coran. . . . At least not yet, he hasn't."

"No? Is she—"

"We have a body, and yes, it's a woman all right, but she's seventy if she's a day, and our collective thinking says it's Mrs. Purdy, Isaiah's wife. Apparently she died out here, and he buried her without any fanfare, and certainly without bothering authorities."

"One more charge to level at the old devil," she replied.

"We're taking the body in for an autopsy, just to be certain it's death from natural causes."

"It's what I'd do if I were there, I can assure you," she replied.

"Could be what set Purdy off," suggested Richard Sharpe, now standing alongside Jessica. "You know, loss of a lifetime partner? Does strange things to people's heads," finished Richard.

Jessica asked, "No sign whatsoever of another burial site? We had assumed he'd return to safe ground to bury his son and the judge on his farmstead."

"Maybe you're assuming too much. Or like one of my boys here said, maybe the suspect's still on his way. It's a long way for an old man to drive alone with two coffins in the rear of his van, all the way to Huntsville, then he's gotta detour to D.C. to abduct the judge. That's a g'damn marathon in itself, and this guy's no spring chicken."

"Which means he could still be on the road back to the farm. So you will keep an eye on the place, right?"

"Course we're going to keep surveillance on the place for a few days. And we're going to cover every inch of ground out here and pry open anything remotely curious, and any*one* remotely connected with the old man before we're done."

"Again, my thanks, Chief . . . and thanks for all the effort. This old man is shrewd like a fox," she said.

"Well, Iowans are known for that." She detected a note of sadness in his voice when he added, "Can't believe what this old fool's gone and done."

"He must have known we'd target his place sooner or later. He saw us coming."

"From the time line you gave me, I'd say your people have moved remarkably fast on this. Don't beat yourself up about it, Doctor, and in the meantime, I'll be in touch. Let you know if anything new develops at this end."

"And we'll keep you apprised, Chief. Again, thanks."

"Sure . . . don't mention it."

Blind alley, Jessica thought, as she hung up the phone.

"LEW," Jessica called out, startling Clemmens. "I want to know what all was said at Jimmy Lee's trial."

"You mean his appeal?"

"No, his trial, what? Nine, ten years ago?"

"A transcript that old may be hard to come by."

"Tap into our friend in Houston. You said he had some cyber inroads in the system there."

"Yeah, I can put him onto the relic stuff, which could be complicated. We can only pray Houston's up to date with scanning that stuff to disk and putting it into electronic files."

"Fact is, Houston's one of the leaders in putting old cases onto computer disk. But are you saying it could be inaccessible?"

"Buried in a hard file or on microfiche someplace, yes. Meantime, I can track down the appeal transcript. It shouldn't be tough to get it electronically. It's a matter of public record. Besides, you'll want both for what you gotta do."

"I think it's time we learned a great deal more about Jimmy Lee Purdy," suggested Sharpe. "Perhaps it will indicate our next move."

"Oh, and what's that?" Shannon Keyes joined them. "Are you actually proposing we do a profile on a dead man? Jimmy Lee Purdy?"

"So far as we know from people around Judge DeCampe, there's no known public pronouncement out of the old man. He was never arrested for so much as disturbing the peace, and he never disrupted the court proceedings," Sharpe countered. "Suppose the old man's driven by his dead son's motives now?"

Keyes shook her head. "Never a word out of the old man? He has no brain of his own? Whataya want to do, provide him with a defense? My dead son made me do it?"

"From all we've learned, the elder Purdy never said word one during all the court appearances he made," said Jessica. "Maybe Richard is onto something here. Stonecoat and Sanger both mentioned that Jimmy Lee was pulling strings from his prison cell."

"So . . . you're supposing that the old man is doing just what his son wanted, fulfilling Jimmy Lee's last wishes?" asked Keyes.

"Parents are funny that way, yes," replied Richard. "So perhaps if we understand Jimmy Lee better, then we'll better understand his father Isaiah and his plan and maybe his moves."

Jessica jumped in, saying, "We've got to understand as much about Jimmy Lee's psyche as possible, then maybe . . . maybe we'll have some idea what the old man is thinking, and if we can determine what he is thinking then . . . maybe . . ."

"Good strategy," Keyes finally relented, agreeing. "Let me help you with it."

"We need to know about every and any contact whatsoever that either of the Purdys may have had in any way with Judge DeCampe," said Jessica.

Keyes nodded, a finger playing with the dimple in her chin. "Yes, perhaps something there will give up an overlooked clue."

"The sins of the son shall the father inherit," added Richard. "Kind of a twist on an old theme."

"More a reversal," countered Jessica.

Keyes bit her pouting lower lip and added, "Perhaps you're right, Sharpe, perhaps the son's transgressions can tell us what this old fool is up to."

"And maybe where he is?" Richard volunteered.

"First we need the transcripts. Lew? What're you standing around for?" asked Jessica.

Lew's eyebrows raised in consternation. "On it, Jess."

J. T. found Jessica still working out of the ops room, looking tired and pale. He brought in fast food from a Chinese restaurant, and as he unpacked the little boxed dinners filled with moo goo gai pan, sweet and sour chicken, beef lo mein, spring rolls, and egg rolls, he informed Jessica that Marsden's story about euthanizing his dog and flipping out as a result had checked out.

"I'll be damned." A wide smile replaced her glum features.

"He did leave some serious bills and confused people in his wake, but he's not wanted for murder or anything like that, thank God."

They all had a light laugh over the Marsden story.

"But Jess, there's something else you need to know."

She stared at J. T. "Lay it on me. What is it?"

"It's about the Claude Lightfoot case."

"Go on."

"Hosea Crooms, our guy in the field asking all the questions, phoned in."

"OK . . . and what'd Hosea say?" Jessica pictured the enormous black agent.

"Seems our snitch, the guy who's been feeding us information about the Lightfoot case, is dead . . . apparent overdose of J&B Scotch and quaaludes."

"Malcolm McArthur, dead?"

"One and the same."

"Only one who was talking in the whole damned county."

" 'Less I miss my guess, someone decided he'd already talked to Hosea long enough."

"Murdered?"

"Yeah, Hosea suspects murder. The scene was a foul mess. It could've been he tore up the place in a drunken stupor like the M.E. wants to believe, but he spilled an awful lot of the J&B."

"How many bottles?"

"M.E. said he consumed three 1.5-liter bottles of the stuff along with enough quaaludes to choke an elephant."

"Sonsabitches silenced him."

"That'd be my guess."

The phone rang, and Keyes caught it. "Jessica, it's Iowa calling back."

"Put it on the con," she replied. In a moment, she asked, "Chief Gorman, what news have you?"

"We got a new wrinkle here, Dr. Coran."

"Shoot."

"Two things, actually. A note left with the wife with a biblical injunction we're all familiar with: an eye for an eye, a tooth for a tooth."

"We'll want it sent here for analysis, Chief."

"Got it."

"And the other thing?"

Gorman breathed deeply before speaking. "One of my cruisers was sitting atop a For Sale sign, doctor. A RE/MAX sign. They didn't discover it until they backed off it. Sorry, but that means Purdy unloaded the place before he left."

"How long?"

"The Purdy farm has been sold for a little over a month, according to our local realtor."

"He sold the place? Over a month ago?"

" 'Bout how long the wife has been under the ground, according to our M.E."

"Think I'm getting the picture."

"You can rest assured we'll check every possible lead here locally. Let you know anything else we uncover as we get it. My guess is the wife's death pulled out some sort of linchpin in the man's head, probably about the time his son was to be executed. Losing both of them at once like that...but then I'll leave that sort of guesswork to the shrinks. Still, I imagine he lit out for Huntsville just after burying his wife and selling the old place."

"So he'd been planning this for at least a month, the abduction, all of it."

"Appears so, yes."

"He must've been disappointed to learn that Judge DeCampe was no longer in Houston," she replied. "He went there to pick up two pine boxes and one body. He meant to find her and abduct her in Houston."

"But he had to detour and delay, come back entirely across the country to D.C. to find her and attack her there."

Keyes, listening in, said, "The man's a walking textbook definition of obsessive-compulsive behavior."

"Stalking with a capital *S,* yes," agreed Sharpe, "but it's not for sexual motives."

Gorman cleared his throat. "Well . . . seeing as how he sold the place, he never intended using it again, so he will have had to hole up somewhere else. We're going to be on any relatives in the area, you can be certain."

"Wait a minute," Jessica said, a flash of light illuminating the darkness. "We all agree that it stands to reason—given his selling his property—that he planned to abduct De-Campe in Houston, right? And if he had abducted her there, she'd be close to where he picked up his son's remains."

Richard picked up on her thread. "Which stands to reason he'd then do it here, in or around D.C."

"Sounds logical," said Gorman from Iowa.

"Following that logic," said Keyes, "hell . . . yes, if he means to bury her with his son, an eye for an eye, then it damn well may be in our own neck of the woods, Jessica. Somewhere in the vicinity of where he abducted her—in the D.C. area."

"And all this time we've been digging in the wrong place. . . ." muttered Gorman, sounding disgruntled.

"Literally diggin' in the wrong place," added J. T. with a shake of his chopsticks.

"What do you do when you need a place to stay, but you don't know the area?" asked Jessica.

"Talk to the locals," replied Gorman.

"Yeah ... like the local realtors. You said he sold it through RE/MAX?"

"Yeah, right, RE/MAX."

"Make the max of your real estate with RE/MAX." She thanked Vigil Gorman and hung up.

J. T. stared at her, knowing her mind was racing. "Whataya think, Jess?"

"I think if you're satisfied with a service provided in Iowa, you're likely to look for the same service provider in the District of Columbia."

"RE/MAX?"

"RE/MAX!"

J. T. picked up another ringing line and after a moment said, "Hey Jess, it's your reporter friend O'Brien on the line."

"Not now!"

"Says he has something pertains to the case."

Jessica reluctantly took the call. She had to bite her lip to keep from cursing O'Brien out. Reporter O'Brien's story, in which Jessica had been quoted as calling the killer a sexual pervert, had by now made several of the wire services, and it had also traveled the continent and back again via television newscasts.

"You asshole, O'Brien," she burst out. "Do you have any idea the light your asinine story has put me in with my superiors?"

"If you'll stop barking long enough, I have a bone to throw your way, Agent Coran."

Jessica closed her luminous eyes and willed her anger down. She again bit her lip and fumed a moment in silence, saying nothing in return for now, knowing that if she did, she would explode.

"Aren't you going to ask what I have?" O'Brien teased, and she pictured his smug, leprechaun grin. All he needed was a green hat and vest.

"O'Brien, I've been ordered to not speak with the press whatsoever during the duration of the DeCampe Missing Persons case. Do you understand that?"

"Your boss put a gag order on you?"

"Do not characterize this as a gag order, and nothing I say to you from now on is for public record unless I say so, O'Brien. Is that clear?"

"Perhaps not clear but . . . but it is interesting."

If she could reach through the line, she'd strangle him. She never knew when he was kidding and when he was serious. She wondered if it were an Irish trait. "All right, damnit, what's this bone you're so generously sharing?"

"It's a doozy-do, believe me! You sitting down?"

"Spill it or get off the line, O'Brien! I'm working here."

"All right, all right . . . I have a letter *purporting* to be from the creep that abducted Judge DeCampe postmarked Nokesville, Virginia."

She dared not breathe; she felt stunned, as if slapped. "You what?"

"You heard me. And I came directly to you with it."

"What's it say? No, never mind. I want to see it; it's got to be authenticated."

"I think it's authentic, all right."

"How can you tell? Does the letter make demands?"

"Some, yeah, but not a single reference to money."

"What kind of demands does he make?"

"He wants us to retract some of the things we've said about him based on your FBI profile of him."

"I didn't give you a profile, O'Brien. I gave you a handful of words. Words that anyone who's read your paper could repeat verbatim. So don't waste my time. Time is a commodity I don't have much of right now." She thought of how time was running out for Kim Desinor and De-Campe.

"Jessica, it's him. I know it."

"How? How do you know it?"

"I don't know. You'll just have to take my word for it until you see it yourself. Something . . . just so right-on *chilling* about it."

"Where is it now?"

"Under glass in my editor's office. We've made some blowup shots, and we've called in a graphologist to tell us what she can about the handwriting."

"What're you guys up to? Trying to do our job for us?"

"Do you want to see it or not?"

"We're on our way. Be right there."

Jessica sent two agents to Nokesville, Virginia, to investigate. Then a wave of fear for Kim washed over her.

Jessica wished she could confer with the psychic FBI detective, realizing that Kim might well get some images from the document if she handled it. Psychometric reading was her specialty. However, in Kim's current condition, she was hardly going to be doing any readings, especially in a public place like a newspaper office.

The others on the team had begun to ask about Kim, and Jessica was running out of excuses. Kim had not been seen by any of them for over twenty-four hours, and there was some notion circulating that she was not well.

"Is everything all right?" asked Keyes, who had just returned. She stared at Jessica, as if studying her breaking point.

"It's Dr. Desinor . . . Kim. She's . . . she needs me. I'm going to see her before going to see O'Brien."

"Sounds to me like you may want someone along," suggested Keyes.

Jessica considered this. "All right, if it suits you."

"You told O'Brien that you'd be right over," J. T. told Jessica.

"I know what I told O'Brien, but I need to touch base with Kim, and maybe, just maybe," she said, turning to Keyes, "you can be of help." She called over to Richard, who was busy following up leads on a telephone, asking, "Will you call O'Brien and tell him we'll be delayed but that we're on our way?"

He replied, "Of course, and I'll meet you there when I get free."

Outside they found the car that had been assigned to Jessica for her personal use for as long as she remained in D.C.

on the case. They climbed in, and Jessica tore off and out of the underground lot, tires barking as if to speak her agitation.

"What's up?" asked Keyes.

"The *Washington Post* claims they have an authentic letter from DeCampe's abductor. However, he makes no ransom demands."

"Shit . . . if only it were about money," said Shannon. "But I actually meant what's up with Dr. Desinor?"

Jessica had not confided all the details of Kim Desinor's illness to Santiva or anyone other than Richard Sharpe and J. T. Now a twinge of doubt invaded her mind as to Keyes's interest, her motives. Jessica knew that being tired clouded one's judgment, and earlier she had had no such thoughts about Keyes, but now she did. She was unsure why. Some nagging little voice told her to not completely trust Keyes to keep a confidence, so she avoided the question. "Sounds like from what O'Brien said that Purdy wants to know how we dare call him a sex pervert. Meanwhile, we're tracing the letter from its postmark."

"Are you intentionally avoiding the question about your friend because I'm a shrink? Trust me, I am only interested in helping, Jessica."

Jessica asked Keyes point-blank, "Tell me, Dr. Keyes, did Santiva put you on this case to watchdog me and to report back my team's every move?"

"That's not entirely true, no, but he did ask me for a special report. You have good instincts, Dr. Coran."

"I thought so."

"But I'm not spying on you."

"Fair enough. Thanks for the honesty."

"So how can I help your friend Desinor?"

Jessica took in a deep breath of air. "I'm not so sure you can. Not sure any of us can."

The lights of Washington Memorial Hospital shone in the night sky ahead of them. A siren wail sounded. "Kim's something of an empath, and it takes a terrible toll on her when she does a psychometric reading."

"I can only imagine the depth of her feeling."

"This case in particular has had a dire effect on her sense of well-being."

Keyes nodded repeatedly. "Some places in the human psyche no one should go, not even by proxy."

"She once told me about the suffering she'd had to endure in Houston, Texas, when she worked the Snatcher case there; the victim was a young boy, who somehow sent out messages—psychic images—of what he was enduring. She received every detail, and it still haunts her to this day. After that, she worked a case with me in Philadelphia, and it took an additional toll on her."

Keyes sighed heavily and fidgeted in the passenger seat. "And now this."

"Now this. I think she may very well be getting images of what's happening to Maureen DeCampe—delayed images."

"Or subconsciously blocked images from her earlier reading of the crime scene," suggested Keyes. "Must be truly difficult for her, indeed."

"Difficult isn't the word for it; it's abhorrent to the tenth power. A lesser person, I suspect, it could kill over time."

"I suspect you're right."

Outside the cocoon of the car, the lights of Washington, D.C., gave way to the gloomy darkness of a spiritless gray sky, the blackness seeming to press down around the car they shared. Jessica parked and they hurried toward the doors.

Inside the hospital, Dr. Shoate told Jessica that Kim Desinor was conscious only for short periods of time, and when conscious, she insisted on no visitors other than her fiancé. "She simply wants to die at this point. She doesn't want anything else."

"You stay here," Jessica told Keyes. "If she'll talk to anyone, it'll be me."

Keyes nodded, frowned, and clasped her hands together. "I'm sure the last thing she needs is an introduction to a stranger who happens to be a psychiatrist."

"She's a shrink herself, along with being psychic, so she has a healthy respect for what a good therapist can do, believe me. Once I get to the bottom of this, maybe we can talk introductions, and who knows, maybe she could benefit from seeing you—professionally."

"Shrink, heal thyself, you mean?"

"Something like that."

"It's not uncommon that a psychiatrist needs psychiatric care. We're only human, after all."

Jessica left Keyes standing in the hallway outside Kim's door at Intensive Care. Coming out was Detective Alex Sincebaugh of the Baltimore police, Kim's lover and fiancé, who spent every weekend with her when he drove in from Baltimore, where he worked homicide. They'd met in New Orleans, where Sincebaugh had combined on the Heartthrob Murders in the French Quarter. Kim and Jessica had teamed with Sincebaugh to bring an end to the killer's career there.

Sincebaugh had fallen in love with Kim, and he had moved across the country to be close to her. He stared Jessica in the eyes now and said, "I knew you people would kill her one day."

"Alex, I'm sorry for what's happening to her as much as you. No one could have foreseen this."

"She's literally dying of no apparent cause, but we both know what the cause is, don't we? What the fuck're you people doing about locating and putting an end to this case involving Judge DeCampe?"

She put out a hand to him, but he brushed past, saying, "I've got to call in. Tell them I'm taking time off. I'm going to be with her night and day." He then rushed away, shaken to the core.

Jessica stepped into the darkened ICU, and seeing the usually vibrant, strong woman reduced to a shell of herself gave Jessica a chill. She went to Kim, whose lesions were covered in bandages, Dr. Shoate using his best elixirs on the continuing decay spots. Shoate whispered now in Jessica's ear that the problem seemed to be arrested at one point, but on further monitoring, this proved false. Nothing seemed to be working.

Kim looked up at Jessica, her eyes blinking. Jessica tearfully said hello.

No answer, only an attempt at a crooked smile.

Jessica wanted to break something. "Kim, we've got to talk. You're scaring me with this bullshit. You've gotta help me here. What the hell am I missing? You've got to pull yourself out of this."

"Now that you've seen me again," Kim croaked out each word separately, "please leave, Jessica. I don't feel up to seeing anyone."

"Kim, you're too strong for this, to let this happen. This is ridiculous. Fight back . . . fight back."

"Please, Jess . . . just go."

Jessica held firmly to Kim's bandaged hand now. "I wanted to come and reassure you, Kim. We are so close to finding and putting an end to Judge DeCampe's abduction. You are going to be all right, Kim. I'm going to make sure you're all right."

"I thank you, Jess, for caring so much." Her eyes fluttered, and she looked as if she might go back into a sleep. Dr. Shoate checked her vital signs.

"You're wasting time here," said Alex Sincebaugh now, in Jessica's ear. "Every minute wasted is a minute that Kim can't afford to lose. Now, go, Dr. Coran, and do your job. Plug into those FBI resources at your beck and call."

Jessica silently cursed and thought how the considerable resources of the FBI had been put to work, but how little had come of it all. She wanted to pound her fist through a wall.

"I've become DeCampe, Jessica," muttered Kim. "Whatever is going on, wherever she is, she's alive, but she's starving to death and she's decaying."

More than ever now, Jessica hated the news that had come out of Iowa. Had they found DeCampe's body, it would have been at least closure, and then Kim would be out of this horrid danger as well.

Jessica's cellular phone went off, and she rushed from the room, leaving Alex Sincebaugh, Kim, and Dr. Shoate behind. The call was from Richard, who said, "They really do have something useful over here at the *Post*, Jessica. You really ought to be here."

Jessica looked up to see Keyes staring at her as an idea

formed in her mind. "What about the power of suggestion? If Kim is told we've located DeCampe alive and we have her in protective custody now, will that help her condition?"

"It's possible," replied Keyes.

"Are you saying that the deception is worth a shot?"

"Yes, it is."

"Anything at this point."

"It would appear so, Jessica."

Jessica returned to Kim's bedside and told her, "That call, Kim . . . we've located her," Jessica lied. "Iowa authorities have found a grave site on the old man's property and have recovered her body. It's over."

Kim took in a deep breath of air. "I want to go home then. Sit out on my porch in my rocker . . . stare at the stars. Thank God . . . thank God . . . now maybe I can heal. No one knows how to treat empathic stigmatalike occurrences like this, Jess."

"I know."

"Dr. Shoate has done all he can. Bless him."

"I had hoped he could arrest the physical problem while you dealt with the mental issues. I've called in a psychiatrist, too, Kim, a Dr. Shannon Keyes, to help you with the recuperation process. I won't let you be alone with this."

Kim somehow managed a weak laugh and said, "You mean friends don't let friends drive themselves to decay? We could call that a new high in friendship."

Shannon Keyes cautiously joined them as Jessica had asked her to do, and Jessica explained the psychosomatic syndrome that her best friend was suffering under. "Fortressing yourself up and being alone," Keyes said, "is not going to be as helpful as drawing on others like your friend here for help, Dr. Desinor. Let us help."

"Do you two think you can help?"

"Yes, we do," Keyes firmly replied. "You'll need a lot of support now that this is over."

As Dr. Shoate was changing the bandage, Shannon Keyes now saw the disfigurement to the right cheek. The sight made Keyes swallow hard; she bit her lower lip to keep from gasping.

Kim had similar bruises and discoloration at each wrist,

the abdomen area, the right breast, the ankles, and the knees.

"How did you locate DeCampe? What was her condition? How alive is she?" asked Kim.

"DeCampe suffered horribly, just as you. She was dehydrated, starving, and decaying . . . decaying—"

"Alive, decaying alive," said Kim. "As I said all along. Her killer wanted to watch her decay alive. He somehow managed to cause decay in her where he kept her."

"Alive . . . yeah . . . alive, and she's going to get well, Kim. Early reports confirm this."

"Great . . . great news."

"Now you can put your mind to stopping this thing in you."

She nodded. "My mind just has to put a stop to this. I have always feared this—that my mind would one day become my worst enemy, that it would in the end destroy me."

Jessica again saw that her friend was weak, terribly weak. "Now maybe you can keep something down?"

"Some liquids . . . nothing solid."

"Hell," joked Jessica, "you've got that on IV." She pointed to the IV glucose drip.

Kim managed a smile at this. "Maybe some chicken soup."

"We've got to go now, Kim, but we'll be back, soon."

Outside, Jessica began to cry, seeing what a skeleton Kim had become in this short time since the parking garage reading. "She looks so emaciated."

"But she was boosted by our story. This could be a turning point for her."

"Yeah, until she turns on a TV and learns the truth."

On the ride to the *Washington Post* offices, Jessica and Shannon were made aware of just how far along Kim Desinor's "psychic" wounds were, as the smell of decay filled the automobile. It had attached itself to them, to their clothes, and they simultaneously began wiping their noses, when Jessica said, "My God, what if Desinor is right about what's going on with DeCampe? That she is literally being killed via decay?"

"I can't begin to imagine such a horrid death."

FOURTEEN

Perfect order is the forerunner of perfect horror.

—CARLOS FUENTES

TWENTY minutes down the Beltway, and Jessica turned into the office of the *Washington Post*. With Keyes, they walked into the *Washington Post* newsroom, calling out for Tim O'Brien. He shouted back from the rear, now angry with Jessica.

"Where the hell've you been?"

Jessica told him in no uncertain terms that their delay had been over a life-and-death situation.

"I'd like to hear about it some time," he replied.

"Not from me, you won't."

They stepped into a private conference room, where Richard Sharpe stood and pulled out a seat for Jessica and then for Shannon.

O'Brien introduced himself and his city editor, a man named Al Cirillo, and he then proceeded to introduce them all to Carolyn Nagby, who might have looked comfortable behind a desk at any library. She was O'Brien's expert handwriting analysis person, a graphologist. Using a magnifying glass, she was scanning the letter still under glass. "No one's been allowed to touch the letter, not since the moment I realized what I had," O'Brien told them.

On viewing the letter, both the one under glass and its blowup counterpart thrown against a wall by an overhead projector, Jessica learned the author wanted to say a good deal more than how dare they. Keyes wryly said, "Says here, Jessica, that you're a harlot, a jezebel, the daughter of Cain, a coward who wouldn't dare call him a sex pervert to his face." The letter threatened that Jessica Coran would be his next victim for slandering him, for making him out to be a sexual deviant.

In the letter, the writer revealed a great deal of himself, Nagby told the others. Then the expert in graphology added, "He makes a number of biblical references before getting down to his immediate message: an eye for an eye, and a notation on Romans 7:24–5."

"Romans 7:24–5. Somebody get me a Bible, now!" said Jessica.

"We've already run it down," said O'Brien. "Having been raised on the Bible, I thought I recognized it. Let me tell you, it's scary to contemplate what this woman must be going through with this guy as her keeper." He lifted a large Bible and pushed it down the length of the table to Jessica. "I keep it at the office for just such occasions."

Jessica and Shannon saw that it was opened to Romans, and each found the passage, and O'Brien said in his most booming voice, sounding like a minister, "This is from the epistles of Paul, written to the saints in Rome around A.D. 57."

"I know the passage," said Shannon Keyes. She then read it aloud: " 'Oh unhappy and pitiable and wretched man that I am! Who will release and deliver me from this body of death that is my shackle? Oh, thank God! Whose will is won through Jesus Christ, the Anointed, our Lord! So then indeed I, of myself with the mind and heart, serve the Law of God, but with the flesh, the law of sin.' "

"What the hell does that mean?" asked Jessica. "Serve the law of sin?"

Keyes explained its significance and meaning. "It seems benign enough," she began, "but it has had conflicting interpretations."

"I'll say," added O'Brien.

"Most interpretations sugarcoat it," agreed Shannon.

Jessica repeated the last phrase, " ' . . . but with the flesh, the law of sin.' What is the literal meaning of that? What does that mean, Shannon?"

"Render unto Caesar."

"Yeah, I get it, but I thought they were talking about taxes."

They examined the passage further, and O'Brien said, "I've sent for a Bible scholar, a real expert, a priest to verify this, but God help me if I don't believe this madman has not only buried her alive but buried her strapped to his decaying son, likely in the same coffin."

"Christ, how do you get that from this biblical passage?" asked Jessica, feeling ill at the mental image O'Brien had created in her brain, Kim Desinor's sores flashing like red flags in her mind's eye.

"It comes out of my interpretation of the passage."

"Well let's hope you're entirely off base."

A knock at the door, and they were joined by a man in the priesthood, a Father Joseph Pinwaring. He looked like the actor Max Von Sydow, and he also looked completely lost and out of place here at the *Washington Post*. "I am here, Tim, just as you requested," he said, taking O'Brien's hand and firmly shaking it.

O'Brien thanked the minister profusely for coming so quickly. They obviously had some history between them. After introductions, the Bible scholar set immediately to work, his dark, piercing eyes instantly fascinated with the selection of Romans 7:24-5.

"It's a highly unusual citing, even for a clergyman, much less a lay person."

He hemmed and hawed and read and reread the selection, trying to place it in the context of the letter, and what he knew of the case from the papers, and from his young friend, O'Brien. "Highly unusual," he repeated, looking dumbfounded, snatching his wire-rimmed glasses off and cleaning them with a handkerchief. "I'm surprised. It's a passage usually . . . that is normally left alone . . . a sleeping dog in the literature, you might say. One of those footnotes we'd all as soon forget."

"Really, no kidding, Father. Why do you think I called you down here? None of us knows what to make of it." O'Brien's remark must have sounded more caustic than he'd intended, as it made the white-haired clergyman stare at him and half grin. "Tim, you were always the boy in the choir I worried most about."

Jessica said, "We're all on edge, sir." She could not believe she was making apology for O'Brien. "You can imagine the frustration since the abduction. It has taken a terrible toll on Tim's pleasant side."

Laughing lightly at this, Father Pinwaring seemed to take no offense. He continued on, while nervously pulling at his bearded chin and caressing his throat. He stood as tall as Jessica and had piercing black eyes with multicolored specks that looked like shards of broken glass meant to surprise and dazzle as they reflected any color. "Little is spoken about it," he softly began, "but the Romans, well known for creating horrid ways to destroy any enemy to the state, refined various methods of impaling and crucifixion. That much is general knowledge, yes?"

The others nodded almost in unison.

"But the Romans reserved one method for convicted murderers," Pinwaring added with a sad shake of the head, his luminous eyes now downcast, taking on a deep sorrow.

Jessica asked, "And you believe this is what the passage is about?"

"I do indeed."

"And that method of punishment?" asked Jessica.

"They would strap the murderer to his victim."

"Tie the dead man to the living?"

"Precisely, usually onto the back. Why? So that the poor devil could not possibly undo the decaying dead man or woman from his flesh, and once the dead flesh began to eat away at the living flesh, believe me, the murderer made every attempt to free himself of the 'monkey on his back' because not only did his life depend upon it, so did his sanity and level of pain."

"He was literally eaten alive by decay," added O'Brien.

"Can't imagine a more horrible way to die," said Keyes, going pale. She exchanged a look with Jessica, both of them realizing what Kim had been saying all along.

Jessica, who had seen every kind of evil imaginable, now

tried to imagine how Old Man Purdy might exact such a price from Judge Maureen DeCampe. The thought made her want to vomit, but she pushed on, considering O'Brien's take: *Bury her alive with Jimmy Lee's rotting corpse.* Obviously, O'Brien thought no one would believe him unless his interpretation of the passage was in sync with and supported by a man of the cloth.

"But then . . . why did the old man take two coffins from the Huntsville Penitentiary?" Jessica asked.

"Perhaps he's dug a hole for himself as well, for when it's over," suggested Keyes.

O'Brien disagreed. "A hole for himself. Not likely if he's threatening to make Jessica his *next* victim."

"Hence death on my shoulder," Pinwaring now said. Pinwaring, a stoop-shouldered, once tall man had been made slighter by age. His large chin and long jaw set him apart. He replaced his glasses and again studied the letter and the reference from the Holy Book. He next snatched the glasses off again and punctuated his remarks with the pointed ends. "It's where the phrase *monkey on my back* originates—the black monkey being the decaying corpse—a euphemism for the most cruel of capital punishment man has ever devised. I mean compare this slow cruelty to a lethal injection or the electric chair. There is no comparison."

"But Dr. Keyes here says the passage was about rendering that pound of flesh unto Caesar—that which is his, taxes, all that," Jessica countered, wanting to believe the old minister wrong.

"Well . . . yes. . . . And that has been a time-worn and I suspect more easily palatable interpretation; unfortunately, the truth of the matter is this is a direct reference to the Roman method of *just* retribution for murder—an ancient concept even to the Romans—to punish in the manner most fitting."

"How's that?" asked Richard Sharpe.

"In murdering someone, you consign him to the worms— decay. So how should you be punished but by decay? Most people are far more agreeable to the kinder interpretation of this passage, but this version is quite within the realm of the

Roman world. Notice it does not refer to it as the law of men nor the law of man, but rather the law of sin."

"Yeah, that's what struck me," agreed Jessica, finding that she liked Pinwaring.

"Given what I know of original texts—I've studied in Rome—I have to disagree with those who soft-sell the passage. My take on the passage makes the most hardened criminal grimace with the thought of such a horrid punishment: being killed by the decay of a rotting corpse from which you have no hope of escape until you, too, rot to death, but you do it *alive.* Trust me, being buried alive, able soon to die of asphyxiation, while horrible in itself, is a cakewalk to this sort of end."

"God, and I thought all the really bad and horrible stuff was caused by modern-day stressors, the times, alienation, disenfranchisement, big cities, isolation in an uncaring, jaded *modern* world," said Sharpe.

Pinwaring vigorously shook his head. "Those who fail to understand the lessons of the past are doomed to commit its errors over and over, and perhaps those who do understand the lessons of the past are doomed to repeat them as well. I'm not sure. Jury is still out on that one, but in the Roman mind, the laws governing murder—the most inescapably despicable act on the planet—were quite simple, really: If you bring on someone else's decay—the pollution of the temple of the soul of another human being—then you repay murder in exact kind. In fact, they believed a murderer paid over and over throughout eternity; that there was no forgiveness for a capital crime, and there was no escaping one's punishment for the greatest crime man can commit."

"A far cry from our judicial system today," complained O'Brien. "Christianity's influence."

"Perhaps we need a little more Roman thinking in our courts today," Jessica agreed.

"Can I quote you on that, Jessica?" asked O'Brien.

"No, you may not. I've got enough problems left over from the last time you quoted me."

"Hey, that story brought our man out, didn't it?" asked

O'Brien. "Just as you had hoped, if I don't miss my guess."

"No comment."

"Fair enough."

"You realize that if this madman from Iowa is reading his Bible literally, he will interpret the passage in the same sense that I have," said Pinwaring.

A silence fell over them all. They were left alone with a terrible image and their thoughts.

Pinwaring added, "While this epistle has been interpreted in various ways throughout biblical history, the particularly pernicious interpretation that troubles you all so greatly now is a viable one for anyone reading the passage. It is perhaps a most twisted version of 'render onto Caesar that which is his'—your very flesh if you are found guilty of the law of ultimate sin. In other words, when convicted of murder in Rome, Caesar exacted a horrifying price. The Roman authorities saw to it that a killer's sinful flesh was baptized in the decay of his victim, and to assure this, the convicted was lashed hand to hand, foot to foot, cheek to cheek, if not to the back. Believe me, the Romans experimented with every conceivable position—some quite crude, to be sure."

"Where was this done?"

"Always out in the sun, in an arena or plaza as an object lesson for the populace."

"So barbaric," said Richard Sharpe.

The graphologist, Nagby, began to squirm and hold back her last meal. Finally, she jumped up and rushed from the room, threatening to vomit, no doubt in search of the ladies' room.

"Before there was Nazi Germany, there was Rome," commented O'Brien. "Absolute power corrupts absolutely."

Pinwaring sadly added, "I'm afraid your worst fears may be ongoing as we speak, that Judge DeCampe's abductor means to make his victim slowly, painfully, and torturously decay to death via the decaying remains of his son."

"It fits with every step he has taken." Jessica admitted aloud what they were all hopefully thinking: "If she is alive, she must be going insane."

Everyone pictured DeCampe still alive, still enduring this horrendous torture. It had only been two days since the abduction.

The thought of Kim learning the truth frightened her now more than ever. How soon would Kim come to the truth? That DeCampe was indeed alive, yes, but also strapped to a decaying corpse.

"God, I hope we're wrong," moaned Shannon Keyes, whom Jessica guessed to be thinking in the same direction as she. "I mean, since the guy's kid was electrocuted in the Texas chair, why wouldn't the old man retaliate in kind? I mean Marsden said the old man had a cattle prod, right? And . . . and he did use it, didn't he? Used electricity to overpower her. She's likely already been zapped and fried by this SOB."

"It would be a merciful alternative to . . . to slowly decaying to death, lashed to a corpse," Jessica agreed. Still, she could not get Pinwaring's words out of her head long enough to believe in Keyes's alternative theory, and she guessed that not even Keyes was buying it.

"To carry out his plan, he has to have a place where he feels safe, at some distance from the rest of the world," Jessica said aloud. "He's had to vacate Iowa, and he was wily enough to know that it would be the first place we'd descend upon once we learned about his son's recent execution and the part DeCampe played in it, his going there for the body, and taking away two coffins with him. So he's had to have planned out carefully where he is holding Judge DeCampe, and it will have to be an isolated piece of real estate."

"Real estate somewhere in the vicinity of D.C.?" asked O'Brien.

"We suspect so. Listen, we've got to get back to the command post, O'Brien, Father Pinwaring. Give our regards to Dr. Nagby." Jessica ushered Richard and Shannon out, whispering in Keyes's ear, "No wonder Kim is still suffering psychic hurts."

Keyes replied, "DeCampe is still alive and still suffering."

"Undergoing Roman justice, I should say," added Richard.

"Vengeance."

"Unnatural revenge if ever there was."

They made their way back to the waiting car. Jessica said, "This means Kim's going to continue to weaken along with DeCampe, should she find out the truth, and perhaps even if she doesn't."

"I fear you're right," Keyes agreed.

Jessica explained to Richard what had occurred at the hospital with Kim. "Has she any chance of pulling out of it?" he asked.

"There's always a chance," she replied.

Keyes added, "I'm sorry about your friend."

"People can die from so-called psychosomatic wounds, can't they?" asked Sharpe.

"They can . . . and they have," replies Keyes.

Jessica had read of documented cases. Her heart felt like the proverbial dead lump of coal so often referred to—cold and hard. She feared to allow herself to feel, and she feared what her mind proposed.

FIFTEEN

Unfathomable to mere mortals is the lore of fiends.

—NATHANIEL HAWTHORNE

WHEN Jessica, Richard, and Shannon returned to the operations room, Jessica called the task force together, saying, "It's a new game, people." Jessica paced the ops room. She told them what had come of the visit to the *Washington Post* newsroom, cursing under her breath as she finished. "This SOB sold his house through RE/MAX, they tell us from Iowa. The letter to the *Post* was mailed from Virginia. We're going to concentrate our search in the D.C. area and all around D.C. That's every state surrounding us: Maryland, Virginia, Pennsylvania, New York. We canvas every RE/MAX realty in the book within a hundred mile radius of D.C."

"What about other realtors?" asked one of the team.

"RE/MAX. . . . RE/MAX! That's our connection. Get hold of the 800 RE/MAX number, and put them to work. Chief Gorman in Iowa said his guys had run over a For Sale sign, said it was RE/MAX. Suppose he shopped RE/MAX for his safe location? Suppose he has one of those telephone book–sized available listings through RE/MAX, which he planned to use in Houston but then had to use in our area instead. Suppose the g'damn old fox never left the D.C. area?"

"Else he had a place here all along," suggested Keyes. "We should call Iowa back, have them run down if the family had any land holding in the D.C. area."

"We'll do that; in the meantime, we have to contact every realtor in the area."

"That's a lot of real estate offices to cover," replied J. T.

"Lew, get on the police band and ask after any crimes that might have a connection with real estate in any way, shape, or form in the past, say, seventy-two hours."

"He could be in Virginia, Pennsylvania, New York. We've got to alert authorities in all the surrounding jurisdictions," said Keyes.

"Then let's do it. DeCampe is dead if she spends one more night in this man's control. As it is, if Father Pinwaring is correct, she may have already gone insane."

"I hope your hunch is right then," Keyes said, their eyes meeting.

"I know I'm right. Logically, if he's sold the farm in Iowa, purchased a brand-new, wide-bodied van for the express purpose of committing this crime, then he had no plans to return to Iowa. He had to've taken time to familiarize himself with some close by 'safe place' to take her."

"Then we need to check out realtors and real estate sales and rentals—yes, rentals most of all," Richard Sharpe concurred.

Tim O'Brien stood in the doorway and shouted, "We've got experts in real estate on the paper, Jess."

"What the hell're you doing here? This is a secure area, O'Brien."

"I only want to help."

"You only want a story."

"Damnit, Jess, don't you think I feel for this woman? After what Pinwaring said? Look, our guys in real estate know the territory from here to Nokesville, believe me. I can get them looking into it. They'd have some good ideas on just how to proceed, who to start with, where to go from there. I can call them. Tell them to concentrate attention on RE/MAX, if you'll let us help. Maybe our guys can unearth something. Who knows? Maybe this guy Purdy put in an ad a month ago in search of a secluded place, or perhaps he saw one in the realty section of the *Post*."

Jessica sighed in response, and saying nothing but saying everything with her body language, she went to Lew Clemmens, who had gone to a computer and was furiously keying in a search of RE/MAX listings in remote areas around D.C. Meanwhile, all the others, including O'Brien, had taken to the phones, talking to every realtor and realty expert in town.

"Lew," Jessica said in her friend's ear, "what about the check on any violence done to anyone in the real estate business the past seventy-two hours?"

"Our guys at Quantico are running it. Promise to get back pronto."

She nodded, breathed heavily, and collapsed in the seat next to Lew, waiting for a hit. "Just on the off chance, have them search for anyone in the realty business who has turned up as Missing Persons, as well."

"Gotcha, boss." Lew gave her a teddy bear smile.

SOME things no one wanted to ever contemplate, such as the process of decay in one's own body, and so it was with Jessica, but she had to face it if she were to help Judge DeCampe and Kim Desinor. She called on an expert on decay, a forensic anthropologist who stood at the top of the profession, also on the FBI payroll.

The man was the head of the most bizarre scientific research facility on the face of the earth, a one-of-a-kind place officially called the University of Tennessee's Forensic Anthropology Research Facility, but unofficially known as the Body Farm. And while they did not grow bodies there, they did grow maggots and decay. Everyone in the forensic community knew of the gruesomely genuine "back to nature" open air laboratory created by Dr. Will Bass, who at seventy-two still showed up for work to oversee training of young forensic scientists in the art and science of discovery through time of rot. A lot of jokes abounded about the farm and its creator, who at an early age had felt so incompetent at the task of determining time of death when faced with a corpse that he determined instead to devote his life to the question of how to read decaying bodies for clues. In a case that had embarrassed him, he'd been off time of death by 113 years, when it was determined the body was that of a Civil War veteran whose coffin had been disturbed in error during a disinterment.

Jessica telephoned the facility only to learn that Bass was in Zurich, lecturing; not surprised by this, she asked for whoever had been left in charge of the farm. Syd Fielding replied that she was talking to the right man. Fielding was one of Bass's disciples. There were some sixty forensic anthropologists who specialized in human degeneration, and Bass had trained two-thirds of them.

Jessica got right to the point, telling Dr. Fielding what they were faced with in the DeCampe kidnapping. He was appalled at the idea of someone being strapped to "one of those bodies we have in the field in advanced stage of decay."

"We fear the worst for good reason, sir. I need to know what kind of time we have left. If I bring you everything we have on when she disappeared and where we suspect she is, and the distances, times for both her and the body she's strapped to, maybe we can have some idea how much time she has left."

"Of course, we'll do all that we can here. You know if it has to do with decay, this is the place to ask your questions. How soon can you be here?"

"I have a helicopter standing ready and have been cleared for the trip ASAP."

"We'll keep the facility open late then; you'll want to come to the main building. The pilot will know where to land."

They hung up, and Jessica rushed to the waiting helicopter atop FBI headquarters. She'd hugged and kissed Richard good-bye, asking him, "Please, keep me abreast of any new developments, Richard. Don't hesitate to call."

She then waved to Keyes and J. T., who had walked up with them. The trio stood on the shoulder of the helipad and waved her off.

*   *   *

AN hour and a half later, Jessica heard the pilot's voice break into her sleep; having had no sleep for twenty-four hours, she'd nodded off to the hum of the rotors. "We're on approach for the Body Farm. Thought you'd want to be awake now," he told her. "There."

She shook off the drowsiness and saw that Pilot Marks was pointing ahead of them. She followed his gesture down to the ground, to a two-acre patch of dense woods—mostly thick oak, maple, and sycamore—the canopy thick and impenetrable. It was all one big swelling or hillside, bracketed on all sides by a stockade-style fence, large even from here, likely ten feet high. Overlaying the spikes of this stockade, a razor wire mesh meant to keep the dead in and the living out.

Jessica had read a great deal about Bass and his extensive research into decay and time-of-death assessment. She knew from her reading how many cases had been won by prosecutors across the country as a result of this facility, and that the information gleaned here had become textbook commonality among medical examiners, forensic scientists, and pathologists alike. Nowhere on the planet did corruption of the flesh do so much to help so many than here in the controversial Tennessee facility.

The place was, in fact, extremely controversial from the day Bass had set up shop on university grounds, with public opinion—as usual—running high at the thought that such a place existed. People demanded to know where the bodies were harvested from, and it outraged people to learn that the bodies were placed in various staged scenarios: held below stagnated black water by chains, held in shallow sunlit water by weights, placed in deep burial pits, shallow graves, or merely half buried. Other "donor" bodies had been left entirely to the elements, and wild animals were left to their own devices to feed. Still other rancid bodies were placed inside burned-out Chevys, and in the trunks of Fords, all to advance the science of understanding rotting flesh—putrefaction.

Now the helicopter passed over the city, and Jessica felt a jolt of surprise at how close the Body Farm was to downtown Knoxville; in fact, it stood just across the Tennessee River from downtown. On a badly sultry day, she wondered what the wind would carry into the city. She knew that at any given time, at least forty bodies lay decomposing in their various poses beneath the canopy of trees, behind the stockade. There was even one pit called the mass grave, wherein slept a tangle of bodies. All to further science, so that when such sites occur in Albacore, Mississippi; Peoria, Illinois; Bonfire, New Mexico; Salem, Oregon; Worcester, Massachusetts; Senegal; or Bangladesh, then doctors on the scene might make some intelligent decisions on how and when the victims of murder met their end.

In 1977, Will Bass realized a need for the farm, when he determined scientists simply did not know enough about normal and abnormal decay in human flesh. Bass was a visionary, a pioneer. He had turned the attitude and the tools of anthropology toward forensics long before anyone else connected the two fields. He made the tools of excavation and skeletal examination into one of the major modern weapons against crime.

All of Bass's best people were now sought after, and Syd Fielding was among the most sought after. Although Bass remained the paterfamilias of the Body Farm at age seventy-two, still held onto a set of keys, and kept close tabs on all the goings on, especially with the residents, Fielding had become the day-to-day manager of the facility. Aside from his duties here, Fielding was in demand on the lecture circuit, addressing M.E.'s and morticians, as well as consulting widely with law enforcement agencies, insurance investigators, and attorneys.

The farm had taught untold lessons to untold people in the field, lessons about whether or not larvae remained on the body, or whether or not empty pupae cases were left behind by maggots as they matured into flies. Such empty insect casings told a savvy forensics person whether or not at least one generation of flies had hatched and matured in the body or bodies, a cycle requiring two weeks or more.

Such information, along with milk labels, meat labels, the mold on the bread, the accumulated mail, all helped to point to a probable time of death, sometimes so accurate as to put a killer away.

On the ground now, the helicopter blades whining and winding down, Jessica was greeted behind the University of Tennessee Medical Center by a surprisingly young-looking Fielding, who had been sitting on the tailgate of a Dodge pickup. After introductions and handshakes, he led her to a large gate posted with Keep Out and No Trespassing signs. The stockade fence had not replaced an earlier chain-link fence but rather reinforced the interior chain-link fence, and it had the added feature of hiding from view what was going on inside. This Syd Fielding explained, adding, "We've had some attempts at sabotage; the new fence cost mightily, but it became necessary after the press got hold of our using bodies here that—in the local opinion—don't deserve our desecrating them as we do."

Fielding was a short man with large hands and wide eyes behind thick glasses. An overbite gave him the appearance of a snapping turtle, and he had to work hard to get up a smile. His set of keys marked him as important here. He unlocked the stockade fence and snatched it open wide, but then he had to unlock the chain-link fence, and this gate pushed inward. Beyond these two gates, a huge wooden structure like something out of *King Kong* confronted them.

"I see you've taken a great deal of precaution."

"Some fears never die. Fear of a rotting corpse in the neighborhood that is not under a cement slab to keep it in place is as alive here as it is in Transylvania, I can assure you. But we've also had attempts at break-ins, some serious protestor types, but more often local high schoolers."

"High schoolers, really?"

"They don't call 'em the Wildcats for nothing. Place has become a beacon for Saturday night dares, a place to visit after the prom, you get the picture. Should something happen to a kid around here, you can bet we'd be shut down in a heartbeat, despite all the good we've done."

"Yeah, I can imagine."

"Place is not for the squeamish, Dr. Coran, and it's certainly not Peabody's Tomb or any other urban legend. It's a scientific experiment that has had multiple benefits for forensic science."

"You don't have to sell me. I know your work is necessary to the advancement of our understanding of decay, and that's precisely why I've come to you."

"Sorry Dr. Bass isn't here to meet you. Your reputation is well known here, however, and he did express his regrets."

"Likewise, sorry I missed him, but I'm sure you can help me."

"As we go through, you will see residents at work; most arrive before daybreak and leave early for classes. The lucky ones get to shower before they leave."

He led her into the facility, and on entering, she was reminded of going to a private zoological garden. A thick layer of foliage encroached on the small pathway leading deeper into the wild forest, the foliage attempting to retake the road, to make it once more part of the hillside landscape. Here and there, Jessica saw a silent old automobile, weeds claiming it, that had been run up into the bushes. She saw another one in a small pond, half submerged.

At one clearing, she saw a handful of students with shovels, rakes, wire mesh screens, cameras, prongs, and specimen bags, all working away like a group of archeologists over a find, but the find here was a body, the skeletal remains of a decayed corpse.

"They're simulating a case."

"Fascinating. How close is the simulation?"

"As real as we can make it. They'll collect all the bone fragments from a victim who was set afire and then left to rot in a shallow grave. They'll take all the parts back with them to a clean, well-lit lab at the research facility. There they'll go at it like a jigsaw puzzle, putting the victim back together again and determining time of death, working backward, and learning exactly how he died."

"I would have killed for such training when I was younger," she said.

"Careful how you phrase that," he joked. "Of course, our John Doe really didn't die of his burns."

"Oh, really?" She kept pace with Fielding, whose feet moved like they had eyes over the well-worn path.

"You see, the body came to us via an incident report in which a homeless man doused himself with gasoline and set himself aflame. However, on closer inspection, I determined the man had been decaying for two weeks before he was set aflame, so he could not have doused himself with the gasoline or lit the match. He was a bit too dead to have pulled that off."

She laughed at this. Fielding had an entertainer's delivery when he spoke of his first love, anthropological forensics.

"He was torched two weeks after being killed?"

"Not someone but a gang of someones—teens who came on the body where it lay in a drain pipe, and they decided it would be fun to watch it burn. After my determination, police set out to find the culprits. They weren't exactly up on charges of murder, but that kind of depraved act can't go unpunished."

They now rounded a corner, and there ahead of them in a shallow backwash of a pond, lying faceup and staring out at them, floated a decomposing, eyeless corpse, its lifeless sockets like Jell-O by this point. Jessica felt a surge of emotions commingle deep within; while on the one hand, she applauded what the facility did for science and forensics in particular, she also despised what was necessary in reaching the findings—a kind of willful disrespect for the human remains.

Instead of dwelling on the eyeless man whose clothes still clung to its now-formless flesh beneath, thinking how like a character in *Night of the Living Dead* the corpse appeared, she said, "Of course, the resident students aren't told the true history of how the bodies came to their respective ends, right?"

"Right, and that means those who piece the truth together from the remains become our brightest among the class."

"They'll know from the green bone effect that Bass discovered," she said.

"That's right. Green bone fractures differently in a fire than drier bone. They'll know—or should know—John Doe's fractures match those of a burned body, not someone burned alive."

"Dry bones are more brittle, so the fracture pattern will be different."

"And only a microscope will tell you that."

"Appears you are doing a lot here . . . down on the farm."

He smiled at this and said, "You bet we are."

They walked on. Nothing in Jessica's experience could have prepared her for the sights and odors of the body farm. Commingled with the thick scent of dogwood and honey-suckle came the sickening sweet odor of decay in the wind. *Animals here must have a field day,* she thought. But then, the animal patterns of disturbance on and around the body were also major concerns of the anthropological forensics specialists. Jessica heard the rummaging and scurrying of any number of rodents, squirrels, and rabbit. She knew from her reading that they had foxes, wild boars, even a family of bears living on the compound in an attempt to simulate natural phenomena as much as possible.

Jessica had once visited a Civil War battleground within driving distance of Quantico, Virginia, and the place exuded the same eerie feeling as the Body Farm. But, as with the battlefield, vegetation and animal life had reclaimed the place, and here the thistle and bramble bush and rat and squirrel ruled. The incidental work of humans here, to fur-ther knowledge of death, dying, and decay in order to both dissuade murder and to catch murderers after the fact, seemed of less importance than the next leaf to be replaced. Birds hummed and chased one another here as if it were a gay, weekend park for families and children to play in. The death and the decay being studied—the concerns of man—were kept at bay by life.

They finished the quick tour of the facility, and Jessica was pleased to see they had found the gate again; a part of her mind found the place like a macabre maze from which she might never find her way.

Fielding broke her reverie now, asking, "Would you like

to get some coffee? We can go over what you've brought in my office."

"That sounds good, yes."

They exited the Body Farm, and he locked up behind them. "I do hope someone else has a key?" she mused.

"Oh, sure, the instructor working with the group you saw. Any problems, they can reach my beeper number."

Now outside the Body Farm, Jessica began to breathe normally again.

INSIDE the nearby laboratory facility at the Body Farm, Jessica found that Bass and Fielding and their students were blessed with state-of-the-art equipment, hardware, and software. They had developed a cutting-edge laboratory here in the Bible belt, and they must be congratulated for it.

Over coffee, she sat across from Fielding while he delved into the DeCampe case file, noting the details with rapid eye movements. Finally, he looked up at her and said, "I see why you called us. This . . . this is horrible if it can be believed."

"Believe it."

Among the documents, findings, and suppositions made about the DeCampe case, Jessica had placed photos of Kim Desinor's wounds, photos taken by Dr. Shoate, which she had gotten copies of. "And these welts or bruises on Dr. Desinor? They're real?"

"As real, I fear, as those on DeCampe."

He breathed in deeply. "How long has the victim gone missing?"

"Two days, two nights now."

"How long since Desinor's first psychosomatic bruising?"

"Twenty-four hours later."

"Then perhaps she has twenty-four hours that DeCampe doesn't have, if she's running a day behind, so to speak."

"You think so?"

"Something as bizarre as this? I am guessing at best. Sorry."

She nodded, accepting this, sipping at her coffee. She felt a well of fear for Kim that filled her being.

"And how long has Jimmy Lee Purdy's body been in his father's hands?"

"Picked it up Sunday."

"Five days."

"He likely kept it on ice for as long as he could do so," she said, adding, "Can you imagine a cop pulling him over and asking him what he's got in the rear?"

Fielding mused. Then he said, "For that matter, imagine pulling over in a highway oasis, and some old guy is replacing ice in the bottom of a coffin."

"If he kept it on ice until he reached D.C., and if the body decay on Purdy were forestalled as long as say the fourth or fifth day, and if she's been forced into contact with the decay for two days and two nights, what kind of estimate on her life span can you give me?"

"So much depends on . . . on, well, on so much."

"What does that mean? I need some help here."

"It means, my dear Dr. Coran, that to determine what sort of clock you have to work with . . . well . . . given the dryness of the season in the D.C. area—you did say you suspect he is keeping her in the D.C. area, right?' "

"We've come to that conclusion, yes."

"Then, given conditions, and if she and the corpse to which she is lashed are being kept in an enclosed, confined space with a floor, that is one thing; atop soil is another, and we'd need to know the type of soil. Sorry, but this is all backward from our usual case. Our usual case involves—"

"A dead body, I know, I know."

"After the fact of murder, yes." He looked genuinely sorry at seeing her distress. For a moment, their eyes met. His eyes said he wanted to pull a miracle out of the hat for her but that he had none. "Evenings have been cool and dry as have been the days there, right? This will delay the process. If Jimmy Lee Purdy's body is not completely decomposed, as you suspect, she's got some time."

"How much time?" Jessica persisted.

"Again, I don't know if she's been made wet, if she's been made to sweat, if she's in direct or indirect, prolonged or intermittent contact with the corpse—the decay, to be exact."

"What do you give her chances of being alive this time tomorrow?" Jessica pleaded. "Nil or nil?"

"You're asking for an opinion I can't give." He sat back in his chair and pushed off strands of thinning blond hair from his forehead. "We usually deal with fractures and gunshot wounds and insect activity here, not . . . What would you call this sort of murder? Induced decay? It's hard to contemplate how anyone could carry out such a sentence."

"A time, Doctor, a best guesstimate."

"Depends on if the old man wants to hasten it or not. If he cut her, for instance, at the areas of contact, it would hasten her gangrene, decay, and death. But if he wants it torturously slow, then he just lets the little microbes of decay do their own work. That would take more time, most certainly. If he's chosen the latter, then I give her maybe twenty-four hours more before the gangrene is likely to be irreversible. She may be helped to a clean bed and her bruises helped by skin grafts, but if infected, gangrene works fast. It will kill her."

"We get the sense that this guy wants her to suffer over as long a period as he can make her suffer. It's about revenge."

"In that case . . . Yeah, I'd say then you have twenty-four, forty-eight hours tops."

"You can't be any more specific than that?"

"Too many variables. Is she getting water? Is she getting any nutrients? Has he tied her back-to-back, face-to-face, face-to-back? Has he placed her in the sun? The corpse's weight used against her? The level of putrefaction to begin with, yet another unknown. We're working with too many unknowns here."

"Then our time clock is forty-eight hours max."

"I believe so."

Fielding blinked as he spoke and as he thought, with a wisp of light strands over a pale face. She had to admire the man. He had made his life's work the study of human decaying flesh in all its permutations and in every circumstance. He had been instrumental in creating the FBI's infamous Body Farm. And there was not a working M.E. in the country who had not benefited, directly or indirectly, knowingly or unknowingly, from the work of men like Bass and Fielding.

A body left for days in the sun, in the shade, in water, in sandy soil, in humus, inside the trunk of a car—they all showed different rates of decay. Fielding had been among the men who had catalogued these fine differences, and in effect had brought many fugitives to justice as a result. However, the corpses used in the experiments—primarily prison inmates who had donated their bodies to the advancement of science while in no way knowing just how science would use them—had that fundamental difference from DeCampe. DeCampe was presumably lashed to Jimmy Lee Purdy's rotting corpse, but her flesh was alive, healthy, a vital heart pumping blood to every capillary. Her body would fight off the decay to some degree before eventually losing the battle. So Jessica had to know how much time she had left. Only a man of Fielding's experience might be able to give her a time line. The word *deadline,* she had avoided; it had taken on a whole new meaning in this case since she had met and spoken with Father Pinwaring.

Fielding now wanted to show her some insect data, larvae that hatched from one of his bodies out at the Body Farm, determining some special facts about the type of mite he was currently fascinated with. He mumbled something about larval sacs having a kind of beauty all their own.

"Yeah, I expect they do, Dr. Fielding."

"Are you staying over long enough to have dinner?" he then asked. "I would love to take you to dinner."

She realized now how hard he had been staring at her, and why. She did not interest him as much as his insect findings, but she did interest him. "No, I'll be going directly back. Time being so limited, you see."

"Of course. Maybe you'd like to return for another visit? Really get familiar with what we do here."

"Perhaps in the future."

"It does indeed sound like a most impossible case, an absolute horror. I certainly do not envy you your job, Dr. Coran."

The man works nine to five studying decay in corpses, and he's pitying me, she glumly thought.

She stood to leave, and he insisted on walking her back to the waiting helicopter. "You know, all the variables that make it impossible for me to be precise on how long Maureen Decampe has to live could also be working in her favor, you realize?"

"The nights of dry lightning, no rain, drought conditions, yes, they have worked in her favor, I'm sure." Jessica knew that decay fed more rapidly in dampness.

"But then a barn like you describe is in itself a microecology," countered Dr. Fielding, ushering her along the corridor and out into the light, "and it will be dimly lit, no sunshine, and little wind blowing through, if he's using it as a prison, a place to keep someone locked inside, and to keep others out."

Jessica nodded several times. "Then we must find her tonight."

"But you understand, this is all assuming she has had no respite from contact with the decaying corpse."

"What do you mean?"

"If her captor is wishing to prolong her agony, he will feed her, give her water, drag it out." Fielding gritted his teeth and shook his head as if to shake out an image. "My God, all the years I've worked with decaying corpses, and it would never have occurred to me that someone could concoct so horrid a murder as you are suggesting."

"Vengeance is a strong motivator, Syd, and often it acts as the mother of invention."

Dr. Fielding's eyes opened beyond the sad, fleshy slits they had become with early middle age, working in the field he did. "You think the killer inventive? Imaginative?" He actually smiled like a teacher trying to embarrass her. Was it a trick question?

"Not really; he's just very familiar with images he's taken from the Bible."

"I should like to learn more about this citizen among us."

"I would love to tell you more, but I have to get back to the task force."

"Sorry I couldn't have been of more help to you," he said, accepting her hand in his, shaking it, and warmly smiling. "You remind me of a tenacious colleague of mine."

"Oh, and who would that be?"

"Dr. Bass, of course, another jack bull."

"Me . . . a terrier? Funny, I do seem to recall someone characterizing me as a tenacious bitch on more than one occasion."

"Oh, no, I only meant it in the best possible light, that you are tenacious—a good quality to have for a medical examiner and seeker of truth."

"Why, thank you, Doctor. I've been called just about everything, but that is the nicest thing I've heard in a long time."

"You have a high PQ."

"PQ?"

"Persistence quotient."

She smiled and again thanked him. They parted with promises to see one another again, Jessica telling him that when she could find the time, she would come for a longer visit to the facility.

The helicopter flight back gave Jessica the freedom to think; she weighed up everything they knew at this point, including what Fielding had said about the variables quite possibly favoring that DeCampe remained alive still.

SIXTEEN

*A case of serial murder is heinous, a hate crime
awful, and a case of self-righteous and fanatical
vengeance just as brutal as any . . .*

—FROM THE CASEBOOKS OF
DR. JESSICA CORAN

TIME passed, and a number of possible leads were looked
into without result. Everyone in and around the Washington, D.C., area having anything to do with crime fighting
by now had learned what the task force was interested in.
In fact, RE/MAX had become a half-joking battle cry. Then
a phone call came in from the D.C. Police Department's
Missing Persons Unit. A Detective Charles Price grumbled
out that he had gotten wind they were interested in any
Missing Persons case involving a realtor.

"What have you got for us?"

"Got your APB, so when a report came in sounding like
the ball park . . ." After listening to what Price had to say,
she replied, "And you say this is a RE/MAX local office?
Give me the address where she works." Jessica jotted the
information down.

When Jessica looked up, she saw that all the others in
the ops room were staring at her. "It's a case recently called
in, a daughter worried about her mother. She coincidentally
works for RE/MAX; left work and never got home. I'm
going to interview her coworkers."

*   *   *

THE realtor's name was Nancy Willis, and she had gone missing, and no one knew why. The partner's name was Carmella Drew, a leggy, well-dressed, and businesslike person with fine features and an unfortunate nose. Jessica asked her a series of questions, but Carmella made it clear that she knew nothing; in fact, she appeared to be so clueless that Jessica began to wonder if her business partner's disappearance had nothing whatever to do with Purdy and the De-Campe case, and all to do with a case of murder unraveling before her, one that involved getting rid of the bothersome business associate.

"So you have no idea whether she went out on a call or not?"

"No."

"No record of an appointment?"

"None, no."

"I see. Did she keep a calendar? An appointment book?"

"She kept her appointment book with her at all times."

"A desk calendar?"

"Yeah, her office. This way."

Jessica scanned the calendar for a week before De-Campe's abduction. A look at her watch told her it was nearing nine P.M. She'd had to drag Carmella back to the closed office to have a look at Nancy's desk. "Any new clients recently who looked like this man?" Jessica asked, holding out the newly drawn composite of Isaiah Purdy.

"She didn't always check with me when she rented out a place. We each generate our own business, you see, and at the end of the month, we give out perks and benefits and bonuses if things are going well. Lately, we've had few things to cheer about."

"So she didn't always bring clients into the office?"

"That, and I wasn't always here. I've only just returned from some time off."

Jessica saw several names of prospective customers and appointments on the calendar. She read them off to the partner. "Any of these clients rent property out of the way, in a remote setting?"

"Lately, that's all anyone wants: remote, preferably with a moat."

Jessica read the names aloud. "Gideon Brown, Mark and Marilou Piper, Damon Shaw." They were all jotted down on days just before the abduction.

"Any of them ring a bell?"

"She closed deals with all of them. Let me see."

"No, let me see your sales records."

"That might speed things up," she replied.

"I hope they're up to date and in order."

"Around here? Don't bet on it."

Jessica exchanged an exasperated look with Richard, who had stood back and allowed Jessica to deal with the frustrating woman.

"Here's the file room," said the partner.

They looked into a closet in which boxes were piled high, most wedged between two upright filing cabinets. "Always going to get around to the filing next week," she muttered, "but next week never comes. Well . . . knock yourselves out."

"Whoa up . . . wait a minute. Are you in the least interested in locating your partner?"

She took in a deep breath. "The woman lives alone with her cat, and she's seeing someone, and by this time tomorrow, she'll come waltzing in here, a big smile on her face, and Nancy will wonder what all the fuss has been about. Her daughter is a little, you know, overprotective. You know how that is."

"Has anyone called her boyfriend?"

"Her daughter said Dave doesn't know where she is either, but Nancy's, you know, a free spirit."

"Was she upset with any of the people on that list I read you?"

"Come to think of it, she was complaining about one of them."

"What kind of complaint was it? And which one?"

"Usual second-guessing. She did a lot of that. Not sure the person renting would be a good tenant, 'fraid he might destroy the place in one fashion or another. She'd go on about such things forever, so I always quit listening after a while."

"Which tenant was she complaining about the loudest?" Sharpe's voice was the epitome of unmasked dislike, but it went right over this woman's head.

"Gee . . . I don't know. I remember it was one of the single men, Shaw or Brown, but which one, I couldn't tell you."

"Can you tell us which properties the two men took?"

She scrunched her petite face into a wadded little ball and said, "Sorry."

Richard had to fight the urge to strangle the woman.

"Look, where are the most recent contracts, ahhh . . . placed in here?" Jessica asked.

"Look in the in-bin, there in the corner." She pointed but remained in the doorjamb.

"Gotcha, and thanks."

"Don't mention it."

"Don't worry. . . ."

Jessica and Richard tore into the stack of papers found below another stack covering the in-basket. "You want to order in some coffee?" asked Richard. "This could take some time."

"No, let's work through. Here, you take this stack, and I'll take the other half."

"Contracts are mixed with junk mail," Richard complained.

"Watch for anything with Brown or Shaw on it."

They fell silent, searching.

After a moment, finding nothing, Richard said, "You realize this could all be a blind alley, don't you?"

"Yeah . . . I know that, but I also keep thinking about Kim Desinor and the clock continues to run out for De-Campe."

Richard bit his lower lip and nodded and continued to pore over papers.

Jessica then said, "On meeting Miss Manners in there, I thought maybe she did away with her partner or bored her to death, but now I admit, she's too stupid to murder someone and properly hide the body, and she likely knows this better than anyone, so . . ."

"Are you kidding, Jessica? Two or three bodies could be below all this paper."

"Yeah, reminds me of my days in the dorm when everyone was sweating final research papers. The room was jammed with paper and books. Didn't see my roommate for three days. She was there . . . I could hear her . . . we called out to one another from time to time, but no . . . couldn't see her for all the paper."

"Maybe we should just call out Nancy Willis's name. See if we get a faint voice from the other side," joked Richard.

Jessica laughed aloud. It felt good; she hadn't had much to smile about lately.

"Mr. Gideon Brown! I got handwriting on a phone form here," said an excited Richard. "It's requesting a rural or remote rental, something resembling a farm, he says, something with a barn. Wants a place he won't be bothered in his old age, where he can raise chickens and tend a few animals like when he was a boy in Illinois—says here."

They took the note to Willis's partner, read it to her, and asked if she recalled anything unusual about this man Brown. Carmella said, "I did think him a bit odd, as I recall. Didn't care for the client in the least, and Nancy kept wondering what he could possibly want the old Killough place for. She told me she didn't like the feel of it—the deal that is, but again, I was only half listening. I had heard it all before, you see."

Jessica turned to Richard and indicated the correspondence. "Tell me there's a response clipped to it, an address?"

"No . . . says he will be in on the eighteenth and that he would be pleased if she had some suggestions for him."

Jessica again tried jogging the memory of Miss Manners, but she had nothing further she could add, until Jessica's stare bore a hole into her head.

"All right. Let me see it," said the partner, who had prepared two cups of steaming coffee for the FBI agents.

After handing the two law enforcement people their coffees, the woman studied the letter for some time. "Oh, yes, I do remember something else of Mr. Brown now. He called in once while Nancy was at lunch. Gruff, callous voice, raw, actually. He was in heat to speak to her, finalize things, and I couldn't help him, and he became angry with me."

"Let me guess. He wanted to rent by the month?" asked Jessica.

"How'd you know? Oh, yes, of course, you are a detective, aren't you. But it was worse. He also wanted a kill fee."

"A kill fee? Isn't that unusual?"

"Shows he was a shrewd man when it came to property. If things didn't in the end suit him, he could step out of the contract and regain most of his down payment, you see."

"Why didn't you alert us to this earlier if it's so unusual?" asked Jessica.

"You . . . you didn't ask if anything unusual had occurred in the context of client contract."

"Oh . . . oh, I see," mocked Jessica, but again the ridicule was wasted on this woman.

"Look, I told Nancy I didn't half blame him—about the kill fee, I mean."

"Oh, and why's that?"

"The property abuts a chemical factory—actually, a paint factory. It's rather a wasteland. It fronts a dump site. Place has been cited so many times for environmental damage by so many different agencies that no one knows who's handling the lawsuits anymore."

Jessica said, "I think I remember reading something about it, but that was years ago."

"They've somehow managed to keep it in court all these years, and the place is producing less product, but still . . ."

Jessica replied, "If this man Brown is Purdy using an alias, I imagine the place suits the old man's needs perfectly."

Richard concurred. "I can just see the old man disposing of two bodies there."

"You think your partner, Willis, may have had second

thoughts on renting the property to Brown? That she might have gone out there to have a look at how he was using the property?" Jessica asked.

"Actually, she does that sort of thing from time to time . . . all the time when things are slow. She's a bit of a busybody that way. Costs us a lot of clients. She's a dear, you know, a kind, big-hearted soul, but she has this one fatal flaw in this business."

"Oh, what's that?"

"After the sale, you don't meddle. She meddles. Nancy can't really help herself; it's rather a compulsion with her. Every instinct against it, and yet she goes and meddles after the sale. Like some people have a compulsion to rewrite procedure manuals from one day to the next, she has this compulsion to know *how* a client uses the damned property, especially a rental."

"Here's an agreement signed by Brown," said Richard, waving it overhead, pleased with himself. "I think we can match the handwriting; it looks like the letter sent to the *Post*."

Jessica studied the agreement. "Too bad he didn't bother to include a photo ID. The guy ponied up cash, though. No plastic. Isn't that unusual these days?" asked Jessica.

"Yes, but we don't look down on the old-fashioned way. Money is money."

"What about Shaw?" asked Sharpe, who now sipped at his coffee.

"Shaw?"

"The other lone renter. Did Nancy have any misgivings about him?"

"No more than the usual."

"Let's keep digging for the Shaw property as well. Just in case," said Jessica, and together, she and Richard went back to work on it.

In a moment, they came across papers on Shaw's rental. The property here, too, was in a remote area.

Jessica asked Carmella, "Show me on the map where these two properties are located."

After a moment's study of the respective rental papers

and a bit of glaring at the county map, she stuck a tack into two exact spots. "The one Brown bought into beside the chemical factory is just here, east of Killarney Farms Road and right at the apex of Cresswell and Cornflower. Two dirt roads maintained by Ravenshire County. Here alongside is the dump site and commercial plants I told you about. Shaw, on the other hand, is here. Off County Line Road just outside Sweetwater, Maryland."

"Brown is closer to Nokesville, Virginia," Richard pointed out.

"We'll need this map and the contracts. We'll want to compare the signatures to handwriting we have from a man who abducted a D.C. judge two days ago. We think Nancy's disappearance may have some connection to the abduction of this earlier victim."

"Oh, my God . . ." The woman turned a shade of pale that threatened them with a fainting. Jessica helped her to an office chair. "You all right?" she asked the woman.

"Until now, it just didn't really register with me that Nancy might . . . that she could really be missing, you know, or hurt, maybe dying somewhere."

JESSICA and Richard made their way back to FBI headquarters, and Jessica sat silent for most of the ride. Richard finally broke the silence, saying, "We go rushing in there and—"

"Alarms, bells, and whistles are sure to tip him off long enough that he could kill her outright—if she's alive. Even if we're as quiet as we can be, he might have the land around booby-trapped. We have to go in cautiously but fast, extremely fast."

"Yes, I agree . . . if he's alerted to our coming, he's likely to kill her."

"It's a moonless night. That'll cover us," Jessica said. "We go in black commando gear. We take control of the compound and the factory beside the farm. We have to take charge before Purdy knows what's happening."

"We've got probable cause, and we'll have a search war-

rant this time. We'll use the factory next door as a staging
area. Arrange it with the owners." Richard drove on, but he
looked across at Jessica, seeing the concern creasing her
features. "You're as worried about Kim as you are De-
Campe, I know."

"You read minds, too?"

"I figure it had to do with your making a call back there."

Jessica had taken a moment to wonder how Kim Desinor
was doing about now. An earlier phone call to her doctors
revealed that she was sitting up, taking liquids by mouth,
and that while her lesions hadn't gotten any worse, neither
had they begun to heal. Jessica imagined that some part of
her brain did not fully accept the placebo lie, that she must
first see hard evidence. Dr. Shoate continued his treatment
of ice and antibiotic gels, still treating it as a strange out-
break of an Ebola-like disease, for which he could only
make the patient as comfortable as possible.

Jessica then contacted the famous psychic Edward Lighttoller, who lived in the D.C. area. Peter Hurkos had been
Lighttoller's mentor. Lighttoller was said to have remarka-
ble gifts as a psychic, and Jessica knew that Kim had great
admiration and respect for the man. Jessica started out by
flattering the man and telling him about Kim Desinor's curious case, and in doing so, she made him curious about the
DeCampe case as well.

"How can I help you, Dr. Coran?" he finally asked.

"If you would just see Dr. Desinor. I have no expectations, but if you could just see her, see what condition she
is in, speak with her, offer her what you can."

"I'm not sure what I can offer her."

She asked, "Is there any way to reach out to Kim to
convince her that she can and should disengage from the
thing that holds her enthralled, the thing that is slowly killing her?"

"And this thing . . . is it not also slowly killing De-
Campe?" he asked.

Jessica felt a sense of the man's power even over the
phone. "Yes . . . yes, we are working under that assumption,
sir."

"How do you do this for a living, Dr. Coran?"

"Do this?"

"Dance with the lunatic and the satanic?"

"I do it. I just do it. I don't slow down to ask why or how; if I did, I'd likely go mad myself."

"Careful that you don't find yourself, in the end, dancing with the devil."

"Will you help Dr. Desinor?"

"I will go see her, speak to her, offer what I can, yes. I have always held her in the greatest esteem."

"Thank you."

"No, Dr. Coran, thank you."

SEVENTEEN

. . . he who finds a certain proportion of pain and evil inseparably woven up in the life of the very worms, will bear his own share with more courage and submission.

—THOMAS H. HUXLEY

MAUREEN DeCampe whimpered and pulled away from the old man's touch. She'd been returned to the awful prison of being bound to the dead man. The old man now roughly slapped her in the back of the head and shouted for her to be still as he worked.

"Jimmy tells me he's real proud how you still got spirit, Maureen . . . but he also wants now to hear you a-moaning and a-pleading, so he wants me to leave the gag outta your mouth."

He then returned to his three-legged stool, watching the slow progression of her death, the unmistakable look of fatigue and glee intermingling on his otherwise dour countenance. "No one can save you, Miss Maureen. No one in the whole world even exists for you now, nor nobody in all of Hell itself 'cept you and me—and Jimmy Lee, of course." He then lifted the RE/MAX woman's cell phone over his head and said, "It's deader'n a doornail, this thing. I know that bitch lying yonder didn't reach nobody else." He then hurled the cell phone into a black corner, the result a metallic rattle.

He began humming and then singing a hymn, "I looked over Jordan . . ." to the sound of crickets and scurrying mice . . . "and what'd I see? But a band-a-angels, coming for me. . . ."

He somehow looked comfortable enough on the three-legged stool to easily remain there for eternity, and after a few bars of "Jordan," he closed his eyes and appeared the picture of peace. He muttered under his breath, "I do right by you, Jimmy Lee. I do right by you."

Maureen DeCampe wondered if she could withstand a moment longer of this horror, this torture. She felt her mind slipping from reality. She'd experienced one, two, three blackouts, possibly more. The blackouts began with thoughts of loved ones, of seeing them again, of one day being reunited both with those who'd gone before her and those remaining behind. It was all she thought about now. She did not think about Isaiah Purdy perched like a gargoyle nearby; she did not think of Jimmy Lee's decaying body below her. She did not think about why the old man placed her on top so that the torture might last longer. She did not question why he had held her here in a dark, cooler area rather than in a sun-baked field or on some sun-baked roof-top, so as to hasten the decay. She no longer wished to ask such questions, questions that all seemed answered in one fell swoop: "It's Jimmy Lee's wish . . ." And she no longer cared to know the answers to such inquiries. It was useless, a waste of precious time. She chose rather to visit with her grandmother, her mother, her father, her grandfather, and other loved ones who'd passed over so many years before.

She chose to not allow the putrefaction of her body to control her mind; chose not to allow her mind or soul one more single hopeless or negative thought, concentrating in-stead on the people she loved, her children and grandchil-dren.

These thoughts gave her solace and peace and allowed her to drop off; he could not hurt her further if she were at peace. This much she knew; some voice from far beyond this place had posited that fact in her brain, and she felt certain it had been her mother's voice. While the old bastard that had done this horrible thing to her heard Jimmy Lee in his head, she heard her mother's voice in hers. She hoped that Isaiah Purdy's punishment—his personal hell—would be Jimmy Lee forever in his head. That would be just retribution; she kept telling herself that somewhere beyond this world, a sure justice awaited the old farmer, one that was already dealing with his son.

As a result of her acceptance, her peace with her impending death and the manner of her death, she had found the one weapon the old man had not suspected. She had found silence. She had become too quiet, too content for him, not making enough discomfiting noise. She no longer swore or moaned or whimpered. She would use the one weapon left her: her silence, her serenity, her peace. A small place in her soul told her that this above anything else she might do would make him crazy with rage and anger, and if it worked well enough, he might put the pitchfork through her and put her out of this misery. So now that Jimmy Lee wanted the gag out of her mouth, she would hold onto silence like a life rope thrown to her by her very soul—thrown out to her where she floated amid the pain, the suffering, and humiliation.

Accepting the inevitable, she sublimated all her high emotions at having had a near escape, the death of Willis, her hatred for her tormentor and his dead son, this time, and this place.

Where she lay, if she opened her eyes, she would see again that the devil had returned the pitchfork to Willis, standing it up neatly through her three wounds, using the woman's stiff body now as a kind of instrument, a place to keep the prongs sheathed. This scene of horror no longer created tears in her, although Purdy made sure that she lay within inches of Nancy Willis's dead eyes. Nothing touched her any longer. Not the smell of decay, not the touch of it against her skin. Her mind and strength of will to not care, to not smell, to not see, to not feel a thing, negated it all.

Still, she knew that she had not given in or given up; quite the contrary, she had accepted her imminent death, and she had made peace with it, with her Maker, a God who could allow this curse to be placed upon her in her final hours. She still held onto her inner resolve, her inner strength, believing she would need all the energy she could muster to find her way along the blinding path to the true light shining down from the hands of her ancestors, a light she believed would lead her to their arms, to that safe harbor, God's kingdom. Mother had always called it a safe harbor with a sturdy lighthouse—her euphemism for the other side. Funny it should seem so obviously true now. She could smell the surf, and she smelled the chemistry that was home, the odors of her mother and the house she kept. Whatever form that kingdom took—lighthouse or home, shore or doorstep—she meant to be a part of it, and she meant to see her children there, to greet them on arrival when they would come. *When all dreams would this way come,* she thought.

Yet she still found strength to condemn the old man in the deepest recesses of her heart, to mark him for God's special attention in a future arena. She silently condemned his soul to the farthest rung of Hades.

He merely continued his hymn: "Looked over Jordan . . ." But something about his missing a beat here, a beat there, told her that the silence, the peace she had come to, had begun to disturb Isaiah Purdy to his core. . . . "What did I see. . . ."

She secretly, inwardly smiled. She felt that even in death she would win the final victory over Isaiah and Jimmy Purdy—the lice of Iowa. Purdy could no longer hurt her.

Take me any time, Lord, she thought, resolved to never speak another word or make another plea.

"What? What'd you say?" asked Isaiah, trying to coax words from her now, agitated because Jimmy Lee wanted to hear her beg more.

"Go ahead, curse me, woman." Isaiah hoped to hear more tortured sounds from her as he worked to rig a booby trap for anyone else who might come snooping.

But Maureen would not give him the satisfaction. *Silence is golden,* she thought.

*   *   *

JESSICA knew that DeCampe was likely to be killed quickly if the old man smelled a threat to his game. She would have to orchestrate the perfect raid, a commando-style hit on two locations: the house and the barn, if Maureen DeCampe had any hope whatsoever of living through this nightmare. Jessica and Richard had rushed back to the center of operations, and before she had even arrived, Jessica had assembled her entire team for debriefing and planning, using her cell phone. She had assembled as much firepower as they could muster for the raid.

A map of the two suspect locations, Brown's rental and Shaw's rental, were already on the wall when she stepped into the ops room. Everyone was front and center, and at the back of the room stood Santiva, carefully taking in every detail.

Jessica told them, "We need to move on the Shaw address and the Brown address. We'll need an aerial attack as well as a ground attack—aerial helicopters equipped with megalights and infrared. Whatever else happens, I don't want this bastard slipping off into the night or getting into those woods and costing us days of manhunt. I want him locked down immediately. I've asked the military for support. They have infrared telephoto lenses that will tell us where the heat sources are, even through rooftops. We'll concentrate our ground attack where the choppers tell us to. We can't go in blind."

"He'll hear the choppers."

"We've contacted the factory beside the property to make enough noise to cover the choppers' approach. He won't be able to distinguish the sounds until late in our arrival. The factory is equipped with a sound system and a horrible old work whistle that will likely blow out our ears as well. They have an alarm system that we intend on using simultaneously as well."

"It's going to sound like an air raid over London in '44," said Richard.

"We've done a lot of old-fashioned homework already. One of the guards out at the plant has spoken to this man claiming to be Gideon Brown, and he characterized him as talkative but weird and antigovernment, the sort that might blow up a federal building. Maybe there's some truth in it, maybe not, but the man has ID'd Brown by the sketch artist's depiction we've been going by."

Jessica then told the assembled force, "While we're awaiting the paperwork, I want two teams assembled, one at each location, ready and waiting to go in, and I want you all to pray we have the right location in one of these choices."

"We can't afford another Iowa," muttered J. T.

"Iowa lost us time, but it was a logical step, and the noose we're about to put out there makes good sense as well. We'll pair off and go at each location with SWAT team backup."

ONE entire unit went for the Shaw residence, the other for the Brown rental. Nothing was spared. Both sites received equal attention. They needed results, and there was no room for error.

Jessica's instincts told her, however, that the Brown place would be where they would find Maureen DeCampe, or what was left of the poor woman. Their first stop was the chemical/paint factory, which, at a glance, must be breaking sixteen federal laws. Having no time for such concerns, they worked out a timing with the owners to blare their whistle and alarm at once. The shock of noise would at first alert Purdy aka Brown, but he would just as quickly determine the noise to be coming from the factory, and as such, he would likely ignore it. At precisely ten seconds after the factory alarm, the hovering helicopters were to move in with minimum running lights and noise, searching infrared cameras seeking body heat, at which point Jessica would be given a go.

Jessica and the others were in radio contact with the helicopters. Once given a report as to where the warm bodies were, they would simultaneously hit the lights and kick in doors.

Everyone was aware of the risk of booby traps.

Jessica and Santiva were in constant contact with the helicopters. Santiva insisted on leading the team at the house, Jessica at the barn. Keyes remained close at Jessica's side, J. T. and Sharpe with Santiva.

Jessica gave the nod to the factory boss, who called his man to let loose with the enormous noisemakers. Jessica and the others had ready earplugs. In the allotted ten seconds, the helicopters moved into place to begin scanning the structures for signs of life. Meanwhile, Jessica and the others, backed by SWAT teams, descended on the farmstead like an army seeking out its front lines.

They moved rapidly to encircle both structures, and they had been able to do so efficiently, given the location of the chemical firm from which they poured. In less than forty seconds, with the helicopter lights now creating an eerie daylight scene outside the barn and homestead, Jessica got word through her earphones that the only signs of life were coming from the barn. The copilot shouted, "Possibly two life forms of any size."

Jessica knew that Santiva had gotten the same message, but his force still meant to enter and secure the house before joining the second squad at the barn. They proceeded there with caution, being alert for any traps the old man might have laid for them.

J. T. went straight in behind Eriq Santiva, followed by Richard and the others. At the same time, the first strike force was entering the house, Jessica signaled for more men to go around to the rear of the barn to secure any exits there. When Eriq Santiva had learned of their plan to move on the two locations simultaneously, he knew there were inherent risks, but Jessica's argument that tonight was DeCampe's last night of life if they did not act had persuaded him to climb down the throat of a reluctant federal judge who had given the warrant to move on the Iowa location. The judge, understandably, wanted far more to go on than they had, but Eriq put on all the pressure of his office, and finally the warrant came through some twenty minutes after they had arrived within sight of the chemical factory abutting the targeted farmstead.

"The realtor was right to be suspicious of anyone willingly paying up front cash money for this place," Jessica noted in Shannon's ear.

Still, they had found no sign of Nancy Willis's car or the woman. If she had come out here to learn more about the man to whom she'd rented the property, there was no evidence of it. The infrared had, however, picked up two living people inside the barn. Perhaps the realtor was being held hostage alongside DeCampe. But that still left Purdy. Was he one of the red flares on the infrared, or was he gone from this place already? His van was then spotted, parked to the rear of the house, beneath a stand of trees. Jessica got the report from Richard, who broke into her frequency.

They inched forward. The decision had been made to blast the place with the alarms and sirens, and to turn the place from pitch black to daylight; nothing was held back now. Their cards had been laid on the table. Still, Jessica feared the crazed old man might in a moment of panic kill DeCampe outright. Shannon Keyes had warned that if he felt cornered, threatened even, she believed he might well strike out at DeCampe, "to assure her death before he is taken alive."

For that reason, they had come on foot, equipped with earphone radios. Now they had reached their objective, coming up on the old man to take him by surprise.

Just back of them where the road had risen up to meet them, an ambulance awaited Maureen DeCampe, but no one knew if it would be used to comfort her or merely to cart away her remains.

Jessica had left nothing to chance; inside the ambulance, she had both a minister of DeCampe's faith and one of D.C.'s leading physicians dealing with gangrene. Everyone was on standby. Inwardly, Jessica prayed for a good outcome tonight. She prayed for Kim Desinor and Maureen DeCampe, and she prayed for them all.

The air around them had filled with an electric energy. A storm of dry lightning strikes occasionally lit up the terrain. It felt like a scene out of *All Quiet on the Western Front*.

Everybody, it seemed, wanted to be in on the kill.

Everybody was itching to get their chance at Purdy.

Everyone knew the stakes.

They stood under the glare of the helicopters, the chemical factory alarms still ringing out, the atmosphere like that of a war zone that masked a sky above that had gone from clear and filled with stars only moments before to an ominous gray confusion of swirling clouds.

The old man, if he were inside the barn with the dying judge, must be freaking out by now, expecting a rain of gas and fire. Jessica took some delight in terrifying the old bastard.

All this under a suddenly angry, moonless night, the sky again filled with lightning bolts and clouds, yet no rain. Still, Jessica picked up the scent of ozone in the air. Rain could come at any time, and she hoped it would be a cleansing shower. Or would it be a mourning shower, a rain wake for Maureen?

EIGHTEEN

*The hungry sheep look up, and are not fed, but swoln
with wind and the rank mist they draw, Rot inwardly and foul contagion spread . . .*

—JOHN MILTON

"ISAIAH Purdy! Federal agents!" shouted Jessica over the
noise they'd created. "Step outside! You are surrounded!"
Jessica's order to Isaiah Purdy brought everyone's gun up
and ready. "Come out with your hands held high."

No response.

"We know you are inside, Purdy!" shouted Keyes.

"And we know you have the judge," added Jessica.

"She has suffered long enough. It's over."

No response.

Jessica ordered the men beside her with the battering ram
to take down the door. They charged it but were repelled,
not by bullet fire or resistance, but by give and take. The
door was loosely fastened, making a ramming effort nearly
impossible.

"We've wasted too much precious time," Jessica told
Keyes.

"What're you going to do?" She could see in Jessica's
eyes that she meant to do something now.

"The door is lashed together with some sort of pliable
binding. I'm going up and over," she said, pointing to the
window loft overhead. One of the SWAT leaders, seeing
what she wanted, without a word sent a grappling hook
overhead, and it secured itself to the wood around the loft
window, biting into it. "I'll go first," he said.

Jessica agreed, following up the rope behind the man

whose nameplate had read Luther Pratt. Three-fourths of the way up the rope, Jessica felt the vibration of the explosive that sent Luther hurling into her and almost knocking her off the rope. Luther fell to the ground in agony, his face splintered by the homemade device that meant to keep them out. The device seemed to have touched off a fire as well, for now the cracks all about the doorway and the walls were alight with a blazing interior.

Jessica pulled herself up and up. Keyes cried out to her, "Be careful! There's a fire inside!"

Jessica only half saw an explosion at the house, where the second team, led by Santiva, stormed the home. The house had been booby-trapped, and the men had rushed in too quickly, the result a blazing inferno. Wherever Isaiah Purdy was at this moment, it looked as if the old man meant to go out in a blaze of glory, to die in a fire of his own making, taking Jimmy Lee's and Maureen DeCampe's and possibly Nancy Willis's remains with him.

From Jessica's vantage point at the window loft now, she saw someone being carried out of the flaming house and across the yard. Keyes looked to where Jessica's eyes had gone, and now she, too, took in what Jessica had witnessed. It appeared someone in the second team had been as hurt as Luther, if not more so. Below her, Jesssica saw that Luther appeared stunned, the wind knocked from him, burns on hands and face, but the man was fending off any help—a good sign.

Keyes shouted, "The old monster's not going down without a battle."

Jessica clawed her way through the window loft, and for a moment, feeling the growing heat inside, she felt paralyzed on hearing a scream that made her blood solidify. The scream wafted across from the house, the sound shattering Jessica's nerve as it sounded like Richard Sharpe's voice—a second injury at the house. Jessica hoped she was wrong.

"Damn . . . booby traps everywhere," Shannon cursed. Keyes now stared up at the frozen Jessica, and she paced in a little circle, unsure what to say, how to begin to urge her friend and colleague on, fearful Jessica might be hurt next.

When Jessica disappeared from the window, making her way into the interior of the loft, Shannon Keyes racked her brain for how to keep the maniac in the barn distracted, to hopefully help Jessica out. Other SWAT team members took Luther Pratt's place, climbing up after Jessica.

There were no guarantees, but for now, Jessica needed all the help she could get. Maybe some noise at this point would help greatly, so Keyes loudly said, "We know you're in there, Mr. Purdy! And it's time you gave it up. I'm a doctor with the authorities, and we know you are in need of help. Now, I'm not discounting how brilliant, how ingenious you must be, to execute the abduction and this plan of vengeance. Fact is, I admire your cunning, your superior intelligence, but I know it all started when your wife died." She paused for an answer, but none came.

"We know how you so lovingly buried Eunice with a biblical passage, Mr. Purdy . . . Mr. Purdy . . ." She worked to play on the old man's last, perhaps final concern in this life. "We know you want to do right by your son, Jimmy Lee, sir."

Keyes feared she was getting nowhere, and that time was running out along with her delaying strategies. Words came more haltingly as her nerves increased. Still, she somehow kept speaking extemporaneously through the stout wooden doors, continuing to engage the old man's attention, to direct it at her and away from Jessica.

"I mean, you have devised the perfect punishment for Judge DeCampe—let her rot! Great idea, Mr. Purdy. I'd love to talk to you about where you got the idea of strapping your victim to your son's rotting corpse."

Finally, a response came back in a gruff male voice from the other side of the door. "You people know about how Mother died? She pined away for years. Died a broken woman, died over what they done to Jimmy Lee, her only child."

Keyes took in a deep breath of air, realizing she had struck a nerve.

"We know everything, Mr. Purdy. It's our job. But we don't know why you chose such a . . . this method of pun-

ishment for Judge DeCampe. Tell me, was it your idea, or
was it Jimmy Lee's?"

"You said you knowed everything, ha! Whataya really
know?"

"I know the passage in the Bible that told you what to
do. Did Jimmy Lee stumble on it while he was in prison?
Please, it's personal with me now. I gotta know, Mr. Purdy . . .
I just have to know."

"You the one wrote them awful things about me in the
newspapers?"

"No, no, that was a colleague of mine, and she was taken
off the case. Now, tell me, Mr. Purdy . . . was it Jimmy Lee
who told you to do all this? Did he come up with the idea
after he—you know—got religion, right?"

"He come across't it, yes . . . but was guided to it, actually. Guided by God's own hand, he was."

Figures, she thought, but she said, "God . . . really? Can
you tell me, sir, exactly how God contacted Jimmy Lee?"
How did He find him in a Texas prison? she wondered.

The old man began to elucidate loudly and sternly,
sounding like an Iowa preacher now. She had gotten the
desired effect, hoping he would be distracted from the
movement of the SWAT team and Jessica now in the loft
overhead.

JESSICA had by this time cautiously moved across the loft
overhead. She could clearly hear the old man spouting off
about God's will be done . . . thankful that Keyes had en-
gaged Purdy so thoroughly. Still, she could not see the old
man from her vantage point. She cautiously moved forward,
now coming into a line of vision that clearly informed her
as to exactly what had happened to the realtor, Nancy Willis.
The dead woman lay like wood in the middle of the barn
with a three-pronged pitchfork nailing her to the ground; a
purplish pool of blood discolored the hay-littered ground
around her. Neither movement nor sound came from her,
but a sickening, animal keening began to rise in crescendo,
coming from somewhere out of Jessica's sight, no doubt

Maureen DeCampe realizing help had found her. Jessica inched along, attempting to locate both Purdy and De-Campe.

Maureen DeCampe, having heard Dr. Shannon Keyes's banter with Isaiah Purdy, was now attempting to make some outcry, but either she was gagged or did not have the strength to speak, or possibly both.

Jessica's next step revealed the most horrid act she'd ever witnessed that any human had ever taken against another, and she felt an emotional body blow. Her every sense assaulted, she stared, mouth agape, at the sight of the judge lashed to the dead man, face-to-face, hand-to-hand, torso-to-torso.

Smoke and flame continued to grow all around the hellish scene below Jessica. It was like looking into the bowels of Hades, like an awful scene out of a Hieronymus Bosch painting, wherein devils tortured the living souls of the damned.

Jessica felt nausea welling up in her as the stench she had been breathing now hit her full force, as if Jimmy Lee's fetid spirit had personally assailed her here in the loft. At the same instant, she heard a sudden, jarring noise, and she felt the noose snatch her ankle, and it efficiently lifted her out of the loft, her head dangling upside down as she swayed out over the barn, ten or eleven feet off the ground.

Cursing, she realized that she'd been snatched by one leg, and a pulley had sent her over the edge of the loft, sending her forehead against a rough board in the bargain. Caught in a rope snare set by the old man, she cursed herself for not being more vigilant. Still, she tenaciously held onto her .38 Smith & Wesson, even as she hurtled into the wall and smashed into its splintered wood surface. Jessica absorbed the full force of the blow against the wall, gasping as a result. Upside down and dazed, she heard Shannon Keyes's voice shouting, "Jessica! Jess!"

Even as she heard others coming in through the loft overhead, she again saw the realtor's body, minus the pitchfork. Where was Purdy? Where was the pitchfork? She half saw the shadow with the three-pronged fork in its hands as it came directly at her. But it wasn't Purdy, only his shadow dancing amid the flames. She forced her body to twist and twirl 180 degrees to make the shot at the real Purdy.

She opened fire just as the pitchfork was raised overhead—three rounds to Purdy's face, sending the old man into hell. His body slammed against a stall, breaking through it and disappearing into the blackness of one corner. The dark swallowed him up as if claiming one of its own.

The others finally broke through the door, the action setting off a kerosene fire that splashed flame over their clothing. Many of the rescuers had now to be rescued from the flames eating away at their clothes and threatening to engulf them entirely.

The old sly fox knew how to strike back, even in death—like father, like son. Or was this a case of like son, like father?

The dry old barn went up in flames, and Jessica, still dangling by one foot, felt helpless as the flames licked all around her. Keyes, and two of the SWAT team members who weren't hit by the kerosene that'd been propped over the doorway made their way to Jessica.

Jessica fought to get control of her swaying body, and someone overhead at the loft was halted in any attempt to cut her down, choking now on the rising fumes. "Forget about me! Help the judge out, now!" she shouted. "Get that fucking decaying thing off her!"

Jessica, still holding firmly to her weapon, hoisted herself up, then holstered her weapon in her shoulder holster. She then located the scalpel her father had given her—which she kept on her at all times—and she pulled herself up to a position where she could cut the rope around her ankle. At the angle she was at, this proved difficult at best. In addition, on pulling herself up, she'd had to breathe in the smoke that had risen above, hugging the ceiling and loft. SWAT team members there had been suddenly forced back, one helping the other out of the strangling smoke. Had she been tied by two legs, the process would have been far easier. Two other SWAT team members were below her, and they caught her fall when the scalpel made its final cut. She fell from her rope prison into smoke and choking gases that had had time to accumulate throughout the barn. Helped to her feet, she coughed and shouted, "Help Keyes! I'm all right! Get Judge DeCampe free of here!"

But everyone was succumbing to the smoke and finding it impossible to breathe, much less see how to help another. Using the scalpel, Jessica ripped her blouse and covered her mouth and nose with the makeshift cotton mask. She next helped Keyes to slice through the remaining bonds, which Purdy had placed on the terrorized woman, but this was taking too much time.

Together, they worked furiously to extricate Maureen DeCampe from the horrid prison, while flames rose higher and closer, like angry demons all around them.

DeCampe, too, was now choking on the smoke. Jessica shouted, "Get her out of here! Now!" even as she worked with the scalpel. Keyes had hold of a clean, white woolen blanket brought for just this moment, and she readied it to cover the victim.

For a moment, Jessica feared they would have to drag out the entire four-legged, two-backed creature in order to save DeCampe from dying of smoke inhalation.

Areas of gangrene and decay showed all about her body, all needing immediate attention, all needing to be covered with a clean cloth. Finally, Jessica's last cut freed De-Campe's nude form from the monstrous creature that Jimmy Lee had become, an electrocuted, decayed corpse. Jessica and Shannon grabbed DeCampe by each arm, disallowing the injured woman any opportunity to place any weight against her own frame. They gently, carefully began to guide her out of the fire, but by now it was too hot, too blistering, the flames searing Jessica's eyebrows and snatching at the trailing blanket. Twice flames tried to claim the blanket, and a fleeting flash of thought bolted through Jessica's mind: *Wouldn't she be better off burned to death at this point? How much reconstructive surgery and additional pain will she face, should she survive this night?*

Jessica had seen that Maureen DeCampe's hands, feet, and right cheek were discolored from the first stages of decay. If she lived through this, Jessica knew she'd need a great deal of psychiatric support, family support, and plastic surgery. In the meantime, Purdy's swan song of fire, which basically and graphically said that they could all go to hell, screamed and roared around them. It was as if the fire fed on Jimmy Lee's and Isaiah's bodies, transforming them into a kind of pure evil within the confines of the fiery barn. At least, she hoped the two sons of bitches would go up in flame in the here and now, and throughout eternity. In the confusion, she also wondered about Nancy Willis's body, but for the moment, she must focus on the living.

Then Jessica saw a pair of SWAT team members attempt to drag the old man out. "He's dead! Fuck 'im!" shouted Jessica. "Leave him to go to hell with his son! Get the dead woman's body out of here if you can, but otherwise, save yourselves!"

An overhead beam came crashing down only feet from them.

"Get out of here, all of you!"

Together, the two women hustled Judge DeCampe through the fire and out into the open air. Others poured in to take DeCampe to the waiting ambulance, while Shannon and Jessica dropped to the ground, coughing and trying to catch their breaths. At the same time, a thick black cloud billowed from the burning barn like a huge black bird of prey that had taken sudden flight. This black soot swallowed up and blotted out the night sky. Meanwhile, lights continued to shower down from the helicopters above.

"Get those other medic teams in here, now!" shouted Eriq Santiva as he came close to the two women now on their knees, still gasping for air. "Now!" he repeated. He came to his knees and held Jessica, but when she smelled Richard Sharpe and not Eriq, she looked up into Richard's eyes. He held her so tightly that she again had to battle for breath. Beside them, Santiva was helping Keyes to the waiting ambulance.

"John Thorpe's been injured," Richard informed her.

Jessica instantly met his gaze. "How bad is it?"

"Knife . . . could've been knives if he hadn't reacted as well and as fast as he did."

"How damned bad is it?"

"Not sure."

She got to her feet and battled her way to Santiva, coughing and bending over as she did so, still having trouble inhaling and exhaling. "Eriq? What's J. T.'s prognosis?"

"One of the knives grazed his head, a glancing blow, but a second one caught him here, clipped his jugular. He bled a lot before the medics got to him. Turned white as a sheet."

Richard again had his arms around her. He said in her ear, "Thorpe's lost consciousness. He's lost a lot of blood. In shock, they said. But his pulse is good, and he's been stabilized, dear. He's going to make it out of this trouble."

She choked and coughed uncontrollably, and a medic placed an oxygen mask over her face. Again, Richard held her. She snatched away the oxygen mask and said, "I've got to be with J. T." This brought on another coughing spasm, but she forced out the question, "What hospital?"

Richard firmly said, "Take it easy. He's in shock, Jess."

Coma due to blood loss, she feared.

"He isn't going to miss you for a while, Jess. Slow down."

She stumbled but pulled away from Richard. "I gotta be there for J. T."

Keyes, also in bad shape from smoke inhalation, on her back in the nearby ambulance, pulled up to her elbows and shouted, "They're taking us to the same hospital, Jess. Don't worry."

Richard gritted his teeth and said, "Don't be so stubborn, Jessica. You are into a case of the seriously ill leading the seriously ill." He guided her to the second bed in the waiting ambulance, but Jessica failed to climb in, instead taking several steps toward Santiva as he approached. Meanwhile, another ambulance pulled up toward the open area fronting the barn, this one kicking up yet another cloud of sand and gravel.

"Exactly what you need," Richard said to her. "More bloody smoke filling your lungs."

Jessica noticed for the first time that Eriq Santiva was bleeding from the forehead and shoulder. Still, he somehow managed to be overseeing everything. Jessica saw him bend over the somewhat charred body of Nancy Willis, her RE/MAX badge discolored with grimy soot, the puncture holes in her chest caked with dried blood. Her body would also leave here by ambulance.

Jessica met Eriq halfway, asking about his wounds.

"Swinging ax almost took off my head," he grumbled. "I was just ahead of J. T., and if he hadn't shoved me ahead . . . well, I would not be here talking to you . . . or anyone else, at least not in this life."

JESSICA'S head bandaged now, she and Keyes having had plenty of oxygen by this time, both women concerned themselves with Eriq Santiva's obvious wounds. Both refused any further attention, instead wanting to not be treated as invalids. Both also wanted to know how DeCampe was doing.

Seasoned paramedics, who had seen almost every kind of wound imaginable, had difficulty dressing Maureen DeCampe's wrists, ankles, her cheek, and several abdominal areas where the skin had broken down, where the pericardial glue of the cells had dissolved and become part of the decay. They were busy pumping her with fluids and antibacterial and antibiotic medications. She'd been hooked up to an IV drip. Jessica believed her to be in good hands. Looking down at the still figure beneath the blanket, flanked by Eriq and Keyes, Richard Sharpe asked, "Is she . . . do you have any hope for . . . will she make it? How bad is . . . the decay?"

"It's not good, and she's damn near out of her mind, and she'll need repeated surgeries to repair the damage done her skin, but for now, she needs to be stabilized," replied Jessica. "And she's going to need a great deal of psychological help, believe me."

The medics began working furiously on DeCampe's heart, as it suddenly began to falter. The medics roared into life and rallied, pleading with DeCampe to stay with them as they did what they were trained to do. The scene riveted Jessica's attention, and she thought how very sad if that monstrous Isaiah Purdy had won after all.

These thoughts began to filter in when suddenly, from out of the flaming barn, a screaming, clothes-smoking banshee with a giant red poker—a flaming pitchfork that was scorching the flesh of Isaiah Purdy's hands—lunged straight at the ambulance holding DeCampe. Afire yet determined, Purdy came straight for DeCampe, resolved to drive the pitchfork into her where she lay. Eriq was thrown off balance when Jessica turned at the disturbance, her shoulder smashing into Santiva as she wheeled and fired a single round. The single bullet bit into the man's brain, precisely between his eyes, sending him and his pitchfork down with a thud. The pitchfork still smoldered in the cool night air. Richard Sharpe, who had also reacted with gunfire, had sent a bullet through the old man's heart.

"God damn it! We should throw his stinking carcass back into the flames," shouted Jessica, raising a fist to the dead man.

"No, no . . . better that we can ID him beyond a reasonable doubt," Santiva countered, as he climbed to his feet, his gun in his hand, looking dizzy now from loss of blood and the recent excitement. Richard Sharpe now took charge, running on adrenaline, ordering one of the medics to look after Chief Santiva's wounds. He and Jessica both realized only now that Eriq had been in a state of walking trauma, and that the loss of blood he had sustained threatened to kill him.

"How is he?" Jessica asked the medic attending Eriq now, and she thought what a mess the lot of them were. *All brought to you by the Purdys of Iowa City.*

"Bleeding badly. An ax on a pulley severed an artery in his arm, and the blow to the head is causing internal bleeding. I gotta tend the arm first, then we need to get him to Holy Cross stat—do something about the head injury."

"Get yourselves attended to," said the medic. "You still haven't gotten an all clear for that smoke inhalation."

Richard guided Jessica and Shannon back to their own waiting ambulance.

EPILOGUE

Three Months Later

JUDGE Maureen DeCampe sat up in bed, receiving visitors
for the first time since her hospitalization. She would see
no one except her immediate family until now. She had sent
word that she wanted to see Dr. Jessica Coran. And now
Jessica was here, looking in at the door, and DeCampe was
smiling and laughing with her daughter. She appeared to be
doing well in her therapy. She looked strong, and she was
coping both physically and psychologically.

At least on the surface. Jessica wondered what it was like
inside DeCampe's mind at three A.M., when she was alone.
Jessica knew she needed extended, serious therapy, despite
outward appearances. No one could suffer the indignities she
had and come out unscathed.

She spied Jessica, who stood hesitant, not sure she
wanted to intrude. But DeCampe called her name and waved
her into the room, saying she must introduce her to her
daughter.

"Mother, Dr. Coran and I know each other."

"Of course you would have met."

"I'll just leave you two to chat." Evangeline, the daughter, hugged Jessica and left.

The judge thanked Jessica for coming by.

"No problem whatsoever," she replied.

DeCampe pointed out a seat, and Jessica came further
into the room. "I wanted to . . . well, I never had the opportunity to thank you, Dr. Coran."

"No need, Judge DeCampe."

"Oh, but there is. From what everyone tells me, you were
the bulldog that never slept, the one who finally caught on
to who had me and why and most importantly where."

"I did my job. I did what I am trained to do."

"Not from what I hear. You went without sleep, you put

your life on hold for me, and then you put your life in danger for me, going into that barn for me, braving Purdy and fire."

"Please, I only wish I could've done more—a lot sooner."

DeCampe waved this off. "I want you to know that if ever I can repay you . . . Well, we both know that is impossible."

"All of us down at the bureau just want to see you back on the bench, Judge. That would be reward enough."

Jessica thought that DeCampe's skin grafts had healed beautifully, and that the healthy tissue below that which had decayed had bonded perfectly with the skin taken from other areas of the woman's body. "You look wonderful, by the way," she told the judge.

"Thanks, the doctors here are the best."

"I know. We flew them in from Johns Hopkins and the Mayo Clinic."

"Oh, I had no idea."

"The FBI and the U.S.A. are footing your medical bills, Judge DeCampe."

"So my daughters have told me."

"But there's a catch."

"And that being?"

"You also continue with psychotherapy."

DeCampe half smiled and nodded. "Thank you for caring so much, Jessica, and as it happens, I will have plenty of time to pursue psychological help along with the rehab."

"That's good to hear, Judge."

"Maureen, please . . . please call me Maureen."

"You do look remarkably well, Your Honor."

"You can stop that."

"But I mean it."

"I mean the 'Your Honor' stuff. I'm no longer a judge. I'm done with that life. I won't be returning to the bench, not after this."

"I . . . I had no idea."

"No one does. You're the first to know. I don't know why it is important for me to tell you this, but . . . well . . .

you gave me my life back; you granted me a second chance with my children, with life itself. I'm retiring early to enjoy what is left to me."

"That's commendable . . . good news, I think."

"Well . . . when you've really got one foot literally in the grave—something few of us ever really experience—it does change your outlook."

"I just didn't want that bastard to win," Jessica said through gritted teeth.

Maureen shook her head. "Trust me, he didn't win. He isn't taking me off the bench. I am. I am taking control of my life again, and I'll never allow anyone ever to do it for me again in any way, shape, or form."

"There's someone I would like you to meet, Judge DeCampe," said Jessica.

Kim Desinor entered the room, going to DeCampe and extending a hand that lightly fell over the judge's forearm. The touch was magical. Somehow DeCampe knew that Desinor was extremely important and instrumental in finding her, but only a handful of words were shared: "How are you," and "You are looking fine," and "I know you will be on your feet soon."

Kim had made a full recovery, not a psychic wound evident, but this strange miracle had occurred only after Judge DeCampe was truly found. Kim had earlier thanked Jessica for "saving my life" as she put it. They had hugged and cried together, and Kim had wanted a full description of how they had found DeCampe, and how Purdy had been dispatched.

Richard Sharpe stepped into the room just as Jessica was trying to determine exactly the price exacted from Maureen DeCampe at the hands of the madman who'd abducted and tortured her in so heinous a fashion. Jessica caught the facial expression, the glint in the eye that rose and waned all in a millisecond, one that spoke of DeCampe's honest indecision about this decision made for her, most likely, by the worried family.

Richard warmly greeted DeCampe, asking after her comfort, asking if he could get her anything from the hospital commissary.

DeCampe declined, and they said their pleasant good-byes. On leaving the hospital, Jessica confided in Richard, holding his hand as they walked, "I believe that the nightmare ordeal that woman has gone through will decide her entire future."

He nodded. "One way or another, I am sure it will." They made their way down in the elevator.

"Don't you see?" continued Jessica.

"See what, sweetheart?"

"That at the back of her mind, she knows that the horror she endured will always be—in one form or another—in control of her."

"So, what're you saying, Jess? That she can't get past this? Ever?"

"I couldn't."

"But you'd have to, to live a normal life."

"Richard, she is adept at deflecting the depth of her pain."

"Isn't that preferable to the alternative? No control? To live the rest of one's life in fear?"

"She thinks she chooses to no longer be a judge."

"That will be her decision."

"No, don't you see? She only thinks she's making the decision," Jessica replied, throwing her hands up.

Past the information desk now and out into the light of a crisp day, they made their way to the parking lot. "She thinks she knows her mind." All the way to the car, she kept spinning the same thought: *The judge intends instead to devote all her time to her family. The family now is all around her, and outwardly all is serenity. Maybe she needs the illusion of serenity, and she even believes it herself at this time, but in six months, in a year, she might well have a change of heart and wish to return to her passion, the law.*

"But in the meantime, in a way, Jimmy Lee and Isaiah won," Jessica said to Richard as he slipped inside the car beside her. "Those bastards will continue to run through her nightmares and continue to win, unless the woman can take real advantage of good professional help."

"Shannon Keyes is working on that department, my worried sweetheart. You can't do it all alone, Jess."

She leaned into him and they kissed, and he held her firmly against his chest. "Time we got some alone time, Richard."

"I'm in absolute agreement, Jess. Absolutely."

JOHN Thorpe had returned to consciousness but remained in the hospital for long-term observation. One of his doctors feared he could lapse into a coma again. Another said this was highly unlikely. A third said there was no way to know at this point. J. T. only wanted to find his pants, get up, and get back to his lab in Quantico, vowing never to leave it ever again, feeling a great deal safer in the confines of its walls. He believed himself fully recovered from his life-threatening wound, and when he came out of the coma, he found Jessica at his bedside, fast asleep, holding his hand. He'd called this his best medicine.

Jessica insisted on remaining until she knew for certain that J. T. was out of any trouble. J. T. had been sleeping fitfully on and off since his "return."

Eriq Santiva had come to Jessica the day after J. T. had come out of the coma. He had come to see J. T. but also to tell her again what an excellent job she had done on the DeCampe case, and that her superiors were extremely pleased with the results and her performance in particular. She had won over her worst critics in the department, according to Eriq. And then he launched into a confession of sorts, admitting how close he came to pulling her off the case when things looked at a standstill.

"Eriq, you never fooled me."

"What do you mean?" He feigned ignorance.

She walked him just outside J. T.'s room and lashed out at him. "Eriq—boss—I've known since you took over the office that your ambition superseded all else, including anything we might call a relationship."

"Now, Jess, that's not really fair."

"I know you have done secret *info reports* on me to our superiors to—"

"Only to . . . only because . . ."

"I know why! To keep the bastards at bay. I know I have enemies at the highest levels of the bureau." People milled about them where they stood in the hallway, visitors in search of room numbers, patients combating boredom, walking the corridor. Santiva's eyes followed every move made around him, a sign of paranoia, she thought. Did he really believe they were being watched?

Finally, he said in a near dead whisper, "No one can achieve as much as you have, Jess, and expect to have no enemies. Despite the good you do. Hell, we both have enemies. The higher you climb . . . all that . . ."

"The more success you achieve, yeah, I know. Look, Eriq, like it or not, I know you're between a rock and a . . . a love: *me.* I know you would not intentionally do anything to harm me. I know we've been through hell and back together." She had taken up his hands in hers, unable to recall the last time they had touched. "And despite you and your behavior, I love you anyway, so quit sweating the small stuff." She gave him a wide smile and a laugh.

He laughed hard at her good nature. "Well, you survived this litmus test that asshole Nicholson and the others put us through."

"And you will, too, Eriq. I know you will."

"Not so certain of that, Jess, but to add injury to insult, they're combing over my records in quite a determined way these days. Of course, they will find some expedient information and twist it to their ends."

Jessica had seen it before. There seemed a constant need for top-level administration to grow antsy and develop polyps up their asses and to get a burr under their collective skin whenever someone below them shone too brightly and did too well. It occurred in many a profession, and FBI work was no more an exception to this Rule of Intended Harm than the medical, legal, or even the education field where top-flight teaching became a "menace" to administrators who could not understand how top-flight teaching came about.

"Maybe you and I are just too damned good for this place, Eriq. Ever consider private practice? We'd make a hell of a team."

"Nice of you to say so, Jess, but the bureau is where you belong."

"And so it is with you, Eriq. You've got to fight any attempt to replace you. I will do all I can to help you and stand by you; you know that."

"You're already under scrutiny, Jess. You'll want to distance yourself from me as much as possible."

"To hell with that."

Eriq laughed again.

"Good to hear you laugh."

"You know your every decision for the past five, maybe ten years, Dr. Coran, will be looked into, not to mention your personal life."

"Let 'em look." She also knew that her personal life had somehow become the talk of the higher-ups, and that some in the bureau believed that it had in some bizarre twist of bureaucratic illogic been shown to interfere with her judgment on the DeCampe case.

"All the gossip, all the innuendo, all things nonsensical, our new fearless leader—Jeffrey Allen Nicholson—believes, or wants to believe. He wants to believe the worst and pursue it as such; he doesn't give a rat's ass about the source or the motive behind the source."

"And that source being other so-called professionals, my colleagues, people I thought my friends."

Eriq's tight-lipped frown and groan were answer enough.

"I've had my suspicions for some time. Carl Wittinger for one, not to mention complaints from police autopsiests like DeAngelos in Philadelphia and elsewhere."

"I blame the boss. The man's got the ears of a goddamn rabbit, and the brain to boot." He laughed again. "Maybe private practice isn't such a bad idea, you know, for me, I mean."

She put him at ease by joining in. "The newly appointed

head of the FBI wanted to hear all about me. I should be
flattered," she said.

"I tell you, Jess, betrayal, even on a small scale, it doesn't
sit well in my stomach. I can't do this job if I have to betray
confidences and friends."

Jessica realized only now the depth of Eriq's friendship,
for the betrayal seemed more painful for Santiva than his
physical injury from which he had fully recovered.

"FBI's a hard place to maintain perspective," he finished.

She hugged him in response and told him to get some
rest. "Besides, I've known, Eriq. It isn't as if you aren't
completely transparent, getting in my way like you do on
case after damned case."

"You knew what was going on all along? From the beginning?"

"I did—since the Phantom case that took us all over the
American West, I've known, although I suspect it's been as
long as when you and I teamed up on the Night Crawler
case in Florida." But in fact, she lied. She hadn't known for
certain until now. She had been far too fixated and obsessed
with saving DeCampe from certain death to play the petty
politics game, but a white lie now would assuage his feelings.

"How is J. T. this morning?" he asked.

"He's out of the coma and doing well. His doctors are
pleased with his progress."

"Well, I'd best go. Lot of garbage to take out today.
Meeting again with new management."

"Sounds like gut-wrenching fun."

"Just wanted you to know to watch your back, Jess, especially with that old South Dakota case you were pursuing
before all the shit hit the fan with Judge DeCampe."

She nodded and watched Eriq walk away. She wondered
if she'd be working with him again, or if the ongoing shuffle
would change the dynamics at their Quantico headquarters.
She also wondered how the strange case of Claude Lightfoot
figured into the mix; she sensed that her limited interest in
the case had sparked some questions in the highest circles
of the bureau. Was there some potential embarrassment to

the FBI if the Lightfoot case were reopened and the truth crawled out from beneath the boulder that someone or some-*ones* had placed over it? Perhaps . . . perhaps it wasn't worth pursuing, or it ought to be left to someone else, someone in a better position to drag out the ugly truth. Perhaps it was altogether someone else's problem. So why was it so snake-like and threatening? Why did it threaten like a cobra trying to find escape from the confined space of her brain? More importantly, was it worth the loss she faced? Was it worth losing everything she had built up over the years: her rep-utation, her career, her relationships, her every comfort zone?

Jessica had had some inkling before now that the higher ups were curious as to why she had involved herself in the South Dakota case. They would want to know the answers to the standard questions: Why are we footing the bills here? Why are we keeping field operatives in South Dakota busy? Was this a pet project of hers? What were the details? The names and numbers of the situation. And why had she asked field operatives in South Dakota to question a whole pop-ulation in connection with the death of a young Native American named Claude Lightfoot. It had been a case shunted aside in the '80s, but when a local man came for-ward to tell the story in toto, and he then mysteriously died before anything was recorded. Previous to his death, two others suspected of being involved in the murder of Light-foot had died under questionable circumstances. Jessica did not know who might be behind the "sudden death syn-drome" of the men she believed to have killed Lightfoot so many years ago, but she feared, unless operatives in Sioux Falls, South Dakota, pursued the case, that no one would ever know the full extent of the story there.

She took a deep breath, turning to go back inside to be with J. T. when she saw a man at the end of the corridor staring. He looked as if he'd been watching with intensity. The stranger then averted his eyes and lifted a newspaper, a sure sign she was under surveillance. Eriq had not been wrong to feel paranoid, after all.

She heard her father's voice in her ear remind her, *"When*

you have a good reason to be paranoid, it's a healthy response."

She stepped into J. T.'s room.

MEANWHILE, back in Houston, Texas, Lucas Stonecoat did not appreciate the fact that the Houston Police Department's Internal Affairs cops were looking at him for the killings taking place in Sioux Falls, South Dakota, a place where he had friends and maintained a getaway residence. IAD could not abide the smell of so close a coincidence. Of course, they could not prove it, but Lucas had known cases to be built against an innocent man that had stuck, sending people to prison on flimsy evidence.

Lucas wasn't in the business of making life easy for IAD, and so he presented them with multiple alibis for his whereabouts on the successive nights that four men were found killed—execution style—in their homes. One had supposedly been an FBI informant wannabe, who planned to rat out the other three.

Four deaths in two weeks proved an enormous statistic in a city of moderate size and permanent residents. The first death was that of a man who had begun opening talks with local FBI agents. Some of the same men in Sioux Falls, knowing of Lucas Stonecoat's reputation as a tough, uncompromising Texas Cherokee firebrand, believed along with HPD's Internal Affairs that Lucas might well be somehow connected to the series of deaths there. They suspected it was some sort of Native American vengeance-is-mine thing. So, naturally, Lucas fit the ready bill.

"This is all I need," Lucas complained to Meredyth, where they sat in Tebo's Bar and Grill, having a drink. "I can't believe that IAD is seriously looking at me for what's going on in Sioux Falls."

"They're looking closely at every step you take," she told him. "But then, haven't they always? Ever since you became a Houston cop."

"Since I didn't play ball with Dallas over their stripping me of my benefits, you mean. If I can sue Dallas for what they owe me, they figure I can sue Houston. That I'm one motherfucking litigious red man, right?"

She laughed at this, and he grudgingly joined her, but after a sip of his Budweiser, he grew serious again. "Why is it that everybody is so freaking interested in investigating my activities? What's the goddamn fascination? Sometimes, just sometimes I wish I were this . . . this outlaw that everyone paints me."

"Really, now?"

"Then maybe I could have half the fun everyone *thinks* I'm having."

"Fun as in killing those men in South Dakota?"

He stared hard into her eyes. "You're not among the fools who have me running around on some blood feud, are you?"

"You know they're talking to the FBI about you?"

"Are you serious?"

"Absolutely."

"And just how have you come by this information, Mere?" He watched her closely for her reply and how she would say it, and what she would do with her eyes, her hands—clenched or opened—and how she would look when she said it—eyes averted or straight on. She grabbed hold of his hands with a grip that hurt, and she stared deeply into his eyes—both good signs.

"They came to me . . . with a lot of questions."

"Who? Who exactly came to you?"

"Houston field operatives from the local FBI."

"Sonsofbitches at IAD are collaborating with them?"

"Most likely, yes."

"But you're not sure?"

"Lucas, they think I might know something that could hurt you."

He laughed. "You've always known something that could hurt me."

"But you told me the blackouts had ceased."

"They have ceased. You can hurt me far worse than telling my enemies my weaknesses. You can hurt me by becoming my enemy. How long ago did this meeting take place, Mere?"

"I didn't know what to think. They laid out their case against you, and it sounded—sounds—fairly strong."

"You're kidding. This has to be like the worst joke you ever tried to pull on me, right?"

"I tell you, they really believe you had something to do with those killings, and that if you did not pull the trigger, then you had a hand in . . . in arranging things."

"And you believe them?"

"I . . . I don't know what to believe. I've seen you enraged. Don't forget, I've seen you on more than one occasion kill a man, and you do it, Lucas, with . . . with a kind of raw . . . delight. It . . . that . . . that side of you . . . scares me. You scare me."

"Best fucking excuse I've ever had leveled at me by a woman to walk away from me, sweetheart. So . . . why are you still sitting here? Go . . . go . . ."

She hesitated. He snatched his hand from hers.

"For all I know, you're wearing a wire on me right now."

"That's not fair, Lucas."

"Fair, you want to talk about what's fair now?" The conversation had risen to such a crescendo that everyone in the place now eavesdropped, including the owner-bartender Tebo, his cigarette ashes going unattended.

"The local FBI didn't frighten me, Lucas. I flatly turned them down when they begged me to get something on you."

"Then I should be thanking you? Taking you upstairs to my bed again?"

"Damn you, Lucas! I got a call from our mutual friend, Dr. Desinor in Quantico, and she got it from Dr. Jessica Coran that FBI headquarters is looking at you. This goes far beyond Houston."

"Desinor? Dr. Coran?"

"They called Coran to corroborate some portions of your alibi."

"I gotta make a call." Stonecoat immediately went to the phone and called Quantico, Virginia's FBI headquarters for Jessica. He was surprised when he got her. He had fully expected to be leaving a message; instead, she came on the line.

"So good to hear from you, Lieutenant," she said.

"I called to congratulate you on the fine job your team did in locating and saving Judge DeCampe. I had meant to do so earlier, but it's been busy as hell around here."

"Why, thank you, Lieutenant. I appreciate the sentiments and the invaluable help you and Dr. Sanger provided."

He then cleared his throat and said, "Contrary to any-thing—anything whatever—that you hear about my being a rogue cop on a vendetta, killing randomly and at will, you can't accept such nonsense on face value, Dr. Coran."

"What are you talking about?"

"The series of deaths in Sioux Falls. Your field operatives there have me down for the killings, some sort of vengeance thing on behalf of Lightfoot. I didn't know the man, and he's not of my tribe, and even if he were, I would not be taking the law into my own hands—not for someone I didn't personally know. Also, my own Internal Affairs Division is coming after me. But that's nothing new."

"You know who is behind the killings?"

He hesitated, saying, "I just want you to know, Dr. Coran, that it isn't me and that I have no knowledge of these executions." He hung up.

When Lucas stepped to the bar, calling for another round for Meredyth and himself, Tebo grunted and cast his eyes at Lucas's table. Meredyth's exit through the door had left it slightly ajar, something Tebo kept claiming he was going to fix. Lucas cursed the situation, on the one hand knowing who was behind the four killings but feeling the killings justifiable homicide in retaliation for what young Claude Lightfoot had suffered. It felt like a fitting end to yet another Cold Room file.

Zachary Roundpoint, a local Native American mob boss and a sometimes acquaintance of Lucas's, wished to make up for all the white injustices over the decades. It would have to be a life's work, so much had been perpetrated against the red man. While Lucas didn't condone Round-point's actions, he did understand them.

Lucas took a six-pack of Bud with him to his room up-stairs. He did so via the back stairs. Once ensconced in his room, he lit up a peyote-stuffed, hand-rolled cigarette. He wanted two things: a good black-and-white western so he could watch "his people" through the pathetic eyes of Hollywood, and to get totally wasted in order to put everything and everyone out of his mind. Even so, he wished that Meredyth would knock at his door this moment. But she did not.

"Be damned if I'd chase her out a door," he told the empty room.

On his fourth beer since leaving the bar, Lucas again thought of his antithesis, Zachary Roundpoint. Lucas had good reason to feel angry at Zachary, a man never to be trusted, a man he could never call a friend, but a man to whom he owed much. Zachary had come through for him when he had needed a friend the most, when Lucas's dying grandfather had need of Roundpoint's power and influence.

Zachary had been a Texas Cherokee gun for hire before he had his boss assassinated. The boss had acted as a father to Roundpoint out of a deep-seated guilt for having murdered Roundpoint's mother. When Lucas first began to investigate the case, he had no idea that Roundpoint would take measures into his own hands and then grant Lucas a lucrative reward along with a job offer for his trouble. That had been then, and now this.

In the case involving Roundpoint's murdered mother, Zachary had taken over his boss's throne after summarily executing the man. Now Roundpoint controlled a small army of men, running the largest Native American cartel in the country right here in Houston. His organization had long tentacles, perhaps long enough to reach Sioux Falls, South Dakota.

Lucas guessed that the FBI knew of his past connection to Roundpoint. Because of his connection to Zachary Roundpoint, he had become an FBI suspect.

Zachary certainly had the manpower and the Cherokee chutzpah to carry out a series of hits anywhere in America. Lucas had no proof, but he could well imagine Zach Roundpoint being involved and possibly ordering the executions.

Lucas's gut reaction was that Zachary had once again

taken the law into his own hands to avenge a perceived wrong to all Native Americans, and in doing so, he had again placed Lucas Stonecoat in a perilous and vulnerable position.

The phone rang, and Lucas grabbed it up, thinking it was Meredyth, hoping so.

"It's Jessica Coran," said the whiskey voice that had become so familiar to Lucas since the DeCampe case. "Hold a moment for me, will you?"

"Sure . . . sure."

She came back on. "I couldn't talk to you on the other line. It wasn't a secure line."

"And this one is?"

"Yes, detective, it is."

"How do I know that?"

She hesitated. "I guess you'll just have to take my word as good."

He remained silent. She heard his breathing come over like thought.

"Listen, detective, what you and your friend Zachary Roundpoint arranged for in Sioux Falls . . ."

"I don't know what you're talking about." His thoughts conflicted with his words. *Does everybody in creation know about my connection to Roundpoint? And if so, does anyone in creation know the nature of that relationship? Fuck!*

"I just wanted you to know that any chance of creating a case died with McArthur. He was going to testify. Next thing we hear is that the other three were murdered."

"I still have no connection with what you're talking about."

"Sure . . . I understand. If I were you, I'd wonder who my friends were, too. Fact is, you have no idea how similar our situations are with respect to people looking over our shoulders."

"I've gotten a double dose since all this crap in Sioux Falls has come down on my head. I've got nothing whatever to do with it."

"I believe you, but I'd distance myself from Zachary

Roundpoint. If they ever get anything to stick to him . . . well . . ."

"I know we did great police work on the DeCampe case together, and for that I think I can trust you, Dr. Coran."

"You can . . . you can."

"I am not associated with Roundpoint in any way, shape, or form."

"Your close relative, a man named Hawk, Billy Hawk, works for Roundpoint."

"So I've been told."

"Billy Hawk is suspected of being the trigger man in at least one if not all of the Sioux Falls executions, Lucas."

"Christ . . . the . . ." Billy Hawk was Lucas's mawkish cousin who would do anything for money and anything to please Zachary Roundpoint.

Jessica Coran hung up, and Lucas listened to the dial tone. It felt like the voice of a nightmare gnome screwing with his brain. The drink and peyote designed to erase his physical pain—pain like a badge he wore from a near-death experience while on the job—were now conspiring to create hallucination. He pictured his cousin in the room, gun in hand, executing an enemy felt to be a threat to Zachary Roundpoint. Lucas focused on the victim of Roundpoint's and Billy Hawk's combined wrath, the man on his knees with hands tied and ankles tied, bent into the deacon's position of prayer. Someone who deserved a bullet to the brain for having literally ripped a young boy apart, using pickup trucks and rope. But the man in the pathetic position now looked up, and his face revealed itself, and it was Lucas's own face staring back at him.

JESSICA Coran hung up and leaned back into her chair in her office at Quantico, Virginia, giving some thought to Lucas's predicament, and what a now-healthy Dr. Kim Desinor had told her about the Texas Cherokee detective. Kim had had a full recovery only after DeCampe had been found alive and saved from Isaiah Purdy and Jimmy Lee's death grasp. While her "psychic disease" had halted on Jessica's lie, it had not improved until the reality of DeCampe's nightmare had come to an end.

Kim had taken a long, deserved leave, but before leaving for St. Sebastian Island, she had confided in Jessica that she had given some dream time over to the Claude Lightfoot case. Even while suffering with the psychic wounds that had threatened to kill her, even as she was in a coma, she said, "I saw someone like Lucas do the killings, but in my heart I knew it was not Lucas Stonecoat. He is not responsible for the vengeance murders being wreaked on Lightfoot's killers."

Jessica now wanted Stonecoat to know that he could count on her, or call on her at any time for any reason in the future. He had proven a valuable ally now in two cases he had been associated with. She feared, however, that he now thought she had him on tape, and with the current level of paranoia normal in a person in his position, he most likely only heard what he wanted to hear.

"You may go down for this, Stonecoat, but not by my hand," she said to the empty room.

When an elite prosecutor faces the most lethal predator
she's ever encountered,
it all comes down to a choice between justice and…

RETRIBUTION

Turn the page for a taste of one of the
most exciting debuts in years!
Jilliane Hoffman's first novel, *RETRIBUTION*,
is guaranteed to have you holding your breath
until you turn the very last page.

On January 5, 2004, retribution will be claimed!

PROLOGUE

June 1988
New York City

C HLOE Larson was, as usual, in a mad and blinding rush. She had all of ten minutes to change into something suitable to wear to *The Phantom of the Opera*—currently sold out a year in advance and the hottest show on Broadway—put on a face, and catch the 6:52 P.M. train out of Bayside into the city, which was, in itself, a three-minute car ride from her apartment to the station. That left her with only seven minutes. She whipped through the overstuffed closet that she had meant to clean out last winter, and quickly settled on a black crepe skirt and matching jacket with a pink camisole. Clutching one shoe in her hand, she muttered Michael's name under her breath, while she frantically tossed aside shoe after shoe from the pile on the closet floor, at last finally finding the black patent-leather pump's mate.

She hurried down the hall to the bathroom, pulling on her heels as she walked. *It was not supposed to happen like this*, she thought as she flipped her long blond hair upside down, combing it with one hand, while brushing her teeth with the other. She was supposed to be relaxed and carefree, giddy with anticipation, her mind free of distractions when the question to end all questions was finally asked of her. Not rushing to and fro, on almost no sleep, from intense classes and study groups with other really anxious people, the New York State Bar Exam oppressively intruding upon her every thought. She spit out the toothpaste, spritzed on Chanel No. 5, and practically ran to the front door. Four minutes. She had four minutes, or else she would have to catch the 7:22 and then she would probably miss the curtain. An image of a dapper and annoyed Michael, waiting outside the Majestic Theater, rose in hand, box in pocket, checking his watch, flashed into her mind.

It was not supposed to happen like this. She was supposed to be more prepared.

She hurried through the courtyard to her car, rushing to put on the earrings she had grabbed off the nightstand in her room. From the second story above, she felt the eyes of her strange and reclusive neighbor upon her, peering down from behind his living room window, as he did every day. Just watching as she made her way through the courtyard into the busy world and on with her life. She shook off the cold, uncomfortable feeling as quickly as it had come and climbed into her car. This was no time to think about Marvin. This was no time to think of the bar exam or bar review classes or study groups. It was time to think only of her answer to the question that Michael was surely going to ask her tonight.

Three minutes. She had only three minutes, she thought, as she cheated the corner stop sign, barely making the light up on Northern Boulevard.

The deafening sound of the train whistle was upon her now as she ran up the platform stairs two at a time. The doors closed on her just as she waved a thank-you to the conductor for waiting and made her way into the car. She sat back against the ripped red vinyl seat and caught her breath from that last run through the parking lot and up the stairs. The train pulled out of the station, headed for Manhattan. She had barely made it.

Just relax and calm down now, Chloe, she told herself, looking at Queens as it passed her by in the fading light of day. Because tonight, after all, was going to be a very special night. Of that she was certain.

PART ONE

ONE

June 1988
New York City

THE wind had picked up and the thick evergreen bushes that hid his motionless body from sight began to rustle and sway. Just to the west, lightning lit the sky, and jagged streaks of white and purple flashed behind the brilliant Manhattan skyline. There was little doubt that it was going to pour—and soon. Buried deep in the dark underbrush, his jaw clenched tight and his neck stiffened at the rumble of thunder. Wouldn't that just put the icing on the cake, though? A thunderstorm while he sat out here waiting for that bitch to finally get home.

Crouched low under the thick mange of bushes that surrounded the apartment building there was no breeze, and the heat had become so stifling under the heavy clown mask that he could almost feel the flesh melting off his face. The smell of rotting leaves and moist dirt overwhelmed the evergreen, and he tried hard not to breathe in through his nose. Something small scurried by his ear, and he forced his mind to stop imagining the different kinds of vermin that might, right now, be crawling on his person, up his sleeves, in his work boots. He fingered the sharp, jagged blade anxiously with gloved fingertips.

There were no signs of life in the deserted courtyard. All was quiet, but for the sound of the wind blowing through the branches of the lumbering oak trees, and the constant hum and rattle of a dozen or more air conditioners, precariously suspended up above him from their windowsills. Thick, full hedges practically grew over the entire side of the building, and he knew that, even from the apartments above, he could still not be seen. The carpet of weeds and decaying leaves crunched softly under his weight as he pulled himself up and moved slowly through the bushes toward her window.

She had left her blinds open. The glow from the street lamp filtered through the hedges, slicing dim ribbons of light across the bedroom. Inside, all was dark and still. Her bed was unmade and her closet door was open. Shoes—high heels, sandals, sneakers—lined the closet floor. Next to her television, a stuffed-bear collection was displayed on the crowded dresser. Dozens of black marble eyes glinted back at him in the amber slivers of light from the window. The red glow on her alarm clock read 12:33 A.M.

His eyes knew exactly where to look. They quickly scanned down the dresser, and he licked his dry lips. Colored bras and matching lacy panties lay tossed about in the open drawer.

His hand went to his jeans and he felt his hard-on rise back to life. His eyes moved fast to the rocking chair where she had hung her white lace nightie. He closed his eyes and stroked himself faster, recalling in his mind exactly how she had looked last night. Her firm, full tits bouncing up and down while she fucked her boyfriend in that see-through white nightie. Her head thrown back in ecstasy, and her curved, full mouth open wide with pleasure. She was a bad girl, leaving her blinds open. Very bad. His hand moved faster still. Now he envisioned how she would look with those long legs wrapped in nylon thigh-highs and strapped into a pair of the high heels from her closet. And his own hands, locked around their black spikes, hoisting her legs up, up, up in the air and then spreading them wide apart while she screamed. First in fear, and then in pleasure. Her blond mane fanned out under her head on the bed, her arms strapped tight to the headboard. The lacy crotch of her pretty pink panties and her thick blond bush, exposed right by his mouth. *Yum-yum!* He moaned loudly in his head and his breath hissed as it escaped through the tiny slit in the center of his contorted red smile. He stopped himself before he climaxed and opened his eyes again. Her bedroom door stood ajar, and he could see that the rest of the apartment was dark and empty. He sank back down to his spot under the evergreens. Sweat rolled down his face, and the latex suctioned fast to the skin. Thunder rumbled again, and he felt his cock slowly shrivel back down inside his pants.

She was supposed to have been home hours ago. Every single Wednesday night she gets home no later than 10:45 P.M. But tonight, *tonight*, of all nights, she's late. He bit down hard on his lower lip, reopening the cut he had chewed on an hour earlier, tasting the salty blood that flooded his mouth. He fought back the almost overwhelming urge to scream.

Goddamn mother-fucking bitch! He could not help but be disappointed. He had been so excited, *so thrilled*, just counting off the minutes. At 10:45 she would walk right past him, only steps away, in her tight gym clothes. The lights would go on above him, and he would rise slowly to the window. She would purposely leave the blinds open, and he would watch. Watch as she pulled her sweaty T-shirt over her head and slid her tight shorts over her naked thighs. Watch as she would get herself ready for bed. *Ready for him!*

Like a giddy schoolboy on his first date, he had giggled to himself merrily in the bushes. *How far will we go tonight, my dear? First base? Second? All the way?* But those initial, exciting minutes had ticked by and here he still was, two hours later—squatting like a vagrant with unspeakable vermin crawling all over him, probably breeding in his ears. The anticipation that had fueled him, that had fed the fantasy, was now gone. His disappointment had slowly turned into anger, an anger that had grown more intense with each passing minute. He clenched his teeth hard and his breath hissed. No, siree, he was not excited anymore. He was not thrilled. He was beyond annoyed.

He sat chewing his lip in the dark for what seemed like another hour, but really was only a matter of minutes. Lightning lit the sky and the thunder rumbled even louder and he knew then that it was time to go. Grudgingly, he removed his mask, gathered his bag of tricks, and extricated himself from the bushes. He knew that there would be a next time.

Headlights beamed down the dark street just then, and he quickly ducked off the cement pathway back behind the hedges. A sleek silver BMW pulled up fast in front of the complex, double-parking no less than thirty feet from his hiding spot.

Minutes passed like hours, but finally the passenger door opened, and two long and luscious legs, their delicate feet wrapped in high-heeled black patent-leather pumps, swung out. He knew instantly that it was she, and an inexplicable feeling of calm came over him.

It must be fate.

Then the Clown sank back under the evergreens. To wait.

TWO

Times Square and Forty-second Street were still all aglow in neon, bustling with different sorts of life even past midnight on a simple Wednesday. Chloe Larson nervously chewed on a thumbnail and watched out the passenger-side window as the BMW snaked its way through the streets of Manhattan towards Thirty-fourth Street and the Midtown Tunnel.

She knew that she should not have gone out tonight. The tiny, annoying voice inside her head had told her as much all day long, but she hadn't listened, and with less than four weeks to go before the bar exam, she had blown off a night of intense studying for a night of romance and passion. A worthy cause, perhaps, except that the evening hadn't been very romantic in the end, and now she was both miserable and panic stricken, suffering from an overwhelming sense of dread about the exam. Michael continued to rant on about his day from corporate hell, and didn't seem to notice either her misery or her panic, much less her inattention. Or if he did, he didn't seem to care.

Michael Decker was Chloe's boyfriend. Possibly her soon-to-be ex–boyfriend. A high-profile trial attorney, he was on the partner track with the very prestigious Wall Street law firm of White, Hughey & Lombard. They had met there two summers ago when Chloe was hired as Michael's legal intern in the Commercial Litigation Department. She had quickly learned that Michael never took no for an answer when he wanted a yes to his question. The first day on the job he was yelling at her to read her case

law more closely, and the next one he was kissing her hot
and heavy in the copy room. He was handsome and brilliant
and had this romantic mystique about him that Chloe could
not explain, and just could not ignore. So she had found a
new job, romance had blossomed, and tonight had marked
the two-year anniversary of their first real date.

For the past two weeks Chloe had asked, practically
begged, Michael if they could celebrate their anniversary
date after the bar exam. But instead, he had called her this
same afternoon to surprise her with theater tickets for tonight's performance of *The Phantom of the Opera*. Michael
knew everyone's weakness, and if he didn't know it, he
found it. So when Chloe had first said no, he knew to immediately zero in on the guilt factor—that Irish-Catholic
homing device buried deep within her conscience. *We hardly see each other anymore, Chloe. You're always studying.
We deserve to spend some time together. We need it, babe,
I need it.* Etc., etc., and etc. He finally told her that he'd
had to practically steal the tickets from some needy client,
and she relented, reluctantly agreeing to meet him in the
city. She'd rushed into Manhattan all the while trying to
quiet that disconcerting voice in the back of her head that
had suddenly begun to shout.

After all that, she had to admit that she wasn't even surprised when, ten minutes after curtain call, the elderly usher
with the kind face handed her the note that told her Michael
was stuck in an emergency meeting and would be late. She
should have left right there, right then, but, well . . . she
didn't. She watched now out the window as the BMW slid
under the East River and the tunnel lights passed by in a
dizzying blur of yellow.

Michael had shown up for the final curtain call with a
rose in his hand and had begun the familiar litany of excuses
before she could slug him. A zillion apologies later he had
somehow managed to then guilt her into dinner, and the next
thing she knew, they were heading across the street together
to Carmine's and she was left wondering just when and
where she had lost her spinal cord. How she hated being
Irish-Catholic. The guilt trips were more like pilgrimages.

If the night had only ended there, it would have been on a good note. But over a plate of veal marsala and a bottle of Cristal, Michael had delivered the sucker punch of the evening. She had just begun to relax a little and enjoy the champagne and romantic atmosphere when Michael had pulled out a small box that she instantly knew was not small enough.

"Happy Anniversary." He had smiled softly, a perfect smile, his sexy brown eyes warm in the flickering candle-light. The strolling violinists neared, like shark to chum. "I love you, baby."

Obviously not enough to marry me, she had thought as she stared at the silver-wrapped box with the extra-large white bow, afraid to open it. Afraid to see what wasn't in-side.

"Go ahead, open it." He had filled their glasses with more champagne, and his grin had grown more smug. Obviously, he thought that alcohol and jewelry of any sort would surely get him out of the doghouse for being late. Little did he know that at that very moment he was so far from home, he was going to need a map and a survival kit to get back. Or maybe she was wrong. Maybe he had just put it in a big box to fool her.

But no. Inside, dangling from a delicate gold chain, was a pendant of two intertwined hearts, connected by a brilliant diamond. It was beautiful. But it wasn't round and it didn't fit on her finger. Mad at herself for thinking that way, she had blinked back hot tears. Before she knew it, he was out of his seat and behind her, moving her long blond hair onto her shoulders and fastening the necklace. He kissed the nape of her neck, obviously mistaking her tears for those of hap-piness. Or ignoring them. He whispered in her ear, "It looks great on you." Then he had sat back in his seat and ordered tiramisu, which arrived five minutes later with a candle and three singing Italians. The violinists soon got wind of the party downtown and had sauntered over and everyone had sung and strummed "Happy Anniversary" in Italian. She wished she had just stayed home.

The car now moved along the Long Island Expressway

toward Queens with Michael still oblivious to her absence
from the conversation. It had started to sprinkle outside, and
lightning lit the sky. In the side-view mirror Chloe watched
the Manhattan skyline shrink smaller and smaller behind
Lefrak City and Rego Park, until it almost disappeared from
sight. After two years, Michael knew what she wanted, and
it *wasn't* a necklace. *Damn him*. She had enough stress in
her life with the bar exam that she needed this emotional
albatross about as much as she needed a hole in the head.

They approached her exit on the Clearview Expressway
and she finally decided that a discussion about their future
together—or lack thereof—would just have to wait until after she sat for the bar. The last thing she wanted right now
was the heart-wrenching ache of a failed relationship. One
stress factor at a time. Still, she hoped her stony silence in
the car would send its message.

"It's not just the depo," Michael continued on, seemingly
oblivious. "If I have to run to the judge every time I want
to ask something as inane as a date of birth and Social Security number, this case is going to get buried in the mountains of sanctions I'm going to ask for."

He pulled off onto Northern Boulevard and stopped at a
light. There were no other cars out on the street at this hour.
Finally he paused, recognized the sound of silence, and
looked over cautiously at Chloe. "Are you okay? You
haven't said much at all since we left Carmine's. You're not
still mad about my being late, are you? I said I was sorry."
He gripped the leather steering wheel with both hands, brac-
ing himself for the fight that hung heavy in the air. His tone
was arrogant and defensive. "You know what that firm is
like. I just can't get away, and that's the bottom line. The
deal depended on me being there."

The silence in the small car was almost deafening. Before
she could even respond, he had changed both his tone and
the subject. Reaching across the front seat, he traced the
heart pendant that rested in the hollow of her throat with
his finger. "I had it made special. Do you like it?" His voice
was now a sensuous inviting whisper.

No, no, no. She wasn't going to go there. Not tonight. *I*

refuse to answer, Counselor, on the grounds it may incriminate me.

"I'm just distracted." She touched her neck and said flatly, "It's beautiful." The hell she was going to let him think that she was just being an emotional bitch who was upset because she didn't get the ring she'd told all her friends and extended family she was expecting. He could take what she said and chew on it for a few days. The light changed and they drove on in silence.

"I know what this is about. I know what you're thinking." He sighed an exaggerated sigh and leaned back in the driver's seat, hitting the palm of his hand hard against the steering wheel. "This is all about the bar exam, isn't it? Jesus, Chloe, you have studied for that test almost nonstop for two months, and I have been really understanding. I really have. I only asked for one night out . . . Just one. I have had this incredibly tough day and all during dinner there has been this, this tension between us. Loosen up, will you? I really, really need you to." He sounded annoyed that he even had to bother having this conversation, and she wanted to slug him again. "Take it from someone who has been there: Stop worrying about the bar exam. You're tops in your class, you've got a terrific job lined up—you'll do fine."

"I'm sorry that my company at dinner did not brighten your tough day, Michael. I really am," she said, the sarcasm chilling her words. "But, let me just say that you must suffer from short-term memory loss. Do you remember that we spent last night together, too? I wouldn't exactly say that I have neglected you. Might I also remind you that I did not even want to celebrate tonight and I told you as much, but you chose to ignore me. Now, as far as having fun goes, I might have been in a better mood if you hadn't been two hours late." Great. In addition to the guilt pangs her stomach was digesting for dessert, her head was beginning to throb. She rubbed her temples.

He pulled the car up in front of her apartment building, looking for a spot.

"You can just let me out here," she said sharply.

He looked stunned and stopped the car, double-parking in front of her complex.

"What? You don't want me to come in tonight?" He sounded hurt, surprised. Good. That made two of them.

"I'm just really tired, Michael, and this conversation is, well, it's degenerating. And quick. Plus I missed my aerobics class tonight, so I think I'll take the early one in the morning before class."

Silence filled the car. He looked off out his window and she gathered her jacket and purse. "Look, I'm really sorry about tonight, Chloe. I really am. I wanted it to be special and it obviously wasn't, and for that, I apologize. And I'm sorry if you're stressed over the bar exam. I shouldn't have snapped like that." His tone was sincere and much softer. The "sensitive guy" tactic took her slightly by surprise.

Leaning over the car seat, he traced a finger up her neck and over her face. He ran his finger over her cheekbones as she looked down in her lap, fidgeting for the keys in her purse, trying hard to ignore his touch. Burying his hand in her honey-blond hair, he pulled her close and brushed his mouth near her ear. Softly he murmured, "You don't need the gym. Let me work you out."

Michael made her weak. Ever since that day in the copy room. And she could rarely say no to him. Chloe could smell the sweetness of his warm breath, and felt his strong hands tracing farther down the small of her back. In her head she knew she should not put up with his crap, but in her heart, well, that was another story. For crazy reasons she loved him. But tonight—well, tonight was just not going to happen. Even the spineless had their limits. She opened the car door fast and stepped out, catching her breath. When she leaned back in, her tone was one of indifference.

"This is not going to happen, Michael. I'm tempted, but it's already almost one. Marie is picking me up at eight forty-five, and I can't be late again." She slammed the door shut.

He turned off the engine and got out of the driver's side. "Fine, fine. I get it. Some great fucking night this turned out to be," he said sullenly and slammed his door in return. She glared at him, turned on her heel, and marched off across the courtyard toward her lobby.

"Shit, shit, shit," he mumbled and ran after her. He caught up with her on the sidewalk and grabbed her hand. "Stop, just stop. Look, I'm frustrated. I'm also an insensitive clod. I admit it." He looked into her eyes for a sign that it was safe to proceed. Apparently, they still read caution, but when she did not move away he took that as a good sign. "There, I've said it. I'm a jerk and tonight was a mess and it's all my fault. Come on, please, forgive me," he whispered. "Don't end tonight like this." He wrapped his hand behind her neck and pulled her mouth to his. Her full lips tasted sweet.

After a moment she stepped back and touched her hand lightly to her mouth. "Fine. Forgiven. But you're still not spending the night." The words were cool.

She needed to be alone tonight. To think. Past her bedroom, where was this whole thing headed anyway? The streetlights cast deep shadows on the walkway. The wind blew harder and the trees and bushes rustled and stirred around them. A dog barked off in the distance, and the sky rumbled.

Michael looked up. "I think it's going to pour tonight," he said absently, grabbing her limp hand in his. They walked to the front door of the building in silence. On the stoop he smiled and said lightly, "Damn. And here I thought I was so smooth. Sensitivity is supposed to work with you women. The man who's not afraid to cry, show his feelings." He laughed, obviously fishing for a smile in return, then he massaged her hand with his and kissed her gently on the cheek, moving his lips lightly over her face toward her lips. Her eyes were closed, her full mouth slightly parted. "You look so good tonight I just might cry if I can't have you." *If at first you don't succeed . . . try, try again.* His hands moved slowly down the small of her back, over her skirt. She didn't move. "You know, it's not too late to change your mind," he murmured, his fingers moving over her. "I can just go move the car."

His touch was electrifying. Finally, she pulled away and

opened the door. Damn it, she was going to make a statement tonight and not even her libido was going to stop her.

"Good night, Michael. I'll talk to you tomorrow."

He looked as if he had been punched in the gut. Or somewhere else.

"Happy Anniversary," he said quietly as she slipped into
the foyer door. The glass door closed with a creak.

He walked slowly back to the car, keys in hand. Damn
it. He had really screwed things up tonight. He really had.
At the car, he watched as Chloe stood at the living room
window and waved to him that all was okay inside. She still
looked pissed. And then the curtain closed and she was
gone. He climbed in the BMW and drove off toward the
expressway and back toward Manhattan, thinking about how
to get back on her good side. Maybe he'd send her flowers
tomorrow. That's it. Long red roses with an apology and an
"I love you." That should get him out of the doghouse and
back into her bed. With the crackle of thunder sounding
closer still and the storm fast moving in, he turned onto the
Clearview Expressway, leaving Bayside way behind him.